# 细读八大古典名著

# Close Reading of Great Classical Novels

## （双语版）

(bilingual edition)

刘雪玲 编著

CFP 中国电影出版社

## 图书在版编目（CIP）数据

细读八大古典名著 / 刘雪玲编著，—北京：中国电影出版社，2013.9

ISBN 978-7-106-03724-6

Ⅰ.细… Ⅱ.①刘… Ⅲ.①中国文学—古典文学—文学欣赏 Ⅳ.①1206.2

中国版本图书馆 CIP 数据核字 (2013) 第 206965 号

责任编辑：贾 伟
封面设计：视域品牌设计机构
版式设计：李 利
责任校对：何 梅
责任印制：庞敬峰

**细读八大古典名著**
刘雪玲 编著

---

**出版发行** 中国电影出版社（北京北三环东路 22 号）邮编 100013
电话：64296664（总编室） 64216278（发行部）
64296742（读者服务部）Email:cfpygb@126.com
**经　　销** 新华书店
**印　　刷** 济南天舜彩色印刷有限公司
**版　　次** 2013 年 9 月第 1 版 2013 年 9 月第 1 次印刷
**规　　格** 开本 /880×1230 毫米 1/32
印张 /9 字数 /180 千字

---

**书　　号** ISBN 978-7-106-03724-6/I · 0858
**定　　价** 30.00 元

# 目录

# 前言

魔鬼词典里给名著的定义是：没人去读，却希望别人说起时，自己可以宣称“我读过的”书。仔细考虑一下，不无道理。一则名著很多；二则很少有人静下心来读。但是，名著的影响却是普遍的，往往是一国文学的酵母，它会不断地自我更新，任凭各个时代各种人群各等领域做出各种取舍。从文字角度说，名著是典范，是语言优化使用的最佳体现，常常被节选，进入课堂教学；从美学角度说，名著是恣意汪洋的想象力的最复杂瑰丽的体现，它会像名画一样激发更多的想象；从翻译角度看，语言之间的互换在名著的翻译中攀升为最高形式的竞技，能流传下来并被广泛认可的译作一定是两种语言最完美的交融与结合。可想而知读名著的译本有一举多得的功效，除了“宣称”自己读过名著，最有意义的莫过于真正读读名著，因此也就催生了《细读八大古典名著》的诞生。

本书选取的八部名著都是古典小说。选取小说来细读是出于这种文学样式的以下两大特征：第一，小说有四大要素：人物，环境，情节，事件；人物总是在特定的自然和社会环境下，按照小说家设计好的情节进行特定的事项。小说的这些要素，使其能够塑造源于现实的人物，能够根据情节的推进有选择性的反映某些实际存在或者想象中的问题，能够旁征博引地把某个时代的突出问题引人入胜地呈现出来。第二，小说的篇幅。本书选取的都是长篇小说，往往是作者耗费了极大的精力甚至毕生心血才创造出来的传世佳作。四大要素在长篇小说里被发挥到了极致，在人物刻画方面，不仅主要人物的性格要鲜明丰满，次要人物甚至是一闪而过的人物也要令人过目不忘；情节的设计也要是动态的且更加令人信服；事件的描绘叠加并置，更加复杂；环境的变迁更加体现了历史感。这两大特征保证了小说阅读的趣味性，挑战性，传承性和知识性。

中国小说孕育于先秦两汉的古代神话传说和寓言故事，成形于魏晋南北朝时期的志人、志怪小说，成熟于唐代的传奇；宋代的话本和明代的拟话本，使古典小说的题材更加广泛，情节更加曲折，描写更加细腻；而明清章回体小说将古典小说逐渐推向了顶峰。本书节选的中国四大古典名著更是小说题材登峰造极的代表作。

英语小说也是一个逐渐成长的过程，一般认为丹尼尔·笛福的《鲁滨逊漂流记》（1719）是第一本比较成熟的小说，紧接着是斯威夫特的《格列夫游记》（1726）；司各特笔下的历史传奇是浪漫主义时期的一大特色，而简·奥斯丁作为第一个女性小说大家使小说的发展更加复杂细腻。古典英语小说在维多利亚时期 (1837——1901) 成了主流文学样式，各种题材各种风格的小说的出现，把英语文学推向了一个新高潮，其中女性作家的贡献功不可没。本书节选的英文四大名著《大卫·科波菲尔》《名利场》《呼啸山庄》《米德尔马契》，有两部就出自女性作家之手。

2003年BBC在英国全境进行了公众最喜爱的小说调查（The Big Read），超过75万人参加了投票，被称为是“到目前为止最大规模的对公众阅读口味的调查”。我们所选的英国四大古典小说都榜上有名，其中《呼啸山庄》第12名，《米德尔马契》第27名，《大卫·科波菲尔》第34名，《名利场》第122名。

从小说在两个国家的简史中，我们至少可以得出两个结论：中文小说比英文小说早熟（罗贯中和英国文学之父乔叟大致同时代）；英国有非常成功的女性小说家。除了这两个显而易见的特征，小说在两个不同国家的不同时代的呈现形式如何？两种文字各自激发了什么样的美的享受？为我们保留了什么样的历史情怀？相信在读完本书后读者会找到自己的答案。

语言障碍是欣赏外国文学的一大憾事，有幸的是，我们有辛勤的辗转于两种语言间的译者，他们使我们可以用同一种文字欣赏两种风情，跨越两个国度。文字是文学的载体，而载体本身就是一种携带着意义的象征符号，中国的四大古典名著在英文里有了哪些微妙的变化？英文的四大名著在转换成方块字后是否也产生了令人意想不到的效果？

翻译最有资格被称为遗憾的艺术，不管是直译还是意译，都会与原著出现差距。大家在买名著译作前习惯性地问：谁的译本最好？是张玲的还是杨必的？是杨宪益，戴乃迭的还是方平的？是朱生豪的还是张谷若的？是罗慕士（Moss Roberts）的还是邓罗（C. H. Brewitt-Taylor）的？真是不好回答。但是有一点是可以肯定的，好的译本应该最大限度地传递原意义，原风格，原美感。鉴于此，本书对八大古典名著的译本作了如下选择：

中文四大名著《红楼梦》、《西游记》、《三国演义》、《水浒传》:

*A Dream of Red Mansions translated by* Yang Xianyi and Gladys Yang

*Three Kingdoms translated by* Moss Roberts

*Outlaws of the Marsh translated by* Sidney Shapiro

*Journey to the West translated by* W.J.F. Jenner

英语四大名著 *David Copperfield, Vanity Fair, Wuthering Heights, Middlemarch:*

《名利场》 **杨 必 译**

《大卫·科波菲尔》 **张谷若 译**

《呼啸山庄》 **方 平 译**

《米德尔马契》 **项星耀 译**

学术界里谈翻译，免不了要追究翻译理论，诸如中国的“信、达、雅”，忠实，通顺；西方的功能理论，交际理论，归化、异化等等。本书的目的是实践性的，普及性的和推广性的。首先，我们来“读”原著和译本，然后才能“悟”理论。但是切记，翻译是带着遗憾的创作，如果在对比阅读中你有更高明的见解，甚至跃跃欲试，想冒天下之大不韪，把某个译本推翻重来的话，说明你对其中的一种语言已经有了相当的敏感度，恭喜你。但是这样的发现通常是细读的结果。“细读”一词借用了文学理论新批评 ( new criticism) 的用法。《文学术语汇编》中给“细读”(close reading) 的解释是：对作品中文字和修辞方面的模糊性和复杂的相互关系的仔细分析。“细读”用在这里主要是引起读者的注意，不能走马观花，中英对照看完学几个单词而已，而是要用研究生的眼光审视原作和译本，体会其选词的精到，修辞的巧妙，人物刻画的高超，以及字里行间渗透出来的文字美，意象美和其他许多只可意会的美。

为了减少阅读障碍，便于细读，本书在排版上采用中英文对照的形式，并且把较长的段落都为分解为句子，好让读者一目了然。同时为了保持原文的版块结构，只有原段落才使用缩进的格式，以区别于便于阅读而分解出来的句子。另外，作为细读的一个手段，每个节选中都会挑选出一些或易或难的句子，用下划线的方式突出，让读者在阅读时细细揣摩，体会语言转换的微妙；对比阅读前，为了拓展思路而设置了一些思考题。总之，本书的宗旨就是要激发大家积极阅读，深度思考，品味文学经典的至纯至美。

以这八大名著为蓝本的影视作品比比皆是，老版新版搞笑版，恨不得穷尽名著的看点，但是影视所表现的只是文字表现中可以用影像演绎的部分，在广度和深度上远不及文字。尽管这八部名著都不停地被翻拍，真正的滋味却深深地埋藏在对文字的品味里。

精心挑选的这些译本，最大限度地缩小不同文字产生的阅读偏误，但是译文永远不是原文，除了遗憾之外，可以提醒自己：很幸运，我读了两部作品。好的译文本身就是创作，那么读了这本书就等于读了十六本古典小说的精华，何乐而不为呢！

# 第一章

# 三国演义
# *Three Kingdoms*

聊寄傲于琴书兮，以待天时。

## 背景介绍

成书于元末明初，全书一百二十回，是作者罗贯中（约1330——约1440）根据《三国志》、《后汉书》、《三国志平话》和一些民间传说写成。是中国文学史上“最有成就的历史小说”，描述了从东汉中平元年的黄巾起义，到西晋武帝司马炎太康元年统一中国的将近一个世纪中，魏、蜀、吴三国间的政治和军事斗争历史。

《三国演义》中最令人们津津乐道的莫过于桃园三结义的故事：春暖花开的时候，三个大男人焚香、磕头、跪拜，在桃花园里结为异姓兄弟。老大刘备，爱哭也会哭，他硬是把诸葛亮给哭出来了，有了这文武全才，三国之中的蜀国就有了着落。这么鲜活的故事还只是冰山的一个小角，一本《三国演义》把中国冷兵器时代的军事、外交、权谋写得是深入浅出，淋漓尽致。人物的刻画也是个个鲜明：自负的曹操、小气的周瑜、脾气大的张飞、神机妙算的诸葛亮、如花似玉的大小乔，哪一个不是栩栩如生，呼之欲出！

罗慕士（Moss Roberts）是纽约大学东亚研究的教授，对中国文化有深刻的认识。他翻译的《三国演义》（Three

Kingdoms）的第一版于 1995 年由外研社出版，已经再版了十几次。从再版的次数上可以推测，这个译本相当成功。

## 细读节选

本书节选了“三顾茅庐”片段，只有等诸葛亮出山了,《三国演义》才算正式开演。不管他是人是妖，卧龙的名头可不是假的，一旦腾空而起，就掀动了整个三国的大棋盘。铺陈的手段在节选里被全面运用，我们跟着刘备他们兄弟三人风里来雪里去，求诸葛亮而不得，但是卧龙岗的风土人情都让我们铁了心一定要找到他，因为他的才思、智慧、谋略已经被他们一一渲染，何止三顾，刘备连四顾的心都有。

这个片段中还有一个令人不可思议的烈女，她的悬梁自尽从一个侧面让我们看到了曹操的品行。

中国古典小说有一个特色，这些写小说的人本身都是才情相当的诗人，所以有时候情绪发散得无法收拾的时候，就赋诗作曲，把读者从琐碎的故事中提拔出来，升华一下。《三国演义》的本次节选中就有 9 首诗歌，有的叙事，有的赞景，有的抒情。不言而喻，对这些诗作的翻译是一个难点，也是语言转换中最难琢磨的部分，我们一起来看看罗慕士是怎么处理的，是否能传递原意的十之八九。

### 拓展思考：

1. 凭借记忆，写出 3 句划线的原文与译文。

| 原文 | 译文 |
|---|---|
| | |
| | |
| | |

2. 刘备拜访时，诸葛亮是碰巧不在吗？

3. 本节选中的诗歌翻译是否传递了原文的意思？举例说明。

4. 罗贯中对卧龙冈的描述可谓充满深情，这对诸葛亮出山有何寓意？

# 第三十七回

## 司马徽再荐名士
## 刘玄德三顾草庐

却说徐庶趱程赴许昌。曹操知徐庶已到，遂命荀彧、程昱等一班谋士往迎之。庶入相府拜见曹操。

操曰："公乃高明之士，何故屈身而事刘备乎？"庶曰："某幼逃难，流落江湖，偶至新野，遂与玄德交厚，老母在此，幸蒙慈念，不胜愧感。"操曰："公今至此，正可晨昏侍奉令堂，吾亦得听清诲矣。"庶拜谢而出。

# Chapter 37

*Still Water Recommends Another Noted Scholar*
*Liu Xuande Pays Three Visits to Zhege Liang*

Riding at breakneck speed, Shan Fu reached the capital. Informed of his arrival, Cao Cao had Xun Wenruo, Cheng Yu, and other advisers greet him at the city gate. From there Shan Fu went to the ministerial residence and paid his respects to Cao Cao.

Cao Cao said to him, "How could so noble and enlightened a scholar as you, sir, lower himself to serve Liu Bei?" "In my youth," Shan Fu responded, "I fled my village and drifted through all sorts of places. Chance brought me to Xinye, where I formed a strong friendship with Xuande. But since my mother is here now in your care, I feel overcome with shame and gratitude." "Now that you are here," the prime minister said, "you will be able to tend and care for your honorable mother at dawn and at dusk as ritual prescribes. And I, too, perhaps may benefit from your superior learning." Shan Fu expressed his thanks and withdrew to his mother's chamber.

(1) 急往见其母，泣拜于堂下。母大惊曰："汝何故至此？"庶曰："近于新野事刘豫州；因得母书，故星夜至此。"

Shan Fu prostrated himself tearfully before his mother. "What brings you here?" she exclaimed in amazement. "I was in the service of Liu Xuande," he explained, "When your letter came. I rushed here at once."

徐母勃然大怒，拍案骂曰："辱子飘荡江湖数年，吾以为汝学业有进，何其反不如初也！汝既读书，须知忠孝不能两全。岂不识曹操欺君罔上之贼？刘玄德仁义布于四海，况又汉室之胄，汝既事之，得其主矣，今凭一纸伪书，更不详察，遂弃明投暗，自取恶名，真愚夫也！吾有何面目与汝相见！汝玷辱祖宗，空生于天地间耳！"

Mother Xu exploded in fury, swearing as she struck the table. "You disgraceful son," she shouted, "flitting hither and thither for so many years. I thought you were finally making progress with your studies. Now you've ended up worse than you started out! As a scholar, you should be aware that loyalty and filial devotion may conflict. How could you have failed to see Cao Cao for what he is——a traitor who has abused and ruined his sovereign——while Liu Xuande is widely known for humanity and righteousness? Moreover, he is a scion of the royal house. You had found yourself a proper master, but trusting a forged scrap of paper, which you never bothered to verify, you left the light for the dark and have earned yourself a name beneath contempt. Oh, you utter fool! With what kind

骂得徐庶拜伏于地，不敢仰视，母自转入屏风后去了。少顷，家人出报曰：“老夫人自缢于梁间。”徐庶慌入救时，母气已绝。

后人有《徐母赞》曰：

“贤哉徐母，
流芳千古：
守节无亏，
于家有补；
教子多方，
处身自苦；
气若丘山，
义出肺腑；
赞美豫州，
毁触魏武；
不畏鼎镬，
不惧刀斧；
唯恐后嗣，
玷辱先祖。

of self-respect am I supposed to welcome you, now that you have shamed the spirit of your ancestors and uselessly wasted your own life?”

During his mother's tirade Shan Fu cowered on the ground, hands clasped over his head, not daring to look up. Suddenly, she turned and vanished behind a screen. Moments later a house servant appeared and called out, “The lady has hanged herself from the beams!” Beside himself, Shan Fu rushed to her, but her breath had ceased. Later someone wrote “In Praise of Mother Xu”:

*Mother Xu's integrity*
*Will savor for eternity.*
*She kept her honor free of stain,*
*A credit to her family's name.*
*A model lesson for her son,*
*No grief or hardship would she shun.*
*An aura like a sacred hill,*
*Allegiance sprung from depth of will.*
*For Xuande, words of approbation*
*For Cao Cao, utter condemnation,*
*Boiling oil or scalding water,*
*Knife or axe could not deter her.*
*Then, lest Shan Fu shame his forbears*

伏剑同流，
断机堪伍；
生得其名，
死得其所：
贤哉徐母，
流芳千古！”

*She joined the ranks of martyred mothers.*
*In life, her proper designation;*
*In death, her proper destination.*
*Mother Xu's integrity*
*Will savor for eternity.*

徐庶见母已死，哭绝于地，良久方苏。曹操使人赍礼吊问，又亲往祭奠。徐庶葬母柩于许昌之南原，居丧守墓。(2) 凡曹操所赐，庶俱不受。

Seeing his mother dead, Shan Fu lay broken on the ground. Much time passed before he recovered. Cao Cao sent him ritual gifts of condolence and personally attended the sacrificial ceremonies. The coffin was interred in the high ground south of the capital. Shan Fu fulfilled the mourning and guarded the grave site. Everything that Cao Cao proffered he declined.

时操欲商议南征。荀彧谏曰：“天寒未可用兵；姑待春暖，方可长驱大进。”操纵之，乃引漳河之水作一池，名玄武池，于内教练水军，准备南征。

At this time Cao Cao was considering a southern expedition. But Xun Wenruo warned, “Winter is no time for that. After the spring thaw we can make an all-out attack.” Cao Cao agreed. He then diverted water from the River Zhang to make a lake for naval training for the attack on the south. The lake was called the Pool of the Dark Tortoise.

却说玄德正安排礼物，欲往隆中谒诸葛亮，忽人报：“门外有一先生，峨冠博带，道貌非常，特来相

As Liu Xuande was preparing his gifts for his visit to Kongming in Longzhong, the arrival was announced of an unusual-looking Taoist with a tall hat and broad

探。"玄德曰："此莫非即孔明否？"遂整衣出迎。

视之，乃司马徽也。玄德大喜，请入后堂高坐，拜问曰："备自别仙颜，因军务倥偬，有失拜访。今得光降，大慰仰慕之私。"徽曰："闻徐元直在此，特来一会。"玄德曰："近因曹操囚其母，似母遣人驰书，唤回许昌去矣。"

徽曰："此中曹操之计矣！吾素闻徐母最贤，虽为操所囚，必不肯驰书召其子；此书必诈也。元直不去，其母尚存；今若去，母必死矣！"玄德惊问其故，徽曰："徐母高义，必羞见其子也。"玄德曰："元直临行，荐南阳诸葛亮，其人若何？"徽笑曰："元直欲去，自去便了，何又惹他出来呕

sash. "Why, this must be Kongming himself!" Xuande said and attired himself formally to welcome him.

It turned out, however, to be still water. Delighted, Xuande took him into his private quarters and led him to the seat of honor. Xuande said, "Since leaving your saintly presence, I have been beset by military concerns and thus failed to pay a courtesy call. Now I am honored by this visit, which gratifies my deeply felt longing and admiration." "I had heard," Still Water replied, " that Shan Fu was here and came especially to see him." "He went to the capital," Xuande explained, "in response to an appeal from his mother, whom Cao Cao had jailed."

"So he felt for the ruse!" Still Water said. "Mother Xu is known for her absolute integrity. Even if Cao imprisoned her, she would never agree to call for her son. The letter has got to be a forgery. By not going he could have saved her; his going dooms her." Agitated, Xuande asked for an explanation. "Shc livcd according to the highest ethic," Still Water said, " and would be ashamed for her son." "As he was leaving," Xuande said, "he recommended

心血也？”玄德曰：“先生何出此言？”

徽曰：“孔明与博陵崔州平、颍川石广元、汝南孟公威与徐元直四人为密友。此四人务于精纯，惟孔明独观其大略。尝抱膝长吟，而指四人曰：“公等仕进可至刺史、郡守。众问孔明之志若何，孔明但笑而不答。(3) 每常自比管仲、乐毅，其才不可量也。”

玄德曰：“何颍川之多贤乎！”徽曰：“昔有殷馗善观天文，尝谓群星聚于颍分，其地必多贤士。”

Zhuge Kongming of Nanyang. What do you know about him?” “If Shan Fu had to leave, he had to leave,” Still Water replied. “But why did he have to drag Kongming into this to sweat out his heart's blood?” “What do you mean by that, good master?” Xuande asked.

Still Water said, “Kongming befriended Shan Fu and three others: Cui Zhouping of Boling, Shi Guangyuan of Yingchuan, and Meng Gongwei of Ruan. These four dedicated themselves to esoteric rituals of spiritual refinement. Kongming, however, was the only one who contemplated the doctrine in its entirety. Once while sitting embracing his knees and chanting invocations he remarked to his three friends: “In official service any of you might advance to inspector or governor.' But when they asked what ambitions he had, he only smiled. He was wont to liken himself to Guan Zhong and Yue Yi. His ability is beyond measuring.”

“I wonder,” Xuande commented, “why the Yingchuan area has produced so many great men.” “Long ago,” Still Water replied, “Yin Kui, a skilled observer of the constellations, remarked that with so many stars congregated in

时云长在侧曰："某闻管仲、乐毅乃春秋、战国名人，功盖寰宇；孔明自比此二人，毋乃太过？"徽笑曰："以吾观之，不当比此二人；我欲另以二人出之。"云长问："那二人？"徽曰："可比兴周八百年之姜子牙、旺汉四百年之张子房也。"

众皆愕然。徽下阶相辞欲行，玄德留之不住。徽出门仰天大笑曰："卧龙虽得其主，不得其时，惜哉！"言罢，飘然而去。玄德叹曰："真隐居贤士也！"

次日，玄德同关、张并从人等来隆中。遥望山畔数人，荷锄耕于田间，而作歌曰：

its part of the sky, the district was sure to have many worthy men."

Lord Guan, who had been listening to this conversation, interjected, "To my knowledge Guan Zhong and Yue Yi were outstanding figures of the Spring and Autumn and Warring States periods, men whose merit overarched the realm. Is it not presumptuous for Kongming to compare himself to them?" "To my mind," Still Water replied smiling, "he might rather be compared to Jiang Ziya, who helped founded the eight-hundred-year Zhou dynasty, or Zhang Liang, whose advice was responsible for the Han's four hundred years of glory."

This praise left all hearers astonished. Still Water then took his leave, declining Xuande's invitation to stay. But on reaching the gate, he gazed upward and laughed aloud, "Sleeping Dragon has found his lord but not his time. A pity!" So saying, he was gone like breeze. "Truly a recluse of great worth," Xuande said with a sigh.

The next day Xuande, Lord Guan, and Zhang Fei went to Longzhong. On the hills men were carrying mattocks to their acres, singing:

"苍天如圆盖，
陆地似棋局；
世人黑白分，
往来争荣辱：
荣者自安安，
辱者定碌碌。
南阳有隐居，
高眠卧不足！"

玄德闻歌，勒马唤农夫问曰："此歌何人所作？"答曰："乃卧龙先生所作也。"玄德曰："卧龙先生住何处？"农夫曰：(4)"自此山之南，一带高冈，乃卧龙冈也。冈前疏林内茅庐中，即诸葛先生高卧之地。"

玄德谢之，策马前行。不数里，遥望卧龙冈，果然清景异常。后人有古风一篇，单道卧龙居处。诗曰：

"襄阳城西二十里，
一带高冈枕流水：
高冈屈曲压云根，
流水潺潺飞石髓；

*The sky's a curving vault of blue,*
*The level earth a chessboard,*
*Where men their white and black divide,*
*Disgrace or glory to decide.*
*For the winner, peace and comfort,*
*For the losers, tiring toil.*
*In Nanyang someone lies secluded,*
*Securely sleeping, Stay abed!*

Xuande reined in and asked who had composed the song. "Why, Master Sleeping Dragon," was the reply. "Where does he live?" Xuande asked. A farmer answered, "A short way south runs a high ridge called Sleeping Dragon Ridge. In front is a thin wood where you'll find the little thatched lodge that he's made his refuge."

Xuande thanked the man and rode on. Soon the ridge came into view. It was a soothing scene of extraordinary peace, as depicted in this old-style ballad:

*West of Xiangyang county twenty li,*
*A rising ridge leans over a flowing stream.*
*The twisting, turning ridge bears heavy clouds;*
*The frothing, churning stream is liquid jade.*

| | |
|---|---|
| 势若困龙石上蟠， | *Caught between the rocks, this dragon winds;* |
| 形如单凤松阴里； | *Shadowed by the pines, this phoenix hides.* |
| 柴门半掩闭茅庐， | *A wattle gate half-screens a thatched retreat:* |
| 中有高人卧不起。 | *Undisturbed, the recluse rests within.* |
| 修竹交加列翠屏， | *The bamboo forms a veil of green outside.* |
| 四时篱落野花馨； | *Where year-round hedgerows exhale flowery scents.* |
| 床头堆积皆黄卷， | *Learned works are piled around his bed;* |
| 座上往来无白丁； | *No common men have come before his seat.* |
| 叩户苍猿时献果， | *Now and then a gibbon taps to offer fruit;* |
| 守门老鹤夜听经； | *A crane, his gateguard, attends his nightly chants.* |
| 囊里名琴藏古锦， | *A brocade sack contains the precious lute;* |
| 壁间宝剑挂七星。 | *The seven-star sword is hung upon the wall.* |
| 庐中先生独幽雅， | *In this refined seclusion the master waits* |
| 闲来亲自勤耕稼： | *And works his acres in his leisure hour,* |
| 专待春雷惊梦回， | *Until spring thunder starts him from his dream* |
| 一声长啸安天下。” | *To calm the kingdom with one impassioned cry.* |
| 玄德来到庄前，下马亲 | Xuande arrived at the farmstead and knocked at the brush- |

叩柴门，一童出问。玄德曰："汉左将军宜城亭侯领豫州牧皇叔刘备，特来拜见先生。"童子曰："我记不得许多名字。"

玄德曰："你只说刘备来访。"童子曰："先生今早少出。"玄德曰："何处去了？"童子曰："踪迹不定，不知何处去了。"玄德曰："几时归？"童子曰："归期亦不定，或三五日，或十数日。"

玄德惆怅不已。张飞曰："既不见，自归去罢了。"玄德曰："且待片时。"云长曰："不如且归，再使人来探听。"玄德从其言，嘱咐童子："如先生回，可言刘备拜访。"

(5) <u>遂上马，行数里，勒马回观隆中景物，果然山不</u>

wood gate. A lad answered the door and asked his name. "General of the left under the Han," Xuande declared, "Lord of Yicheng Precinct, Protector of Yuzhou, Imperial Uncle Liu Bei comes to pay his respects to your master." "Too many names to remember," said the youth. "Just say Liu Bei is paying a call," Xuande urged him. "My master," the lad said, "went out for a bit earlier this morning." "Where to?" Xuande asked. "His movements are uncertain; I don't know where he has gone," was the reply. "When will he be back?" Xuande asked. "I don't know that, either," the lad said, "It could be three or four days or ten or more."

Xuande was greatly disappointed. Zhang Fei said, "Since we have failed to see him, let's go home and have done with it!" Xuande was for waiting a little longer, but Lord Guan also said, "We might as well be off. We can send someone later to inquire." Xuande finally agreed and told the lad, "When your master returns, will you say Liu Bei came to call?"

The brothers remounted and rode off. Several li later they reined in and looked back on the scenic figurations of Longzhong.

高而秀雅，水不深而澄清；地不广而平坦，林不大而茂盛；猿鹤相亲，松篁交翠。

Now the hills seemed more elegant than lofty, the streams more sparkling than deep, the land more smooth than spacious, the woods more lush than large, with gibbons and cranes joining in play, pine and bamboo blending their green.

观之不已，忽见一人，容貌轩昂，丰姿俊爽，头戴逍遥巾，身穿皂布袍，杖藜从山僻小路而来。

Xuande could not take his eyes away. Suddenly a man appeared his countenance imposing, his bearing stately yet simple. A scarf was wound casually around his head: a plain black gown covered his frame. With a staff of goose-foot wood he trod down a hillside path.

玄德曰："此必卧龙先生也！"急下马向前施礼，问曰："先生非卧龙否？"其人曰："将军是谁？"玄德曰："刘备也。"其人曰："吾非孔明，乃孔明之友博陵崔州平也。"玄德曰："久闻大名，幸得相遇。乞即席地权坐，请教一言。"

"This must be Master Sleeping Dragon," Xuande said eagerly as he dismounted and made a gesture of respectful greeting. "Could you be Sleeping Dragon, master?" he asked. "Your name, General?" the man responded. "Liu Bei," he answered. "I am not Kongming," the man went on, "but a friend of his, Cui Zhouping of Boling." "Your name has been long known to me," Xuande said. "This is a meeting ordained by fortune. I would like to benefit from your instruction if you could find the time…"

二人对坐于林间石上，关、张侍立于侧。州平曰：

The two men sat on some rocks in the woods; Lord Guan and Zhang Fei stood to either

“将军何故欲见孔明？”玄德曰：“方今天下大乱，四方云扰，欲见孔明，求安邦定国之策耳。”

州平笑曰：“公以定乱为主，虽是仁心，但自古以来，治乱无常。自高祖斩蛇起义，诛无道秦，是由乱而入治也；至哀、平之世二百年，太平日久，王莽篡逆，又由治而入乱；光武中兴，重整基业，复由乱而入治；至今二百年，民安已久，故干戈又复四起：此正由治入乱之时，未可猝定也。将军欲使孔明斡旋天地，补缀乾坤，恐不易为，徒费心力耳。岂不闻顺天者逸，逆天者劳；数之所在，理不得而夺之；命之所在，人不得而强之乎？”

side. Cui Zhouping began, “For what reason, General, do you wish to see Kongming?” “There is such disorder in the empire,” Xuande replied. “The four quarters are as unsettled as clouds. I would seek of Kongming the strategy to secure and stabilize the government and the country.”

“My lord,” Cui Zhouping responded with a smile, “ you are bent on bringing the disorder of our day to an end? However benevolent your intentions, since ancient times periods of disorder and civic order have come and gone quite unpredictably. When the Supreme Ancestor of the dynasty slew the white serpent and embarked on the rising that destroyed the despotic Qin, that interval, which led to the founding of the Han, was a time of transition from disorder to civil order. Two hundred years of peace and prosperity followed. Then, in the time of the Emperors Ai and Ping, Wang Mang usurped the throne and brought us again, from order to disorder. But the first emperor of the Later Han, Guang Wu, revived the dynasty and, righting its foundations, brought us out of disorder and back to civic order.

“Now after another two hun-

玄德曰："先生所言，诚为高见。但备身为汉胄，合当匡扶汉室，何敢委之数与命？"州平曰：(6)"山野之夫，不足与论天下事，适承明问，故妄言之。"玄德曰："蒙先生见教。但不知孔明往何处去了？"州平曰："吾亦欲访之，正不知其何往。"玄德曰："请先生同至敝县，若何？"州平曰："愚性颇乐闲散，无意功名久矣；容他日再见。"言讫，长揖而去。玄德与关、张上马而行。张飞曰："孔明又访不着，却遇此腐儒，闲谈

dred years, during which the population has enjoyed peace and contentment, we find sword and shield around us. This only shows that we are moving again into a period of disorder, and one which cannot be quickly ended. For Kongming to try to reverse the course of events or mitigate what fortune has in store would be, I am afraid, a futile expense of mind and body. It is said, "Adapt to Heaven and enjoy ease; oppose it and toil in vain." It is also said, "None can deduct from the reckoning, or force what is fated."

"There is great insight in your words," Xuande conceded. "But I, a Liu, scion of the Han, committed to maintain the dynasty's rule, may not leave the task to fate or reckoning." "A mountain rustic like myself," Cui Zhouping responded, "is hardly fit to discuss the affairs of empire. You honored me with your profound question and I expressed myself rashly." "You have favored me with your insight and instruction," Xuande said, "but I would know where Kongming has gone." "I, too, was hoping to pay a call on him," Cui Zhouping replied, "so I could not tell you where he is." "Would you be interested, master," Xuande in-

许久！”玄德曰：“此亦隐者之言也。”

quired, “in coming back with me to our humble county seat?” “My uncultured nature,” Cui Zhouping replied, “has grown too fond of leisure's freedom to give thought to success and fame. But there will be occasion for us to meet again.” With that, the man left after making a deep bow. “We have failed to find Kongming,” Zhang Fei said, “and bumped into that rotten pedant instead. Too much idle talk!” “That is how men in seclusion express themselves,” Xuande admonished him.

三人回至新野，过了数日，玄德使人探听孔明。回报曰：“卧龙先生已回矣。”玄德便教备马。

A few days after returning to Xinye, Xuande made inquiries and was told that Kongming had come back from his rambles. Xuande ordered the horses readied for another visit.

张飞曰：“量一村夫，何必哥哥自去，可使人唤来便了。”玄德叱曰：“汝岂不闻孟子云：欲见贤而不以其道，犹欲其入而闭之门也。孔明当世大贤，岂可召乎！”遂上马再往访孔明。关、张亦乘马相随。

“Do you have to go yourself for that village bumpkin?” Zhang Fei demanded. “Have him summoned.” “It looks,” Xuande said sharply, “as if you do not know what the sage Mencius meant when he said, “Trying to meet a worthy man in the wrong way is as bad as closing the door on an invited guest,” Kongming is one of the greatest men of our time, and yet you expect me to send out a summons?” And so a second time, attended by his brothers, Xuande went to Sleeping Dragon Ridge.

时值隆冬，天气严寒，彤云密布。行无数里，忽然朔风凛凛，瑞雪霏霏：山如玉簇，林似银妆。

张飞曰："天寒地冻，尚不用兵，岂宜远见无益之人乎！不如回新野以避风雪。"

玄德曰："吾正欲使孔明知我殷勤之意。如弟辈怕冷，可先回去。"

飞曰："死且不怕，岂怕冷乎！但恐哥哥空劳神思。"玄德曰："勿多言，只相随同去。"

将近茅庐，忽闻路旁酒店中有人作歌。玄德立马听之。其歌曰：

"壮士功名尚未成，
呜呼久不遇阳春！

君不见东海者叟辞荆榛，

It was the dead of winter, severely cold. Dense, somber clouds covered the sky. The brothers rode into a cutting northern wind. A heavy snow made the mountains gleam like arrowheads of white jade and gave the woods a silvery sheen. "The air is bitter," Zhang Fei said, "and the ground frozen solid. A bad time even for military operations, and yet you think we should be going this distance to meet someone of no use to us at all? Let's go back and get out of the storm."

"I am determined," Xuande replied, "to show Kongming my earnest intentions. If you can't stand it, brother, go on back yourself."

"If death doesn't frighten me," Zhang Fei retorted, "why should the cold? I just hate to see my elder brother waste his energy." "Then stop complaining," Xuande said, "and follow me."

As they approached the thatched cottage, they were surprised to hear someone singing in a roadside wine shop:

*No deeds, no fame achieved at manhood's prime:*
*Shall he ever find his lord or meet his time?*
*Remember when Jiang Ziya,*

| | |
|---|---|
| 后车遂与文王亲； | *The old sage of the Eastern Sea, quit his hazel wood And followed Zhou' s first king, Wen, as servant and as kinsman?* |
| 八百诸侯不期会， | *When, uncalled, eight hundred lords converged,* |
| 白鱼入舟涉孟津； | *And a white fish flew into King Wu' s boat As he forded at Meng* |
| 牧野一战血流杵， | *To battle the Shang at Grazing Field, Where he shed a tide of blood That bore off sword and shield,* |
| 鹰扬伟烈冠武臣。 | *As, fierce and majestic, an eagle on the wing, He towered above King Wu' s martial vassals?* |
| 又不见高阳酒徒起草中， | *And when The tippler from Gaoyang (as he liked to call himself), Li Yiji, came and made a common bow* |
| 长揖芒砀隆准公； | *To the "Big Nose Governor" in those dark hours* |
| 高谈王霸惊人耳， | *And spoke such startling truths of reign and rule* |
| 辍洗延坐钦英风； | *That the king-to-be dismissed his footwashers? And feasted Li Yiji, honoring his splendid spirit?* |
| 东下齐城七十二， | *The surrender of the east soon followed: Seventy –two cities and towns.* |

天下无人能继踪。

二人功绩尚如此，

至今谁肯论英雄？”

歌罢，又有一人击桌而歌。其歌曰：

“吾皇提剑清寰海，

创业垂基四百载；

桓灵季业火德衰，

奸臣贼子调鼎鼐。

青蛇飞下御座傍，

又见妖虹降玉堂；

群盗四方如蚁聚，

奸雄百辈皆鹰扬，

吾侪长啸空拍手，

闷来村店饮村酒；

独善其身尽日安，

何须千古名不朽！”

二人歌罢，抚掌大笑。玄德曰：“卧龙其在此间

*What man has followed in those footsteps?*
*Such were the deeds of Jiang Ziya and Li Yiji,*
*Heroes unsurpressed unto this very day.*

As soon as this song was finished, another man tapped the table and began to sing:

Han's first king took the realm by sword;

*The house he founded lasted twenty score.*
*With Huan and Ling, Han' s fire-virtue waned.*
*And evil men the chancelorship profaned.*
*They saw a serpent coiled beside the throne;*
*A rainbow in the consort-querters shone.*
*Ant-like, outlaws gathered everywhere;*
*Villains rose like raptors in the air.*
*We pound our hands and keen, but all in vain;*
*Our sorrow take us to the village inn*
*Leading lives of simple decency,*
*Who needs a name that lasts eternally?*

Their songs sung, the two men clapped and laughed aloud. Con-

乎！”遂下马入店。见二人凭桌对饮：上首者白面长须，下首者清奇古貌。

vinced that Sleeping Dragon was within, Xuan dismounted and entered the wineshop. The singers were leaning over a table drinking. One had a light complexion and a long beard, the other a fresh, ageless look.

玄德揖而问曰：“二公谁是卧龙先生？”

Xuande saluted them and asked, “Which of you is master Sleeping Dragon?”

长须者曰：“公何人？欲寻卧龙何干？”玄德曰：“某乃刘备也。欲访先生，求济世安民之术。”

“Who are you, sir?” the long-bearded one responded. “And what have you to do with him?” “I am Liu Bei,” was the reply, “and I need the master's skill to aid my cause and succor our age.”

长须者曰：“我等非卧龙，皆卧龙之友也：吾乃颍川石广元，此位是汝南孟公威。”

“I am not the man you seek,” the long-bearded man replied, “nor is he. But we are friends of his. I am Shi Guangyuan of Yingchuan, and this is Meng Gongwei of Runan,”

玄德喜曰：“备久闻二公大名，幸得邂逅。今有随行马匹在此，敢请二公同往卧龙庄上一谈。”

“Noble names long known to me,” Xuande exclaimed with delight. “I am favored by this fortunate encounter, and I have extra honors if you gentlemen would be willing to accompany me to Sleeping Dragon's farm.”

广元曰：“吾等皆山野慵懒之徒，不省治国安民之事，不劳下问。明公请自上马，寻访卧龙。”

“Country idlers like us,” Shi Guangyuan replied, “have no knowledge of the weighty matters that concern you. Do not waste time on the likes of us, sir, but resume your search yourself.”

玄德乃辞二人，上马投卧龙冈来。到庄前下马，叩门问童子曰："先生今日在庄否？"童子曰："现在堂上读书。"玄德大喜，遂跟童子而入。至中门，只见门上大书一联云：

(7)"淡泊以明志。

宁静而致远。"

玄德正看间，忽闻吟咏之声，乃立于门侧窥之，见草堂之上，一少年拥炉抱膝，歌曰：

"凤翱翔于千仞兮，
非梧不栖；
士伏处于一方兮，
非主不依。
乐躬耕于陇亩兮，
吾爱吾庐；
聊寄傲于琴书兮，

Xuande bade the drinkers good-bye and rode toward Sleeping Dragon Ridge. He dismounted at Kongming's farm and, finding the youth at the gate, asked, "Is your master in today?" "In the house reading," was the reply. Excitedly, Xuande followed the lad. Coming to the inner gate, they stopped before a couplet on the wall that read:

"Only through austerity and quiescence can one's purpose shine forth;

only through concentration and self-control can one's distant goal be reached."

As Xuande was studying the words, he heard someone singing inside. Standing attentively by the door of the thatched house, he peered in and saw a young man with his arms about his knees, chanting:

*The phoenix winging on the air*
*Will choose no tree*
*Except the wu.*
*The scholar keeping to his lair*
*Will have no lord Except the true.*
*Oh, let me till these furrowed fields,*
*By this sweet home*
*That I call mine.*
*In books and song I place my dreams*
*And wait the time*

以待天时。”

*The fates assign.*

玄德待其歌罢，上草堂施礼曰：“备久慕先生，无缘拜会。昨因徐元直称荐，敬至仙庄，不遇空回。今特冒风雪而来。得瞻道貌，实为万幸，”

When the singer stopped, Xuande entered and extended his courtesies. “I have long held you in admiration,” Xuande began. “but wanted occasion to express it personally. The other day, thanks to Shan Fu’s suggestion, I came to pay my respects at this retreat of yours. Unable to meet you, however, I went home dispointed. Now I come a second time, undaunted by the storm. This glimpse of your learned countenance is an untold blessing.”

那少年慌忙答礼曰：“将军莫非刘豫州，欲见家兄否？”玄德惊讶曰：“先生又非卧龙耶？”少年曰：“某乃卧龙之弟诸葛均也。愚兄弟三人：长兄诸葛瑾，现在江东孙仲谋处为幕宾；孔明乃二家兄。”

Fulstered by this speech, the young man returned the greeting and then replied, “General, you must be Liu Yuzhou and, I believe, wish to see my elder brother.” “Master,” Xuande said in astonishment, “then you are not Sleeping Dragon, either?” “No, I am his younger brother, Zhuge Jun. There are three of us brothers. The eldest, Zhuge Jin, is in the Southland advising Sun Quan. Kongming is the second brother.”

玄德曰：“卧龙今在家否？”均曰：“昨为崔州平相约，出外闲游去矣。”玄德曰：“何处闲游？”均曰：

“Is the Sleeping Dragon at home?” Xuande inquired. “Yesterday,” Zhuge Jun replied, “he was invited by Cui Zhouping to

"或驾小舟游于江湖之中，或访僧道于山岭之上，或寻朋友于村落之间，或乐琴棋于洞府之内：往来莫测，不知去所。"

玄德曰："刘备直如此缘分浅薄，两番不遇大贤！"均曰："少坐献茶。"

张飞曰："那先生既不在，请哥哥上马。"玄德曰："我既到此间，如何无一语而回？"因问诸葛均曰："闻令兄卧龙先生熟谙韬略，日看兵书，可得闻乎？"均曰："不知。"

张飞曰："问他则甚！风雪甚紧，不如早归。"玄德叱止之。均曰："家兄不在，不敢久留车骑；容日却来回礼。"

go on a jaunt." "Do you know where?" Xuande asked. "They might have gone rowing down some lake or river," Zhuge Jun anaswered. "Or to visit some Buddhist or Taoist on his hilltop retreat. Or to look for friends in the villages. Or they might have simply decided to entertain themselves with lutes and chess in some cavern den. My brother comes and goes quite unpredictably, and I have no idea where he might be."

"How meagre my lot!" Xuande exclaimed. "Twice now have I missed this excellent man!" "Sit awhile," Zhuge Jun suggested. "Let me offer you tea."

But Zhang Fei broke in, "The master in not here. Let's get going!" "Why go back," Xuande answered him, "Without having spoken to anyone?" With that, Xuande turned to Zhuge Jun and said, "Your esteemed brother is known for his mastery of military arts. They say he applies himself to the subject daily. Can you tell me more about this?"

When Zhuge Jun said he know nothing about it, Zhang Fei spoke again. "Look at that storm," he said. "Better be starting back." But Xuande told him sharply to

玄德曰："岂敢望先生枉驾。数日之后，备当再至。愿借纸笔作一书，留达令兄，以表刘备殷勤之意。"均遂进文房四宝。玄德呵开冻笔，拂展云笺，写书曰：

"备久慕高名，两次晋谒，不遇空回，惆怅何似！窃念备汉朝苗裔，滥叨名爵，伏睹朝廷陵替，纲纪崩摧，群雄乱国，恶党欺君，备心胆俱裂。虽有匡济之诚，实乏经纶之策。仰望先生仁慈忠义，慨然展吕望之大才，施子房之鸿略，天下幸甚！社稷幸甚！先此布达，再容斋戒薰沐，特拜尊颜，面倾鄙悃。统希鉴原。"

be quiet. "Since my brother is not here," Zhuge Jun said, "I should not detain your officers. He will return your courteous call at a future time."

"I would not want him to have to travel," Xuande replied. "I expect to be coming again in a few days . Could I trouble you, though, for a brush and paper? As an expression of the earnestness of my wish, I shall leave your elder brother a letter." The writing instruments were brought.

Xuande thawed the frozen hairs of the brush with his breath and unrolled the writing paper. His letter read:

A longtime admirer of your hnored name. I, Liu Bei, have come twice to present myself, only to leave again without having met you-a keen disppointment. I am humbly mindful that as a remote kinsman of the court, I have enjoyed prestige and rank far beyond my merits. When my thoughts turn to the rude displacement at court-our laws and customs crumbling and swept aside while countless contenders subvert the state and vicious factions abuse the sovereign-my heart breaks, my gall is rent. Whatever sincerity I may offer to the cause of delivering the Han is wasted for want of strategy. I admire your humane compassion, your sense of loyalty and honor. If in your greatness of spirit you would unfold your mighty talents, talents comparable to those of Jiang Ziya, and apply your grand strategy in the manner of Zhang Liang then the empire and the sacred shrines of the royal house would doubly blessed. I am forwarding this to convey my intention, after further ceremonial purification, to pay homage yet again to your honored presence, respectfully offering my poor, simple sincerity and entreating your discerning consideration.

玄德写罢，递与诸葛均收了，拜辞出门。均送出，玄德再三殷勤致意而别。

Xuande handed the letter to Zhuge Jun, bade him goodbye, and left. Zhuge Jun accompanied him past the gate, listening to his earnest reiterations. Finally they parted.

方上马欲行，忽见童子招手篱外，叫曰："老先生来也。"玄德视之，见小桥之西，一人暖帽遮头，狐裘蔽体，骑着一驴，后随一青衣小童，携一葫芦酒，踏雪而来；转过小桥，

口吟诗一首。诗曰：

Xuande was starting homeward when he saw the lad beyond the fence waving and shouting, "The old master is coming!" Ahead, past a small bridge, a man in winter headdress and fox furs was riding a donkey through the descending snow. He was followed by a youth in simple black carrying a gourd of wine. Turning on to the bridge, the rider sang:

“一夜北风寒，
万里彤云厚。
长空雪乱飘，
改尽江山旧。
仰面观火虚，
疑是玉龙斗。
纷纷鳞甲飞，
顷刻遍宇宙。
骑驴过小桥，
独叹梅花瘦！”

*Nightlong, north winds chill,*
*Myriad-leagued, dusky clouds expand.*
*Capering snow through an infinite sky*
*Transforms the never-changing land.*
*He looks into the ether' s vastitude:*
*Are jade dragons at war up there,*
*Strewing their scales every which way,*
*And filling up the hollow sphere?*
*Alone,*
*Sighing for the plum trees' battered blooms.*

玄德闻歌曰：“此真卧龙矣！”滚鞍下马，向前施礼曰：“先生冒寒不易！刘备等候久矣！”那人慌忙下驴答礼。

Certain that Sleeping Dragon was coming, Xuande leaped from the saddle to extend his greetings. “It must be hard for you, master,” he said, “to brave this bitter cold. I have long been awaiting you.” The startle rider climbed off his beast and returned the salutation.

诸葛均在后曰：“此非卧龙家兄，乃家兄岳父黄承彦也。”

Then Zhuge Jun came up and said, “This is not Sleeping Dragon; it is his father-in-law, Huang Chengyan.”

玄德曰：“适间所吟之句，极其高妙。”承彦曰：“老夫在小婿家观《梁父吟》，记得这一篇；适过小桥，偶

“I happened to hear you chanting just now,” Xuande said. “It sounded so elevated and poignant.” “I was reading the

见篱落间梅花，故感而诵之。不期为尊客所闻。”玄德曰：“曾见令婿否？”承彦曰：“便是老夫也来看他。”

玄德闻言，辞别承彦，上马而归。正值风雪又大，回望卧龙冈，悒怏不已。后人有诗单道玄德风雪访孔明。

诗曰：

“一天风雪访贤良，
不遇空回意感伤。
冻合溪桥山石滑，
寒侵鞍马路途长。
当头片片梨花落，
扑面纷纷柳絮狂。
回首停鞭遥望处，
烂银堆满卧龙冈。”

"Liangfu Elegies" in my son-in-law's home," the man replied. "I had that stanza in mind as I crossed the bridge; the plum blossoms near the fence moved me to sing. I never imagined an honoured guest might hear me." "Have you seen your esteemed son-in-law?" Xuande asked. "Actually, I am coming to see him," was the reply.

With that, Xuande took his leave, remounted and headed home. The wind and snow grew fiercer. Giving a last look back over Sleeping Dragon Ridge, Xuande felt overwhelmed by sadness and uncertainty. As a poet of later times wrote:

*That stormy day he sought the sage in vain,*
*And sore at heart, he started home again.*
*The creek bridge, frozen; the land, sheer ice.*
*His trembling horse has many li to cross.*
*Pearl-petal flakes descending from the skies,*
*Antic willow puffs darting at his eyes,*
*He turns and halts to view the scene behind:*

*Banked with snow, the silvered ridges shine.*

玄德回新野之后，(8)光阴荏苒，又早新春。乃令卜者揲蓍，选择吉期，斋戒三日，薰沐更衣，再往卧龙冈谒孔明。关、张闻之不悦，遂一齐入谏玄德。

Back in Xinye time crept by until it was again spring. Xuande ordered the diviners to cast for a propitious time to visit Kongming. After three days' abstinence from meat and wine, Xuande bathed, smeared himself with ritual oils, changed his clothes, and went back to Sleeping Dragon Ridge. His two brothers expressed intense displeasure and protested. Indeed:

正是：

高贤未服英雄志，

屈节偏生杰士疑。

The worthiest has yet to bend the hero's will;

Servility could shake his fighters' confidence.

未知其言若何，下文便晓。

What would Xuande say to them?

Read on.

# 第二章

# 水浒传

# *Outlaws of the Marsh*

义胆包天，忠肝盖地，四海无人识。

## 背景介绍

成书于元末明初，作者施耐庵（1296 年——1371 年）（还有一种说法是施耐庵与罗贯中合著）。是作者在《宣和遗事》及相关话本、故事的基础上创作而成的。是中国文学史上“第一部描写农民起义”的小说，讲述的是北宋仁宗皇帝时官逼民反的故事。洋洋洒洒一百回的《水浒传》写尽了江湖义气。在中国文学史上，犯了法的人第一次被提高到了“好汉”的高度，108 名来自不同行业，不同地位，不同背景的人被一个及时雨宋江撮合到了一块。他们似乎无法无天，在梁山泊上逍遥自在；可是他们的存在本身就是一个悖论，“忠义”是他们的名头，为了这个名头，宋江带着他们去招安，反身又投入他们逃离的奸佞当道的社会。最后的悲剧是不可避免的，死的死、散的散，曾经轰轰烈烈的占山为王的事业，最后只剩了山头旗杆上晃晃荡荡的半只旗子。人们只好从佛教里寻找一点慰藉，那个悖论也在供奉宋江的庙宇里不了了之。

《水浒传》流行最广的译本是沙博理（Sidney Shapiro）翻译的 *Outlaws of the Marsh* 。译者是美国出生的中国人，自从

1947 年就在中国居住，他在两种文字上的造诣和对中国历史文化的深切体会使他的译本独具特色。

## 细读节选

本书节选了原著的第七十二回，在这一回里，我们从梁山好汉们的厮杀呐喊中抽身出来，跟着宋江一行去京城逛灯会，挤在熙熙攘攘穿着长袍，束着发髻的古人堆儿里，忍不住也要驻足赏东观西，或者吃几颗开封的汤圆；然而，此行的目的让人想起来就觉得沉重，连青楼女子莲步轻移的曼妙也不能阻止英雄们的命运一路下滑。

与罗慕士不同，沙博理对原著中的诗歌采取了回避的处理（不排除他用的中文版本本身就没有这些诗歌）。这对原意的传达是否会产生影响？我们一边看，一边来琢磨这个问题。

## 拓展思考

1. 凭借记忆，写出 3 句划线的原文与译文。

| 原文 | 译文 |
|---|---|
| | |
| | |
| | |

2. 宋江此行的目的是什么？达到了吗？

3. 英文版和中文版在故事情节方面是否一致？读两种语言的感觉有何不同？

4. 请尝试把沙博理没有翻译的部分翻译出来。难点在哪里？

# 第七十二回

柴进簪花入禁院

李逵元夜闹东京

# Chapter 72

*Chai Jin Wears a Cockade and Enters the Forbidden Courtyard*
*Li Kui on Festival Night Disturbs the Eastern Capital*

诗曰：

圣主忧民记下四凶，
施行端的有神功。
等闲冒籍来官内，
造次簪花入禁中。
潜向御屏剜姓字，
更乘明月展英雄。
纵横到处无人敌，
谁向斯时竭寸衷？

无译文

话说当日宋江在忠义堂上分拨去看灯人数："我与柴进一路，史进与穆弘一路，鲁智深与武松一路，朱仝与刘唐一路。只此四路人去，其余尽数在家守寨。"

In Loyalty Hall that day Song Jiang announced the disposition of those who would go to see the lanterns : "I will travel with Chai Jin, Shi Jin with Mu Hong, Sagacious Lu with Wu Song, and Zhu Tong with Liu Tang. The rest of you will remain and guard the fortress."

李逵便道："说东京好灯，我也要去走一遭。"(1)

"They say the lanterns of the Eastern Capital are a pretty sight," said Li Kui. "I want to go

宋江道："你如何去得？"李逵守死要去，那里执拗得他住。宋江道："你既然要去，不许你惹事，打扮做伴当跟我；就叫燕青也走一遭，专和李逵作伴。"

too." "Impossible," said Song Jiang. Li Kui insisted stubbornly. There was no refusing him. Finally, Song Jiang relented. "All right. But only on condition that you don't make any trouble. Dress as a servant." He told Yan Qing to accompany them also, with the specific task of keeping a watchful eye on Li Kui.

看官听说，宋江是个文面的人，如何去得京师？原来却得"神医"安道全上山之后，却把毒药与他点去了，后用好药调治，起了红疤；再要良金美玉，碾为细末，每日涂搽，自然消磨去了。那医书中说："美玉灭斑"，正此意也。

You will remember, reader,, that Song Jiang's face bore the tattoo of the criminal. How could he appear in the capital city? After the skilled doctor An Daoquan had arrived at the stronghold he had removed the mark with a powerful caustic. Later, he treated the wound with good medicines. When a red scar formed he removed this gradually with daily applications of poultices containing powdered gold and ground jade. That is what medical books refer to when they talk of "obliterating blemishes with fine jade."

当日先叫史进，穆弘作客人去了，次后便使鲁智深，武松，扮作行脚僧行去了，再後宋江，朱仝，刘唐，也扮作客商去了。各人跨腰刀，提朴刀，都藏暗器，不必得说。

Song Jiang instructed Shi Jin and Mu Hong to go first, disguised as travellers. Sagacious Lu and Wu Song would go next, as wandering monks. Lastly would be Zhu Tong and Liu Tang, in the garb of merchants. All wore swords and carried halberds and, needless to say, had concealed weapons on their persons.

且说宋江与柴进扮作间凉官，再叫戴宗扮作承局，也去走一遭，有些缓急，好来飞报。

李逵，燕青扮伴当，各挑行李下山，众头领都送到金沙滩饯行。军师吴用再三吩咐李逵道：“你闲常下山，好歹惹事，今番和哥哥去东京看灯，非比闲时，路上不要吃酒，十分小心在意，使不得往常性格。若有冲撞，弟兄们不好厮见，难以相聚了。”李逵道：“不索军师忧心，我这一遭并不惹事。”

相别了，取路登程，抹过济州，路经滕州，取单州，上曹州来，前望东京万寿门外，寻一个客店安歇下了。

Song Jiang himself and Chai Jin pretended to be vacationing officials. Dai Zong went as a lieutenant. In the event of any emergency, he could rush back to the stronghold with a report.

Li Kui and Yan Qing, the "servants," transported the luggage of the "officials" down the mountain on carrying-poles. The chieftains saw the travellers off to the Shore of Golden Sands. Wu Yong cautioned Li Kui. "Whenever you set out on your own you get into a jam. This time you're going to the Eastern Capital with Big Brother to see the lanterns.It's not your usual jaunt.You're not to drink on the road.Behave with caution and curb your temper. If you provoke any clashes, we brothers may have to terminate our relationship." "Don't worry, Military Advisor," said the Black Whirlwind, "I won't stir up anything."

They parted, and the travellers set out. They touched Jizhou, passed Tengzhou, went through Danzhou, reached Caozhou, and at last arrived at an inn outside the Wanshou Gate of the Eastern Capital, where they took quarters. It was the eleventh day of the first lunar month.

宋江与柴进商议，此是正月十一日的话，宋江道：“明日白日里，我断然不敢入城，直到正月十四日夜，人物喧哗，此时方可入城。”柴进道：“小弟明日先和燕青入城中去探路一遭。”宋江道：“最好。”

次日，柴进穿一身整整齐齐的衣服，头上巾帻新鲜，脚下鞋袜干净；燕青打扮，更是不俗。两个离了店肆，看城外人家时，家家热闹，户户喧哗，都安排庆赏元宵，各作贺太平风景。来到城门下，没人阻挡，果然好座东京去处。怎见得：

州名汴水，府号开封。逶迤按吴楚之邦，延亘连齐鲁之境。山河形胜，水陆要冲。禹画为豫州，周封为郑地。层叠卧牛之势，按上界戊己中央；崔嵬伏虎之形，像周天二十八宿。金明池上三春柳，小苑城边四季花。十万里鱼龙变化之乡，四百座军州辐辏之地。

Song Jiang conferred with Chai Jin. “I don't dare enter the capital tomorrow in daylight,” he said. “I'll wait until the evening of the fourteenth, when the celebration is noisiest, and go in then.” “I'll scout out a route for you with Yan Qing tomorrow.” “Excellent.”

The following day Chai Jin dressed handsomely, bound his head in a fresh kerchief, and put on clean shoes and stockings. Yan Qing also garbed himself fashionably. The two left the inn. The suburban households were festive and gay as they prepared to enjoy the lantern festival and celebrate the peaceful atmosphere. Chai and Yan reached the gate without incident and entered the city.

无译文

霭霭祥云笼紫阁，融融瑞气照楼台。

当下柴进，燕青两个入得城来，行到御街上，往来观，转过东华门外，见往来锦天花帽之人，纷纷济济，各有服色，都在茶坊酒肆中坐地。柴进引燕青，迳上一个小小酒楼，临街占个阁子，栏望时，见班直人等多从内里出入，头边各簪翠叶花一朵。

柴进唤燕青，附耳低言，你与我如此如此。燕青是个点头会意的人，不必细问，火急下楼。出得店门，恰好迎著个老成的班直官，燕青唱个喏。

那人道："面生并不相识。"燕青说道："小人的东人和观察是故交，特使小人来相请。"原来那班直姓王，燕青道："莫非足下是张观察？"那人道："我自姓王。"

They strolled along Imperial Road, taking in the sights, and came to the area adjoining the palace's East Glory Gate. Here were many taverns and tea—houses, patronized by people richly garbed in silks and satins, each in a distinctive color. Chai Jin led Yan Qing to a small tavern. They went upstairs and sat down in a room overlooking the street. They could see attendants going in and out of the palace grounds. Each wore a cockade in the shape of a flower with jade-green leaves tacked to the side of his head kerchief.

Chai whispered some instructions in Yan's ear. Yan nodded, went swiftly down the stairs and left the tavern. Fortunately, the attendant he approached was rather simple-minded. Yan hailed him respectfully.

"I don't know your face," the man said. "We've never met."

"My master is an old friend of yours. He's sent me to invite you to join him. Aren't you Inspector Zhang?"

"My name is Wang."

"Oh, Inspector Wang, of

燕青随口应著："正是教小人请王观察，贪慌忘记了。"

那王观察跟随著燕青来到楼上，燕青揭起帘子，对柴进道："请到王观察来了。"燕青接了手中执色，柴进邀入阁儿里相见，各施礼罢，王班直看了柴进半晌，却不认得。说道："在下眼拙，失忘了足下，适蒙呼唤，愿求大名。"

柴进笑道："小弟与足下童稚之交，且未可说，兄长熟思之。"一壁便叫取酒肉来，与观察小酌。酒保安排到肴馔果品，燕青斟酒，殷勤相劝。

酒至半酣，柴进问道："观察头上这朵翠花何意？"那王班直道："今上天子庆贺元宵，我们左右内外共有二十四班，通类有五千七八百人，每人皆赐衣袄一领，翠叶金花一枝，上有小小金牌一个，凿著(2)"与民同乐"四字，因此每日在这里听候点视。如有宫

course. That's the name. I was in such a hurry, I forgot."

Wang went with Yan into the tavern and up the stairs. Yan raised the door curtain and announced: "Inspector Wang is here." He gave Chai a hidden signal with his hand. The two men exchanged courtesies. Wang looked at Chai Jin. He didn't know him. "My eyesight is poor," he said. "I'm afraid I don't remember Your Excellence. Would you be good enough to tell me your name?"

Chai Jin smiled. "We were friends as children. You'll think of it without me saying." He summoned the waiter and ordered wine. Tasty dishes were served, and Yan Qing saw to it that the attendant's cup remained filled.

When the man was half drunk, Chai questioned him.

"What is the meaning of that cockade?"

"Today, the emperor is celebrating the first full moon. There are twenty-four companies of us palace attendants, nearly fifty-eight hundred men in all. We've each been issued a new robe, a cockade in the shape of green leaves and a golden flower, and a small metal badge pinned above

花锦袄，便能勾入内里去。”

柴进道：“在下却不省得。”又饮了数杯，柴进便叫燕青，你自去与我旋一杯热酒来吃。

无移时，酒到了，柴进便起身与王班直把盏道：“足下饮过这杯小弟敬酒，方才达知姓氏。”王班直道：“在下实想不起，愿求大名。”王班直拿起酒来，一饮而尽。恰才吃罢，口角流涎，两脚腾空，倒在凳上。

柴进慌忙去了巾帻，衣服，鞋袜，却脱下王班直身上锦袄，踢串，鞋之类，从头穿了，带了花帽，拿了执色，吩咐燕青道：“酒保来问时，只说这观察醉了，那官人未回。”燕青道：“不必吩咐，自有道理支吾。”

且说柴进离了酒店，直

it reading: 'Celebrate with the People.' We're on call at all times. Only those with this palace cockade and robe are allowed in."

"I didn't know that," said Chai Jin. They downed several more cups, and Chai said to Yan Qing: "Get us a pot of warm wine."

Before long, Yan brought the wine. Chai Jin rose and addressed Attendant Wang, cup in hand.

"Drink this round I respectfully offer and you'll know my name."

"I just can't think of it. Please tell me."

Wang raised his cup and drained it. Almost instantly he began to drool from the corners of his mouth. His feet flailed, and he fell back off his bench.

Chai quickly stripped Wang of his head kerchief, clothing and footwear, and put them on, including the cockade and the colored silk robe. "If the waiter should ask," he said to Yan Qing, "tell him the attendant is drunk, and that the other gentleman will be back soon."

"No need to instruct me. I'll handle it."

Chai Jin left the tavern and went to the East Glory Gate of

入东华门去看那内庭时，真乃人间天上，但见：

祥云龙凤阙，瑞霭罩龙楼。琉的瓦砌鸳鸯，龟背帘垂翡翠。正阳门迳通黄道，长朝殿端拱紫垣。浑仪台占算星辰，待漏院班分文武。墙涂椒粉，丝丝绿柳拂飞甍；殿绕栏杆，簇簇紫花迎步辇。疑身在蓬莱岛，仿佛神游兜率天。

柴进去到内里，但过禁门，为有服色，无人阻当，直到紫宸殿。转过文德殿，殿门各有金锁锁着，不能勾进去，且转过凝晖殿。从殿边转将入去，到一个偏殿，牌上金书“睿思殿”三字，此是官家看书之处，侧首开著一扇朱红□子。

柴进闪身入去看时，见正面铺着御座，两边几案上放着文房四宝，象管，花笺，龙墨，端砚，书架上尽

the palace. Because of the cockade and the color of his robe, no one stopped him from entering. It was a splendid, lavish place of glorious hues, a paradise on earth.

无译文

Chai passed a number of compounds whose gates were closed and fastened with golden locks. Then, off to a side, he saw a sign in letters of gold, "Hall of Deep Thought." This was the imperial library. Its vermilion doors of ornately carved wood were open.

Chai Jin entered. Directly opposite was an imperial chair, flanked by tables on which lay brush-pens with ivory handles, decorated paper, imperial ink-

是群书，各插着牙签；正面屏风上堆青叠绿画着山河社稷混一之图。转过屏风后面，但见素白屏风上御书四大寇姓名，写着道：

山东宋江 准西王庆 河北田虎 江南方腊

柴进看了四大寇姓名，心中暗忖道："国家被我们扰害，因此时常记心，写在这里。"便去身边拔出暗器，正把山东宋江那四个字刻将下来，慌忙出殿，随后早有人来。

柴进便离了内苑，出了东华门，回到酒楼上看那王班直时，尚未醒来，依旧把锦衣，花帽，服色等项，都放在阁儿内。柴进还穿了依旧衣服，唤燕青和酒保计算了酒钱，剩下十数贯钱，就赏了酒保。

临下楼来吩咐道："我和王观察是弟兄，恰才他醉

slabs, and the famous grinding stones from Duanxi. Innumerable sets of books lined the walls, each with ivory fastenings. Behind the chair was a screen decorated with a scenic panorama in lovely colors. Chai Jin walked around to the back of the screen. It was blank, except for a listing of the four major outlaws, as follows: "Song Jiang of Shandong, Wang Qing west of the River Huai, Tian Hu of Hebei, Fang La south of the Yangzi."

"We are the ones who are ravaging the country," Chai Jin reflected. "It has been written here so that no one will forget." He drew a concealed knife and cut out the words "Song Jiang of Shandong" and hastily quit the building. Others were already entering.

Chai Jin left the inner grounds, departed through the East Glory Gate, and returned to the tavern. Attendant Wang was still in a drugged slumber. Chai took off Wang's clothes and put on his own. He directed Yan Qing to pay the bill and give the waiter a large tip.

As he and Yan were leaving he said to the waiter: "At-

了，我替他去内里点名了回来，他还未醒。我却在城外住，恐怕误了城门，剩下钱都赏你，他的服色号衣都在这里。”酒保道：“官人但请放心，男女自服侍。”柴进，燕青离得酒店，迳出万寿门去了。

tendant Wang and I are close friends. He's drunk, so I signed in for him at the palace. He still hasn't come to, but I have to go outside the city and must leave before the gates close. You can keep the change. Wang's clothing and identification are all here." "I'll take care of everything, sir," the waiter assured him. Chai and Yan left the tavern and exited from the city through the Wanshou Gate.

王班直到晚起来，见了服色，花帽都有，但不知是何意。(3) 酒保说柴进的话，王班直似醉如痴，回到家中。

Towards evening the attendant awakened, Since his identifying robe and cockade were still with him, he didn't suspect what had happened. The waiter told him what Chai Jin had said. Still befuddled with drink, Wang returned home.

次日有人来说：“睿思殿上不见山东宋江四个字，今日各门好生把得铁桶般紧，出入的人，都要十分盘诘。”王班直情知是了，那里敢说。

The next day a colleague informed him: "The words 'Song Jiang of Shandong' have been removed from the Hall of Deep Thought. Today security at every gate is as tight as the bands on a bucket. Anyone going in or out is closely checked." Wang at last understood. But he didn't dare breathe a word.

再说柴进回到店中，对宋江备细说内宫之中，取出御书大寇“山东宋江”四字，与宋江看罢，叹息不

On reaching the inn, Chai told in detail what he had seen in the palace, and handed over the "Song Jiang of Shandong" which he had cut from the imperial writ-

已。十四日晚，宋江引了一干人入城看灯。怎见得好个东京？有古乐府一篇，单道东京胜概：

ing. Song Jiang examined it with many sighs. On the evening of the fourteenth he and several of his men went into the city to view the lanterns.

一自梁王，初分晋地，双鱼正照夷门。卧牛城阔，相接四边村。多少今明陈迹，上林苑花发三春。绿杨外溶溶汴水，千里接龙津。潘樊楼上酒，九重宫阙，风阙天阍。东风外，笙歌嘹亮堪闻。御路上公卿宰相，天街畔帝子王孙。堪图画，山河社稷，千古汴京尊。

无译文

故宋时，东京果是天下第一国都，繁华富贵，出在道君皇帝之时。当日黄昏，明月从东而起，天上并无云翳，宋江，柴进扮作闲凉官，戴宗扮作承局，燕青扮为小闲，只留李逵看房。

During the Song Dynasty the Eastern Capital was the leading metropolis. It grew prosperous and rich under the Taoist Sovereign. At dusk that day a bright moon rose in the east in a cloudless sky. Song Jiang and Chai Jin were disguised as vacationing officials. Dai Zong wore the garb of a lieutenant. Yan Qing tagged along as servant. Only Li Kui remained at the inn.

四个人杂在社火队里，取路哄入封丘门来，遍玩六街三市，果然夜暖风和，正

The four men mingled with the noisy crowds swarming in through the Fengqiu Gate and

好游戏。转过马行街来，家家门前扎缚灯棚，赛悬灯火，照耀如同白日，正是楼台上下火照火，车马往来人看人。

wandered about the streets and marts. It was a warm evening with gentle breezes, ideal for strolling. On the main thoroughfare sheds had been erected in front of every door and hung with lanterns, which vied for beauty and turned the night into day. The buildings too were decked with lanterns, and the streets thronged with carriages and people.

四个转过御街，见两行都是烟月牌，来到中间，见一家外悬青布幕，里挂斑竹帘，两边尽是碧纱窗，外挂两面牌，牌上各有五个字，写道：

The four men turned away from Imperial Road to a street lined on both sides with signboards denoting establishments of "misty moonlight." The four were struck by one house midway down. Its doorway was covered by a blue cloth drape, behind which was a curtain of spotted bamboo. Green silk gauze screened the windows on either side. Between them and the doorway hung two vertical plaques reading: "A Fairy Maid of Song and Dance, A Flower of Surpassing Grace."

(4)“歌舞神仙女，风流花月魁。”

宋江见了，便入茶坊里来吃茶，问茶博士道：“前面角妓是谁家？”

Song Jiang and his companions went into a tea—house opposite and sat down. "Which courtesan's place is that?" they asked the waiter.

茶博士道：“这是东京上厅行首，唤作李师师。间壁便是赵元奴家。”

"The leading lady of her profession in the Eastern Capital, Li Shishi. And in the house next door to us is Zhao Yuannu."

宋江道："莫不是和今上打得热的。"茶博士道："不可高声，耳目觉近。"

"Isn't Li the one who's having a hot affair with the emperor?" Song Jiang asked.

"Not so loud," said the waiter. "There are eyes and ears all around."

宋江便唤燕青，附耳低言道："我要见李师师一面，暗里取事，你可生个婉曲入去，我在此间吃茶等你。"宋江自和柴进，戴宗在茶坊里吃茶。

Song Jiang leaned close to Yan Qing and whispered: "I want to meet Li Shishi and arrange something with her privately. Invent some story to get us in. We'll wait for you here." He remained with Chai Jin and Dai Zong, drinking tea.

却说燕青迳到李师师门首，揭开青布幕，掀起斑竹帘，转入中门，见挂著一碗鸳鸯灯，下面犀皮香桌儿上，放着一个博山古铜香炉，炉内细细喷出香来。

Yan Qing walked up to the door of the courtesan's residence, pushed aside the drape, raised the bamboo curtain, and entered. He saw fine smoke rising from a bronze incense burner on a rhinoceros—hide table beneath a hanging duck and drake lamp.

两壁上挂着四幅名人山水画，下设四把犀皮一字交椅。燕青见无人出来，转入天井里面，又是一个大客位，设着三座香楠木雕花玲珑小床，铺着落花流水紫锦褥，悬挂一架玉棚好灯，摆着异样古董。

On two of the walls were scenic paintings by four famous artists. Below stood four armchairs, also covered by rhinoceros hide. There didn't seem to be anyone around. Yan Qing crossed a small courtyard into another parlor. Here were three small beds of ornately carved camphor wood, cushioned with purple mattresses bearing a fallen-petals-in-a-lowing-stream design. A fine lamp hung on a jade stand, here

燕青微微咳嗽一声，只见屏风背后钻出一个丫鬟来，见燕青道个万福，便问燕青："哥哥高姓哪里来？"

燕青道："相烦姐姐请妈妈出来，小闲自有话说。"梅香入去不多时，转出李妈妈来。燕青请她坐了，纳头四拜。李妈妈道："小哥高姓？"

燕青答道："老娘忘了，小人是张乙的儿子，张闲的便是，从小在外，今日方归。"原来世上姓张姓李姓王的最多，那虔婆思量了半晌，又是灯下，认人不仔细，猛然省起，叫道："你不是太平桥下小张闲么？你哪里去了？许多时不来！"

燕青道："小人一向不在家，不得来相望。如今服侍个山东客人，有的是家私，说不能尽。他是个燕南河北第一个有名财主，今来此间：一者就赏元宵，二者来京师

and there were rare antiques.

Yan Qing coughed softly. A serving maid rounded a folding screen, saw Yan Qing and curtsied.

"What is your name, big brother? Where are you from?"

"Can I trouble you, sister, to ask mama to come out? I have something to say."

The girl left and, a few moments later, returned with the bawd. Yan urged her to be seated. He kowtowed four times. "What is your name, young brother?"

"You've forgotten me, mother. I'm Zhang Xian, son of Zhang the Second. I've been away from the city since childhood. I only returned today." Zhang was a very common name. The bawd thought for several moments. She couldn't see the young man clearly in the lamplight. Suddenly, she imagined she remembered.

"Not little Zhang Xian near the Taiping Bridge? Where have you been? I haven't seen you in ages."

"Of course not. I've been away. Today, I'm looking after a guest from Shandong. He's got more property than words can say. He's probably the richest man in his province. He's here on business. One, he wants to enjoy the

省亲，三者就将货物在此做买卖，四者要求见娘子一面。怎敢说来宅上出入，只求同席一饮，称心满意。不是少闲卖弄，那人实有千百两金银，欲送与宅上。”

那虔婆是个好利之人，爱的是金宝，听的燕青这一席话，便动了念头，忙叫李师师出来，与燕青厮见。灯下看时，端的好容貌。燕青见了，纳头便拜，有诗为证：

芳年声价冠青楼，玉貌花颜是罕俦。
共羡至尊曾贴体，何惭壮士便低头。

那虔婆说与备细，李师师道：“那员外如今在那里？”燕青道：“只在前面对门茶坊里。”李师师便道：“请过寒舍拜茶。”燕青道：“不得娘子言语，不敢擅进。”虔婆道：“快去请来。”

lantern festival; two, he's visiting relatives here in the capital; three, he's buying and selling merchandise; and four, he's longing to meet your lady. He asks only to sip tea at the same table, and he'll be satisfied. I wouldn't dare ask otherwise. I'm not kidding-that man has thousands in gold and silver, and he'd like to present some of it to this house."

The greedy bawd was very fond of money. Yan Qing's story went to her heart. She hastily called out Li Shishi and introduced her to Yan. He could see in the lamplight that the girl truly had a form that could sink fish and down geese, a face that eclipsed the moon and put the flowers to shame. Yan dropped to his knees and kowtowed.

无译文

The bawd relayed his story to Shishi.

"Where is the gentleman now?" asked the girl.

"In that tea house across the way," said Yan.

"Invite him to have some tea here."

"He wouldn't dare enter without your permission."

"Hurry over and ask him," said the bawd.

燕青迳到茶坊里，耳边道了消息，戴宗取些钱，还了茶博士，三人跟着燕青，迳到李师师家内。入得中门相接，请到大客位里，李师师敛手向前动问起居道："适间张闲多谈大雅，今辱左顾，绮阁生光。"

Yan Qing went to the tea house and related the news in Song Jiang's ear. Dai Zong paid the bill and the three men followed Yan to the courtesan's house, On entering, they were escorted to the main parlor, where Li Shishi stood with hands folded demurely. She greeted Song Jiang politely and said: "Zhang Xian has just been talking about your munificence. Your visit brings luster to our humble dwelling."

宋江答道："山僻村野，孤陋寡闻，得睹花容，生平幸甚。"

"I'm an ignorant man from an obscure mountain hamlet," replied Song. "To be able to gaze upon your beauty is my greatest good fortune."

李师师便邀请坐，又看着柴进问道："这位官人，是足下何人？"宋江道："此是表弟叶巡简。"就叫戴宗拜了李师师。

The courtesan asked him to be seated. "Who is this other gentleman?" she queried, indicating Chai Jin. "My nephew Sheriff Ye," said Song. He also instructed Dai Zong to greet the girl.

宋江，柴进居左，客席而坐；李师师右边，主位相陪。奶子捧茶至，李师师亲手与宋江，柴进，戴宗，燕青换盏，不必说那盏茶的香

Song Jiang and Chai Jin were ushered to guest seats on the left Side of the table, and Li Shishi took her place on the right, as hostess, while the bawd brought in the tea things. The girl poured for each of the four men person-

味，细欺雀舌，香胜龙涎。

ally. The tea leaves were finer than birds' tongues, the brew was as fragrant as dragon's saliva.

茶罢，收了盏托，欲叙行藏，只见 子来报："官家来到后面。"

When they had finished and the tea service was removed, they chatted pleasantly. The bawd entered and said: "His Majesty is waiting in the rear."

李师师道："其实不敢相留，来日驾幸上清宫，必然不来，却请诸位到此，少叙三杯。"

"I'm afraid I can't keep you any longer, today," the courtesan said to her guests. "But he's due to visit the Upper Purity Temple soon and won't be able to come here for some time. Once he goes, you gentlemen will be welcome to call again and join me in a few cups of wine."

宋江喏喏连声，带了三人便行。出得李师师门来，与柴进道："今上两个表子，一个李师师，一个赵元奴。虽然见了李师师，何不再去赵元奴家走一遭？"

Song Jiang bid her a respectful farewell and departed with his three companions. When they had left her door Chai Jin said: "The emperor has two mistresses, Li Shishi and Zhao Yuannu. We've met one, what about the other?"

宋江径到茶坊间壁，揭起帘幕，张闲便请赵婆出来说话。燕青道：

They went to the building next to the tea house and raised the door curtain. Yan Qing spoke to Zhao Yuannu's bawd.

"我这两位官人，是山东巨富客商，要见娘子一面，一百两花银相送。"

"These two gentlemen are wealthy merchants from Shandong. If they could meet your lady, they would present her with a hundred ounces of silver."

赵婆道："恰恨我女儿没缘，不快在床，出来相见

"My girl hasn't any luck. She's sick in bed and can't receive com-

不得。”宋江道：“如此却再来求见。”赵婆相送出门，作别了。

pany."

"We'll try again another time," said Song Jiang. The bawd saw them to the door and bid them farewell.

四个且出小御街，迳投天汉桥来看鳌山。正打从樊楼前过，听得楼上笙簧聒耳，鼓乐喧天，灯火疑眸，游人似蚁。

Leaving the street, they headed towards Tianhan Bridge to view the massed lanterns display. As they neared the Fanlou Restaurant building they heard the shrilling of pipes and the beat of drums. Lanterns dazzled the eye, people swarmed in and out like ants.

宋江，柴进也上樊楼，寻个阁子坐下，取些酒食肴馔，也在楼上赏灯饮酒。吃不到数杯，只听得隔壁阁子内有人作歌道：

Song Jiang and Chai Jin went upstairs, found a room and sat down. They ordered drinks and side dishes. Sipping their wine, they admired the lanterns gleaming outside in the night. They had downed only a few cups when they heard someone making up lyrics and singing them in the adjoining room:

浩气冲天贯斗牛，
英雄事业未曾酬。
手提三尺龙泉剑，
不斩奸邪誓不休！

*Though our courage surges to the stare,*
*Our heroic task is unfulfilled.*
*With dragon sword grasped firm in hand,*
*We won't quit till every scoundrel's killed!*

宋江听得，慌忙过来看时，却是“九纹龙”史进，“没

Song Jiang knew that voice. He hastily entered. There was

遮拦”穆弘，在阁子内吃得大醉，口出狂言。

宋江走近前去喝道：(5)“你这两个兄弟吓杀我也！快算还酒钱，连忙出去！早是遇着我，若是做公的听得，这场横祸不小。谁想你这两个兄弟也这般无知口糙！快出城，不可迟滞。明日看了正灯，连夜便回，只此十分好了，莫要弄得撅撒了！”史进，穆弘默默无言，便叫酒保算还了酒钱。两个下楼，取路先投城外去了。

宋江与柴进四人微饮三杯，少添春色，戴宗计算还了酒钱，四人拂袖下楼，迳往万寿门来客店内敲门。

李逵困眼睁开，对宋江道：“哥哥不带我来也罢了，既带我来，却教我看房，闷出鸟来。你们都自去快活。”

Nine Dragons Shi Jin and Mu Hong the Unrestrained, quite drunk and talking wildly.

"You brothers frightened the wits out of me," Song Jiang said sharply. "Pay your bill and get out. If it was some policeman instead of me who heard you, you'd have been in a fine mess. I never expected you two to be so careless. Leave the city without delay. After the formal lantern display tomorrow night, I'm leaving too.

That's the best way. We don't want to stir up any trouble." Shi Jin and Mu Hong had nothing to say. They paid their bill, went down the stairs, and departed from the Eastern Capital.

Song Jiang and his three companions had a few more cups. They were a bit tipsy. Dai Zong paid the bill. Flipping their long sleeves, they left the restaurant. They returned to the inn outside Wanshou Gate and pounded on the door.

Li Kui peered at them with sleepy eyes. "What's the good of letting me come to the Eastern Capital?" he grumbled to Song Jiang. "You only makc mc stay here and watch the room. While I'm penned up in this frigging place, you fellows are out having a good time."

宋江道："为你生性不善，面貌丑恶，不争带你入城，只恐因而惹祸。"李逵便道："你不带我去便了，何消得许多推故！几曾见我那里吓杀了别人家小的大的！"宋江道："只有明日十五日这一夜带你入去，看罢了正灯，连夜便回。"李逵呵呵大笑。

过了一夜，次日正是上元节候，天色晴明得好。看看傍晚，庆贺元宵的人不知其数，古人有篇《绛都春》单道元宵景致：

融和初报，乍瑞霭霁色，皇都春早。翠　竞飞，玉勒争驰，都闻道鳌山彩结蓬莱岛，向晚色双龙衔照。绛霄楼上，彤芝盖底，仰瞻天表。缥缈风传帝乐，庆玉殿共赏，群仙同到。迤逦御香飘满，人间开嘻笑，一点星球小。隐隐鸣梢声杳，游人月下归来，洞天未晓。

这一篇词，称颂道君皇

"It's because you have a bad disposition and are so ugly. I'm afraid if I take you into the city you'll only create a disturbance." "Don't take me, then! Why make a lot of excuses? When did my looks ever scare anybody's family to death?" "All right, tomorrow night, the fifteenth, and no more. We'll see the lanterns and leave immediately." Li Kui laughed happily.

The next day, Lantern Festival Day itself, was bright and clear. Towards evening, huge crowds of celebrants gathered. It was a time of national peace and prosperity, when peasants toiled contentedly in their fields.

无译文

帝庆赏元宵，与民同乐。此时国富民安，士农乐业。

当夜宋江与同柴进，依前扮作闲凉官，引了戴宗，李逵，燕青五个人，迳从万寿门来。

是夜虽无夜禁，各门头目军士全付披挂，都是戎装帽带，弓弩上弦，刀剑出鞘，摆布得甚是严整。高太尉自引铁骑马军五千，在城上巡禁。

宋江等五个向人丛里挨挨抢抢，直到城里，先唤燕青，附耳低言，与我如此如此，只在夜来茶坊里相等。

燕青迳往李师师家扣门，李妈妈，李行首都出来接见燕青，便说道：“烦达员外休怪，官家不时间来此私行，我家怎敢轻慢。”

燕青道：“主人再三上覆妈妈，启动了花魁娘子，

Song Jiang and Chai Jin, in the guise of vacationing officials, followed by Dai Zong, Li Kui and Yan Qing, went into the city through the Wanshou Gate.

Although there was no curfew that night, each of the gates was guarded by soldiers in full armor, equipped with weapons at the ready. Their bows were strung, their swords were unsheathed, and every post was manned. Five thousand cavalry under the personal command of Marshal Gao Qiu patrolled atop the city walls.

Song Jiang and his four companions jostled through the crowds into the Eastern Capital. He whispered some instructions in Yan Qing's ear, and added: "I'll be waiting in the tea house."

Yan Qing went to the home of Li Shishi and knocked on the door. The prime-ranking courtesan and her bawd received him.

"Ask your master, the magnate, to please forgive us," they said. "We never know when His Majesty is liable to drop in privately. We must be diligent."

"My master apologizes for disturbing you. Shandong is only a remote province by the sea. It

山东海僻之地，无甚希罕之物，便有些出产之物将来，也不中意，只教小人先送黄金一百两，权当人事；随后别有罕物，再当拜送。”

doesn't have anything of value. What it does produce wouldn't be worth presenting to you. All he can do is send you one hundred ounces of gold as a token of his esteem. Perhaps the lady can have ornaments made out of them for her hair. If he comes across something attractive later on, he'll send it with his respects."

李妈妈问道：“如今员外在那里？”燕青道：“只在巷口等小人送了人事，同去看灯。”世上虔婆爱的是钱财，见了燕青取出那火炭也似金子两块，放在面前，如何不动心！

"Where is the magnate now?" asked the bawd.

"He's waiting for me at the end of the lane. We're going to see the lanterns." There was nothing the bawd loved more in the world than wealth. When Yan Qing took out two gold nuggets, gleaming like live coals and put them on the table, she was overjoyed.

便道：“今日上元佳节，我子母们却待家筵数杯，若是员外不弃，肯到贫家少叙片时，不知肯来也不？”

"This is Lantern Festival Day," she said, "and my girl and I are celebrating it at home with a few cups of wine. If the magnate wouldn't think our fare too meager, perhaps he'd visit our humble abode for a chat. Do you think he might come?"

燕青道：“小人去请，无有不来。”说罢，转身回到茶坊，说与宋江这话了，随即都到李师师家。宋江教戴宗同李逵只在门前等。

"I'm sure he will. I'll pass on your invitation."

Yan Qing went to the tea house and informed Song Jiang. They all repaired to the home of Li Shishi.

Song Jiang told Dai Zong and Li Kui to wait at the front door.

三个人入到里面大客位里，李师师接着，拜谢道："员外识荆之初，何故以厚礼见赐，却之不恭，受之太过。"

宋江答道："山僻村野，绝无罕物，但送些小微物，表情而已，何劳花魁娘子致谢。"

李师师邀请到一个小小阁儿里，分宾坐定，奶子侍婢，捧出珍异果子，济楚菜蔬，希奇按酒，甘美肴馔，尽用锭器，摆一春台。李师师执盏向前拜道：

"夙世有缘，今夕相遇二君，草草杯盘，以奉长者。"

宋江道："在下山乡虽有贯伯浮财，未曾见如此富贵，花魁的风流声价，播传寰宇，求见一面，如登天之难，何况亲赐酒食。"

The three entered the large parlor where Li Shishi received them. "We've only just met," she said to Song Jiang. "You shouldn't give such an expensive gift. It really isn't right."

"We have nothing of value in my rustic mountains. I can only offer this trifle as an expression of thanks."

The courtesan invited them into a small adjoining room, and asked them to be seated. Maids served rare fruits, fine food, vintage wine, and tasty delicacies. The crockery was of the best, the table was laid beautifully.

Shishi approached them and bowed, wine cup in hand.

"I must have been lucky in my previous incarnation or I wouldn't be able to meet you two gentlemen today. With this simple wine, I pledge to you, my elders."

Song Jiang said: "Although I have a bit of property in my mountain area, I have never seen anything so lavish as you have here. Your fame is known throughout the land, lovely and charming lady. An interview with you is more difficult to obtain than reaching Heaven. Yet here I am, actually chatting and drink-

李师师道："员外奖誉太过，何敢当此。"都劝罢酒，叫奶子将小小金杯巡筛。但是李师师说些街市俊俏的话，皆是柴进回答；燕青立在边头和哄取笑。

ing with you personally!"

"How extremely kind of you, magnate. You praise me too highly. I am unworthy!" Both drank, and Shishi directed her personal maid to pour wine in tiny gold cups. Then the courtesan relaxed and gossiped about members of her profession. To all her remarks it was Chai Jin who replied. Yan Qing, who was standing off to one side, offered quips that made everyone laugh.

酒行数巡，宋江口滑，把拳裸袖，点点指指，把出梁山泊手段来。柴进笑道："我表兄从来酒后如此，娘子勿笑。"

After several rounds Song Jiang became more loquacious. He rolled up his sleeves and gesticulated as he talked in the free manner of the brigands of Mount Liangshan. "My brother is always like this after he's had some wine," Chai Jin smiled. "Pray don't laugh at him, lady."

李师师道：(6)"酒以合欢，何拘于礼。"

"Drinking is for pleasure," said Shishi. "Why stand on ceremony?"

丫鬟说道："门前两个伴当：一个黄髭须，且是生的怕人，在外面喃喃呐呐地骂。"

"One of those two servants at the front door," a young maid said, "the one with the yellow beard who's so weird-looking he scares you, is muttering curses."

宋江道："与我唤他两个人入来。"只见戴宗引着李逵到阁子里。李逵看见宋江，柴进与李师师对坐饮酒，自肚里有五分没好气，

"Tell them both to come in," said Song Jiang. Dai Zong soon entered the side room with Li Kui. When the Black Whirlwind saw Song Jiang and Chai Jin sitting and drinking with Shishi, he

圆睁怪眼，直瞅他三个。

李师师便问道："这汉是谁？恰像土地庙里对判官立地的小鬼。"众人都笑。李逵不省得他说。宋江答道："这个是家生的孩儿小李。"李师师笑道："我倒不打紧，辱没了太白学士。"

宋江道："这厮却有武艺，挑得三二百斤担子，打得三五十人。"

李师师叫取大银赏锺，各与三锺，戴宗也吃三锺。燕青只怕他口出讹言，先打抹他和戴宗依先去门前坐地。

宋江道："大丈夫饮酒，何用小杯，就取过赏锺，连饮数锺。"

李师师低唱苏东坡《大江东去词》。宋江乘着酒兴，索纸笔来，磨得黑浓，蘸得笔饱，拂开花笺，对李师师道："不才乱道一词，尽诉胸中郁结，呈上花魁尊听。"

glared.

"Who is this fellow?" Shishi asked. "He looks like one of those imps standing before the judge in the temple statuary." Everyone laughed except Li Kui. He didn't know what she was talking about.

"He's the son of one of our family servants," said Song Jiang. "It doesn't matter," said the courtesan with a laugh. "I have no refinement."

"The lout is a skilled warrior," Song explained. "He can tote two or three hundred catties and fight forty or fifty men."

Shishi called for large silver flagons and gave Li Kui and Dai Zong three rounds each. Yan Qing was afraid Li Kui would say something coarse, and he directed the two to return to their posts at the front of the house.

"When a real man drinks," said Song Jiang, "he doesn't use small cups." He picked up a large silver flagon and downed several rounds.

In a low voice Shishi murmured a song by the poet Su Dongpo to the melody of Xijiangyue. His senses heightened by wine, Song Jiang called for brush-pen and paper. He ground the ink thick and black, dipped

当时宋江落笔，遂成乐府词一首，道是：

天南地北，
问乾坤何处可容狂客？
借得山东烟水寨，
来买凤城春色。
翠袖围香，
绛绡笼雪，
一笑千金值。
神仙体态，
薄幸如何消得？
想芦叶滩头，
蓼花汀畔，
皓月空凝碧，
六六 雁行连八九，
只等金鸡消息。
义胆包天，
忠肝盖地，
四海无人识。

his pen, and spread the paper. "Though I have no learning," he said to the courtesan, "I'd like to scrawl a few words to express the sadness in my heart. I beg of you to hear me, foremost flower." Taking up his pen, Song Jiang, then and there composed a yuefu poem. It ran as follows:

*North and south,*
*Where under Heaven is there a place for this wild traveller?*
*My misty mountain stronghold*
*Is but a base for future status in the imperial capital.*
*Jade sleeves and swirling incense,*
*Red brocades and snow-white cuffs...*
*One smile from you is worth*
*A thousand ounces of gold.*
*Fairy maid, your beauty*
*Is more than I can bear!*

无译文

*Six times six in wild goose formation,*
*Plus eight times nine,*
*Waiting only for news*
*From the Golden Cock.*
*Our chivalry Heaven-embracing.*
*Earth-shaking our loyalty,*
*Yet recognized by none*

离愁万种，

醉乡一夜头白。

写毕，递与李师师反复看了，不晓其意。宋江只要等她问其备细，却把心腹衷曲之事告诉，只见奶子来报："官家从地道中来至后门。"

李师师忙道："不能远送，切乞恕罪。"自来后门接驾，奶子丫环连忙收拾过了杯盘什物，扛过台桌，洒扫亭轩，宋江等都未出来，却闪在黑暗处，

张见李师师拜在面前，奏道起居，圣上龙体劳困。只见天子头戴软纱唐巾，身穿滚龙袍，说道："寡人今日幸上清宫方回，教太子在宣德楼赐万民御酒，令御弟在千步廊买市，约下杨太尉，久等不至，寡人自来，爱卿近前与朕攀话。"

*Within the Four Seas.*
*Morose and sad at separation,*
*I drink,*
*And in a single night*
*My hair turns white.*

When he had finished, he handed the poem to Li Shishi. She read it a few times, but didn't understand. He was about to explain when the courtesan's personal maid entered. "His Majesty has arrived at the rear door through the tunnel," she announced.

"I won't be able to see you off," Shishi said hastily to her guests. "Please forgive me." She hurried to receive the emperor. The young maid quickly gathered the cups and utensils, carried away the small table, and swept the floor. Song Jiang and the others concealed themselves in a dark corner of the side room.

From it they could see Shishi in the parlor kneeling before the sovereign. "Your Majesty must be weary from affairs of state." The emperor's head was covered by a silk gauze kerchief in the Tang style. He wore an imperial dragon robe. "I've just returned from the Upper Purity Temple," he said. "I directed my son the prince to dispense wine to the populace at

Xuande House and my younger brother to attend the fair at the Thousand Paces Esplanade. I had arranged to meet Marshal Yang, but he never showed up, though I waited a long time. So I came here. Approach, beloved, let us talk together."

宋江在黑地里说道：(7)"今番挫过，后次难逢，俺三个就此告一道招安赦书，有何不好！"

"If we miss this chance, we may never get another," Song Jiang whispered to his cohorts in the darkness. "Why don't we three go forward and beseech an amnesty? What would be wrong with that?"

柴进道："如何使得？便是应允了，后来也有翻变。"三个正在黑影里商量。

"Impossible!" said Chai Jin. "Even if he agreed, he could always reverse himself later."

却说李逵见了宋江，柴进和那美色妇人吃酒，却教他和戴宗看门，头上毛发倒竖起来，一肚子怒气正没发付处，只见杨太尉揭起帘幕，推开扇门，迳走入来，见了李逵，喝问道："你这厮是谁？敢在这里？"

Meanwhile, Li Kui's wrath was growing. Song Jiang and Chai Jin had sat drinking with the beauty, but he and Dai Zong had been sent to watch the door! Li Kui's hackles rose. His fury reached a boiling point. Just then, Marshal Yang raised the hanging screen and pushed open the double doors. He was about to Step in when his eyes Ml on Li Kui, Standing inside the entry. "Who are you, knave? How dare you come here?" he barked.

李逵也不回应，提起把交椅，望杨太尉脸打来。杨太尉倒吃了一惊，措手不

Without a word, Li Kui picked up an armchair and flung it at Yang's head. The startled marshal

及，两交椅打翻地下。戴宗便来救时，那里拦挡得住。李逵扯下幅画来，就蜡烛上点着，东捽西捽，一面放火，香桌椅凳，打得粉碎。

宋江等三个听得，赶出来看时，见“黑旋风”裩下半截衣裳，正在那里行凶。四个扯出门外去时，李逵就街上夺条棒，直打出小御街来。

宋江见他性起，只得和柴进，戴宗先赶出城，恐关了禁门，脱身不得，只留燕青看守着他。

李师师家火起，惊得赵官家一道烟走了。邻佑人等一面救火，一面救起杨太尉，这话都不必说。

城中喊起杀声，震天动地。高太尉在北门上巡警，听了这话，带领军马，便来追赶。燕青伴着李逵，正打之间，撞着穆弘，史进，四

tumbled backwards, knocking over another two chairs. Dai Zong rushed to intervene, but he was too late. Li Kui ripped pictures off the wall and set fire to them with a candle. Smashing left and right, he spread the blaze. Incense table, chairs, benches-he pulverized them all.

Song Jiang and his companions hurried out when they heard the tumult. They found the Black Whirlwind, stripped to the waist, going on a rampage. By the time they got outside the door, Li Kui was tearing down the street with a cudgel he had grabbed somewhere.

Song Jiang decided to leave the city immediately with Chai Jin and Dai Zong, lest the gates be closed before they could escape. He directed Yan Qing to remain behind and look after Li Kui.

The moment the fire broke out in Li Shishi's home, the emperor was off like a streak of smoke. Neighbors who hurried to fight the blaze also rescued Marshal Yang. Of that no more need be said.

The sounds of the yelling and shouting reached Marshal Gao, who was patrolling above the North Gate. He hastened down with his soldiers to give chase.

人各执枪棒，一齐助力，直打到城边。

Li Kui, battling madly, ran into Mu Hong and Shi Jin. They were joined by Yan Qing, and the four fought their way to the inner side of the city wall.

把门军士急待要关门，外面鲁智深轮铁禅仗，武行者使起双戒刀，朱仝，刘唐手捻着朴刀，早杀入城来，救出里面四个。方才出得城门，高太尉军马恰好赶到城外来。

Soldiers rushed to close the gate. But from the outside up charged Sagacious Lu with his iron staff, Wu Song with his double swords, and Zhu Tong and Liu Tang, swinging halberds. They hacked a path into the city and saved their four mates. They got through the gate just about the time Gao and his mounted force were reaching it.

八个头领不见宋江，柴进，戴宗，正在那里心慌。

Song Jiang, Chai Jin and Dai Zong had vanished. The eight chieftains grew alarmed.

原来军师吴用已知此事，定教大闹东京，克时定日，差下五员虎将，引领带甲马军一千骑，是夜恰好到东京城外等接，正逢着宋江，柴进，戴宗三人，带来的空马，就教上马，随后众人也到。正都上马时，於内不见了李逵，高太尉军马冲将出来。

Now it so happened that Wu Yong, the outlaws' military advisor, suspecting Song Jiang would have difficulty, had decided to raid the Eastern Capital. He fixed a time and dispatched a thousand armored cavalry under the five Tiger Chieftains. In the outskirts they met Song Jiang, Chai Jin and Dai Zong, and provided them with horses they had brought for that purpose. Then the other eight arrived and were also given mounts. But there was no sign of Li Kui. Marshal Gao and men were preparing to charge forth.

宋江手下的五虎将：关

胜，林冲，秦明，呼延灼，董平突到城边，立马於壕堑上，大喝道：(8)“梁山泊好汉全伙在此！早早献城，免汝一死。”高太尉听得，哪里敢出城来，慌忙教放下吊桥，众军上城堤防。

宋江便唤燕青吩咐道：“你和黑厮最好，你可略等他一等，随后与他同来。我和军马众将先回，星夜还寨，恐怕路上别有枝节。”

不说宋江等军马去了，且说燕青立在人家房檐下看时，只见李逵从店里取了行李，拿着双斧，大吼一声，跳出店门，独自一个，要去打这东京城池。

正是：声吼巨雷离店肆，手提大斧劈城门。

毕竟“黑旋风”李逵怎的去打城，且听下回分解。

Five of Song Jiang's commanders-Guan Sheng, Lin Chong, Qin Ming, Huyan Zhuo and Dong Ping, galloped up to the edge of the moat.

"All the gallants of Mount Liangshan are here," they shouted. "Surrender the city and save yourselves from death!" Gao dared not come out. He hurriedly pulled up the drawbridge and retreated with his soldiers to defensive positions atop the city wall.

"You're Li Kui's best friend," Song Jiang said to Yan Qing. "Wait for the swarthy oaf and bring him back. I want to return to the stronghold with our men tonight before the foe can intercept us."

Song Jiang and the outlaws departed. Yan Qing, watching beneath the eaves of a house, saw Li Kui emerging from the inn with his luggage on his back. An ax in either hand, he leaped forth from the inn gate with a yell and headed, alone, to attack the Eastern Capital.

Truly, he left the inn roaring like thunder, flourishing axes to split the city gate.

How did Li Kui the Black Whirlwind assault the Eastern Capital? Read our next chapter if you would know.

# 第三章

# 西游记

## *Journey to the West*

“我乃齐天大圣，就请我老孙做个尊席，有何不可？”

### 背景介绍

《西游记》成书于明代，作者吴承恩(1501 年——1582 年)。是一本以唐僧西天取经为主线的集历史事实、神话传说和丰富想象为一体的，长达 100 回的古典小说名著。天地人，人鬼神，神佛道，被串联成一个有机整体，相互映照着，以极大的魅力冲击读者的想象空间和传统的审美规范，是神话小说最活灵活现的代表作。

毫无疑问，孙悟空是世界文学史上独一无二的角色。他张扬的性格、好动的特性、无法无天却忠心事主的行为，都造就了他喜剧、动感的形象，他是人所能想象得到的最自由自在的状态。西天取经的情节设计既是宗教事实也是浪漫情怀的释放，一路上师徒四人过五关斩六将，终成正果，人生不也如此吗？所以《西游记》就是一部寓言小说，我们从里面得到的除了乐趣，还有智慧和勇气。

詹纳尔（W · J · F · Jenner）是著名的英国汉学家。毕业于牛津大学，从二十世纪 70 年代年着手《西游记》的翻译，1993 年第一版在外研社出版，再版十多次。他的译本语言通俗，洒脱，能够较好地传达原文的形和神。

## 细读节选

带上紧箍咒之前的美猴王，是自由主义的化身，在他眼里没有上下等级之分。他是快乐的孩子，无拘无束的顽童，是受不得半点管制的自由意识的具体化。可惜，不久他就要被压在五指山下，一压就是五百年。我们抓紧这最后一刻，随着美猴王一起去大闹天宫。

## 拓展思考

1. 凭借记忆，写出 3 句划线的原文与译文。

| 原文 | 译文 |
|---|---|
| | |
| | |
| | |

2. 齐天大圣屡犯天条，他可有罪恶感？
3. 译文是否传意，是否传神？举例说明。
4. 大闹天宫的“闹”指的是猴子的哪些举动？

# 第五回

## Chapter 5

乱蟠桃大圣偷丹

反天宫诸神捉怪

*After Chaos Among the Peaches the Great Sage steals the Pills*
*In the Revolt Against Heaven the Gods Capture the Demons*

话表齐天大圣到底是个妖猴，更不知官衔品从，也不较俸禄高低，但只注名便了。

The story goes on to relate that the Great Sage Equealling heaven, a mere monkey devil after all, was quite satisfied that his name was on the register of office without caring about the grading of his job and his own rank, or the size of his salary.

那齐天府下二司仙吏，早晚扶侍，只知日食三餐，夜眠一榻，无事牵萦，自由自在。

The Immortal clerks in the two offices in his residence were in constant attendance on him, he had three meals a day and a bed to sleep on at night, and he lived a free and easy life without worries.

（1）闲时节会友游宫，交朋结义。

In his spare time he would visit the other palaces, get together with his old friends, and make new ones.

见三清，称个“老”字；逢四帝，道个“陛下”。

When he saw the Three Pure Ones, he would address them as “venerable”, and when he met the Four Emperors he called them “Your Majesty”.

与那九曜星、五方将、二十八宿、四大天王、十二元辰、五方五老、普天星相、河汉群神，俱只以弟兄相待，彼此称呼。

He was on fraternal terms with the Nine Brighter Shiners, the Generals of the Five Regions, the Twenty-Eight Constellations, the Four Great Heavenly Kings, the Gods of the Twelve Branches, the Five Ancients of the Five Regions, the star ministers of the whole sky, and the countless gods of the Milky Way.

（2）今日东游，明日西荡，云去云来，行踪不定。

Today he would wander east, and tomorrow he would go west, coming and going by cloud, and never staying anywhere for long.

一日，玉帝早朝，班部中闪出许旌阳真人，俯囟启奏道："今有齐天大圣，无事闲游，结交天上众星宿，不论高低，俱称朋友。恐后闲中生事，不若与他一件事管，庶免别生事端。"

When the Jade Emperor was holding his morning court one day the Immortal Xu of Jingyang came forward from the body of officials, kowtowed, and suggested, "The Great Sage Equaling Heaven is spending his time in idle travel, and is making the acquaintance of all the stars in the sky, calling them all his friends irrespective of their rank. It would be as well to give him some responsibility, and prevent his idleness leading to trouble later on."

（3）玉帝闻言，即时宣诏。

The Jade Emperor's response to this suggestion was to send for the Monkey King at once.

猴王欣欣然而至，道："陛下，诏老孙有何升赏？"

He came in a cheerful mood and asked, "What promotion and reward have you summoned me here to receive, Your Majesty?"

玉帝道："朕见你身闲无事，与你件执事。你且权管那蟠桃园，早晚好生在意。"

"Seeing that you are idle and have nothing to do," replied the Jade Emperor, "We are giving you a job. You are to administer the Peach Orchard, and you will give it your attention day and night."

大圣欢喜谢恩，朝上唱喏而退。

The Great Sage was overjoyed, and after expressing his thanks and chanting "na-a-aw" he withdrew.

他等不得穷忙，即入蟠桃园内查勘。本园中有个土地拦住，问道："大圣何往？"

In his eagerness to be at work he went straight to the Peach Orchard to have a look round. When he got there he was stopped by a local tutelary god who asked him, "Where are you going, Great Sage?"

大圣道："吾奉玉帝点差，代管蟠桃园，今来查勘也。"那土地连忙施礼，即呼那一班锄树力士、运水力士、修桃力士、打扫力士都来见大圣磕头，引他进去。但见那：

"I've been put in charge of the Peach Orchard by the Jade Emperor, and I've come to inspect it." The local god hastened to greet him formally, and he called the men who weeded, brought water, looked after the trees, and swept the grounds to come and kowtow to the Great Sage. When Sun Wukong was taken inside this is what he saw:

夭夭灼灼，颗颗株株。

夭夭灼灼花盈树，

颗颗株株果压枝。

*Charming*
*Every tree.*
*Charming and luxuriant the full blossom;*
*Every three weighed down with*

果压枝头垂锦弹，
花盈树上簇胭脂。
时开时结千年熟，
无夏无冬万载迟。
先熟的，
酡颜醉脸；
还生的，
带蒂青皮。
凝烟肌带绿，
映日显丹姿。
树下奇葩并异卉，
四时不谢色齐齐。
左右楼台并馆舍，
盘空常见罩云霓。
不是玄都凡俗种，
瑶池王母自栽培。

*fruit.*
*The fruit-laden branches bend like carding-bows;*
*The blossoming trees are covered with powder and rouge.*
*Always blossoming, always in fruit, they are ripe for a thousand years;*
*They know no summer or winter, but linger for ever.*
*The early ripeners*
*Look red-faced and tipsy;*
*The ones still growing*
*Are green in stalk and skin.*
*When the dew forms, their flesh has a touch of blue,*
*While the sun picks out their vermilion beauty.*
*Below the trees exotic flowers grow,*
*Bright and unfading throughout the year.*
*On either side stand towers and pavilions,*
*And a rainbow always arches the sky.*
*These are not the common breeds of the Dark Earth Capital,*
*But are tended by the Queen Mother of the Jade Pool.*

大圣看玩多时，问土地道："此树有多少株数？"

After taking a good look at this the Great Sage asked the local god, "How many of these trees are there?"

土地道：“有三千六百株：前面一千二百株，花微果小，三千年一熟，人吃了成仙了道，体健身轻。

“Three thousand six hundreds all together,” the local god replied. “The ones growing at the front have tinny blossoms and small fruits, and they ripen every three thousand years. Anyone who eats them becomes an Immortal and understands the Way, and his body becomes both light and strong.

中间一千二百株，层花甘实，六千年一熟，人吃了霞举飞升，长生不老。

The twelve hundred in the middle have multiple blossoms and sweet fruits, and ripen every six thousand years; whoever eats them can fly and enjoy eternal youth.

后面一千二百株，紫纹缃核，九千年一熟，人吃了与天地齐寿，日月同庚。”

The back twelve hundred are streaked with purple and have pale yellow stones. They ripen once every nine thousand years, and anyone eats them becomes as eternal as Heaven and Earth, as long-lived as the Sun and the Moon.

大圣闻言，欢喜无任，当日查明了株数，点看了亭阁，回府。自此后，三五日一次赏玩，也不交友，也不他游。

The Great Sage was beside himself with joy on learning this, and that day he checked the number of the trees and looked over the building in the orchard before going back to his residence. From then on, he went to admire them every three or four days. He dropped his friends, and made on more pleasure jaunts.

(4) 一日，见那老树枝头，桃熟大半，他心里要吃

One day he noticed that the peaches near the end of the branches of one old tree were

个尝新。奈何本园土地、力士并齐天府仙吏紧随不便。

all but ripe, and he felt like trying one; but as the local god, the workmen, and the immortal clerks from his residence were close on his heels it was impossible.

忽设一计道："汝等且出门外伺候，让我在这亭上少憩片时。"

Suddenly he had an idea, and he said, "Go and wait for me outside the gates while I take a nap in this summer house."

那众仙果退。只见那猴王脱了冠着服，爬上大树，拣那熟透的大桃，摘了许多，就在树枝上自在受用。吃了一饱，却跳下来，簪冠著服，唤众等仪从回府。迟三二日，又去设法偷桃，尽他享用。

All the Immortals thereupon withdrew, and the Monkey King took off his official hat and clothes, climbed one of the bigger trees, and chose some large, ripe peaches. When he had picked a good number he sat at his ease in the branches and ate his fill of them, then jumped down from the tree, pinned on his hat, put on his clothes, and shouted for all his attendants to go back to his residence with him. Two or three days later he thought of another trick to steal some more peaches, and he ate his fill of them.

一朝，王母娘娘设宴，大开宝阁，瑶池中做"蟠桃盛会"，即着那红衣仙女、素衣仙女、青衣仙女、皂衣仙女、紫衣仙女、黄衣仙女、绿衣仙女，各顶花篮，去蟠桃园摘桃建会。

One day the Queen Mother arranged a banquet, opening many precious pavilions for a feast of peaches by the Jade Pool. She sent the Red Fairy, the Blue Fairy, the White Fairy, the Black Fairy, the Purple Fairy, the Yellow Fairy, and the Green Fairy to the Peach Orchard with their baskets to pick peaches for the feast.

七衣仙女直至园门首，只见蟠桃园土地、力士同齐天府二司仙吏，都在那里把门。仙女近前道："我等奉王母懿旨，到此携桃设宴。"

The seven fairies went straight to the orchard gates, the workmen of the orchard and the immortal superintendents of the two offices of the Equaling Heaven Residence were guarding the gate. The fairies went up to them and said, "We have come on the orders of the Queen Mother to pick peaches for a feast."

土地道："仙娥且住。今岁不比往年了，玉帝点差齐天大圣在此督理，须是报大圣得知，方敢开园。"仙女道："大圣何在？"土地道："大圣在园内，因困倦，自家在亭子上睡哩。"仙女道："既如此，寻他去来，不可延误。"土地即与同进。寻至花亭不见，只有衣冠在亭，不知何往。四下里都没寻处。

"Wait a moment please, Immortal Beauties," said the local god. "Things are different this year. The Jade Emperor has appointed the Great Sage Equaling Heaven to be the guardian of this orchard, and we must ask him before we can open the orchard to you." "Where is the Great Sage?" the fairies asked, and the local god replied, "Inside the orchard. As he was feeling tired he is having a nap by himself in a summerhouse." "In that case, please find him without delay," requested the fairies, and the local god took them into the orchard. But all they could find of him in the summerhouse were his hat and clothes. They had no idea where he could have gone, and looked everywhere without success.

原来大圣耍了一会，吃了几个桃子，变做二寸长的个人儿，在那大树梢头浓叶

The Great Sage had in fact made himself only two inches long after eating some of the peaches for fun, and he was

之下睡着了。

七衣仙女道："我等奉旨前来，寻不见大圣，怎敢空回？"旁有仙吏道："仙娥既奉旨来，不必迟疑。我大圣闲游惯了，想是出园会友去了。汝等且去摘桃，我们替你回话便是。"

那仙女依言，入树林之下摘桃。先在前树摘了二篮，又在中树摘了三篮；到后树上摘取，只见那树上花果稀疏，只有几个毛蒂青皮的。

原来熟的都是猴王吃了。七仙女张望东西，只见南枝上只有一个半红半白的桃子。青衣女用手扯下枝来，红衣女摘了，却

sleeping under a large leaf at the top of one of the big trees.

"We have come by decree, and we can't go back empty-handed, although the Great Sage is nowhere to be found," said the fairies. One of the immortal superintendents who was standing nearby replied, "As you Immortal Beauties have come by order of the Queen Mother, we must not delay you. Our Great Sage is always wandering off, so I expect that he has gone away to visit some of his friends. You had better pick the peaches; it will be all right if we inform him."

The fairies did as he suggested and went into the orchard to pick peaches. First they filled two baskets from the trees in front, and then they picked three basketfuls from the trees in the middle; but when they came to the trees at the back, they saw that peaches and blossoms were few and far between. Only a few unripe fruits with furry stalks and green skins were left.

All the ripe ones had been eaten up by the Monkey King. The seven fairies looked everywhere, but all they could see was a single red and white peach on a Southern branch. The Blue Fairy

将枝子往上一放。原来那大圣变化了，正睡在此枝，被他惊醒。大圣即现本相，耳朵内掣出金箍棒，晃一晃，碗来粗细，咄的一声道：(5)“你是那方怪物，敢大胆偷摘我桃！”

慌得那七仙女一齐跪下道：“大圣息怒。我等不是妖怪，乃王母娘娘差来的七衣仙女，摘取仙桃，大开宝阁，做‘蟠桃盛会’。适至此间，先见了本园土地等神，寻大圣不见。我等恐迟了王母懿旨，是以等不得大圣，故先在此摘桃，万望恕罪。”

大圣闻言，回嗔作喜道：“仙娥请起。王母开阁设宴，请的是谁？”

仙女道：“上会自有旧

pulled the branch down, the Red Fairy picked the peach, and then they let the branch go again. This woke up the Great Sage, who had changed himself into this peach to take a nap on this branch. He resumed his own form, took his gold—banded cudgel from his ear, shook it till it was as thick as a ricebowl, and shouted at them, "Where are you from, you thieving fiends?"

The seven fairies fell on their knees in confusion. "Please don't be angry with us, Great Sage. We're not fiends but seven fairies sent by Her Majesty the Queen Mother of the West to pick peaches of immortality and open the precious halls here for a Feast of Peaches. When we arrived here we saw the local god and other deities of the place, but we could not find you, Great Sage. We could not delay carrying out the Queen Mother's orders, so we went ahead and picked the peaches without waiting for you, Great Sage. We very much hope that you will forgive us."

These words turned the Great Sage's bad mood into a good one, and he said, "Please rise, Fairy Beauties. Who is the Queen Mother inviting to this feast?"

"There are old rules about

规。请的是西天佛老、菩萨、罗汉，南方南极观音，东方崇恩圣帝，十洲三岛仙翁，北方北极玄灵，中央黄极黄角大仙，这个是五方五老。还有五斗星君，上八洞三清、四帝、太乙天仙等众，中八洞玉皇、九垒、海岳神仙，下八洞幽冥教主、注世地仙。各宫各殿大小尊神，俱一齐赴蟠桃嘉会。”

大圣笑道：“可请我么？”仙女说：“不曾听得说。”大圣道：“我乃齐天大圣，就请我老孙做个尊席，有何不可？”

仙女道：“此是上会会

who attends: The Buddha of the Western Heaven, Bodhisattvas, holy monks, Arhats, the Guanyin of the South Pole, the Merciful and Sage Emperor of the East, the Venerable Immortals of the Ten Continents and the Three Islands, the Mystic Divinity of the North Pole, and the Great Yellow—horned Immortal of the Yellow Pole at the Centre. These make up the Five Venerable Ones of the Five Regions. There will also be the Star Lords of the Five Constellation; the Three Pure Ones, the Four Emperors and the Heavenly Immortal of the Great Monad from the Eight High Caves; the Jade Emperor, the immortals of the Nine Mounds, and the gods of the Seas and Mountains and the Ruler of the Nether World from the Eight Lower Caves; and the terrestrial deities. All the major and minor gods of all the halls and palaces will come to the Feast of Peaches."

"Will I be invited?" asked the Great Sage with an ingratiating smile. "Not as far as we've heard," the fairies replied. "I'm the Grcat Sagc Equaling Heaven, so why shouldn't I be asked?" said the Great Sage.

"That was what happened before: we don't know about this

规，今会不知如何。”大圣道：“此言也是，难怪汝等。你且立下，待老孙先去打听个消息，看可请老孙不请。”

time," the fairies replied.

"You're right," he said. "Just wait here while I go and find out whether I'm invited."

好大圣，捻着诀，念声咒语，对众仙女道：“住！住！住！”这原来是个定身法，把那七衣仙女一个个睖睖睁睁，白着眼，都站在桃树之下。大圣纵朵祥云，跳出园内，竟奔瑶池路上而去。

Splendid Great Sage. Making a magic with his hands as he spoke the words of the spell, he said to the fairies, "Stay where you are! Stay where you are!" As this was an immobilizing spell, the seven fairies were left standing in a daze under the peach tree with their eyes wide open as the Great Sage leapt out of the orchard on a somersault cloud and headed for the Jade Pool.

正行时，只见那壁厢：

As he traveled he saw that

一天瑞霭光摇曳，
五色祥云飞不绝。
白鹤声鸣振九皋，
紫芝色秀分千叶。
中间现出一尊仙，
相貌天然丰采别。
神舞虹霓幌汉霄，
腰悬宝录无生灭。
名称赤脚大罗仙，

*The sky shimmered with auspicious light ;*
*As clouds of many colours streamed across it.*
*The white stork's cry made the heavens shake ;*
*A thousand leaves grew on the purple asphodel.*
*Amid it all an Immortal appeared,*
*Carrying himself with heaven—sent elegance,*
*As he danced on the rainbow, cloaked by the Milky Way,*
*With a talisman at his waist to ward off birth and death.*

特赴蟠桃添寿节。

*His name was Bare-Foot Immortal,*

那赤脚大仙觌面撞见大圣，大圣低头定计，赚哄真仙，他要暗去赴会，却问："老道何往？"大仙道："蒙王母见招，去赴蟠桃嘉会。"大圣道："老道不知。玉帝因老孙筋斗云疾，着老孙五路邀请列位，先至通明殿下演礼，后方去赴宴。"

And he was going to the feast of longevity-giving peaches. As the Bare-foot Immortal saw him, the Great Sage lowered his head and thought of a plan by which to trick the Immortal and get to the banquet himself. "Where are you going, reverend sir?" he asked; and the Immortal replied, "I'm going to the Peach Banquet by the invitation of the Queen Mother." "There is something you do not know, venerable sir," said the Great Sage. "As my somersault cloud is so fast, the Jade Emperor has sent me everywhere to tell all you gentlemen to go to the Hall of Universal Brightness for a ceremony before going on to the banquet."

（6）大仙是个光明正大之人，就以他的诳语作真。道："常年就在瑶池演礼谢恩，如何先去通明殿演礼，方去瑶池赴会？"无奈，只得拨转祥云，径往通明殿去了。

As the Immortal was an open and upright man, he took this lie for the truth, but wondered, "The thanksgiving ceremony is usually held by the Jade Pool, so why are we having the ceremony in the Hall of Universal Brightness before going to the Jade Pool for the banquet?" Nevertheless, he turned his propitious cloud around and went to the Hall of Universal Brightness.

大圣驾着云，念声咒

As the Great Sage rode his

语，摇身一变，就变做赤脚大仙模样，前奔瑶池。不多时，直至宝阁，按住云头，轻轻移步，走入里面。只见那里：

琼香缭绕，
瑞霭缤纷，
瑶台铺彩结，
宝阁散氤氲。
凤翥鸾腾形缥缈，
金花玉萼影浮沉。
上排着九凤丹霞，
八宝紫霓墩。
五彩描金桌，
千花碧玉盆。
桌上有龙肝和凤髓，
熊掌与猩唇。
珍馐百味般般美，
异果佳肴色色新。

那里铺设得齐齐整整，却还未有仙来。这大圣点看

cloud he said a spell, shook himself, took the form of the Barefoot Immortal, and hurried to the Jade Pool. He reached the pavilion there a moment later, stopped his cloud, and went quietly inside. He saw Fabulous perfumes coiling,

*A confusion of auspicious clouds;*
*The jade tower set with color,*
*The precious pavilions scattering mists;*
*The phoenix soars till almost lost to view,*
*And jeweled flowers seem to rise and fall.*
*Above a nine-phoenix screen*
*A rainbow stool of the eight precious things,*
*A coloured golden table,*
*Green jade bowls with a thousand flowers.*
*On the table were dragon livers and marrow of phoenix bone,*
*Bears' paws and apes' lips-*
*A hundred different dishes, and all of them good;*
*Rare fruits and fine delicacies, every one unique.*

Everything was neatly set out, but no Immortals had yet arrived. The Great Sage had not finished

不尽，忽闻得一阵酒香扑鼻；忽转头，见右壁厢长廊之下，有几个造酒的仙官，盘糟的力士，领几个运水的道人，烧火的童子，在那里洗缸刷瓮，已造成了玉液琼浆，香醪佳酿。

looking when he smelt wine; and as he whirled round he saw under a portico to the right several immortal officials in charge of brewing liquor with some workmen who stirred the lees, a number of novices who carried water and some boys who looked after the fires. They were washing the vats and scrubbing the pots, having made jade liquor and a fragrant fermentation of the lees.

大圣止不住口角流涎，就要去吃，奈何那些人都在这里。他就弄个神通，把毫毛拔下几根，丢入口中嚼碎，喷将出去，念声咒语，叫“变！”即变做几个瞌睡虫，奔在众人脸上。你看那伙人，手软头低，闭眉合眼，丢了执事，都去盹睡。

The Great Sage could not stop himself from drooling, and he longed to drink some, but unfortunately all those people were there. So he performed a spell by pulling several hairs from his body, chewing them up, spitting them up, saying the magic words, and shouting "Change"; whereupon the hairs turned into sleep insects, which flew into the faces of all the liquor-makers. Watch them as their hands go limp, their heads droop, their eyes close, and they drop their symbols of office and all fall asleep.

大圣却拿了些百味珍馐，佳肴异品，走入长廊里面，就着缸，挨着瓮，放开量，痛饮一番。吃够了多时，酕醄醉了。自揣自摸道：“不好！不好！再过会，

Whereupon the Great Sage grabbed the rare delicacies and exotic foods, then went under the portico and drank from the vats and pots until he was completely drunk. Only then did he think, "This won't do at all. When the guests come for the banquet

请的客来，却不怪我？一时拿住，怎生是好？不如早回府中睡去也。”

they'll be furious with me, and I'll be for it if I'm caught. I'd better get back to the Residence as soon as I can and sleep it off."

好大圣：摇摇摆摆，仗着酒，任情乱撞，一会把路差了；不是齐天府，却是兜率天宫。

Our dear Great Sage staggered and swayed, charging about all over the place under the influence of the liquor, and going the wrong way. He arrived not at the Equaling Heaven Residence but at the Tushita Heavenly Palace.

一见了，顿然醒悟道：“兜率宫是三十三天之上，乃离恨天太上老君之处，如何错到此间？——也罢！也罢！一向要来望此老，不曾得来，今趁此残步，就望他一望也好。

As soon as he saw this he sobered up and said to himself, "The Tushita Palace is the highest of the thirty-three heavens, where Lord Lao Zi of the Great Monad reigns. However did I get here? Never mind, I've always wanted to see that old chap, and I've never managed to come here before. I might as well go and have a look at him now that I'm passing this way."

即整衣撞进去，那里不见老君，四无人迹。原来那老君与燃灯古佛在三层高阁朱陵丹台上讲道，众仙童、仙将、仙官、仙吏，都侍立左右听讲。

He straightened his clothes and rushed in, but did not see Lord Lao Zi. There was no sign of anyone. This was because Lao Zi and the Ancient Buddha Dipamkara were expounding the Way from a red dais in a triple-storied pavilion, and all the immortal boys, generals, officials and petty functionaries were standing to right and left listening to the lecture.

这大圣直至丹房里面，

The Great Sage went straight to the room in which the elixir

寻访不遇，但见丹灶之旁，炉中有火。炉左右安放着五个葫芦，葫芦里都是炼就的金丹。

was kept, and although he could not find Lao Zi there he saw that there was a small fire in the stove beside the range over which pills were made. On either side of the stove were five gourds, full of golden pills of refined elixir.

大圣喜道："此物乃仙家之至宝，老孙自了道以来，识破了内外相同之理，也要些金丹济入，不期到家无暇；今日有缘，却又撞着此物，趁老子不在，等我吃他几丸尝新。"他就把那葫芦都倾出来，就都吃了，如吃炒豆相似。

"This is the Immortals' greatest treasure," he exclaimed in delight. "I've wanted to refine some of these golden pills to save people with ever since I understood the Way and mastered the principle of the correspondence of the Esoteric and Exoteric, but I've never had time to come here. Today I'm in luck-I've found them. As Lao Zi isn't here I'll try a few." He emptied the gourds of their contents and ate up all the pills as if he were eating fried beans.

一时间丹满酒醒，又自己揣度道："不好！不好！这场祸，比天还大；若惊动玉帝，性命难存。走！走！走！不如下界为王去也！"他就跑出兜率宫，不行旧路，从西天门，使个隐身法逃去。即按云头，回至花果山界。

Before long he was full of pills and quite sober. "This is terrible," he thought, "this is a colossal disaster. If the Jade Emperor is shocked by this, I'm done for. I must get out of here. I'd be much better off as a king in the lower world." He rushed out of the Tushita Palace, avoiding his usual route. Using a spell to make himself invisible, he left by the West Gate of Heaven, and went straight down to the Mountain of Flowers and Fruit by cloud.

When he got there he saw

但见那旌旗闪烁，戈戟光辉，原来是四健将与七十二洞妖王，在那里演习武艺。

flags, banners, spears and halberds gleaming in the sun: the four Stalwart Generals and the seventy-two kings of the monsters were holding military exercises.

大圣高叫道："小的们！我来也！"众怪丢了器械，跪倒道："大圣好宽心！丢下我等许久，不来相顾！"

"Children, I'm back," shouted the Great Sage in a loud voice, and all the fiends dropped their weapons and fell to their knees.

"You don't care, do you, Great Sage?" they said. "It's been so long since you left us, and you never came back to see us."

大圣道："没多时！没多时！"且说且行，径入洞天深处。四健将打扫安歇叩头礼拜毕。俱道："大圣在天这百十年，实受何职？"

"I haven't been long, I haven't been long," protested the Great Sage, and as they talked they walked into the innermost part of the cave. When the four Stalwart General's had tidied the place up and made him sit down, they kowtowed to him and asked, "What office did you hold, Great Sage, during your century and more in Heaven?"

大圣笑道："我记得才半年光景，怎么就说百十年话？"健将道："在天一日，即在下方一年也。"

The Great Sage laughed and said, "As far as I can remember it was only six months, so why do you say it was over a century?" "A day in Heaven is the same as a year on earth," the Stalwart Generals replied.

大圣道："且喜这番玉帝相爱，果封做'齐天大圣'，起一座齐天府，又设

"I was lucky this time," said the Great Sage. "The Jade Emperor took a liking to me and ennobled me as the Great Sage

安静、宁神二司，司设仙吏侍卫。向后见我无事，着我看管蟠桃园。近因王母娘娘设‘蟠桃大会’，未曾请我，是我不待他请，先赴瑶池，把他那仙品、仙酒，都是我偷吃了。走出瑶池，踉踉跄跄误入老君宫阙，又把他五个葫芦金丹也偷吃了。但恐玉帝见罪，方才走出天门来也。”

众怪闻言大喜。即安排酒果接风，将椰酒满斟一石碗奉上，大圣喝了一口，即龇牙咧嘴道：“不好吃！不好吃！”崩、巴二将道：“大圣在天宫，吃了仙酒、仙肴，是以椰酒不甚美口。常言道：‘美不美，乡中水。’”

Equaling Heaven. He had an Equaling Heaven Residence built for me, complete with a Tranquillity Office and a Calm Divinity Office with Immortal functionaries, attendants and guards. Later on, when he saw that I had nothing to do, he put me in charge of the Peach Orchard. Recently the Queen Mother Goddess gave a Peach Banquet, but she didn't invite me. Instead of waiting for an invitation, I went to the Jade Pool and stole all the immortal food and drink. I staggered away from the Jade Pool and blundered into Lord Lao Zi's palace, and there I ate up his five gourds of pills of immortality. Then I got out through the heavenly gates and came here because I was scared that the Jade Emperor was going to punish me."

All the fiends were delighted with what they heard, and they laid on liquor and fruit with which to welcome him back. They filled a stone bowl with coconut toddy and handed it to him, but when he tasted it the Great Sage grimaced and said, "It's awful, it's awful." Two of his Stalwart Generals, Beng and Ba, explained, "You don't find coconut toddy very tasty because you have drunk immortal liquor and

大圣道："你们就是'亲不亲，故乡人。'我今早在瑶池中受用时，见那长廊之下，有许多瓶罐，都是那玉液琼浆。你们都不曾尝着。待我再去偷他几瓶回来，你们各饮半杯，一个个也长生不老。"

众猴欢喜不胜。大圣即出洞门，又翻一筋斗，使个隐身法，径至蟠桃会上。进瑶池宫阙，只见那几个造酒、盘糟、运水、烧火的，还鼾睡未醒。

他将大的从左右胁下挟了两个，两手提了两个，即拨转云头回来，会众猴在于洞中，就做个"仙酒会"，各饮了几杯，快乐不题。

eaten immortal food in the heavenly palace, Great Sage. But as the saying goes, 'Sweet or not, it's water from home.'"

To this the Great Sage replied, "And all of you, whether related to me or not, are from my home. When I was enjoying myself beside the Jade Pool today I saw jars and jars of jade liquor under a portico there. As none of you have ever tasted it I'll go and pinch you a few jars; then you can each have a little drink, and live forever."

All the monkeys were beside themselves with glee. The Great Sage then went out of the cave, turned a somersault, made himself invisible, and went straight to the Peach Banquet. As he went through the gates of the Jade Pool he saw that the men who made the wine, stirred the lees, carried the water, and looked after the fire were still snoring away.

He tucked two big jars of wine under his arms, took two more in his hands, then turned his cloud round and went back to have a feast of immortal wine with the monkey masses in the cave. They all drank several cups and were very happy, but we will not go into this.

The story returns to the seven

却说那七衣仙女自受了大圣的定身法术，一周天方能解脱。各提花篮，回奏王母，说道："齐天大圣使法术困住我等，故此来迟。"

fairies, who were only able to free themselves a whole day after Sun Wukong had immobilized them with his magic. They picked up their baskets and went back to report to the Queen Mother that they were late because the Great Sage Equaling Heaven had held them there by magic.

王母问道："你等摘了多少蟠桃？"

"How many peaches did you pick?" the Queen Mother asked.

仙女道："只有两篮小桃，三篮中桃。至后面，大桃半个也无，想都是大圣偷吃了。及正寻间，不期大圣走将出来，行凶挖打，又问设宴请谁。我等把上会事说了一遍，他就定住我等，不知去向。只到如今，才得醒解回来。"

"Two baskets of little ones and three baskets of medium ones. But when we got to the back we could not find a single big one; we think that they were all eaten by the Great Sage. While we were looking for some the Great Sage suddenly appeared, and he beat and tortured us to make us tell him who had been invited to the banquet. After we had told him he immobilized us there, and we don't know where he went. We only came round and freed ourselves a moment ago."

王母闻言，即去见玉帝，备陈前事。说不了，又见那造酒的一班人，同仙官等来奏："不知什么人，搅乱了'蟠桃大会'，偷吃了玉液琼浆，其八珍百味，亦俱偷吃了。"

On hearing this the Queen Mother went to see the Jade Emperor and gave him a full account of what had happened. Before she had finished, the liquor-makers arrived with their immortal officials to report that an unknown person had thrown the Grand Peach Banquet into confusion and stolen the

又有四个大天师来奏上:“太上道祖来了。”玉帝即同王母出迎。老君朝礼毕,道:“老道宫中,炼了些‘九转金丹’,伺候陛下做‘丹元大会’,不期被贼偷去,特启陛下知之。”玉帝见奏,悚惧。

少时,又有齐天府仙吏叩头道:“孙大圣不守执事,自昨日出游,至今未转,更不知去向。”玉帝又添疑思。只见那赤脚大仙又俯囟上奏道:“臣蒙王母诏昨日赴会,偶遇齐天大圣,对臣言万岁有旨,着他邀臣等先赴通明殿演礼,方去赴会。臣依他言语,即返至通明殿外,不见万岁龙车凤辇,又急来此俟候。”

jade liquor as well as the precious delicacies of a hundred flavors.

Then came Four Heavenly Teachers to announce that the Supreme Patriarch of the Way, Lao Zi, had arrived. The Jade Emperor went out with the Queen Mother to meet him, and after doing obeisance Lao Zi said, "I had refined some Golden Pills of the Nine Transformations in my palace for a Feast of Elixir Pills with Your Majesty, but a thief has stolen them. This is what I have come to report to Your Majesty." This news made the Jade Emperor tremble with fear.

Not long afterwards the immortal administrators from the Equaling Heaven Residence came to kowtow and report: "The Great Sage Sun Wukong abandoned his post and went wandering off yesterday. He has not come back yet and we do not know where he has gone." The Jade Emperor, now more suspicious than ever, then saw the Bare-Foot Immortal bow his head to the ground. "Your subject was going to the banquet on a summons from the Queen Mother," he reported, "when I happened to meet the Great Sage Equaling Heaven. He told me, O Lord of Ten Thousand Years, that you had issued a decree ordering him to tell all the rest of us to go to the Hall of Universal Brightness for a ceremony before going to the banquet. Your subject went back to the Hall of Universal Brightness as he had told me to, but as I did not see the Imperial Dragon and Phoenix Chariot outside I hurried here to await orders."

玉帝越发大惊道："这厮假传旨意，赚哄贤卿，快着纠察灵官缉访这厮踪迹！"

"This wretch has the impudence to invent fraudulent decrees and deceive eminent ministers," exclaimed the Jade Emperor with anger and astonishment. "The Miraculous Investigator is to find out at once what he has been up to."

灵官领旨，即出殿遍访尽得其详细。回奏道："搅乱天宫者，乃齐天大圣也。"又将前事尽诉一番。

The Miraculous Investigator left the palace in obedience to the edict, and by making thorough enquiries he found out all the details of what had happened. "The wrecker of the Heavenly Palace was Sun Wukong," he reported, and he went on to give a full account.

玉帝大恼。即差四大天王，协同李天王并哪吒太子，点二十八宿、九曜星官、十二元辰、五方揭谛、四值功曹、东西星斗、南北二神、五岳四渎、普天星相，共十万天兵，布一十八

The Jade Emperor was furiously angry, and he ordered the Four Great Heavenly Kings along with Heavenly King Li and Prince Nezha to mobilize the Twenty-eight Constellations, the Nine Bright Shiners, the Twelve Gods of the Twelve Branches, the Revealers of the Truth of the Five Regions, the Four Duty Gods,

架天罗地网下界，去花果山围困，定捉获那厮处治。众神即时兴师，离了天宫。这一去，但见那：

the Constellations of the East and West, the Gods of the North and South, the Deities of the Five Mountains and the Four Rivers, the star ministers of all Heaven, and a total of a hundred thousand heavenly soldiers. They were to descend to the lower world with eighteen heaven-and-earth nets, surround the Mountain of Flowers and Fruit, and capture that wretch for punishment. The gods called out their troops at once, and left the heavenly palace.

黄风滚滚遮天暗，
紫雾腾腾罩地昏。
只为妖猴欺上帝，
致令众圣降凡尘。
四大天王，
五方揭谛：
四大天王权总制，
五方揭谛调多兵。
李托塔中军掌号，
恶哪吒前部先锋。

*A gusty sandstorm blotted out the heavens,*
*Purple fog threw the earth into darkness.*
*Just because the monkey fiend offended the Supreme Emperor*
*Heavenly hosts were sent down to the mortal dust.*
*The Four Great Heavenly Kings,*
*The Revealers of the Truth of the Five Regions.*
*The Four Great Heavenly Kings held the supreme command,*
*And the Revealers controlled the soldiers' movements.*
*Li the Pagoda Carrier commanded the central corps,*
*Nezha the deadly led the van.*
*The star Rahu ordered the leading*

| | |
|---|---|
| 罗猴星为头检点， | *rands,* |
| 计都星随后峥嵘。 | *And the star Ketu towered behind.* |
| 太阴星精神抖擞， | *The Sun revealed his divinity,* |
| 太阳星照耀分明。 | *And radiance shone from the Moon.* |
| 五行星偏能豪杰， | *The stars of the Five Elements were mighty in valour,* |
| 九曜星最喜相争。 | *And the Nine Bright Shiners were fond of battle.* |
| 元辰星子午卯酉， | *The stars of the Branches Zi, Wu, Mao and You,* |
| 一个个都是大力天丁。 | *Were all great heavenly warriors.* |
| 五瘟五岳东西摆， | *The Five Plagues and the Five Mountains were drawn up on the East and West,* |
| 六丁六甲左右行。 | *While the Six Ding and Six Jia marched to right and left.* |
| 四渎龙神分上下， | *The Dragon Gods of the Four Rivers stood above and below,* |
| 二十八宿密层层。 | *And the Twenty—eight Constellations were drawn up in serried ranks:* |
| 角亢氐房为总领， | *Horn, Gullet, Base, and Chamber were the officers commanding,* |
| 奎娄胃昴惯翻腾。 | *Strider, Harvester, Stomach, and Mane wheeled and soared;* |
| 斗牛女虚危室壁， | *Dipper, Ox, Woman, Barrens, Roof, House, and Wall,* |
| 心尾箕星个个能， | *Heart, Tail, and Winnower——all able stars——* |
| 井鬼柳星张翼轸 | *Well, Ghost, Willow, Spread, Whig and Axletree* |
| 轮枪舞剑显威灵。 | *Wielded their swords and spears, showed forth their power,* |

停云降雾临凡世，

花果山前扎下营。

诗曰：

天产猴王变化多，

偷丹偷酒乐山窝。

只因搅乱蟠桃会，

十万天兵布网罗。

当时李天王传了令，着众天兵扎了营，把那花果山围得水泄不通。上下布了十八架天罗地网，先差九曜恶星出战。

九曜即提兵径至洞外，只见那洞外大小群猴跳跃顽耍。

星官厉声高叫道：“那小妖！你那大圣在哪里？我等乃上界差调的天神，到此降你这造反的大圣。教他快快来归降；若道半个‘不’字，教汝等一概遭诛！”

*Halted their clouds and descended in mists to the mortal world,*
*Pitching camp before the Mountain of Flowers and Fruit.*
*There is a poem that runs:*
*Many the transformations of the heaven-born Monkey King*
*Happy in his lair after stealing the pills and wine.*
*Just because he wrecked the banquet of peaches,*
*A hundred thousand heavenly troops now spread their nets.*

Heavenly King Li gave the order for the heavenly soldiers to pitch camp and throw a watertight cordon round the Mountain of Flowers and Fruit. Above and below they spread eighteen heaven-and-earth nets, and the Nine Bright Shiners were sent out to start the battle.

They took their soldiers to the outside of the cave, where they saw the monkeys, big and small, leaping and fooling around.

The star officers shouted in harsh voices, "Little goblins, where's that Great Sage of yours? We are gods, sent from the upper world to subdue your mutinous Great Sage. Tell him to surrender at once-and if there's so much as a hint of a 'no' from him, we

那小妖慌忙传入道："大圣，祸事了！祸事了！外面有九个凶神，口称上界来的天神，收降大圣。"

那大圣正与七十二洞妖王，并四健将分饮仙酒，一闻此报，公然不理道："今朝有酒今朝醉，莫管门前是与非！"

说不了，一起小妖又跳来道："那九个凶神，恶言泼语，在门前骂战哩！"大圣笑道："莫睬他。

'诗酒且图今日乐，

功名休问几时成。'"

说犹未了，又一起小妖来报："爷爷！那九个凶神已把门打破了，杀进来也！"

will exterminate every last one of you."

The little monkeys went rushing in to report, "Great Sage, a disaster, a disaster. There are nine evil gods outside who say they've been sent from the upper world to subdue you."

The Great Sage, who was just then sharing the immortal liquor with the seventy-two kings of the monsters and his four Stalwart Generals, paid no attention to the report, saying: "Today we have wine so today we celebrate:To hell with what's happening outside the gate."

But before the words were out of his mouth another group of little devils came in. "Those nine evil gods are using foul and provocative language to challenge us to fight," they announced. "Never mind them," said the Great Sage with a laugh.

"With verse and wine we're happy today;

Who cares when fame will come our way?"

But before these words were out of his mouth yet another group of devils came rushing in. "Sir, those nine evil gods have smashed the gates and are charging in."

"The stinking gods!" exploded

大圣怒道："这泼毛神，老大无礼！本来不与他计较，如何上门来欺我？"即命独角鬼王，领帅七十二洞妖王出阵，老孙领四健将随后。那鬼王疾帅妖兵，出门迎敌，却被九曜恶星一齐掩杀，抵住在铁板桥头，莫能得出。

the Great Sage, "What nerve! I never wanted a fight with them, so why should they come here to push us around?" He thereupon ordered the One-horned Monster King to lead the seventy-two monster kings into battle while he followed them with the four Stalwart Generals. The monster king hastily assembled the devil soldiers and sallied forth to meet the enemy. They were all stopped by a charge by the Nine Bright Shiners, who held the head of the iron bridge so that no one could enter or leave.

正嚷间，大圣到了。叫一声"开路！"掣开铁棒，晃一晃，碗来粗细，丈二长短，丢开架子，打将出来。九曜星那个敢抵，一时打退。

During the tumult the Great Sage came on the scene, and shouting "Make way!" he raised his iron cudgel, shook it till it was as thick as a bowl and twelve feet long, and struck and parried as he came charging out.

那九曜星立住阵势道："你这不知死活的弼马温！你犯了十恶之罪，先偷桃，后偷酒，搅乱了蟠桃大会，又窃了老君仙丹，又将御酒偷来此处享乐。你罪上加罪，岂不知之？"

The Nine Bright Shiners, who were no match for him, fell back. "You reckless Protector of the Horses," they shouted when they were back in the safety of their own position. "You have committed the most terrible crimes. You stole the peaches and the wine, wrecked the Peach Banquet, and pilfered the immortality pills of Lord Lao Zi. On top of all this you brought some of the immor-

大圣笑道："这几桩事，实有！实有！但如今你怎么？"九曜星道："吾奉玉帝金旨，帅众到此收降你，快早皈依！免教这些生灵纳命。不然，就屣平了此山，掀翻了此洞也！"

大圣大怒道："量你这些毛神，有何法力，敢出浪言，不要走，请吃老孙一棒！"

这九曜星一齐踊跃。那美猴王不惧分毫，轮起金箍棒，左遮右挡，把那九曜星战得筋疲力软，一个个倒拖器械，败阵而走，急入中军帐下，对托塔天王道："那猴王果十分骁勇！我等战他不过，败阵来了。"李天王即调四大天王与二十八宿，一路出师来斗。

tal liquor you stole back here. Don't you realize that you have piled crime upon crime?"

The Great Sage laughed. "It's true, it's true," he said, "but what are you going to do about it?" "In obedience to a golden edict of the Jade Emperor," the Nine Bright Shiners replied, "we have led out troops here to subdue you. Submit at once, or else all these creatures of yours will have to pay with their lives. If you refuse, we shall trample this mountain flat and turn your cave upside-down."

"You hairy gods," roared the Great Sage in a fury, "what magic powers have you got to let you talk so big? Clear off, or I'll give you a taste of my cudgel."

The Nine Bright Shiners did a war-dance together, which did not frighten the Handsome Monkey King in the least. He whirled his gold-banded cudgel, parrying to right and left, and fought the Nine Bright Shiners till their muscles were weak and their strength was gone; then each of them broke ranks and fled, dragging their weapons behind them. Thcy rushcd to thc command post of the central corps and reported to the Pagoda-Bearing Heavenly King Li that the Monkey King was so ferocious that they had

大圣也公然不惧，调出独角鬼王、七十二洞妖王与四个健将，于洞门外列成阵势。你看这场混战，好惊人也：

寒风飒飒，
怪雾阴阴。
那壁厢旌旗飞彩，
这壁厢戈戟生辉。
滚滚盔明，
层层甲亮。
滚滚盔明映太阳，
如撞天的银磬；
层层甲亮砌岩崖，
似压地的冰山。
大捍刀，
飞云掣电，
楮白枪，

fled from the battlefield, unable to defeat him Heavenly King Li then sent the Four Heavenly Kings and the Twenty-eight Constellations into battle.

The Great Sage, not at all frightened at this, ordered the One-horned Demon King, the seventy-two kings of the monsters, and the four Stalwart Generals to draw up their line of battle outside the gates of the cave. The ensuing melee was really terrifying.

*Howling winds,*
*Dark, sinister clouds.*
*On one side flags and standards colorfully flying,*
*On the other side the gleam of spears and halberds.*
*Round helmets shine,*
*Layered armour gleams.*
*The shining round helmets reflect the sun,*
*Like silver boulders reaching to the sky;*
*Gleaming layers of armour are built into a wall*
*Like a mountain of ice weighing down the earth.*
*Long-handled swords*
*Flash through the clouds like lightning;*
*Paper-white spears*

度雾穿云。
方天戟，
虎眼鞭，
麻林摆列；
青铜剑，
四明铲，
密树排阵。
弯弓硬弩雕翎箭，
短棍蛇矛挟了魂。
大圣一条如意棒，
翻来覆去战天神。
杀得那空中无鸟过，
山内虎狼奔。
扬砂走石乾坤黑，
播土飞尘宇宙昏。
只听兵兵扑扑惊天地，
煞煞威威振鬼神。

这一场自辰时布阵，混杀到日落西山。那独角鬼王与七十二洞妖怪，尽被众天神捉拿去了，只走了四健将与那群猴，深藏

*Pierce mists and fogs;*
*Heaven-shaped halberds,*
*Tiger-eye chains,*
*Bristling like a field of hemp;*
*Bronze swords,*
*And four-brightness spears*
*Drawn up like a dense forest.*
*Bows and crossbows, eagle-feathered arrows,*
*Short clubs and snaky spears to terrify the soul.*
*Wielding his single As-You-Will cudgel,*
*The Great Sage fights against the heavenly gods.*
*Such is the slaughter that no bird flies over it;*
*And tigers and wolves flee in terror.*
*The swirling stones and clouds of sand make*
*everything dark,*
*The dirt and the dust blot out the heavens.*
*The clash of arms startles the universe*
*As the battle strikes awe into gods and demons.*

The battle started in the morning and went on till the sun set behind the mountains in the West. By then the One-horned Demon King and the seventy-two kings of the monsters had all been

在水帘洞底。

captured by the heavenly hosts. Only the four Stalwart Generals and the monkeys had got away, and they were now hiding in the innermost recesses of the Water Curtain Cave.

这大圣一条棒，抵住了四大天神与李托塔、哪吒太子，俱在半空中，一一杀勾多时，大圣见天色将晚，即拉毫毛一把，丢在口中，嚼将出去，叫声“变!”就变了千百个大圣，都使的是金箍棒，打退了哪吒太子，战败了五个天王。

The Great Sage's solitary cudgel had fought off the Four Heavenly Kings, Li the Pagoda-bearer and Prince Nezha, who were all in the sky. After the battle had gone on for a long time the Great Sage saw that night was drawing on, so he plucked out one of his hairs, munched it up, spat out the pieces and shouted, "Change!" They changed into thousands of Great Sages, all with gold-banded cudgels, who forced Prince Nezha and the five Heavenly Kings to withdraw.

大圣得胜，收了毫毛，急转身回洞，早又见铁板桥头，四个健将，领众叩迎那大圣，哽哽咽咽大哭三声，又唏唏哈哈大笑三声。大圣道：“汝等见了我，又哭又笑，何也？”

After winning this victory the Great Sage put back his hair and hurried back to the cave, where the four Stalwart Generals at once led the monkeys out to kowtow at the head of the iron bridge to welcome him back. They sobbed three times and then laughed three times. "Why are you laughing and crying at the sight of me?" the Great Sage asked.

四健将道：“今早帅众将与天王交战，把七十二洞妖王与独角鬼王，尽被众神

"When we led all the commanders into battle against the heavenly kings this morning," replied the Stalwart Generals,

捉了，我等逃生，故此该哭。这见大圣得胜回来，未曾伤损，故此该笑。”

大圣道：“(7) 胜负乃兵家之常。古人云：‘杀人一万，自损三千。’况捉了去的头目乃是虎、豹、狼虫、獾獐、狐骆之类，我同类者未伤一个，何须烦恼？他虽被我使个分身法杀退，他还要安营在我山脚下。我等且紧紧防守，饱食一顿，安心睡觉，养养精神。天明看我使个大神通，拿这些天将，与众报仇。”四将与众猴将椰酒吃了几碗，安心睡觉不题。

"the seventy-two kings of the monsters and the One-horned Demon King were all captured by the gods, and we had to flee for our lives. That is why we cried. We laughed because you, Great Sage, have come back victorious and unharmed."

To this the Great Sage replied, "Victory and defeat are all the soldier's lot. As the ancients said, 'To kill ten thousand of the enemy you must lose three thousand of your own.' Anyhow, the officers of ours who were captured were all tigers, leopards, wolves, badgers, river-deer, foxes, and raccoon-dogs. Not one of our own kind was even wounded, so there's no need for us to be bothered about it. But although I forced the enemy to withdraw by dividing up my body through magic, they're still encamped at the foot of our mountain, so we'll have to remain on our guard. Meanwhile we must eat a good meal and get a good night's sleep to build up our energy. Tomorrow morning I'll use powerful magic to capture those heavenly generals and avenge our people." After the four Stalwart Generals and the other monkey commanders had drunk several cups of coconut toddy, they went to bed with

那四大天王收兵罢战，众各报功：有拿住虎豹的，有拿住狮象的，有拿住狼虫狐狢的，更不曾捉着一个猴精。当时果又安辕营，下大寨，赏劳了得功之将，吩咐了天罗地网之兵，个个提铃喝号，围困了花果山，专待明早大战。(8) 各人得令，一处处谨守。

此正是：

妖猴作乱惊天地，

布网张罗昼夜看。

毕竟天晓后如何处治，且听下回分解。

their worries calmed.

When the four Heavenly Kings had withdrawn their troops and ended the battle, those who had distinguished themselves reported what they had done. Some had captured tigers and leopards, some lions and elephants, and others wolves and raccoon-dogs, but not one single monkey goblin had been taken. Then they built a mighty stockade around their camp. Commanders who had distinguished themselves were rewarded, and the soldiers who made up the heaven-and-earth nets were ordered to surround the Mountain of Flowers and Fruit, holding bells and shouting, ready for a great battle the next day. Every man heard the orders, and they were strictly obeyed.

Indeed:

A wicked monkey made chaos, shocking heaven and earth,

So they spread their nets and watched by night and day.

Listen to the next installment to hear how he was dealt with the following morning.

# 第四章

# 红楼梦
# *A Dream of Red Mansions*

“你从此可都改了罢！”

## 背景介绍

中国古典文学史上，哪一部作品有诗一般的语言，梦一般的意境，歌一般的柔情？哪一部作品是仙境、梦境、与人景的重叠？ 答案是你我心中那永远的《红楼梦》，它是中国乃至世界古典文学的顶峰。

《红楼梦》成书于清代，全书一百二十回。作者曹雪芹（约 1715——约 1763 年），高鹗（约 1738——约 1815 年）。前八十回由曹雪芹作，后四十回一般认为是由高鹗所作。这是一本人人都可以看，人人都可以读的全才作品。就爱情而言，纵使宝黛爱到以命相许也终究是镜中花，水中月，即使有缘也终虚化；就宗教而言，道佛的超凡脱俗的影子飘荡在所有情节中，映射着小到个人，大到家族的命运；就经济管理而言，一个小女子王熙凤把贾府上下打理得够热闹，在入不敷出的情况下还能张灯结彩；就营养大全而言，燕窝当归茯苓还有那冷香丸，哪一样不是细细地称过，慢慢地品过。

《红楼梦》是中国现实主义大作，曹雪芹笔下的现实是没有任何矫饰的现实。他不做任何解释，只是絮絮叨叨地给我们陈述事实，宝玉的多情颠覆了读者对英雄的认识，他爱的不只是女人，不只是人，而是所有美的事物，他的形象是色彩斑斓的。曹雪芹可能不懂得什么圆形角色方形人物，他只是忠实的陈述者。也因此而给我们留下了关于那个时代的最鲜活的故事。

翻译界的一件幸事是杨宪益 (1915——2009 年 ) 和戴乃迭 (1919——1999 年 ) 的结合。他们成全了大家关于中西合璧的愿望，这种人与人的结合，体现在文化中便是别人无法超越的中英互译的优势，因此他们胆敢着手把《红楼梦》翻译成英语，并且非常之成功。

### 细读节选

在这一回里，宝黛钗都出现了，连薛蟠也漏了脸，贾府上下老爷太太们都行动起来。除了黛玉哭得恓恓惶惶，使得宝黛的情节持续推进，宝黛钗的三角恋被描述得细致入微，不漏痕迹。宝钗有家底，黛玉有泪水，从宝玉赠手帕可以肯定他对黛玉的感情；偏偏薛蟠又戳穿了宝钗的“金石良缘”的秘密。端正娴雅的宝钗也被绑在悲剧的轮子上，和宝黛一起不问未来地往前滚去。这一回里黛玉终于知晓了宝玉对她的真情，可惜呀，“却不知病由此萌”。

### 拓展思考

1. 凭借记忆，写出 3 句划线的原文与译文。

| 原文 | 译文 |
|---|---|
| | |
| | |
| | |

2. 黛玉和宝钗对宝玉挨打的反应有何不同？为什么？

3. 袭人是一个什么角色？

4. 薛蟠可有可取之处？跟电视剧中相比，有哪些不同？

# 第三十四回

情中情因情感妹妹

错里错以错劝哥哥

话说袭人见贾母王夫人等去后，便走来宝玉身边坐下，含泪问他："怎么就打到这步田地？"宝玉叹气说道："不过为那些事，问他做什么！只是下半截疼得很。你瞧瞧打坏了哪里。"

袭人听说，便轻轻的伸手进去，将中衣褪下。宝玉略动一动，便咬着牙叫'嗳哟'，袭人连忙停住手，如此三四次才褪了下来。袭人看时，只见腿上半段青紫，都有四指宽的僵痕高了起来。

袭人咬着牙说道："我的娘，怎么下这般的狠手！你但凡听我一句话，也不得到这步地位。幸而没动筋骨，倘或打出个残疾来，可

# Chapter 34

*Moved by Affection, Baoyu Moves His Cousin*
*A Wrong Report Makes BaochaiWrong Her Brother*

As soon as the others had left, Xiren sat down by Baoyu's side and with tears in her eyes asked the reason for this fearful beating.

"Oh, nothing special. What's the use of asking?" Baoyu sighed. "The lower part of my body hurts terribly. Do see how serious the damage is."

Xiren gently set about removing his underwear, but the least move ment made him grit his teeth and groan so much that she stopped. Only after three or four attempts did she succeed in undressing him. Then she clenched her teeth at the sight of his thighs, all blackand purple with weals four fingers wide.

"Heavens! How could he be so cruel?" she exclaimed. "But, you know, this would never have happened if you'd paid the least attention to my advice. Well, it's lucky no bones are broken. What if you'd been

叫人怎么样呢！”

正说着，只听丫鬟们说：“宝姑娘来了。”袭人听见，知道穿不及中衣，便拿了一床袷纱被替宝玉盖了。只见宝钗手里托着一丸药走进来，向袭人说道：“晚上把这药用酒研开，替他敷上，把那淤血的热毒散开，可以就好了。”

说毕，递与袭人，又问道：“这会子可好些？”宝玉一面道谢说：“好了。”又让座。

宝钗见他睁开眼说话，不像先时，心中也宽慰了好些，便点头叹道：

“早听人一句话，也不至今日。别说老太太，太太心疼，就是我们看着，心里也疼。”刚说了半句又忙咽住，自悔说的话急了，不觉的就红了脸，低下头来。

（1）宝玉听得这话如此亲切稠密，大有深意，忽见他又咽住不往下说，红了脸，低下头只管弄衣带，那

maimed for life?”

Just then Baochai was announced. As there was no time to clothe Baoyu again, Xiren threw a lined gauze coverlet over him as Baochai walked in, a pill in one hand.

“Dissolve this drug in wine this evening and apply it as a salve,” she told Xiren. “That will draw the heat and poison from the bruise and help to cure him.”

Having handed her the pill, she asked, “Is he any better?” Baoyu gratefully assured her that he was and asked her to take a seat.

Seeing he was now able to open his eyes and talk, Baochai nodded in relief.

“If you’d listened to our advice, this wouldn’t have happened,” she sighed. “Now you’ve not only upset the old lady and your mother; when the rest of us see you like this, our hearts ache too… “She broke off abruptly, regretting her indiscretion, and hung her head with a blush.

She had spoken with such intimate, tender concern, although attempt ing to hide her deep emotion, and she looked so indescribably charming in her bashful confusion as she hid her blushing

一种娇羞怯怯，非可形容得出者，不觉心中大畅，将疼痛早丢在九霄云外。

心中自思：“我不过挨了几下打，他们一个个就有这些怜惜悲感之态露出，令人可玩可观，可怜可敬。假若我一时竟遭殃横死，他们还不知是何等悲感呢！既是他们这样，我便一时死了，得他们如此，一生事业纵然尽付东流，亦无足叹惜，冥冥之中若不怡然自得，亦可谓糊涂鬼祟矣。

想着，只听宝钗问袭人道：“怎么好好的动了气，就打起来了？”

袭人便把焙茗的话说了出来。宝玉原来还不知道贾环的话，见袭人说出方才知道。因又拉上薛蟠，惟恐宝钗沉心，忙又止住袭人道：“薛大哥哥从来不这样的，你们不可混猜度。”

宝钗听说，便知道是怕

face and fingered her sash, that Baoyu completely forgot his pain in his elation.

“I just get given a few strokes,” he thought, “and they show such sweet distress and sym pathy. How good and kind they are! How admirable! If I were to meet with some accident and die, they'd surely be quite overcome with grief. But it would be worth dying, even with nothing to show for my life,pro vided I'd won their hearts. Indeed, it would be silly if I wasn't a happy and contented ghost.”

His thoughts were interrupted by a question Baochai put to Xiren:

“What's the reason for this sudden row and beating?”

Xiren passed on what Beiming had said, and this was Baoyu's first inkling of Jia Huan's tale-telling. But when Xue Pan's name came up he was afraid Baochai would be upset.

“Cousin Xue would never do such a thing!” he interposed quickly. “Stop making such wild guesses.“

Baochai understood why he had silenced Xiren. “How tactful

他多心，用话相拦袭人，因心中暗暗想道："打得这个形象，疼还顾不过来，还是这样细心，怕得罪了人，可见在我们身上也算是用心了。你既这样用心，何不在外头大事上做工夫，老爷也喜欢了，也不能吃这样亏。但你固然怕我担心，所以拦袭人的话。难道我就不知我的哥哥素日恣心纵欲，毫无防范的那种心性。当日为一个秦钟，还闹得天翻地覆，自然如今比先又更厉害了。"

想毕，因笑道："你们也不必怨这个，怨那个。据我想，到底宝兄弟素日不正，肯和那些人来往，老爷才生气。就是我哥哥说话不防头，一时说出宝兄弟来，也不是有心调唆：一则也是本来的实话，二则他原不理论这些防嫌小事。袭姑娘从小儿只见宝兄弟这么样细心的人，你何尝见过天不怕地不怕、心里有什么口里就说什么的人。"

袭人因说出薛蟠来，见

and cautious you are in spite of your pain after such a dreadful beating," she thought. "If you can be so considerate of our feelings, why not pay equal attention to important matters outside? For then your father would be pleased, and you wouldn't get into hot water like this. You cut Xiren short for fear of hurting me, but do you suppose I don't know my brother's wild, lawless ways? If such a rumpus was raised that time because of Qin Zhong, much worse things are possible now."

After these reflections she turned to Xiren with a smile.

"Why pin the blame on this person or that?" she said. "I think the master was angry because Cousin Bao doesn't behave well and keeps bad company. Even if my brother did let fall some careless remark about Cousin Bao, he can't have meant to make trouble. For after all, in the first place, it was the truth; in the second, he's the type who can't be bothered to gossip. You're used to Cousin Bao who's so considerate. You haven't met my brother, who fears neither Heaven nor Earth and blurts out whatever happens to be in his mind."

Baoyu's interruption when she spoke of Xue Pan had made

宝玉拦他的话，早已明白自己说造次了，恐宝钗没意思，听宝钗如此说，更觉羞愧无言。（2）宝玉又听宝钗这番话，一半是堂皇正大，一半是去己疑心，更觉比先畅快了。方欲说话时，只见宝钗起身说道："明儿再来看你，你好生养着罢。方才我拿了药来交给袭人，晚上敷上管就好了。"说着便走出门去。

袭人赶着送出院外，说："姑娘倒费心了。改日宝二爷好了，亲自来谢。"宝钗回头笑道："有什么谢处。你只劝他好生静养，别胡思乱想的就好了。不必惊动老太太，太太众人，倘或吹到老爷耳朵里，虽然彼时不怎么样，将来对景，终是要吃亏的。"说着，一面去了。

袭人抽身回来，心内着实感激宝钗。进来见宝玉沉思默默似睡非睡的模样，因而退出房外，自去栉沐。

Xiren realize that her tactlessness must have embarrassed Baochai, whose last remarks abashed her even more. As for Baoyu, he could see that while saying what was right and proper Baochai was also trying to put him at his ease. He felt even more touched. But before he could speak again she rose to leave. "I'll come back tomorrow to see how you are," she assured him. "Have a good rest. I've given Xiren something to make you a salve tonight, and that should help."

With that she left, and Xiren escorted her out of the courtyard.

"Thank you, miss, for taking so much trouble," she said. "When Master Bao's better he'll come himself to thank you." Baochai turned and smiled. "There's nothing to thank me for. Just persuade him to rest properly and not let his imagination run away with him. We don't want the old lady and the mistress and everyone disturbed. For if word of it reached the master's ears, even if he did nothing for the time being, there'd be trouble later on." So saying, she went off.

With a warm sense of gratitude to her, Xiren returned to Baoyu. Finding him in a dreamy, drowsy state, she went to the other room to tidy herself.

宝玉默默地躺在床上，无奈臀上作痛，如针挑刀挖一般，更又热如火炙，略展转时，禁不住“嗳哟”之声。那时天色将晚，因见袭人去了，却有两三个丫鬟伺候，此时并无呼唤之事，因说道：“你们且去梳洗，等我叫时再来。”众人听了，也都退出。

Although Baoyu lay as still as he could, his buttocks were smarting as if scorched by fire, pricked by needles, or cut by knives. The slightest movement wrung a groan from him. Dusk was falling, Xiren had gone, and he dismissed the other maids saying that he would call if he wanted anything.

这里宝玉昏昏默默，只见蒋玉菡走了进来，诉说忠顺府拿他之事，又见金钏儿进来哭说为他投井之情。宝玉半梦半醒，都不在意。忽又觉有人推他，恍恍忽忽听得有人悲戚之声。宝玉从梦中惊醒，睁眼一看，不是别人，却是林黛玉。

Dozing off, he dreamed that Qiguan had come to tell of his capture by prince Zhongshun's steward; after which Jinchuan appeared, in tears, to explain why she had thrown herself into the well. Half sleeping and half waking, he paid only scant attention. But then he felt himself shaken and caught the faint sound of sobbing. He opened his eyes with a start to see Daiyu.

宝玉犹恐是梦，忙又将身子欠起来，向脸上细细一认，(3)只见两个眼睛肿的桃儿一般，满面泪光，不是黛玉，却是哪个？宝玉还欲看时，怎奈下半截疼痛难忍，支持不住，便“嗳哟”一声，仍就倒下，叹了一声，

Suspecting at first that this was another dream, he propped him self up to look at her more closely. Her eyes were swollen, her face was bathed in tears: it was Daiyu beyond a doubt. He would have gazed at her longer, but the pain in his legs was so unbearable that he fell back with a groan.

说道：“你又做什么跑

“You shouldn't have come,” he said. “Though the sun's set,

来！虽说太阳落下去，那地上的余热未散，走两趟又要受了暑。我虽然挨了打，并不觉疼痛。我这个样儿，只装出来哄他们，好在外头布散与老爷听，其实是假的。你不可认真。”

此时林黛玉虽不是嚎啕大哭，然越是这等无声之泣，气噎喉堵，更觉得厉害。（4）听了宝玉这番话，心中虽然有万句言词，只是不能说得，半日，方抽抽噎噎地说道：“你从此可都改了罢！”

宝玉听说，便长叹一声，道：“你放心，别说这样话。就便为这些人死了，也是情愿的！”

一句话未了，只见院外人说：“二奶奶来了。”林黛玉便知是凤姐来了，连忙立起身说道：

“我从后院子去吧，回来再来。”宝玉一把拉住道：“这可奇了，好好的怎么怕起他来。”林黛玉急得跺脚，悄悄地说道：“你瞧瞧我的

the ground is still hot. Walking here and back may make you unwell again. I'm not in any pain after my beating, just putting on an act to fool them so that word of it will get out to my father. I'm shamming actually. Don't you worry about me.“

Daiyu was not crying aloud. She swallowed her tears in silence till she felt as if she would choke. She had a thousand replies to make to Baoyu, but not one word could she utter. At long last she sobbed:

“Never do such things again.”

“Don't you worry,” replied Baoyu with a long sigh. “Please don't talk this way. I would die happily for people like them, and I'm still alive.”

At this point some maids in the courtyard announced Xifeng's arrival. Daiyu at once stood up.

“I'll go out the back way and drop in again later,” she said.

Baoyu caught her hand protesting, “That's a strange thing to do. Why should you be afraid of her?” Daiyu stamped one foot in desperation.

眼睛，又该他取笑开心呢。”宝玉听说赶忙的放手。黛玉三步两步转过床后，出后院而去。凤姐从前头已进来了，问宝玉：“可好些了？想什么吃，叫人往我那里取去。”接着薛姨妈又来了。一时贾母又打发了人来。

至掌灯时分，宝玉只喝了两口汤，便昏昏沉沉的睡去。接着，周瑞媳妇、吴新登媳妇，郑好时媳妇这几个有年纪常往来的，听见宝玉挨了打，也都进来。袭人忙迎出来，悄悄地笑道：“婶婶们来迟了一步，二爷才睡着了。”说着，一面带他们到那边房里坐了，倒茶与他们吃。那几个媳妇子都悄悄的坐了一回，向袭人说：“等二爷醒了，你替我们说罢。”

袭人答应了，送他们出去。刚要回来，只见王夫人使个婆子来，口称“太太叫一个跟二爷的人呢。”袭人

“Look at my eyes,” she whispered. “She'd make fun of me if she saw.” At once he released her and she slipped past his bed and out through the back court just as Xifeng came in from the front.

“Are you better?” she asked Baoyu. “If you fancy anything to eat, send someone to my place for it.” Aunt Xue called next. And then the Lady Dowager sent maids to inquire after the invalid.

When it was time to light the lamps, Baoyu swal¬lowed two mouthfuls of soup and soon dozed off. Then came some of the older maid-servants, the wives of Zhou Rui, Wu Xindeng and Zheng Haoshi, who were in the habit of calling and had dropped in after hearing of today's trouble. Xiren hurried out to greet them with a smile. “You're a second too late, aunties,” she whispered, “Master Bao has just gone to sleep.” She offered them tea in the outer room and after sitting quietly for a while they left, having asked her to let Baoyu know that they had called.

As Xiren was coming back from seeing them off, one of Lady Wang's women accosted her with the message that her mistress wanted to see one of

见说，想了一想，便回身悄悄地告诉晴雯、麝月、檀云、秋纹等说："太太叫人，你们好生在房里，我去了就来。"说毕，同那婆子一径出了园子，来至上房。

Master Bao's maids. Xiren came to a quick decision. Turning softly she told Qingwen, Sheyue, Tanyun and Qiuwen:

"The mistress has sent for one of us. You see to things here. I'll be back presently." She went with the other woman out of the Garden to Lady Wang's apartments, where she found her fanning herself with a palm-leaf fan on the couch "Why didn't you send one of the others?" asked Baoyu's mother. "Who'll look after him in your absence?"

王夫人正坐在凉榻上摇着芭蕉扇子，见他来了，说："不管叫个谁来也罢了。你又丢下他来了，谁服侍他呢？"

袭人见说，连忙陪笑回道："二爷才睡安稳了，那四五个丫头如今也好了，会服侍二爷了，太太请放心。恐怕太太有什么话吩咐，打发他们来，一时听不明白，倒耽误了。"

"Master Bao's sound asleep now, and the other girls know how to look after him," Xiren answered confidently. "Please don't worry, madam. I thought perhaps you had some instructions which one of the others might not understand, and that might hold things up."

王夫人道："也没甚话，就问问他这会子疼得怎么样？"袭人道："宝姑娘送去的药，我给二爷敷上了，比先好些了。先疼得躺不稳，这会子都睡沉了，可见好些了。"王夫人又问："吃了什

"I've no special instructions. I just wanted to know how he is now."

"Miss Baochai brought us a salve, and after I applied it he seemed better. At first the pain kept him awake, but now he's sleeping soundly. It shows he's on the mend."

"Did he eat anything?"

么没有？”

袭人道：“老太太给的一碗汤，喝了两口，只嚷干渴，要吃酸梅汤。我想着酸梅是个收敛的东西，才刚挨了打，又不许叫喊，自然急的那热毒热血未免不存在心里，倘或吃下这个去激在心里，再弄出大病来，可怎么样呢。因此我劝了半天才没吃，只拿那糖腌的玫瑰卤子和了吃，吃了半碗，又嫌吃絮了，不香甜。”

王夫人道：“嗳哟，你真该早来和我说。前儿有人送了两瓶子香露来，原要给他点子的，我怕他胡糟蹋了，就没给。既是他嫌那些玫瑰膏子絮烦，把这个拿两瓶子去。一碗水里只用挑一茶匙儿，就香的了不得呢。”说着就唤彩云来，“把前儿的那几瓶香露拿了来。”

袭人道：“只拿两瓶来吧，多了也白糟蹋。等不够再要，再来取也是一样。”彩云听说，去了半日，果然拿了两瓶来，付与袭人。袭

"Only two mouthfuls of the soup the old lady sent. He complained he was parched and asked for some sour plum juice. But I thought to myself: Sour things are astringent, and when he was beaten and couldn't cry out some choleric humours must have rushed to his viscera; plum juice might affect them, bringing on a serious illness, and that would never do. Finally I talked him out of it and gave him some candied rose petals instead. He only ate half a bowl, though, then found it cloying and insipid."

"Why didn't you send and let me know before?" cried Lady Wang. "The other day I was sent a couple of bottles of scented flower juice and meant to give them to him, but thought he might waste them. If he finds rose petals cloying, take him these. One teaspoon in a bowl of water is delicious." She told Caiyun, "Fetch those bottles of juice which were brought the other day."

"Two bottles will be plenty," Xiren assured her, "More would be wasted. We can always come and ask for more when it's finished." Caiyun went off on this errand, returning presently

人看时，只见两个玻璃小瓶，却有三寸大小，上面螺丝银盖，鹅黄笺上写着“木樨清露”，那一个写着“玫瑰清露。”

with two bottles which she handed to Xiren. They were tiny glass bottles barely three inches high, with silver caps which screwed on, and yellow labels. On one was written “Pure Osmanthus Juice,” on the other “Pure Rose Juice.”

袭人笑道：“好金贵东西！这么个小瓶子儿，能有多少？”王夫人道：“那是进上的，你没看见鹅黄笺子？你好生替他收着，别糟蹋了。”

“What luxury objects!” Xiren laughed. “Such small bottles can't hold much.”

“They're for the Imperial use,” explained Lady Wang. “Don't you see the yellow label? Mind you keep them carefully for him. Don't waste any of the juice.”

袭人答应着，方要走时，王夫人又叫：“站着，我想起一句话来问你。”袭人忙又回来。王夫人见房内无人，便问道：“我恍惚听见宝玉今儿挨打，是环儿在老爷跟前说了什么话。你可听见这个了？你要听见，告诉我听听，我也不吵出来叫人知道是你说的。”

Xiren assented and was about to leave when Lady Wang told her to wait.

“There's something else I want to ask you,” she said.

Having made sure that no one else was about she continued, “There's talk that the master beat Baoyu because of some tale Huan told. Did you hear that? If you did, just tell me what it was. I won't make a rumpus about it. No one will know that it was you who told me.”

袭人道：“我倒没听见这话，为二爷霸占着戏子，人家来和老爷要，为这个打的。”

“No, I didn't hear that,” replied Xiren. “I heard it was because Master Bao kept an actor from some prince's mansion, and they came to ask His Lordship to send him back.”

王夫人摇头说道："也为这个，还有别的缘故。"袭人道："别的缘故实在不知道了。我今儿在太太跟前大胆说句不知好歹的话。论理……"说了半截忙又咽住。

王夫人道："你只管说。"

袭人笑道："太太别生气，我就说了。"

王夫人道："我有什么生气的，你只管说来"袭人道："论理，我们二爷也须得老爷教训两顿。若老爷再不管，将来不知做出什么事来呢。"

王夫人一闻此言，便合掌念声"阿弥陀佛"，由不得赶着袭人叫了一声(4)"我的儿，亏了你也明白，这话和我的心一样。我何曾不知道管儿子，先时你珠大爷在，我是怎么样管他。难道我如今倒不知管儿子了？只是有个缘故：如今我想，我已经快五十岁的人，通共剩了他一个，他又长的单弱，况且老太太宝贝似的，若管紧了他，倘或再有个好歹，或是老太太气坏了，那时上

Lady Wang shook her head.

"That was one reason, but there was another too."

"If there's anything else I really don't know it," rejoined Xiren. She added, "May I make so bold, now that I'm here, to suggest something, madam." She broke off at this point. "Go on."

With a sly smile she went on, "I hope Your Ladyship won't think it presumptuous."

"Of course not. What is it?"

"Actually, Master Bao does need to be taught a lesson. If His Lordship doesn't discipline him, there's no knowing what may happen in future."

On hearing this, Lady Wang clapped her hands together, exclaiming "Gracious Buddha!" Then although so eager to hear more, she confided, "Dear child, I'm glad you are so understanding-that's exactly how I fed. Of course I know the importance of discipline. I haven't forgotten how strict I was with Master Zhu. But there's a reason for my indulgence now. I'm getting on for fifty, and I've only the one son left; besides, he's rather delicate and the old lady dotes on him. If I were too strict so that something happened to him, or

下不安，岂不倒坏了。所以就纵坏了他。我常常掰着口儿劝一阵，说一阵，气得骂一阵，哭一阵，彼时他好，过后儿还是不相干，端的吃了亏才罢了。若打坏了，将来我靠谁呢！”说着，由不得滚下泪来。

if the old lady were upset, the whole household would be turned upside down and that would be even worse. That's why he's been spoiled. I'm always scolding him, pleading with him, getting angry with him or crying over him, but after a short improvement back he slips. He'll never mend his ways unless he's made to smart. Yet if he's badly injured, I'll have no one to depend on in the future." With this she burst into tears.

袭人见王夫人这般悲感，自己也不觉伤了心，陪着落泪。又道："二爷是太太养的，岂不心疼。便是我们做下人的服侍一场，大家落个平安，也算是造化了，要这样起来，连平安都不能了。哪一日哪一时我不劝二爷，只是再劝不醒。偏生那些人又肯亲近他，也怨不得他这样。总是我们劝的倒不好了。今儿太太提起这话来，我还记挂着一件事，每要来回太太，讨太太个主意。只是我怕太太疑心，不但我的话白说了，且连葬身之地都没了。"

And Xiren, seeing her distress, wept in sympathy.

"He's your son, madam, of course you take this to heart. Even those of us who wait on him would be happy if everyone could keep out of trouble. If things go on like this we'll have no peace either. Not a day goes by but I reason with Master Bao, yet it has no effect. It's not his fault if people of that sort make up to him, and he loses patience when we reason with him. Since you've brought this up, madam, I'd like to ask your advice about something that's been worrying me for a long time. I've never raised it before for fear you might misunderstand. In that case, not only would I be wasting my breath but taking an outrageous liberty."

王夫人听了这话内有因，忙问道："我的儿，你有话只管说。近来我因听见众人背前背后都夸你，我只说你不过是在宝玉身上留心，或是诸人跟前和气，这些小意思好，所以将你和老姨娘一体行事。谁知你方才和我说的话全是大道理，正和我的想头一样。你有什么只管说什么，只别教别人知道就是了。"袭人道："我也没什么别的说。我只想着讨太太一个示下，怎么变个法儿，以后竟还叫二爷搬出园外来住就好了。"

王夫人听了，吃一大惊，忙拉了袭人的手问道："宝玉难道和谁作怪了不成？"

袭人连忙回道："太太别多心，并没有这话。这不过是我的小见识。如今二爷也大了，里头姑娘们也大了，况且林姑娘宝姑娘又是两姨姑表姊妹，虽说是姊妹们，到底是男女之分，日夜一处起坐不方便，由不得叫人悬心，便是外人看着也不像。一家子的事，俗语说的

Lady Wang realized there was something behind this.

"Just say what's on your mind, my child," she urged. "I've heard nothing but good of you recently from everyone. I assumed it was just because you looked after Baoyu well and were pleasant to everybody. Such thoughtfulness in little things is good. That's why I treated you like one of the old nurses. Now I see you have principles too and your views coincide with mine. Just say whatever's on your mind, but don't let it go any further."

"It's nothing else, only that I was hoping Your Ladyship might arrange for Master Bao to move out of the Garden."

Lady Wang was shocked. She caught hold of Xiren's hand.

"Has Baoyu been up to anything improper?"

"No, no, madam. Don't misunderstand me. Nothing of that sort. But in my humble opinion, now that he and the young ladies are no longer children and, what's more, Miss Lin and Miss Bao aren't members of the family, cousins of different sexes should live apart. When they spend all their time together every day, it's not convenient for them and we can't help worrying. Besides, it

(5)`没事常思有事',世上多少无头脑的人，多半因为无心中做出，有心人看见，当作有心事，反说坏了。只是预先不防着，断然不好。

二爷素日性格，太太是知道的。他又偏好在我们队里闹，倘或不防，前后错了一点半点，不论真假，人多口杂，那起小人的嘴有什么避讳，心顺了，说的比菩萨还好；心不顺，就贬的连畜生不如。二爷将来倘或有人说好，不过大家直过没事，若要叫人说出一个不好字来，我们不用说，粉身碎骨，罪有万重，都是平常小事，但后来二爷一生的声名品行岂不完了，二则太太也难见老爷。俗语又说`君子防不然'，不如这会子防避的为是。太太事情多，一时固然想不到。我们想不到则可，既想到了，若不回明太太，罪越重了。近来我为这事日夜悬心，又不好说与人，惟有灯知道罢了。”

doesn't look good to people outside. As the proverb has it: Best be prepared for the worst. A lot of foolishness is quite innocent, but suspicious people always think the worst. Better make sure in advance that there's no trouble.

“You know, madam, what Master Bao is like and how he enjoys amusing himself with us girls. If no precautions are taken and he does something the least bit foolish-no matter whether it's true or not there's bound to be talk. Lowclass people will gossip. When they're well disposed, they laud you to the skies; when they're not, they talk as if you were worse than a beast. If people speak well of him, that's as it should be. If a single slighting remark is passed, not only shall we deserve a thousand deaths-that's not important-but his reputation will be ruined for life and how will you answer for it to His Lordship? Another proverb says: A gentleman should show providence. Better guard against this now. You're naturally too busy, madam, to think of these things, and they might not occur to us either. But if they do and we fail to mention it, that would be very remiss. Lately this has been preying on my mind day and night, but

I couldn't mention it to anyone else. Only my lamp at night knew how I worried!"

王夫人听了这话，如雷轰电掣的一般，正触了金钏儿之事，心内越发感受袭人不尽，忙笑道：

Lady Wang felt thunderstruck on hearing this, borne out as it was by the case of Jinchuan. The more she thought, the more grateful she felt to Xiren.

"我的儿，你竟有这个心胸，想的这样周全！我何曾又不想到这里，只是这几次有事就忘了。你今儿这一番话提醒了我。难为你成全我娘儿两个声名体面，真真我竟不知道你这样好。罢了，你且去吧，我自有道理。只是还有一句话：你今既说了这样的话，我就把他交给你了。好歹留心，保全了他，就是保全了我。我自然不辜负你。"

"What a wise child you are to see so far!" she exclaimed. "Of course I've given some thought to this myself, but lately I've had too much else on my mind. Now you've reminded me. I'm glad you're so concerned for our reputation. I really had no idea what a good girl you are! All right, you may go now. Leave everything to me. But I tell you this: after what you've said today, I mean to entrust Baoyu to you. You must look after him and keep him safe. That way, you'll be safeguarding me as well, and I shan't forget our obligation to you."

袭人连连答应着去了。回来正值宝玉睡醒，袭人回明香露之事。宝玉喜不自禁，即令调来尝试，果然香妙非常。

Xiren hastily assented and withdrew. Back in Happy Red Court, she found Baoyu had just woken up. When she told him about the juice he was delighted. He asked to taste some and pronounced it delicious.

因心下记挂着黛玉，满心里要打发人去，只是怕袭人，便设一法，先使袭人往

Because Baoyu had Daiyu on his mind he was eager to send someone over to her, but for fear of Xiren he had to resort to

宝钗那里去借书。袭人去了，宝玉便命晴雯来吩咐道：

“你到林姑娘那里看看他做什么呢。他要问我，只说我好了。”晴雯道：“白眉赤眼，做什么去呢？到底说句话儿，也像一件事。”宝玉道：“没有什么可说的。”

晴雯道：“若不然，或是送件东西，或是取件东西，不然我去了怎么搭讪呢？”宝玉想了一想，便伸手拿了两条手帕子撂与晴雯，笑道：“也罢，就说我叫你送这个给他去了。”晴雯道：“这又奇了。他要这半新不旧的两条手帕子？他又要恼了，说你打趣他。”宝玉笑道：“你放心，他自然知道。”

晴雯听了，只得拿了帕子往潇湘馆来。只见春纤正在栏杆上晾手帕子，见他进来，忙摆手儿，说：“睡下了。”晴雯走进来，满屋魆黑。并未点灯。黛玉已睡在床上。问是谁。晴雯忙答

a trick. He dispatched Xiren to Baochai to borrow some books, and as soon as she had left called for Qingwen.

“Go and see what Miss Lin is doing,” he said. “If she asks after me, tell her I'm better.”

“I can't just go there without any excuse. Is there no message that you want to send?”

“Not that I can think of.”

“Give me something to take then, or ask to borrow something. Otherwise what am I going to say when I see her?”

After a little thought Baoyu picked up two Handkerchiefs and tossed them to her.

“All right, tell her I sent you to give her these.”

“This is even odder!” cried Qingwen. “What would she want two old handkerchiefs for?

She'll flare up again and say you're teasing her."" Don't worry. She'll understand.”

So Qingwen took his gift to Bamboo Lodge,where she found Chunxian hanging some handkerchiefs to dry on the balustrade.Chunxian held up a warning finger “She's gone to bed.” Qingwen slipped into the dark room where the lamps were not yet lit. Daiyu, lying on the

道："晴雯。"

黛玉道："做什么？"晴雯道："二爷送手帕子来给姑娘。"黛玉听了，心中发闷："做什么送手帕子来给我？"因问："这帕子是谁送他的？必是上好的，叫他留着送别人去吧，我这会子不用这个。"

晴雯笑道："不是新的，就是家常旧的。"林黛玉听见，越发闷住，着实细心搜求，思忖一时，方大悟过来，连忙说："放下，去kc吧。"

晴雯听了，只得放下，抽身回去，一路盘算，不解何意。

这里林黛玉体贴出手帕子的意思来，不觉神魂驰荡：(6) 宝玉这番苦心，能领会我这番苦意，又令我可喜；我这番苦意，不知将来如何，又令我可悲；忽然好好的送两块旧帕子来，若不是领我深意，单看了这帕子，又令我可笑；再想令人私相

bed, asked who it was." It's me, Qingwen."

"What do you want?"

"Master Bao has sent you some handkerchiefs, miss." Why should he send me handkerchiefs? Daiyu wondered. "Who gave these to him?" she asked. "I suppose they're specially fine ones. Tell him to keep them for someone else, I don't need them for the time being."

"They're not new," replied Qingwen giggling. "He's often used them." Daiyu was even more mystified at this, but some careful thought cleared up the riddle for her. "Leave them then," she said quickly, "You may go."

So Qingwen put down the handkerchiefs and left, puzzling her head all the way back over this gift.

Meanwhile Daiyu, touched by the meaning of this gift, was lost in reverie. Pleased as she was by Baoyu's insight and sympathy, it was sad to think that all her concern for him might come to nothing. This unex¬pected present of two used handkerchiefs was rather laughable if it were not for the fact that she understood the thought behind it; yet it was scandalous that he should send and she accept a secret gift. And

传递与我，又可惧；我自己每每好哭，想来也无味，又令我可愧。

如此左思右想，一时五内沸然炙起。黛玉由不得余意绵缠，令掌灯，也想不起嫌疑避讳等事，便向案上研墨蘸笔，便向那两块旧帕子上走笔写道：

眼空蓄泪泪空垂，
暗洒闲抛却为谁？
尺幅鲛绡劳解赠，
叫人焉得不伤悲！

其二

抛珠滚玉只偷潸，
镇日无心镇日闲，
枕上袖边难拂拭，
任他点点与斑斑。

其三

彩线难收面上珠，
湘江旧迹已模糊，
窗前亦有千竿竹，
不识香痕渍也无？

林黛玉还要往下写时，

it made her ashamed of her habit of crying so much.

As she mused in this way, her heart was very full, her mind in a turmoil. Having ordered the lamps to be lit, without any thought of the possible consequences she ground some ink on the inkstone, dipped her brush in it and quickly wrote these lines on the handkerchiefs:

*Vain are all these idle tears,*
*Tears shed secretly-for whom?*
*Your kind gift of a foot of gauze*
*Only deepens my gloom.*

*By stealth I shed pearly tears,*
*Idle tears the livelong day;*
*Hard to wipe them from sleeve and pillow,*
*Then suffer the stains to stay.*

*No silk thread can string these pearls;*
*Dim now the tear-stains of those bygone years;*
*A thousand bamboos grow before my window .*
*Is each dappled and stained with tears?*

She would have written more

觉得浑身火热，面上作烧，走至镜台揭起锦袱一照，只见腮上通红，自羡压倒桃花，却不知病由此萌。一时方上床睡去，犹拿着那帕子思索，不在话下。

but her whole body was afire, her face burning. Going to the mirror-stand she removed its silk cover and saw that her flushed cheeks were redder than peach blossom, but failed to realize that this was the first symptom of consumption. She went to bed with the handkerchiefs clasped in her hands and lost herself in dreams.

却说袭人来见宝钗，谁知宝钗不在园内，往他母亲那里去了，袭人便空手回来。等至二更，宝钗方回来。

To return to Xiren and her errand to Baochai, when she found that Baochai was not in the Garden but had gone to her mother's house, she went back empty-handed. And Baochai did not return till the second watch.

原来宝钗素知薛蟠情性，心中已有一半疑是薛蟠调唆了人来告宝玉的，谁知又听袭人说出来，越发信了。究竟袭人是听焙茗说的，那焙茗也是私心窥度，并未据实，竟认准是他说的。那薛蟠都因素日有这个名声，其实这一次却不是他干的，被人生生的一口咬死是他，有口难分。

The fact is that Baochai's knowledge of her brother had led her to suspect that he was behind the visit of the prince's chief steward, and Xiren's report confirmed her suspicion. Xiren of course had this on hearsay from Beiming, who had simply been guessing, not having any proof. But she now was sure of his guilt. The joke was that for all Xue Pan's bad reputation he was not to blame this time, and yet everyone con¬demned him out of hand.

这日正从外头吃了酒回来，见过母亲，只见宝钗在这里，说了几句闲话，因问：

Coming home today after carousing outside, Xue Pan went in to greet his mother and found Baochai with her. After they had

"听见宝兄弟吃了亏，是为什么？"薛姨妈正为这个不自在，见他问时，便咬着牙道："不知好歹的东西，都是你闹的，你还有脸来问！"

exchanged a few words he remarked:

"I hear Cousin Bao got a whacking. What for?"

Aunt Xue was already upset on this score.

"You trouble-maker," she snapped back, gnashing her teeth, "this is all your doing. And you have the impudence to ask!"

薛蟠见说，便怔了，忙问道："我何尝闹什么？"薛姨妈道："你还装憨呢！人人都知道是你说的，还赖呢。"薛蟠道："人人说我杀了人，也就信了罢？"薛姨妈道："连你妹妹都知道是你说的，难道他也赖你不成？"

Xue Pan was genuinely taken aback. "What trouble have I made?" he asked." Still playing the innocent? Everyone knows you were the one who told. Do you still deny it?"" If everyone said I'd killed a man, would you believe it?"" Even your sister knows it was you. Would she make up something against you?"

宝钗忙劝道："妈和哥哥且别叫喊，消消停停的，就有个青红皂白了。"因向薛蟠道："是你说的也罢，不是你说的也罢，事情也过去了，不必较证，倒把小事儿弄大了。我只劝你从此以后在外头少去胡闹，少管别人的事。天天一处大家胡逛，你是个不防头的人，过后儿没事就罢了，倘或有事，不是你干的，人人都也疑惑是你干的，不用说别人，

"Do keep your voices down!" put in Baochai quickly. "It will all be cleared up by and by." She turned to her brother. "Whether you told or not, it's over and done with. Don't let's quibble or make a mountain out of a molehill. Take my advice, though, and stop fooling around outside. Just mind your own business. You waste all your time with those rowdies and you're too careless. If nothing happens, well and good. But if trouble starts everyone is bound to suspect you, whether you caused it or not. Why, even I

我就先疑惑。”

薛蟠本是个心直口快的人，一生见不得这样藏头露尾的事，又见宝钗劝他不要逛去，他母亲又说他犯舌，宝玉之打是他治的，早已急的乱跳，赌身发誓的分辩。又骂众人：

“谁这样赃派我？我把那囚攮的牙敲了才罢！分明是为打了宝玉，没的献勤儿，拿我来作幌子。难道宝玉是天王？他父亲打他一顿，一家子定要闹几天。哪一回为他不好，姨爹打了他两下子，过后老太太不知怎么知道了，说是珍大哥哥治的，好好的叫了去骂了一顿。今儿越发拉上我了！既拉上，我也不怕，越性进去把宝玉打死了，我替他偿了命，大家干净。”

（8）一面嚷，一面抓起一根门闩来就跑。慌的薛姨妈一把抓住，骂道：“作死的孽障，你打谁去？你先打我来！”薛蟠急得眼似铜铃

would suspect you, let alone others.”

Blunt, outspoken Xue Pan could not stand such insinuations. Baochai's warning against fooling about outside and his mother's charge that his careless talk had caused Baoyu's flogging made him stamp with rageand swear he must clear himself.

“Who's been shifting the blame on to me?” he fumed. “I'll smash the scoundrel's teeth. It's obvious that to make up to Baoyu they're using me as a whipping-boy. Is Baoyu the king of heaven? Whenever his father whacks him the whole household's bound to be upside down for days. After my uncle caned him for misbehaving last time, it somehow came to the old lady's ears that Cousin Zhen was behind it and she summoned him to give him a big dressing-down. This time they're picking on me. Well, I'm not afraid. I'll go and kill Baoyu then pay with my life-make a clean sweep!”

He seized the door bar and started rushing out. In desperation his mother dragged him back.” You'll be the death of me, you monster,” she scolded. “Off to pick a fight, are you? Better

一般，嚷道："何苦来！又不叫我去，又好好的赖我。将来宝玉活一日，我担一日的口舌，不如大家死了清净。"

宝钗忙也上前劝道："你忍耐些儿吧。妈急的这个样儿，你不说来劝妈，你还反闹的这样。别说是妈，便是旁人来劝你，也为你好，倒把你的性子劝上来了。"薛蟠道："这会子又说这话。都是你说的！"宝钗道："你只怨我说，再不怨你顾前不顾后的形景。"

薛蟠道："你只会怨我顾前不顾后，你怎么不怨宝玉外头招风惹草的那个样子！别说多的，只拿前儿琪官的事比给你们听：那琪官，我们见过十来次的，我并未和他说一句亲热话，怎么前儿他见了，连姓名还不知道，就把汗巾子给他了？难道这也是我说的不成？"

kill me first." Xue Pan's eyes nearly started from his head in fury." What's all this nonsense!" he bellowed. "You won't let me go, yet pin this thing on me for no reason at all. As long as Baoyu lives, I shall always be his whipping-boy. We'd better all die and be done with it."

"Do have patience," urged Baochai, stepping quickly forward. "Mother's so upset, yet instead of soothing her you raise this rumpus. When people-especially your own mother-advise you, it's for your own good. You shouldn't fly into a temper."

"So you 're nagging again, are you?" he roared. "You're the one who started this."

"You only blame me for nagging, never blame your own thoughtlessness."

"Instead of blaming my thoughtlessness, why don't you blame Baoyu for looking for trouble outside? Let's take just one example-that recent business of Qiguan. I've met Qiguan a dozen times without his making up to me once; but the very first time Baoyu met him, before he even knew his name, Qiguan gave him his girdle. That was my fault too, I suppose?"

薛姨妈和宝钗急得说道："还提这个！可不是为这个打他呢 可见是你说的了。"

"There you go again," cried his mother and sister frantically. "That's why he got beaten. This shows you're the one who told."

薛蟠道："真真的气死人了！赖我说的我不恼，我只为一个宝玉闹的这样天翻地覆的。"

"You want me to burst with anger," growled Xue Pan. "It's not being wrongly accused that enrages me, it's this fearful fuss you make over Baoyu."

宝钗道："谁闹了？你先持刀动杖的闹起来，倒说别人闹。"薛蟠见宝钗说的话句句有理，难以驳正，比母亲的话反难回答，因此便要设法拿话堵回他去，就无人敢拦自己的话了，也因正在气头上，未曾想话之轻重，便说道：

"Who's making a fuss?" retorted Baochai. "You started it by arming yourself and threatening to fight. Now you accuse us of fussing." As all her arguments were so reasonable and even harder to refute than his mother's, Xue Pan cast about for some way to silence her in order to have his say. And being in a towering rage, he did not trouble to weigh his words carefully.

"So you 're nagging again, are you?" he roared. "You're the one who started this."

"You only blame me for nagging, never blame your own thoughtlessness."

"好妹妹，你不用和我闹，我早知道你的心了。从先妈和我说，你这金要拣有玉的才可正配，你留了心，见宝玉有那劳什骨子，你自然如今行动护着他。"

"It's no use flying into a huff with me, my dear sister," he sneered. "I can see into your heart. Mother's told me about your gold locket which has to be matched with jade. Naturally you looked round carefully, and now that you find Baoyu has that rubbishy thing you're bound to take

话未说了，把个宝钗气怔了，拉着薛姨妈哭道："妈妈你听，哥哥说的是什么话！"薛蟠见妹妹哭了，便知自己冒撞了，便赌气走到自己房里安歇不提。

这里薛姨妈气得乱战，一面又劝宝钗道："你素日知那孽障说话没道理，明儿我叫他给你陪不是。"

宝钗满心委屈气忿，待要怎样，又怕他母亲不安，少不得含泪别了母亲，各自回来，到房里整哭了一夜。

次日早起来，也无心梳洗，胡乱整理整理，便出来瞧母亲。

可巧遇见林黛玉独立在花阴之下，问他那里去。薛宝钗因说"家去"，口里说着，便只管走。黛玉见他无精打采的去了，又见眼上有哭泣之状，大非往日可比，便在后面笑道：

"姐姐也自保重些儿。就是哭出两缸眼泪来，也医

his side."

Baochai was speechless at first with indignation. Then catching hold of her mother she sobbed:" Do you hear what he's saying, mother?" At this Xue Pan knew he had gone too far and sullenly retired to his own room.

Though trembling with rage, Aunt Xue tried to comfort her daughter. "You know that monster always talks nonsense," she said. "Tomorrow I'll tell him to apologize."

Bitterly wronged as Baochai felt, she could not make a scene for fear of upsetting her mother. So with tears in her eyes she took her leave and went back to her own apartment to cry all night.

The next morning she rose early and, without troubling to make a careful toilet, simply straightened her clothes and set off to see her mother again.

On the way she happened to meet Daiyu standing alone under the shade of some blossom and was asked where she was going. Baochai, not stopping, said she was on her way home. Daiyu saw that she looked in low spirits, quite unlike her usual self, and had been crying.

She called mischievously after her, "Cousin, look after your

不好棒疮。”

不知宝钗如何答对，且听下回分解。

health! Even if you fill two vats with tears that won’t cure his welts.”

To know how Baochai replied you must read the next chapter.

# 第五章

# Vanity Fair
# 名利场

*"Where have you been, wretch? Here is Emmy crying her eyes out for you. Are you coming to fetch me for the quadiller?"*

## 背景介绍

19 世纪早期的英国风俗画卷出自于萨克雷的小说 Vanity Fair《名利场》，这本绵里藏针的长篇小说讲述了一个出身于艺人家庭的孤女斗智斗勇斗才色，费尽心思地往上流社会爬的传奇故事。夏泼 (Sharp) 这个角色在文学史上是绝无仅有的，但是如果只是成功地塑造了一个人物，是配不上“风俗画卷”这样的称谓的。《名利场》的副标题是：一个没有主角的小说。可见萨克雷也用了相当的心思来塑造其他角色，比如都宾，这个心眼实诚，甘愿为朋友做垫脚石的大个子军官；爱米丽亚和她那死心塌地地爱着的，却并不那么爱她的乔治；夏泼那曾经游手好闲后来却一副慈父模样的丈夫；从印度回国的花里胡哨的乔斯先生；身为贵族却比平民都浮浪的毕脱爵士等等。有人统计了一下，一本《名利场》栩栩如生地刻画了大大小小 150 多个人物。毫无疑问，为人物塑造立下汗马功劳的肯定是萨克雷的语言，所谓的妙笔生花，用在这本书上是一点也不为过。他的语言以辛辣讽刺著名，这样的风格会不会在翻译中失去它的锋利呢？

幸而对上面疑问的回答是：不会的。杨必 (1922—1968 年) 翻译的《名利场》是目前为止最为大众喜欢，也最为翻译界称赞的作品。这位江南女子才气逼人，语言灵动，思路畅达。中文在她的笔下也是热热烈烈的，跟英语原文相得益彰。“布鲁塞尔”这一章是比较难处理的片段，夏泼女士既要卖弄风骚勾引俊哥帅男又要向昔日的老朋友表示的温情脉脉还得不让老公吃醋，这样微妙的表情和心理上的变化都要通过中文的遣词造句再次表达出来，大家来对比阅读一下，就可以明白这个译本的成功之处了。

## 细读节选

选择《布鲁塞尔》这一章来细读是出于以下原因：在情节上，是夏泼费尽心思挤入上流社会后最得意的展示，是爱米丽亚对夏泼的认识发生质的转变的环节，也是未来夏泼用来拯救艾米丽亚的用的那张纸条被传递的时刻。

## 拓展思考

1. 凭借记忆，写出 3 句划线的原文与译文。

| 原文 | 译文 |
|---|---|
| | |
| | |
| | |

2. 译者的方言习惯对翻译有何影响？举例说明。

3. 利蓓加是一个什么角色？ 她对待爱米丽亚的方式有何特征？

4. 对名利的追逐在节选中是怎么体现出来的？

# Chapter xxix

# 第二十九章

## *Brussels*

## 布鲁塞尔

Mr. Jos had hired a pair of horses for his open carriage, with which cattle, and the smart London vehicle, he made a very tolerable figure in the drives about Brussels.

乔斯先生租了两匹马来拉他的敞篷车。时髦的伦敦车子套上了这两匹牲口，在布鲁塞尔的马路上很有点风头了。

George purchased a horse for his private riding, and he and Captain Dobbin would often accompany the carriage in which Jos and his sister took daily excursions of pleasure.

乔治也买了一匹马专为下班以后骑。乔斯和他妹妹天天坐在马车里出去散心，乔治和都宾上尉骑马陪着他们。

They went out that day in the park for their accustomed diversion, and there, sure enough, George's remark with regard to the arrival of Rawdon Crawley and his wife proved to be correct.

那天，他们照常在公园里兜风，发现乔治猜得不错，克劳莱夫妇果然也来了。

In the midst of a little troop of horsemen, consisting of some of the very greatest persons in Brussels, Rebecca was seen in the prettiest and tightest of riding-habits, mounted on a beautiful little Arab, which she rode to perfection (having acquired the

好些个将官骑着马都在那里，有好几个是当时布鲁塞尔最了不起的人物；利蓓加就杂在这群人里面。她骑着一匹神骏的阿拉伯小马，穿一件绝顶俏皮的骑马装，紧紧地贴在身上。她骑马的

art at Queen's Crawley, where the Baronet, Mr. Pitt, and Rawdon himself had given her many lessons), and by the side of the gallant General Tufto.

"Sure it's the Juke himself," cried Mrs. Major O'Dowd to Jos, who began to blush violently; "and that's Lord Uxbridge on the bay. How elegant he looks! Me brother, Molloy Malony, is as like him as two pays."

Rebecca did not make for the carriage; but as soon as she perceived her old acquaintance Amelia seated in it, acknowledged her presence by a gracious nod and smile, and by kissing and shaking her fingers playfully in the direction of the vehicle.

Then she resumed her conversation with General Tufto, who asked "who the fat officer was in the gold-laced cap?" on which Becky replied, "that he was an officer in the East Indian service." But Rawdon Crawley rode out of the ranks of his company, and came up and shook hands heartily with Amelia, and said to Jos, "Well, old boy, how are you?" and stared in Mrs. O'Dowd's face and at the black cock's feathers

本领也很了得，因为在女王的克劳莱，毕脱爵士、毕脱先生、罗登都曾经指点过她好多次。紧靠在她旁边的就是勇敢的德夫托将军。

“嗳呀，那不是公爵本人吗！”奥多太太对乔斯这么一嚷，乔斯立刻把脸涨的通红……“骑栗色马的是厄克斯白立奇勋爵。瞧他多文雅，活脱儿像我兄弟莫洛哀•玛洛内。”

利蓓加并没有走到马上旁边来；她看见爱米丽亚坐在里面，立刻气度雍容地微笑着点点头，向这边飞了一个吻，又开玩笑似的对大家招招手。

这么招呼过以后，她又接着和德夫托将军说起话来。将军问她那戴金边帽子的胖军官是谁，她回答说是东印度部队里的。罗登•克劳莱特离开朋友们跑过来，亲亲密密的和爱米莉亚拉手，跟乔斯说了声：“嗳，好小子，你好啊？”他光着眼看奥多太太，又瞪着她帽子上插的黑鸡毛，奥多太太还只

until she began to think she had made a conquest of him.

George, who had been delayed behind, rode up almost immediately with Dobbin, and they touched their caps to the august personages, among whom Osborne at once perceived Mrs. Crawley. He was delighted to see Rawdon leaning over his carriage familiarly and talking to Amelia, and met the aide-de-camp's cordial greeting with more than corresponding warmth. (1) The nods between Rawdon and Dobbin were of the very faintest specimens of politeness.

Crawley told George where they were stopping with General Tufto at the Hotel du Parc, and George made his friend promise to come speedily to Osborne's own residence.

"Sorry I hadn't seen you three days ago," George said. "Had a dinner at the Restaurateur's rather a nice thing. Lord Bareacres, and the Countess, and Lady Blanche, were good enough to dine with us-wish we'd had you." Having thus let his friend know his claims to be a man of fashion, Osborne parted from Rawdon, who followed the august squadron down an alley into which they cantered, while George and

道他看上了自己。

乔治因为有事给耽搁在后面，立刻和都宾骑马迎上来，对这些大人物行了礼，一眼就看见克劳莱太太夹在他们一群人中间。他瞧着罗登怪亲密地靠着马车和爱米莉亚说话，满心欢喜。那副官很客气地跟他招呼，他回答得更是热和。罗登和都宾互相点了点头，仅仅表示了礼数。

克劳莱告诉乔治说他们和德夫托将军住在一起，都在花园饭店；乔治请他朋友赶快到他家里去玩。

乔治说：“可惜三天前没碰见你，我们在饭店里吃了一餐饭，还不坏。贝亚爱克斯伯爵，伯爵夫人，和白朗茜小姐都赏光了，可惜你没来。”这样一说，奥斯本就让朋友知道自己也是在时髦场上走走的人。最后大家别过，罗登跟着那群大人物跑到一条夹道上去；乔治和

Dobbin resumed their places, one on each side of Amelia's carriage.

都宾一边一个，回到爱米丽亚的马车旁边。

"How well the Juke looked," Mrs. O'Dowd remarked. "The Wellesleys and Malonys are related; but, of course, poor I would never dream of introjuicing myself unless his Grace thought proper to remember our family-tie."

奥多太太说："公爵的气色多好呀。威尔斯莱家里和玛洛内家里原是亲戚。不过呢，可怜的我当然做梦也不会去攀附他，总得他大人愿意认亲戚才好呢。"

"He's a great soldier," Jos said, much more at ease now the great man was gone. "Was there ever a battle won like Salamanca? Hey, Dobbin? But where was it he learnt his art? In India, my boy! The jungle's the school for a general, mark me that. I knew him myself, too, Mrs. O'Dowd: we both of us danced the same evening with Miss Cutler, daughter of Cutler of the Artillery, and a devilish fine girl, at Dumdum."

乔斯见大人物走了，松了一口气，说道："他是个了不起的军人。哪一回打仗比得上萨拉孟战役呢？你说呀，都宾？他的军事技巧是在哪儿训练出来的？在印度呀，孩子！我告诉你吧，印度的大树林才是训练将军的好地方。奥多太太，我也认识他。在邓姆开跳舞会的那天晚上，他跟我都和克脱勒小姐跳舞来着，她是炮兵营克脱勒的女儿，漂亮的不得了。"

（2）The apparition of the great personages held them all in talk during the drive; and at dinner; and until the hour came when they were all to go to the Opera.

看见了这些有名儿的人，话就多了。他们一路回家的时候，吃饭的时候，议论讲究的全是这题目，一直到动身上歌剧院才住口不谈。

It was almost like Old England. The house was filled with

那时的情形和英国差不多，戏院里满是熟悉的英国

familiar British faces, and those toilettes for which the British female has long been celebrated. Mrs. O'Dowd's was not the least splendid amongst these, and she had a curl on her forehead, and a set of Irish diamonds and Cairngorms, which outshone all the decorations in the house, in her notion. Her presence used to excruciate Osborne; but go she would upon all parties of pleasure on which she heard her young friends were bent. It never entered into her thought but that they must be charmed with her company.

"She's been useful to you, my dear," George said to his wife, whom he could leave alone with less scruple when she had this society. "But what a comfort it is that Rebecca's come: you will have her for a friend, and we may get rid now of this damn'd Irishwoman." To this Amelia did not answer, yes or no: and how do we know what her thoughts were?

The coup d'oeil of the Brussels opera-house did not strike Mrs. O'Dowd as being so fine as the theatre in Fishamble Street, Dublin, nor was French music at all equal, in her opinion, to the melodies of her native country. She fa-

脸，太太小姐们也是久已闻名的英国打扮。奥多太太穿戴得十分华丽，竟也不输似别的人。她脑门上装着卷曲的假刘海，戴一套爱尔兰金刚钻和苏格兰烟水晶的首饰。照她看来，戏院里看家的首饰都没有她的漂亮。乔治见了她就头疼，可是她一听到年轻的朋友们出外寻欢作乐，准会赶来凑热闹，满心以为他们对自己欢迎不暇。

有了她，乔治觉得就是把太太丢在一边也没有妨碍。他说：“亲爱的，她对你很有用。可是现在利蓓加来了，你可以跟她做伴，不必再要这讨厌的爱尔兰婆子了。”爱米丽亚听了这话，一声儿不回答，我们也不知道她心里怎么想。

奥多太太把布鲁塞尔的歌剧院打量了一下，说是还不如都柏林弗香勃街的戏馆好看，而且她听着法国的音乐也没有本乡的歌曲入耳。她扯起嗓子，把自己的这些

voured her friends with these and other opinions in a very loud tone of voice, and tossed about a great clattering fan she sported, with the most splendid complacency.

"Who is that wonderful woman with Amelia, Rawdon, love?" said a lady in an opposite box (who, almost always civil to her husband in private, was more fond than ever of him in company).

"Don't you see that creature with a yellow thing in her turban, and a red satin gown, and a great watch?"

"Near the pretty little woman in white?" asked a middle-aged gentleman seated by the querist's side, with orders in his button, and several under-waistcoats, and a great, choky, white stock.

"That pretty woman in white is Amelia, General: you are remarking all the pretty women, you naughty man."

"Only one, begad, in the world!" said the General, delighted, and the lady gave him a tap with a large bouquet which she had.

见解和许多别的感想说给朋友们听，一面得意洋洋地卖弄她的大扇子，把它摇得劈啪劈啪的响。

对面包厢里一位太太问道："罗登亲爱的，爱米丽亚旁边那个了不起的太太是谁？"她在家的时候，总对丈夫十分客气，出外的时候也比以前更显得恩爱。

她又道："你瞧见没有？她穿一件红软缎长袍，戴一只大表，头巾上还有一个黄东西。"

说话的人旁边坐了一位中年男子，纽扣洞里挂着勋章，身上穿了好几件衬背心，脖子上围着一条又大又白、叫人透不过气的领巾。他问道："她是不是坐在穿白的漂亮女人身边？"

"将军，那穿白的漂亮女人叫爱米丽亚。你老是注意漂亮女人，真不老实！"

将军高兴极了，答道："哈，我只注意一个人。"那位太太听罢，用手里的大花球打了他一下。

"Bedad it's him," said Mrs. O'Dowd; "and that's the very bokay he bought in the Marshy aux Flures!" and when Rebecca, having caught her friend's eye, performed the little hand-kissing operation once more, (3) Mrs. Major O'D., taking the compliment to herself, returned the salute with a gracious smile, which sent that unfortunate Dobbin shrieking out of the box again.

At the end of the act, George was out of the box in a moment, and he was even going to pay his respects to Rebecca in her loge. He met Crawley in the lobby, however, where they exchanged a few sentences upon the occurrences of the last fortnight.

"You found my cheque all right at the agent's? George said, with a knowing air.

"All right, my boy," Rawdon answered. "Happy to give you your revenge. Governor come round?"

"Not yet," said George, "but he will; and you know I've some private fortune through my mother. Has Aunty relented?"

"Sent me twenty pound,

奥多太太说道："咦，就是他！那花球就是他在花市场买的。"利蓓加引得朋友往她那面看，便又亲着手指送了一个吻，奥多少佐太太以为利蓓加对她招呼，气度娴雅的微笑着还了一个吻，又把都宾逗得大笑着往包厢外面跑。

第一幕闭幕之后，乔治立刻走到包厢外面，盘算着要到利蓓加包厢里去应酬一下。他在穿堂里碰见克劳莱，说了几句话，彼此问问两星期来别后的情况。

乔治做出很有含蓄的样子问道："我的支票没出毛病吧？我的代理人把钱给你了吧？"

罗登答道："没毛病，孩子。我非常愿意给你一个报仇的机会。你爸爸让步没有？"

乔治道："还没有呢。可是将来总不要紧。你知道我母亲还留给我一些财产呢。姑妈回心转意了吗？"

"老婆子真小气，只给

damned old screw. When shall we have a meet? The General dines out on Tuesday. Can't you come Tuesday? I say, make Sedley cut off his moustache. What the devil does a civilian mean with a moustache and those infernal frogs to his coat! By-bye. Try and come on Tuesday"; and Rawdon was going-off with two brilliant young gentlemen of fashion, who were, like himself, on the staff of a general officer.

我二十镑。咱们什么时候碰头？星期二将军不在家吃饭，你就星期二来好不好？唉，叫赛特笠把胡子剃了吧！一个老百姓，留着两撇胡子，衣服上全是长方大纽扣，成什么样子？再见，星期二请过来。”和罗登一起还有两个时髦风流的年轻军官，也是高级将领的副官。罗登说完话，就打算和他们一起走。

George was only half pleased to be asked to dinner on that particular day when the General was not to dine. "I will go in and pay my respects to your wife," said he; at which Rawdon said, "Hm, as you please," looking very glum, and at which the two young officers exchanged knowing glances. George parted from them and strutted down the lobby to the General's box, the number of which he had carefully counted.

乔治见他特意在将军不在家吃饭的一天请他去，心里不大舒服，说道：“我想去问候问候你太太。”罗登沉着脸答道：“呣，随你的便。”其余的两个军官心里有数，互相使了个眼色。乔治别了他们，大踏步走过穿堂，在将军的包厢面前停了下来，原来他早已数过，把包厢的号码算出来了。

"Entrez," said a clear little voice, and our friend found himself in Rebecca's presence; who jumped up, clapped her hands together, and held out both of them to George, （4） so charmed was she to see him. The General, with

里面说话的人声音不大，可是很清朗，用法文说道：“进来。”我们的朋友一进去，就看见利蓓加坐在那里。她立刻跳起身来，高兴地拍了一下手，随后把两只

the orders in his button, stared at the newcomer with a sulky scowl, as much as to say, who the devil are you?

"My dear Captain George!" cried little Rebecca in an ecstasy. "How good of you to come. The General and I were moping together tete-a-tete. General, this is my Captain George of whom you heard me talk."

"Indeed," said the General, with a very small bow; "of what regiment is Captain George?"

George mentioned the -th: how he wished he could have said it was a crack cavalry corps.

"Come home lately from the West Indies, I believe. Not seen much service in the late war. Quartered here, Captain George?"the General went on with killing haughtiness.

"Not Captain George, you stupid man; Captain Osborne," Rebecca said. The General all the while was looking savagely from one to the other.

手都伸出来拉着乔治。那将军纽扣洞里挂着好些宝星，虎起脸儿，直眉瞪眼的对新来的人看着，好像说："你这东西是谁？"

小蓓基喜欢得不知怎么才好，叫道："亲爱的乔治上尉。多谢你来看我。将军跟我两个人在这儿说话，气闷得不得了。将军，这位就是我说起的乔治上尉。"

将军微微的把腰弯了一下，说道："是吗？乔治上尉是哪一联队的？"

乔治回说属于第一联队，心上自恨不属于第一流的骑兵营。

"我想你们大概刚从西印度群岛回来，在最近的战事中还没有机会上场。驻扎在此地吗，乔治上尉？"将军说话的口气，骄傲的叫人难堪。

利蓓加说道："傻东西，不是乔治上尉，是奥斯本上尉。"将军恶狠狠地轮流看着他们两个人，说道："哦，奥斯本上尉！跟某某地方的奥斯本是一家吗？"

"Captain Osborne, indeed! Any relation to the L-Osbornes?"

"We bear the same arms," George said, as indeed was the fact; Mr. Osborne having consulted with a herald in Long Acre, and picked the L-arms out of the peerage, when he set up his carriage fifteen years before.

"乔治道："我们两家用的纹章是一样的。"他说的是事实；十五年前他父亲奥斯本先生置备马车的时候，曾经和一个专司宗谱纹章的官员商量过，在《缙绅录》里挑了一个纹章，正是某某地方奥斯本家的。

The General made no reply to this announcement; but took up his opera-glass-the double-barrelled lorgnon was not invented in those days-and pretended to examine the house; but Rebecca saw that his disengaged eye was working round in her direction, and shooting out bloodshot glances at her and George.

将军听了不睬，拿起看戏用的望远镜（那时还没有双筒千里镜），假装细细地看那戏院。利蓓加看见他不时的把闲着的那只眼睛溜过来，杀气腾腾地瞧着乔治和她。

She redoubled in cordiality. "How is dearest Amelia? But I needn't ask: how pretty she looks! And who is that nice good-natured looking creature with her-a flame of yours? O, you wicked men! And there is Mr. Sedley eating ice, I declare: how he seems to enjoy it! General, why have we not had any ices?"

她对乔治加倍的亲热起来，说道："最亲爱的爱米丽亚怎么啦？其实我也不用问了，瞧她多漂亮！她旁边的那位好太太是谁？看上去怪和气的。嗳呦，她准是你的情人，你这坏东西。赛特笠先生在吃冰淇淋呢，瞧他吃得多高兴！将军，咱们怎么没有冰淇淋呀？"

"Shall I go and fetch you

将军气鼓鼓地问道："要

some?" said the General, bursting with wrath.

"Let ME go, I entreat you," George said.

"No, I will go to Amelia's box. Dear, sweet girl! Give me your arm, Captain George"; and so saying, and with a nod to the General, she tripped into the lobby. She gave George the queerest, knowingest look, when they were together, a look which might have been interpreted, "Don't you see the state of affairs, and what a fool I'm making of him?" But he did not perceive it. (5) He was thinking of his own plans, and lost in pompous admiration of his own irresistible powers of pleasing.

The curses to which the General gave a low utterance, as soon as Rebecca and her conqueror had quitted him, were so deep, that I am sure no compositor would venture to print them were they written down. They came from the General's heart; and a wonderful thing it is to think that the human heart is capable of generating such produce, and can throw out, as occasion demands, such a supply of lust and fury,

我去给你拿点来吗？”

乔治道：“请让我去吧。”

“不，我想到爱米丽亚的包厢里去瞧瞧她，这宝贝儿真招人疼。乔治上尉，你扶着我吧。”说着，她对将军点了一点头，轻轻俏俏的走到穿堂里。只剩他们两个在一起的时候，她瞧了乔治一眼，那表情含蓄无穷，非常的古怪，好像在向他说：“这是个什么局面你看得出吗？瞧我怎么开他的玩笑！”可惜乔治不能领会她的意思；他一面忙着做种种打算，一面得意洋洋的赞赏自己迷人的本事。

利蓓加跟她心上的人儿走到外面，将军立刻低声咒骂起来。他用的字眼那么难听，就算我写了下来，排字的人也不见得敢把他们印出来。这些恶毒骂人的话全是从将军心里发出来的。人的心里竟能有这样的产物，有的时候竟会发出这么强烈的愤怒、怨恨和淫欲，倒也着实稀奇。

rage and hatred.

Amelia's gentle eyes, too, had been fixed anxiously on the pair, whose conduct had so chafed the jealous General; but when Rebecca entered her box, she flew to her friend with an affectionate rapture which showed itself, in spite of the publicity of the place; for she embraced her dearest friend in the presence of the whole house, at least in full view of the General's glass, now brought to bear upon the Osborne party. Mrs. Rawdon saluted Jos, too, with the kindliest greeting: she admired Mrs. O'Dowd's large Cairngorm brooch and superb Irish diamonds, and wouldn't believe that they were not from Golconda direct.

他们的行为不但挑起了将军的醋劲，连爱米丽亚也不放心，一双温柔的眼睛急巴巴地瞧着他们。利蓓加进了包厢，飞也似的跑到朋友身边。她热情奔放，也顾不得这是众目所注的地方，竟当着全院观众的面——至少是当着将军的面，因为他正凑着望远镜向奥斯本这边的人瞪眼——跟她最亲密的朋友搂抱起来。对于乔斯，克劳莱太太也拿出和气不过的态度来招呼了一声。她又夸赞奥多太太的烟水晶大别针和美丽的爱尔兰金刚钻首饰，说什么也不肯相信这些金刚钻不是从高尔孔达买来的。

（6）She bustled, she chattered, she turned and twisted, and smiled upon one, and smirked on another, all in full view of the jealous opera-glass opposite. And when the time for the ballet came (in which there was no dancer that went through her grimaces or performed her comedy of action better), she skipped back to her own box, leaning on Captain Dobbin's arm this time. No, she

她一刻不得安定，转过来，扭过去，唧唧呱呱的说话，对这个人说话，对那个人抿嘴。对面包厢里，酸溜溜的将军拿着望远镜对这边张望，她便对着望远镜做作，直到芭蕾舞开始的时候，才蹦蹦跳跳地回到自己位子上去。说到挤眉弄眼的张致，轻浮佻达的身段，戏里的舞

would not have George's: he must stay and talk to his dearest, best, little Amelia.

女没一个赶得上她。这一次是都宾上尉扶她回来的。她说她不要乔治送回去，逼他留下来陪着最好的、最亲爱的小爱米丽亚说话。

"What a humbug that woman is!" honest old Dobbin mumbled to George, when he came back from Rebecca's box, whither he had conducted her in perfect silence, and with a countenance as glum as an undertaker's. "She writhes and twists about like a snake. All the time she was here, didn't you see, George, how she was acting at the General over the way?"

老实的都宾像办丧事的人一般，嗒丧着脸儿，一声不响地陪她回去。回来时，他对乔治咕哝道："那女人真会装腔，扭来扭去，活像一条蛇。乔治，你瞧见没有，她在这儿的时候，一直在向对面的将军做戏。"

"Humbug-acting! Hang it, she's the nicest little woman in England," George replied, showing his white teeth, and giving his ambrosial whiskers a twirl. "You ain't a man of the world, Dobbin. Dammy, look at her now, she's talked over Tufto in no time. Look how he's laughing! Gad, what a shoulder she has! Emmy, why didn't you have a bouquet? Everybody has a bouquet."

"装腔——做戏！什么呀，她是全英国最了不起的女人呢！"乔治一面回答，一面拉着喷香的胡子，露出雪白的牙齿，"都宾，你是个不通世故的人。喝，瞧她！要不了一会儿的工夫，已经把德夫托哄得回心转意。瞧他笑得多起劲。天哪，她的肩膀多好看！爱米，人人都拿着花球，你怎么不拿？"

"Faith, then, why didn't you BOY one?" Mrs. O'Dowd said; and both Amelia and William Dobbin thanked her for this

"唷，那么你干吗不给她买一个？"奥多太太说这话的合适，爱米丽亚和都宾

timely observation. But beyond this neither of the ladies rallied. Amelia was overpowered by the flash and the dazzle and the fashionable talk of her worldly rival. Even the O'Dowd was silent and subdued after Becky's brilliant apparition, and scarcely said a word more about Glenmalony all the evening.

都很感激她。这句话说过之后，两位太太再没有鼓起兴致来说什么别的。爱米丽亚的对头是在世路上混熟了的，她打扮的十分张扬，张嘴便是时髦话儿，把爱米丽亚一比就比下去了。就连奥多婆子，看见这么光芒四射的人儿，也自觉矮了一截，说不出话来，整个晚上没有再提葛兰曼洛内。

"When do you intend to give up play, George, as you have promised me, any time these hundred years?" Dobbin said to his friend a few days after the night at the Opera. "When do you intend to give up sermonising?" was the other's reply. "What the deuce, man, are you alarmed about? We play low; I won last night. You don't suppose Crawley cheats? With fair play it comes to pretty much the same thing at the year's end."

看过戏以后几天，都宾对他的朋友说道："乔治，你早就答应我不再赌钱，这话说来说去，总说过一百年了吧。你到底什么时候罢手不赌？"那一个答道："你到底什么时候罢手不训话？你怕什么？我们盘子又不大，昨晚我还赢了钱呢。难道你认为克劳莱会作弊吗？只要赌得公道，一年结下账来，不会有多少出入的。"

"But I don't think he could pay if he lost," Dobbin said; and his advice met with the success which advice usually commands. Osborne and Crawley were repeatedly together now. General Tufto dined abroad almost

都宾道："不过照我看来，他赌输了未必拿得出钱来。"劝人改过的话向来不大有用，都宾这一回也是白费唇舌。奥斯本和克劳莱老在一块儿。德夫托将军差不

constantly. George was always welcome in the apartments (very close indeed to those of the General) which the aide-de-camp and his wife occupied in the hotel.

Amelia's manners were such when she and George visited Crawley and his wife at these quarters, that they had very nearly come to their first quarrel; that is, George scolded his wife violently for her evident unwillingness to go, and the high and mighty manner in which she comported herself towards Mrs. Crawley, her old friend; and Amelia did not say one single word in reply; but with her husband's eye upon her, and Rebecca scanning her as she felt, was, if possible, more bashful and awkward on the second visit which she paid to Mrs. Rawdon, than on her first call.

Rebecca was doubly affectionate, of course, and would not take notice, in the least, of her friend's coolness. "I think Emmy has become prouder since her father's name was in the-since Mr. Sedley's MISFORTUNES," Rebecca said, softening the phrase charitably for George's ear.

"Upon my word, I thought

多常常在外面吃饭，副官夫妇总欢迎乔治到他们旅馆里去——他们的房间离开将军的没有几步路。

有一回乔治带着妻子去拜访克劳莱夫妇，爱米丽亚的态度不好，弄得夫妻俩几乎拌嘴——婚后第一回拌嘴。所谓拌嘴，就是乔治恶狠狠地责骂老婆，而爱米丽亚一声不言语。乔治怪她动身的时候不该那么勉强，而且对于她的老朋友克劳莱太太不客气。她第二次去拜访的时候，觉得利蓓加细细的看着她，自己丈夫的眼睛也紧紧盯着她，又窘又尴尬，竟比第一次做客更加为难了。

利蓓加当然加倍的温存，朋友对她冷淡，她当做不知道。她说："我觉得自从她爸爸的名字在——呃，自从赛特笠先生家里坏了事，爱米反倒骄傲起来了。"利蓓加说到赛特笠的时候，特别的把语气缓和了一下，免得乔治听着刺耳。

罗登太太又说："真的，

when we were at Brighton she was doing me the honour to be jealous of me; and now I suppose she is scandalised because Rawdon, and I, and the General live together. Why, my dear creature, how could we, with our means, live at all, but for a friend to share expenses? And do you suppose that Rawdon is not big enough to take care of my honour? But I'm very much obliged to Emmy, very," Mrs. Rawdon said.

在布拉依顿的时候，承她看得起我，好像对我很有些醋劲儿。现在呢，大概她看见罗登和我跟将军住得那么近，觉得不成体统。唉，亲爱的，我们的钱怎么够开销呢？总得和别人同住，一块儿分担费用才行。有罗登这样的大个儿在旁边，难道还不能保我身名清白不成？可是爱米那么关心我，我真是非常感激。"

"Pooh, jealousy!" answered George, "all women are jealous."

"And all men too. Weren't you jealous of General Tufto, and the General of you, on the night of the Opera? Why, he was ready to eat me for going with you to visit that foolish little wife of yours; as if I care a pin for either of you," Crawley's wife said, with a pert toss of her head. "Will you dine here? The dragon dines with the Commander-in-Chief. Great news is stirring. They say the French have crossed the frontier. We shall have a quiet dinner."

乔治道："得了，都是吃醋。所有的女人全爱吃醋。"

"男人也是一样。看戏的那天晚上，你跟德夫托将军不是彼此吃醋吗？后来我跟着你去瞧你那糊涂太太，他恨不得一口把我吃下去。其实我心上根本没有你们这两个人。"克劳莱的太太说到这里，把脸儿一扬。"在这儿吃饭吧？那厉害的老头出去跟总指挥一块儿吃。消息紧得很，听说法国军队已经过了边境了。咱们可以安安静静地吃一顿饭。"

George accepted the invitation, although his wife was a little

乔治的妻子虽然身体不好，病在家里，他却答应留

ailing. They were now not quite six weeks married. (7) Another woman was laughing or sneering at her expense, and he not angry. He was not even angry with himself, this good-natured fellow. It is a shame, he owned to himself; but hang it, if a pretty woman WILL throw herself in your way, why, what can a fellow do, you know? I AM rather free about women, he had often said, smiling and nodding knowingly to Stubble and Spooney, and other comrades of the mess-table; and they rather respected him than otherwise for this prowess. Next to conquering in war, conquering in love has been a source of pride, time out of mind, amongst men in Vanity Fair, or how should schoolboys brag of their amours, or Don Juan be popular?

So Mr. Osborne, having a firm conviction in his own mind that he was a woman-killer and destined to conquer, did not run counter to his fate, but yielded himself up to it quite complacently. And as Emmy did not say much or plague him with her jealousy, but merely became unhappy and pined over it miserably

下来吃饭。他们结婚还不满一个半月，就听着另外一个女人嘲笑奚落自己的妻子，心里也没觉得生气。他这人脾气好，他心里承认这件事有些岂有此理，可是漂亮女人要和你纠缠不清，叫你也没有办法呀！他常常说："我对于男女的事情相当随便。"一面说，一面笑嘻嘻地对同桌吃饭的斯德博尔，斯卜内，还有别的伙伴作出怪含蓄的样子点点头。他们对于他的本领只有佩服。除了战场上的胜利以外，要算情场上的胜利最光彩了。名利场上的男人向来有这种成见。要不然的话，为什么连没出校门的孩子都喜欢当众卖弄自己的风流韵事？为什么唐璜会得人心？

奥斯本先生自信是风月场上的能手，注定是太太小姐的心上人，因此不愿意跟命运闹别扭，洋洋自得的顺着定数做人。爱米不爱多说话，也不用心里的妒忌去麻烦他，只不过私底下自卑自叹的伤心罢了。虽然他的朋

in secret, he chose to fancy that she was not suspicious of what all his acquaintance were perfectly aware,namely, that he was carrying on a desperate flirtation with Mrs. Crawley.

友都知道他和克劳莱太太眉来眼去，不断的勾搭，他自己总以为爱米丽亚是不知就里的。

He rode with her whenever she was free. He pretended regimental business to Amelia (by which falsehood she was not in the least deceived), and consigning his wife to solitude or her brother's society, passed his evenings in the Crawleys' company; losing money to the husband and flattering himself that the wife was dying of love for him. It is very likely that this worthy couple never absolutely conspired and agreed together in so many words: the one to cajole the young gentleman, whilst the other won his money at cards: but they understood each other perfectly well, and Rawdon let Osborne come and go with entire good humour.

利蓓加一有空闲，他就骑着马陪她出去兜风。对爱米丽亚，他只说联队里有事，爱米丽亚也明明知道他在撒谎。他把妻子仍在一边，有时让她独自一个人，有时把她交给她哥哥，自己却一整天的跟克劳莱夫妇俩混在一起。他把钱输给丈夫，还自以为那妻子在为他销魂。看来这对好夫妻并没有同谋协议，明白规定由女的哄着小伙子，再由男的跟他斗牌赢他的钱。反正他们俩心里有数，罗登听凭奥斯本出出进进，一点也不生气。

George was so occupied with his new acquaintances that he and William Dobbin were by no means so much together as formerly. George avoided him in public and in the regiment, and, as we see, did not like those sermons which his senior was dis-

乔治老是和新朋友混在一起，跟威廉都宾比以前疏远了好些。不论在联队里或是在公共场所，乔治总躲着他。做老大哥的时常教训他，乔治却不爱听。都宾上

posed to inflict upon him. If some parts of his conduct made Captain Dobbin exceedingly grave and cool; of what use was it to tell George that, though his whiskers were large, and his own opinion of his knowingness great, he was as green as a schoolboy that Rawdon was making a victim of him as he had done of many before, and as soon as he had used him would fling him off with scorn? He would not listen: and so, as Dobbin, upon those days when he visited the Osborne house, seldom had the advantage of meeting his old friend, much painful and unavailing talk between them was spared. Our friend George was in the full career of the pleasures of Vanity Fair.

尉看见他行为荒唐，不由得上了心事，对他不似往常亲热。乔治白白的留着一把大胡子，自以为一身好本事，其实却像未出校门的孩子一般容易上当，可是如果你对他这么说，他肯信吗？如果你告诉他罗登哄骗过不知多少人，眼前正在算计他，等到用不着他的时候，就会把他当不值钱的东西那么一脚踢开——这些话他一定听都不愿意听。这些日子，都宾到奥斯本家里拜访的时候难得有机会碰见老朋友，因此倒省了许多难看而无谓的口舌。我们的朋友正在全力追求名利场上的快乐呢。

There never was, since the days of Darius, such a brilliant train of camp-followers as hung round the Duke of Wellington's army in the Low Countries, in 1815; and led it dancing and feasting, as it were, up to the very brink of battle. A certain ball which a noble Duchess gave at Brussels on the 15th of June in the above-named year is historical. All Brussels had been in a state of excitement about it, and I

一八一五年，威灵顿公爵的军队驻扎在荷兰比利时一带，随着军队去了一大批漂亮时髦的人物，这是从大流士大帝以来所没有的。这些人带着军人们跳舞欢乐，一直玩到战争前夕。同年六月十五日，一位高贵的公爵夫人在布鲁塞尔开了一个有历史性的的舞会。整个布鲁塞尔为它疯魔。我曾经听见

have heard from ladies who were in that town at the period, that the talk and interest of persons of their own sex regarding the ball was much greater even than in respect of the enemy in their front. The struggles, intrigues, and prayers to get tickets were such as only English ladies will employ, in order to gain admission to the society of the great of their own nation.

Jos and Mrs. O'Dowd, who were panting to be asked, strove in vain to procure tickets; but others of our friends were more lucky. For instance, through the interest of my Lord Bareacres, and as a set-off for the dinner at the restaurateur's, George got a card for Captain and Mrs. Osborne; which circumstance greatly elated him. Dobbin, who was a friend of the General commanding the division in which their regiment was, came laughing one day to Mrs. Osborne, and displayed a similar invitation, which made Jos envious, and George wonder how the deuce he should be getting into society. Mr. and Mrs. Rawdon, finally, were of course invited; as became the friends of a General commanding a cavalry brigade.

On the appointed night,

当年在场的太太们谈过，据说女人们对于舞会比对前线的敌人还关切，所有的兴趣和谈话都集中在舞会上。大家用手段，走门路，求情，争夺，无非为几张入场券。为了要登本国贵人的门不惜花掉这许多精力，倒是英国女人的特色。

乔斯和奥多太太急迫的想去，可是费了一大把劲也得不到门票，我们其余的朋友运气比较好。譬如说，靠着贝亚爱格思勋爵的面子，乔治得到一张邀请奥斯本上尉夫妇的帖子，得意的不得了，勋爵也就把吃饭欠下的人情还掉了。他们的联队所属的一师的师长恰巧是都宾的朋友，因此有一天都宾去看奥斯本太太，笑着拿出一张同样的帖子。乔斯眼红得很，乔治也觉得诧异，心想：“他算什么，居然也能到上流社会里去了。”罗登夫妇因为是统领骑兵的旅长的朋友，最后当然也得到了请帖。

乔治给太太买了各色的

George, having commanded new dresses and ornaments of all sorts for Amelia, drove to the famous ball, where his wife did not know a single soul. After looking about for Lady Bareacres, who cut him, thinking the card was quite enough-and after placing Amelia on a bench, he left her to her own cogitations there, thinking, on his own part, that he had behaved very handsomely in getting her new clothes, and bringing her to the ball, where she was free to amuse herself as she liked. Her thoughts were not of the pleasantest, and nobody except honest Dobbin came to disturb them.

新衣服新首饰。到请客的一夜，他们坐了马车去赴宴会，那儿的主人客人爱米丽亚一个也不认得。乔治先去找贝亚爱格思夫人，可是她认为给他请帖已经赏足了面子，没有睬他。他叫爱米丽亚在一张椅子上坐下来，自己走开了，让她一个人在那里想心思。他觉得自己真大方，又给她买新衣服，又带她上跳舞会，至于在跳舞会上她爱怎么消遣，只好 随她的便。她的心里可并不怎么愉快，除了老实的都宾之外，也没人来招呼她。

Whilst her appearance was an utter failure (as her husband felt with a sort of rage), Mrs. Rawdon Crawley's debut was, on the contrary, very brilliant. She arrived very late. Her face was radiant; her dress perfection. In the midst of the great persons assembled, and the eye-glasses directed to her, Rebecca seemed to be as cool and collected as when she used to marshal Miss Pinkerton's little girls to church. Numbers of the men she knew already, and the dandies thronged round her. As for the ladies, it was whispered

她进场的时候几乎没人理会，她丈夫因此不大惬意。罗登太太就不是这样，一露面就与众不同。她到得很晚，脸上光艳照人，衣服穿得很得体。四面全是大人物，好些人举着眼镜对着她看，可是她不慌不忙，就好像她从前在平克顿女学校带着小学生上课的时候那么镇定。许多原来认识她的人，还有好些花花公子，都上来围着她。太太小姐们窃

among them that Rawdon had run away with her from out of a convent, and that she was a relation of the Montmorency family. She spoke French so perfectly that there might be some truth in this report, and it was agreed that her manners were fine, and her air distingue. Fifty would-be partners thronged round her at once, and pressed to have the honour to dance with her. But she said she was engaged, and only going to dance very little; and made her way at once to the place where Emmy sate quite unnoticed, and dismally unhappy. And so, to finish the poor child at once, Mrs. Rawdon ran and greeted affectionately her dearest Amelia, and began forthwith to patronise her. She found fault with her friend's dress, and her hairdresser, and wondered how she could be so chaussee, and vowed that she must send her corsetiere the next morning. She vowed that it was a delightful ball; that there was everybody that every one knew, and only a VERY few nobodies in the whole room. It is a fact, that in a fortnight, and after three dinners in general society, this young woman had got up the genteel jargon so well, that a native could not speak it better; and

窃私语，说她是给罗登从修道院办的学校里和人私奔结婚的，又说她和蒙脱莫伦茜一家是亲戚关系。她的法文说的那么好，想来这话有根据。大家认为她举止不凡，仪容也不俗。五十来个男人一起簇拥着她，希望她赏脸，肯和他们跳舞。

可是她说已经有了舞伴，而且不准备多跳，一直走过来找爱米。爱米闷闷不乐地坐在那里，也没人睬她。罗登太太飞跑过来跟她最亲爱的爱米丽亚见面，摆出一副倚老卖老的样子和她说话，弄得这可怜的孩子更加无地自容。她批评朋友的衣服头发，埋怨她的鞋子不像样，说第二天早晨一定要叫她自己的内衣裁缝给爱米做衣服。她说跳舞会真是有趣，到会的全是有名的人物，难得看见几个无名小卒。这年轻女人在上流社会应酬了两个星期，参加过三次宴会，就把时髦人的一套话儿一股脑儿学来了，连这里头根生土长的人也比不过

it was only from her French being so good, that you could know she was not a born woman of fashion.

George, who had left Emmy on her bench on entering the ball-room, very soon found his way back when Rebecca was by her dear friend's side. Becky was just lecturing Mrs. Osborne upon the follies which her husband was committing. "For God's sake, stop him from gambling, my dear," she said, "or he will ruin himself. He and Rawdon are playing at cards every night, and you know he is very poor, and Rawdon will win every shilling from him if he does not take care. Why don't you prevent him, you little careless creature? Why don't you come to us of an evening, instead of moping at home with that Captain Dobbin? I dare say he is tres aimable; but how could one love a man with feet of such size? Your husband's feet are darlings—Here he comes. Where have you been, wretch? Here is Emmy crying her eyes out for you. Are you coming to fetch me for the quadrille?" And she left her bouquet and shawl by Amelia's side, and tripped off with George to dance.

Women only know how to

她。若不是她法文说得那么好，你准会以为她是有身份人家的小姐。

乔治进了跳舞场，把爱米撇在长椅子上转身就走，这时看见利蓓加坐在她好朋友旁边，便又回来了。蓓基正在对奥斯本太太说话，说她丈夫尽做糊涂事。她说："亲爱的，看老天的面子，赶快叫他别再赌钱了。要不然他就完了。他跟罗登天天晚上斗牌，你知道他并不是很有钱，倘若他不小心的话，所有的钱全要输给罗登了。你这小东西，那么不小心，干吗不阻止他呢？你晚上何不到我们那儿去玩？何必跟那都宾上尉闷在家里？当然啰，他这人和蔼可亲，可是他的脚那么大，叫人怎么喜欢他？你丈夫的脚才好看呢。哦，他来了。坏东西，你上哪儿去了？爱米为你把眼泪都哭干了。你来带我去跳八人舞吗？"她把披肩和花球搁在爱米丽亚旁边，轻轻巧巧地跟着乔治去跳舞了。

wound so. There is a poison on the tips of their little shafts, which stings a thousand times more than a man's blunter weapon.（8）Our poor Emmy, who had never hated, never sneered all her life, was powerless in the hands of her remorseless little enemy.

只有女人才会这样伤人家的心。她们放出来的箭头上有毒药，比男人用的钝头兵器厉害一千倍。我们可怜的爱米一辈子不记恨，不会说带刺的话，碰见了这么毒辣的冤家一点办法都没有。

George danced with Rebecca twice or thrice—how many times Amelia scarcely knew. She sat quite unnoticed in her corner, except when Rawdon came up with some words of clumsy conversation: and later in the evening, when Captain Dobbin made so bold as to bring her refreshments and sit beside her. He did not like to ask her why she was so sad; but as a pretext for the tears which were filling in her eyes, she told him that Mrs. Crawley had alarmed her by telling her that George would go on playing.

"It is curious, when a man is bent upon play, by what clumsy rogues he will allow himself to be cheated," Dobbin said; and Emmy said, "Indeed." She was thinking of something else. It was not the loss of the money that grieved her.

乔治和利蓓加跳了两三回舞，反正爱米丽亚也不知道他们跳了几回。她坐在犄角上没人注意。罗登走过来拙口笨腮的和她应酬了几句；后来都宾上尉居然不顾冒昧，不但给她送茶点来，并且坐在她旁边。他没有过问她为什么事不痛快，倒是她要为自己的眼泪找个推脱，搭讪着说克劳莱太太提起乔治仍旧不断的赌钱，所以她心里着急。

都宾说道："真奇怪，赌钱上瘾的人真容易上当，连最笨的流氓也骗得着他的钱。"爱米答道："可不是！"但心里，她另有隐衷，并不是因为银钱亏空而着急。

后来乔治过来拿利蓓加的披肩和花球。原来她要回

At last George came back for Rebecca's shawl and flowers. She was going away. She did not even condescend to come back and say good-bye to Amelia. The poor girl let her husband come and go without saying a word, and her head fell on her breast. Dobbin had been called away, and was whispering deep in conversation with the General of the division, his friend, and had not seen this last parting. George went away then with the bouquet; but when he gave it to the owner, there lay a note, coiled like a snake among the flowers. Rebecca's eye caught it at once. She had been used to deal with notes in early life. She put out her hand and took the nosegay.

家了，竟不肯亲自过来跟爱米丽亚告别。可怜的孩子看着丈夫来了又去，低下头没说一句话。都宾给别人找了去，正在跟他那当师长的朋友密谈，没看见乔治和他太太分手的情形。乔治拿着花球走过去，当他把它交还她的时候，里面却夹了张纸条子，好像一条蛇蜷着身子藏在花朵里面。利蓓加立刻看见了。她知道怎么处置纸条儿，只伸出手来接了花球。

He saw by her eyes as they met, that she was aware what she should find there. Her husband hurried her away, still too intent upon his own thoughts, seemingly, to take note of any marks of recognition which might pass between his friend and his wife. These were, however, but trifling. Rebecca gave George her hand with one of her usual quick knowing glances, and made a curtsey and walked away. George bowed over the hand, said nothing in

他们两个四目相对的当儿，乔治知道她已经看见了花底下的秘密。她丈夫似乎一心想着自己的心事，没工夫理会他妻子和朋友在递眼色，只顾催她快走。他们两个传递的暗号本来不太刺眼，利蓓加伸出手来，像平常一样很含蓄地溜了他一眼，微微的一屈膝，便转身走了。乔治躬着身子拉住她的手，克劳莱对他说话他也

reply to a remark of Crawley's, did not hear it even, his brain was so throbbing with triumph and excitement, and allowed them to go away without a word.

His wife saw the one part at least of the bouquet-scene. It was quite natural that George should come at Rebecca's request to get her her scarf and flowers: it was no more than he had done twenty times before in the course of the last few days; but now it was too much for her. "William," she said, suddenly clinging to Dobbin, who was near her, "you've always been very kind to me-I'm-I'm not well. Take me home." She did not know she called him by his Christian name, as George was accustomed to do. He went away with her quickly. Her lodgings were hard by; and they threaded through the crowd without, where everything seemed to be more astir than even in the ball-room within.

George had been angry twice or thrice at finding his wife up on his return from the parties which he frequented: so she went straight to bed now; but although she did not sleep, and although the din and clatter, and the galloping of horsemen were incessant, she never heard any of these

不回答，竟可说连听都没听见。他兴奋得意的头都昏了，看着他们回家，一句话也不说。

传递花球的一幕戏，他的妻子也看见一部分。乔治给利蓓加拿花球和披肩，原是很平常的事，几天来他当这差使已经不下二十来次，可是那时候爱米丽亚忽然觉得受不住。都宾恰巧在她旁边，她拉着他说道："威廉，你一向待我很好，我——我不大舒服，送我回家吧。"她不知不觉的学着乔治直呼他的名字。他连忙陪她出去。她的家离儿那很近，他们走到街上，看见外面似乎比舞场里还热闹，只好从人堆里穿出去。

这以前，乔治常常出去做客，晚上回家倘若看见妻子还没有睡觉，就要生气，已经发过两三回脾气了。所以她回家以后立刻上床。外面闹哄哄的，马蹄声络绎不绝。她虽然醒着，却不留心

noises, having quite other disturbances to keep her awake.

Osborne meanwhile, wild with elation, went off to a play-table, and began to bet frantically. He won repeatedly. "Everything succeeds with me to-night," he said. But his luck at play even did not cure him of his restlessness, and he started up after awhile, pocketing his winnings, and went to a buffet, where he drank off many bumpers of wine.

Here, as he was rattling away to the people around, laughing loudly and wild with spirits, Dobbin found him. He had been to the card-tables to look there for his friend. Dobbin looked as pale and grave as his comrade was flushed and jovial.

"Hullo, Dob! Come and drink, old Dob! The Duke' s wine is famous. Give me some more, you sir"; and he held out a trembling glass for the liquor." Come out, George," said Dobbin, still gravely; "don' t drink."" Drink! there' s nothing like it. Drink yourself, and light up your lantern jaws, old boy. Here' s to you."

这些声音，因为心里还有许多别的烦恼让她睡不着。

奥斯本得意得发狂，又走到赌台旁边去赌钱，下的赌注大得吓人。他赢了好几次，想道："今晚可说是没一样不顺手的。"他的赌运虽然好，他仍旧坐立不安，不多时又站起来，拿起赌赢的钱，走到茶食柜子旁一连喝了几大杯酒。

都宾走来找他的时候，他正在和柜台旁边的人兴高采烈的大说大笑。都宾刚到赌台那儿去找过乔治；他颜色青白，一脸的心事，跟他那红光满面兴致勃发的朋友刚刚相反。

乔治手抖抖的伸出杯子要酒，一面说："喂，都宾！来喝酒呀，都宾！公爵的酒是有名的。请再给我一点儿。"都宾仍旧心事重重的样子，说道："来吧，乔治，别喝了。""喝吧，喝酒比什么都痛苦。你自己也来一点儿。好小子，别把你那瘦长脸儿绷那么紧呀！我喝一杯祝你健康！"

Dobbin went up and whispered something to him, at which George, giving a start and a wild hurray, tossed off his glass, clapped it on the table, and walked away speedily on his friend' s arm. "The enemy has passed the Sambre," William said, "and our left is already engaged. Come away. We are to march in three hours."

都宾过来凑着他的耳朵说了几句话，乔治一听，霍地跳起来欢呼一声，一口气喝干了酒，把酒杯用力往桌子上一摔，勾着朋友的胳膊就走。威廉说的是："敌人已经过了桑勃，咱们左边一支军队已经在开火了。快回去吧，三点钟以内就得开拔了。"

Away went George, his nerves quivering with excitement at the news so long looked for, so sudden when it came. What were love and intrigue now? He thought about a thousand things but these in his rapid walk to his quarters—his past life and future chances—the fate which might be before him—the wife, the child perhaps, from whom unseen he might be about to part. Oh, how he wished that night' s work undone! and that with a clear conscience at least he might say farewell to the tender and guileless being by whose love he had set such little store!

久已盼望的消息来的真突兀。乔治一面走，一面兴奋得浑身打战。恋爱，调情，在这当儿可算什么呢？他急急回家，一路想着千百件事情——全是和谈情说爱无关的事情。他想到过去的半辈子，未来的机会，可能遭到的危险，行将分别的妻子，可能还没有出世的孩子，来不及见面就要分手了。唉，他真懊悔当天晚上干了那么一件事！不然的话他和妻子告别时还可以问心无愧。他把那温柔天真的人儿给他的爱情看得太不值钱了。

He thought over his brief married life. In those few weeks he had frightfully dissipated his little capital. How wild and reckless he had been! Should any mischance

他回顾结婚以后那几天的日子，觉得自己太荒唐。他名下的财产已经给他花得所剩无几。倘若自己有个闪

befall him: what was then left for her? How unworthy he was of her. Why had he married her? He was not fit for marriage. Why had he disobeyed his father, who had been always so generous to him? Hope, remorse, ambition, tenderness, and selfish regret filled his heart. He sate down and wrote to his father, remembering what he had said once before, when he was engaged to fight a duel. Dawn faintly streaked the sky as he closed this farewell letter. He sealed it, and kissed the superscription. He thought how he had deserted that generous father, and of the thousand kindnesses which the stern old man had done him.

He had looked into Amelia' s bedroom when he entered; she lay quiet, and her eyes seemed closed, and he was glad that she was asleep. On arriving at his quarters from the ball, he had found his regimental servant already making preparations for his departure: the man had understood his signal to be still, and these arrangements were very quickly and silently made. Should he go in and wake Amelia, he thought, or leave a note for her brother to break the news of departure to her? He went in to look

失，叫他的太太怎么过日子？想想自己真配不上她。当初何必娶她呢？像他这样的人。根本不配娶亲。父亲对他那么千依百顺，为什么不听父亲的话呢？他心里充满了悔恨、希望、野心、柔情和自私的惆怅。他记得从前和人决斗的时候说的话，坐下来写了一封信给父亲。等到告别信写完，天已经亮了。他封了信，在父亲的名字上吻了一下。他回忆到严厉的老头儿对他种种行事多么慷慨体贴，懊悔自己丢下他不顾。

他进门的时候先探头进去对爱米丽亚的卧房里瞧了一眼，见她合上眼睛静静的躺着，以为她睡着了，心里很安慰。他从跳舞会回到家里，就见联队里伺候他的佣人在拾掇他的行装。那听差懂得他的手势是不许惊吵别人的意思，轻手轻脚很快地把一切都准备就绪。他想，是把爱米丽亚叫醒了和她告别呢，还是留个条子给她哥哥让他告诉她？想着，又走

at her once again.

She had been awake when he first entered her room, but had kept her eyes closed, so that even her wakefulness should not seem to reproach him. But when he had returned, so soon after herself, too, this timid little heart had felt more at ease, and turning towards him as he stept softly out of the room, she had fallen into a light sleep. George came in and looked at her again, entering still more softly.

By the pale night-lamp he could see her sweet, pale face-the purple eyelids were fringed and closed, and one round arm, smooth and white, lay outside of the coverlet. Good God! how pure she was; how gentle, how tender, and how friendless! and he, how selfish, brutal, and black with crime! Heart-stained, and shame-stricken, he stood at the bed' s foot, and looked at the sleeping girl. How dared he—who was he, to pray for one so spotless! God bless her! God bless her! He came to the bedside, and looked at the hand, the little soft hand, lying asleep; and he bent over the pillow noiselessly towards the gentle pale face.

进去看着她。

他第一次进房的时候，爱米还醒着，可是她紧紧的闭上眼睛，因为如果她不睡，就好像含有责备他的意思了。胆小的小姑娘因为他肯紧跟着自己回家，心上舒服了好些，等他放轻了脚步走出去的时候，就侧过身子朝着了朦朦胧胧的睡着了。乔治第二次进去看她的时候脚步更轻。

在淡淡的灯光底下，他看见她苍白美丽的脸庞儿，眼睛闭着，底下是浓浓的睫毛，眼圈儿有些发黑，一只圆润白皙的手膀子搁在被面上。老天爷！她真是洁白无瑕。她是多么的温柔、脆弱，多么的孤苦伶仃，而自己自私自利，性情又暴戾，简直是浑身污点。他怎么配给这样洁白无瑕的人祷告？求天保佑她！求天保佑她！他走到床旁边，对平放着的小手看着——多软的小手！他轻轻的弯下身子望着她苍白温柔的脸儿。

Two fair arms closed tenderly round his neck as he stooped down. (9) "I am awake, George," the poor child said, with a sob fit to break the little heart that nestled so closely by his own. She was awake, poor soul, and to what? At that moment a bugle from the Place of Arms began sounding clearly, and was taken up through the town; and amidst the drums of the infantry, and the shrill pipes of the Scotch, the whole city awoke.

当他弯下身子来的当儿，两只美丽的膀子软软地勾住了他的脖子。可怜的小姑娘说道："我醒着呢，乔治。"她紧紧贴在乔治胸口，哭得好像她的心快要碎了。可怜的小东西还醒着，醒着又怎么样呢？正在那时，军营里的号角响起来了，声音十分清晰，其余的号角立刻接应，一霎时响遍全城。在步兵营的战鼓声和苏格兰军营的尖锐的风笛声中，所有的居民都醒了。

# 第六章

# *David Copperfield*

# 大卫·科波菲尔

*'Janet! Donkeys!'*

## 背景介绍

狄更斯 (1812 ——1870 年 ) 是维多利亚时期最伟大的小说家。他的伟大不仅在于其产出多，产量高，还在于他对于一个特殊群体的令人无法忘怀的深情描述。对儿童生活的关注贯穿于他的整个写作生涯，他对于孩子的同情不仅仅是对自己悲苦的童年经历无法释怀，更是对弱势群体的一种悲天悯人的深沉情怀。

我们单说他“最宠爱的孩子”——*David Copperfield*，这部篇长 64 章，厚度堪比长城上的砖块的巨著，讲述了一个英国孩子从还没有出生到成家立业的整个过程。这个过程，就像我们的人生一样，不是单线的，而是和别人的人生纵横交织在一起。同时，对狄更斯的风格略有所知的读者一定会嗅到背叛、阴谋的气息，也一定会做好捧腹大笑的准备。戏剧化的表现手法与其说是为了制造悬念，推动故事前进，还不如说是孩子般故弄玄虚的伎俩，我们瞪大眼睛，欣赏他的热忱和勇气。

北京大学教授张谷若 (1903——1994 年 ) 翻译的《大卫·科波菲尔》是一部带有注释的译本，张先生不仅要让读者看懂故事，还要借助注释，了解书中涉及的西方文化，从而加深对原文的理解。

## 细读节选

狄更斯的一大手笔就是对儿童所遭受的艰辛的描写，可能他自己的童年记忆愈久弥新，因此能够把青少年的语言、行为和心理拿捏得非常到位，在成长类小说中，没有人比他更能体会和同情小青年了，这种细致入微的刻画，有时候让人分辨不出作者和他创作出来的人物的界限。《大卫·科波菲尔》是一部长篇成长类小说，大卫的童年只占很小的一部分，但是却是狄更斯最用功最出彩的部分。节选的这一章是整个故事的转折点，大卫在沦为孤儿之后，历尽千辛万苦，终于找到了这世上的唯一的亲人，之后，他终于逃离了继父的魔掌，开始过上正常生活。一个不到15岁的小男孩在逃离途中，怎么地被欺骗、被侮辱、被恐吓，但却像一个小绅士一样地坚忍不拔，终于找到改变自己命运的姨婆，这就是第十三章的大意。让我们怀揣仁爱之心，跟大卫一起踏上童年的孤寂旅程吧。

## 拓展思考

1. 凭借记忆，写出3句划线的原文与译文。

| 原文 | 译文 |
|---|---|
| | |
| | |
| | |

2. 大卫的言行和他的年龄相符吗？

3. 姨婆是个什么样的角色？

4. 译者的方言特征会不会对翻译产生负影响？

# Chapter 13

## *THE SEQUEL OF MY RESOLUTION*

For anything I know, I may have had some wild idea of running all the way to Dover, when I gave up the pursuit of the young man with the donkey-cart, and started for Greenwich. My scattered senses were soon collected as to that point, if I had; for I came to a stop in the Kent Road, at a terrace with a piece of water before it, and a great foolish image in the middle, blowing a dry shell.

Here I sat down on a doorstep, quite spent and exhausted with the efforts I had already made, and with hardly breath enough to cry for the loss of my box and half-guinea.

# 第十三章

## 决心之后

我终于不再追那个赶驴车的青年，而取道往格林威治走去；那时候（我现在想来），我说不定曾有一种荒唐的想法，要一路跑到多佛。不过关于这一点，我那种凌乱散漫、茫无头绪的思路，却不久就有了头绪了（这是说，如果我当真那么想过的话），因为我在肯特路上停下来了，站在一排高台房子面前，那儿有一湾水，水湾中央有一个拙笨可笑的塑像，用嘴吹着一个干涸无水的法螺[1]。

我在那儿一家门前的台

[1] 指希腊神话中海神之子特莱屯（Triton）而言，他通常吹一法螺，犹如号角。所谓"一湾水"，原指那儿有一个喷水池，由法螺嘴儿喷水，现池废水涸，古云"干涸无水"。

阶上坐下，因为拼命地追赶那个青年，累得筋疲力尽，几乎连为我那丢了的箱子和半几尼而哭的劲儿都没有了。

It was by this time dark; I heard the clocks strike ten, as I sat resting. But it was a summer night, fortunately, and fine weather. (1) When I had recovered my breath, and had got rid of a stifling sensation in my throat, I rose up and went on. In the midst of my distress, I had no notion of going back. I doubt if I should have had any, though there had been a Swiss snow-drift in the Kent Road.

那时候天已经黑了，我坐在那儿休息的时候，听见钟正敲十下。不过总算侥幸，那时正是夏天，天气又好。我喘息已定，喉头那种堵得慌的感觉也消失了，我站起身来，往前走去。我那时虽然穷苦无助，却一点想要折回去的意思都没有。我直到现在还不敢说，如果当时我前面的肯特路上，有像瑞士那样的积雪挡住去路，我会不会想要折回去。

But my standing possessed of only three-halfpence in the world (and I am sure I wonder how they came to be left in my pocket on a Saturday night!) troubled me none the less because I went on. I began to picture to myself, as a scrap of newspaper intelligence, my being found dead in a day or two, under some hedge; and I trudged on miserably, though as fast as I could, until I happened to pass a little shop, where it was

我现在通统算起来只有三枚半便士（我现在很纳闷，不知道星期六晚上，我的口袋里，怎么还剩那么点钱！），我虽然直往前走，这种情况仍旧使我非常焦心。我开始想象，在一两天以内，我怎样在树篱下面被人发现，成了“倒卧”，当做一条新闻登在报上。这样一幅景象，虽然并没有使我放慢脚步，

written up that ladies' and gentlemen's wardrobes were bought, and that the best price was given for rags, bones, and kitchen-stuff.

我还是尽力往前快走，但是在我前奔的时候，却使我觉得十分苦恼。我就这样走去，一直到碰巧从一个小铺子旁边经过，只见那儿写着，收买男女旧衣，高价收买破布、骨头和厨房废物。

The master of this shop was sitting at the door in his shirt-sleeves, smoking; and as there were a great many coats and pairs of trousers dangling from the low ceiling, and only two feeble candles burning inside to show what they were, I fancied that he looked like a man of a revengeful disposition, who had hung all his enemies, and was enjoying himself.

铺子的老板只穿着背心和衬衫，坐在铺子的门口那儿抽烟。屋子里低矮的天花板下面，摇摆着许多褂子和裤子，屋里又只点着两只暗淡的蜡，影影绰绰地照在褂子和裤子上，因此我觉得，那个老板好像是一个专事报复的人，把他所有的仇人全吊了起来，因此怨气已消，踌躇满志。

My late experiences with Mr. and Mrs. Micawber suggested to me that here might be a means of keeping off the wolf for a little while. I went up the next by-street, took off my waistcoat, rolled it neatly under my arm, and came back to the shop door.'If you please, sir,' I said, 'I am to sell this for a fair price.'

我新近和米考伯夫妇住在一块儿的经验告诉我，这儿也许可以找到办法，使我暂时免于饥饿。我走到前面一条背静的街道，把背心脱了下来，把它服帖整齐地卷了起来，夹在胳膊底下，然后又回到了那个铺子的门前。"你要是给个公道价儿，掌柜的，"我说，"我就把这件背心卖给你。"

Mr. Dolloby—Dolloby was the name over the shop door, at least—took the waistcoat, stood his pipe on its head, against the door-post, went into the shop, followed by me, snuffed the two candles with his fingers, spread the waistcoat on the counter, and looked at it there, held it up against the light, and looked at it there, and ultimately said:

道勒毕先生——至少道勒毕是写在铺门上面的名字——接过那件背心，把他的烟袋锅儿朝下，倚在门框上，进了铺子里面（我跟在他后面），把那两只蜡用手指头打了打蜡花儿，把背心放在柜台上，在那儿看了一遍，又把背心提起来，迎着亮儿，又看了一遍，最后说：

'What do you call a price, now, for this here little weskit?'

"这个小小的坎肩儿，要卖多少钱？"

'Oh! you know best, sir,' I returned modestly.

"哦，你说多少就是多少好啦，掌柜的，"我谦虚地回答说。

'I can't be buyer and seller too,' said Mr. Dolloby. 'Put a price on this here little weskit.'

"我不能又去那个买的，又去那个卖的，"道勒毕先生说。"这样一件小小的坎肩儿！你说个价好啦。"

'Would eighteenpence be?'I hinted, after some hesitation.

"十八便士值不——？"我迟疑了一会儿试着说。

Mr. Dolloby rolled it up again, and gave it me back. 'I should rob my family,' he said, 'if I was to offer ninepence for it.'

道勒毕先生把背心又卷了起来，把它还给了我。"我要是给你九便士，"他说，"那就等于我打劫了我家里的人一样。"

This was a disagreeable way of putting the business; because it imposed upon me, a perfect

这样做交易，真叫人不愉快，因为强叫我一个和道勒毕先生素不相识的人，为了救

stranger, the unpleasantness of asking Mr. Dolloby to rob his family on my account.

自己的急，逼着他去打劫他家里的人，当然不是好事。

My circumstances being so very pressing, however, I said I would take ninepence for it, if he pleased. Mr. Dolloby, not without some grumbling, gave ninepence. I wished him good night, and walked out of the shop the richer by that sum, and the poorer by a waistcoat. But when I buttoned my jacket, that was not much.

但是我的处境却非常窘迫，所以我就说，你肯给九便士，我就卖。道勒毕先生很不乐意地嘴里咕噜着，给了我九便士。我对他说了一声夜安，走出了他的铺子，手里多了九便士，身上却少了一件背心，不过我把夹克的纽扣扣上了以后，少了什么也并不大显得出来。

Indeed, I foresaw pretty clearly that my jacket would go next, and that I should have to make the best of my way to Dover in a shirt and a pair of trousers, and might deem myself lucky if I got there even in that trim. But my mind did not run so much on this as might be supposed. Beyond a general impression of the distance before me, and of the young man with the donkey-cart having used me cruelly, I think I had no very urgent sense of my difficulties when I once again set off with my ninepence in my pocket.

实在说起来，我早就看得明明白白了，我的夹克也非跟着背心一道而去不可，我得只穿着一件衬衣和一条裤子，尽力地快快往多佛奔，并且如果能那样到得了多佛，还得算是非常侥幸呢。照例说，我对于这一点，也许会死乞白赖地琢磨，但是我却并没那样。我只知道，我前面有远路要走；我只知道，我觉得那个赶驴的青年对我太狠了。我现在想，除了这两点而外，我当时口袋里装着那九便士又上了路以后，并没怎么觉

A plan had occurred to me for passing the night, which I was going to carry into execution. This was, to lie behind the wall at the back of my old school, in a corner where there used to be a haystack. I imagined it would be a kind of company to have the boys, and the bedroom where I used to tell the stories, so near me: although the boys would know nothing of my being there, and the bedroom would yield me no shelter.

(2) I had had a hard day's work, and was pretty well jaded when I came climbing out, at last, upon the level of Blackheath. It cost me some trouble to find out Salem House; but I found it, and I found a haystack in the corner, and I lay down by it; having first walked round the wall, and looked up at the windows, and seen that all was dark and silent within. Never shall I forget the lonely sensation of first lying down, without a roof above my hcad!

Sleep came upon me as it came on many other outcasts,

着我的困难有多迫切。

我脑子里想到一个晚上过夜的办法，我就要按着这个想法实行。原来我母校后身儿的一堵墙后面有一个旮旯，平常老有一个草垛堆在那儿，我想就在那儿睡一夜。我认为，我能离那些学生和我从前说故事的那个宿舍很近，就等于是有人作伴了，虽然那些学生完全不知道我在那儿，那个宿舍也一点没给我遮风挡雨。

我累了一整天了，我后来攀上了布莱克·奚斯的平坦地方的时候，已经累极了。我去找撒伦学舍，很费了点儿事，不过我还是找着了，并且也找着了旮旯那儿的草垛了。我就在草垛旁边躺下，未躺之前，先在学舍四围走了一周，把宿舍的窗户都看了一下，只见里面黑洞洞、静悄悄的。那是我平生第一次在头上没有遮挡的地方躺着过夜，所以那种孤寂的感觉，是我永远也忘不了的！

那天晚上，睡魔光临到我身上，也和光临到许多

against whom house-doors were locked, and house-dogs barked, that night—and I dreamed of lying on my old school-bed, talking to the boys in my room; and found myself sitting upright, with Steerforth's name upon my lips, looking wildly at the stars that were glistening and glimmering above me.

无家可归的流浪者身上一样；对这种人，都是家家的门严扃，所有的犬乱吠。我睡着了的时候，梦见我在学校里旧日的床上躺着，和我同屋的人说话，跟着又只见我只身坐着，嘴里还嘟念着史朵夫的名字，但是眼睛却像疯癫呆傻了一样，看着天空里的星星，在我上面闪烁、眨眼。

When I remembered where I was at that untimely hour, a feeling stole upon me that made me get up, afraid of I don't know what, and walk about. (3) But the fainter glimmering of the stars, and the pale light in the sky where the day was coming, reassured me: and my eyes being very heavy, I lay down again and slept—though with a knowledge in my sleep that it was cold—until the warm beams of the sun, and the ringing of the getting-up bell at Salem House, awoke me.

我当时忽然想到，我原来在异乎寻常的时光里，躺在露天之下，那时候，一种无以名之的恐惧袭我而来，叫我爬起来，到处走了一遍。不过我看到星光比以前微茫稀淡了，曙色来临那一面的天上，又呈现了灰白之色，我的心就放下了；那时我的眼皮发涩，我就又躺下睡了——在睡眠中只觉得冷，一直睡到太阳暖和的光线照到我身上，撒伦学舍的起床钟传到我耳边，我才醒来。

If I could have hoped that Steerforth was there, I would have lurked about until he came out alone; but I knew he must have left long since. Traddles

如果我当时认为史朵夫还能在学校，我就会先躲在一边儿，等他一个人出来的机会，见他一面，不过我知

still remained, perhaps, but it was very doubtful; and I had not sufficient confidence in his discretion or good luck, however strong my reliance was on his good nature, to wish to trust him with my situation. So I crept away from the wall as Mr. Creakle's boys were getting up, and struck into the long dusty track which I had first known to be the Dover Road when I was one of them, and when I little expected that any eyes would ever see me the wayfarer I was now, upon it.

道他早已离开学校了。特莱得也许还在学校，不过那也很靠不住；而且，我对他的好心肠，固然深信不疑，但是对于他这个人的谨慎与运气，并没有足够的信心，所以不打算让他知道我当时的情况。这样一来，在克里克先生的学生起床的时候，我就从墙后的旮旯那儿走开了，跟着上了那条尘土飞扬的长路。我还是撒伦学舍的学生那时候，就知道那是往多佛去的路，不过那时候却万没想到，我自己会在那条路上，作了现在这样的行人。

What a different Sunday morning from the old Sunday morning at Yarmouth! In due time I heard the church-bells ringing, as I plodded on; and I met people who were going to church; and I passed a church or two where the congregation were inside, and the sound of singing came out into the sunshine, while the beadle sat and cooled himself in the shade of the porch, or stood beneath the yew-trcc, with his hand to his forehead, glowering at me going by.

那是一个星期天早晨，但是那个星期天早晨，和我在亚摩斯的星期天早晨多不一样啊！我当时努力往前奔，到了相当的时候，我听见教堂鸣钟，遇到人们上教堂；我走过一两个教堂，听见人们在里面做礼拜；唱诗的声音传到外面的阳光里，事务员就在门廊下面阴凉的地方乘凉，再不就站在水松树下面，用手打着眼罩，皱

But the peace and rest of the old Sunday morning were on everything, except me. That was the difference. I felt quite wicked in my dirt and dust, with my tangled hair. But for the quiet picture I had conjured up, of my mother in her youth and beauty, weeping by the fire, and my aunt relenting to her, I hardly think I should have had the courage to go on until next day. But it always went before me, and I followed.

眉蹙额地看着我走过[2]。

星期日的平安和和平，表现在一切东西上，只有我自己是例外。那就是我和别人不同的地方。我满身尘土，头发凌乱，连自己都觉得是个坏人。如果没有我心里想的那幅恬静的画图——我母亲年轻貌美，坐在炉前垂泣，我姨婆对她怜惜——如果没有这幅画图，我想，我当天几乎没有勇气前进了。但是我却老看见这幅画图在我眼前，我老跟着这幅画图往前走。

I got, that Sunday, through three-and-twenty miles on the straight road, though not very easily, for I was new to that kind of toil.

那个星期天，我在那条很直的大道上，走了二十三英里，不过却很费了些劲儿，因为走远路我还不习惯。

I see myself, as evening closes in, coming over the bridge at Rochester, footsore and tired, and eating bread that I had bought for supper.

天黑下来的时候，只见我走到罗彻斯特的大桥[3]，两脚疼痛，全身疲乏，吃我买来做晚饭的面包。

[2] 这种人是专管维持教堂秩序的，对于小孩，特别严厉。现看到大卫不在教堂做礼拜，而却像个小流氓走过，所以皱眉蹙额。

[3] 罗彻斯特（Rochester）为英国迈德维（Medway）河边的城市，有横桥跨该河。

One or two little houses, with the notice, 'Lodgings for Travellers', hanging out, had tempted me; but I was afraid of spending the few pence I had, and was even more afraid of the vicious looks of the trampers I had met or overtaken. I sought no shelter, therefore, but the sky; and toiling into Chatham,—which, in that night's aspect, is a mere dream of chalk, and drawbridges, and mastless ships in a muddy river, roofed like Noah's arks,—crept, at last, upon a sort of grass-grown battery overhanging a lane, where a sentry was walking to and fro.

有两家小客店，挂着安寓行客的招牌，使我跃跃欲试；但是我却害怕把我所有的那几个便士都花了，更害怕我碰上或者赶上的那些无业游民对我心怀不良的那个样子。因此，除了青天，我没去找别的荫庇。我当时费劲地走到查塔姆[4]——那地方，在那天的夜色里看来，只是朦胧迷离，如在梦中的一片白垩，几座吊桥和一些船只，船只都停在泥水成浆的河里，没有桅杆，却有顶子，像诺亚的方舟[5]那样。我在那儿，爬到一个俯视小巷、满长青草的炮台跟前，小巷那儿有一个卫兵正在来回地走。

Here I lay down, near a cannon; and, happy in the society of the sentry's footsteps, though he knew no more of my being above him than the boys at Salem House had known of my lying by the wall, slept soundly until morning.

我就在那儿，靠着一尊大炮，躺了下去；有卫兵的脚步声和我作伴（虽然他并不知道我在他上面，也就像撒伦学舍的学生不知道我就睡在墙下一样），就觉得够

[4] 查塔姆（Chatham）为英国海军造船场所在地。附近的小山为白垩质。

[5] 诺亚的方舟：见《旧约 创世纪》地6章，这里指摹仿方船形状的儿童玩具。

Very stiff and sore of foot I was in the morning, and quite dazed by the beating of drums and marching of troops, which seemed to hem me in on every side when I went down towards the long narrow street.

Feeling that I could go but a very little way that day, if I were to reserve any strength for getting to my journey's end, I resolved to make the sale of my jacket its principal business. （4）Accordingly, I took the jacket off, that I might learn to do without it; and carrying it under my arm, began a tour of inspection of the various slop-shops.

It was a likely place to sell a jacket in; for the dealers in second-hand clothes were numerous, and were, generally speaking, on the look-out for customers at their shop doors. But as most of them had, hanging up among their stock, an officer's coat or two, epaulettes and all, I was rendered timid by the costly nature of their dealings, and walked about for a long time without offering my merchandise to anyone.

好的了，因而熟熟睡了一觉，一直睡到天亮。

我早晨起来的时候，满身发僵，两腿作疼。我往那条窄而长的街上走去的时候，只听击鼓声和演操声，好像四面八方地把我包围起来了，把我弄得头昏脑涨。

我觉得，如果我要留有余力，把这条路走到头，那在那一天，我就不能走得太多了。因此我决定把卖我的夹克作为我那一天的主要工作。我就把夹克脱了，为的是好先试一试，不穿夹克是不是也过得。我把夹克夹在胳膊下面，开始对各估衣铺巡行考查。

在那个地方，要卖夹克，似乎很合适，因为那儿买卖旧衣服的铺子很多，并且，一般说来，铺子的老板都站在门口瞭望，看是否有主顾来。但是，他们多数之中，都在货物里面挂着一两件军官的制服，全部原样不变，连肩章都带在上面，我就认为他们的买卖一定很阔气，因此就胆怯，不敢过去，来回走了半天，竟没敢把我的货物对任何人兜揽出售。

This modesty of mine directed my attention to the marine-store shops, and such shops as Mr. Dolloby's, in preference to the regular dealers. At last I found one that I thought looked promising, at the corner of a dirty lane, ending in an enclosure full of stinging-nettles, against the palings of which some second-hand sailors' clothes, that seemed to have overflowed the shop, were fluttering among some cots, and rusty guns, and oilskin hats, and certain trays full of so many old rusty keys of so many sizes that they seemed various enough to open all the doors in the world.

我这种虚心，使我注意带卖旧船具的铺子和道勒毕开的那类铺子，而不和正式的铺子打交道。最后我看到一家，看样子可以去问一问。那个铺子，坐落在一个脏胡同的犄角上。铺子的一头是一个空场，里面长满了扎人的荨麻，前面有栏杆；旧的水手衣服好像铺子里满处都是，有的靠着栏杆挂着，在风里飘摆；四面还有小孩子的床，锈了的枪，油布帽子；还有一些盘子，盘子里满是锈了的钥匙，大大小小，各色俱备，好像世界上所有的门，都可以用它们打开似的。

Into this shop, which was low and small, and which was darkened rather than lighted by a little window, overhung with clothes, and was descended into by some steps, I went with a palpitating heart; which was not relieved when an ugly old man, with the lower part of his face all covered with a stubbly grey beard, rushed out of a dirty den behind it, and

这个铺子又小又矮，只有一个小窗户，不但不能使屋子明亮，反倒令屋子更暗，因为那儿挂着衣服。进这个铺子得下好几层台阶。我心里扑腾扑腾地进了这个铺子，进去了以后，心里的扑腾并没有减轻，因为一个很丑的老头子，他那脸的下半截，

seized me by the hair of my head.

(5) He was a dreadful old man to look at, in a filthy flannel waistcoat, and smelling terribly of rum. His bedstead, covered with a tumbled and ragged piece of patchwork, was in the den he had come from, where another little window showed a prospect of more stinging-nettles, and a lame donkey.

'Oh, what do you want?' grinned this old man, in a fierce, monotonous whine. 'Oh, my eyes and limbs, what do you want? Oh, my lungs and liver, what do you want? Oh, goroo, goroo!'

I was so much dismayed by these words, and particularly by the repetition of the last unknown one, which was a kind of rattle in his throat, that I could make no answer; hereupon the old man, still holding me by the hair, repeated:

全是毛烘烘的花白胡子碴儿，从铺子后面一个又脏、又像个窝的小屋子里冲了出来，一下抓住了我的头发。

这个老头子，面目凶恶，看着令人可怕，穿了一件很脏的法兰绒背心，红酒的味大极了。他的床铺，上面乱堆着一块碎块缀成的破烂被头，就安在他刚出来的那个像窝一般的小屋子里。那儿也有一个小窗户，从那儿往看，能看到另一片扎人的荨麻和一头瘸驴。

"哦，你要干什么？"那老头子，龇着牙、咧着嘴说；他的声音像乞怜呼痛、哀鸣长呻，态度却凶狠，语调却单一："哦，我的胳膊腿儿，你要干什么？哦，我的心肝肺，你要干什么？哦，咽噜，咽噜[6]！"

我听了他这种话，害怕极了，特别是他最后那声连声发出、让人不懂的话，那是他嗓子眼儿里像咯啦咯啦

[6] 这里写的这个家伙，表现了患慢性酒精中毒（chronic alcoholism）的症状。

上痰的声音；我吓得说不出话来了，因此那个老家伙，一面仍旧抓着我的头发，一面重复说：

'Oh, what do you want? Oh, my eyes and limbs, what do you want? Oh, my lungs and liver, what do you want? Oh, goroo!'—which he screwed out of himself, with an energy that made his eyes start in his head.

"哦，你要干什么？哦，我的胳膊腿儿，你要干什么？哦，我的心肝肺，你要干什么？哦，咽噜！"这一声咽噜，是他使劲儿憋出来的，使劲的时候，他的眼珠子都差一点儿没从眼眶子里迸出来。

'I wanted to know,' I said, trembling, 'if you would buy a jacket.'

"我想要问一问，"我浑身哆嗦着说，"你要不要买一件茄克。"

'Oh, let's see the jacket!' cried the old man. 'Oh, my heart on fire, show the jacket to us! Oh, my eyes and limbs, bring the jacket out!'

"哦，我瞧瞧你的夹克！"那老家伙喊道。"哦，我的火烧的一般的心，把你的夹克给我瞧瞧！哦，我的胳膊腿儿，把你的夹克拿出来！"

With that he took his trembling hands, which were like the claws of a great bird, out of my hair; and put on a pair of spectacles, not at all ornamental to his inflamed eyes.

他一面这样说，一面把他那两只哆嗦的手（那两只手和大鸟儿的两只爪子一样）从我的头发里拿出来，戴上了一副眼镜。他那发红的眼睛，戴上眼镜，一点也不看些。

'Oh, how much for the jacket?' cried the old man, after examining it. 'Oh—goroo!—how much for the jacket?'

'Half-a-crown,' I answered, recovering myself.

'Oh, my lungs and liver,' cried the old man, 'no! Oh, my eyes, no! Oh, my limbs, no! Eighteenpence. Goroo!'

Every time he uttered this ejaculation, his eyes seemed to be in danger of starting out; and every sentence he spoke, he delivered in a sort of tune, always exactly the same, and more like a gust of wind, which begins low, mounts up high, and falls again, than any other comparison I can find for it.

'Well,' said I, glad to have closed the bargain, 'I'll take eighteenpence.'

'Oh, my liver!' cried the old man, throwing the jacket on a shelf. 'Get out of the shop! Oh, my lungs, get out of the shop! Oh, my eyes and limbs-goroo!-don't ask for money; make it an

"哦，这件夹克要多少钱？"那个老家伙把夹克仔细看了一遍问。"哦——咽噜！——这件夹克要多少钱？"

"给半克朗吧，"我说，这时候我刚定住了神儿。

"哦，我的心肝肺，不值，"那个老家伙喊道。"不值！哦，我的眼睛，不值！哦，我的胳膊腿儿，不值！十八便士好啦。咽噜！"

他每次发出这个声音的时候，他的眼珠子都好像有从眼眶子里迸出来的危险。他每说一句话，都老用一种腔调，前后永远完全一样，起先低，然后高起来，最后又低下去，除了用刮的一阵风来比方，我再就想不出别的比方来了。

"好吧，"我说，我那时认为交易成功了，觉得很高兴。"就是十八便士吧。"

"哦，我的心肝肺！"那个老家伙喊道，同时把夹克扔在架子上。"你到铺子外面去！哦，我的肺！你到铺子外面去！哦，我的胳膊腿儿，咽噜！——别跟我要

exchange.'

I never was so frightened in my life, before or since; but I told him humbly that I wanted money, and that nothing else was of any use to me, but that I would wait for it, as he desired, outside, and had no wish to hurry him. So I went outside, and sat down in the shade in a corner. And I sat there so many hours, that the shade became sunlight, and the sunlight became shade again, and still I sat there waiting for the money.

There never was such another drunken madman in that line of business, I hope. That he was well known in the neighbourhood, and enjoyed the reputation of having sold himself to the devil, I soon understood from the visits he received from the boys, who continually came skirmishing about the shop, shouting that legend, and calling to him to bring out his gold.

'You ain't poor, you know, Charley, as you pretend. Bring out your gold. Bring out some of the gold you sold yourself to the

钱，换东西好啦。”

我从来没像那一次害怕过，不论以前，也不论以后，不过我还是很谦虚地对他说，我需要钱，别的东西都于我没有任何用处。我可以等，在外面等，像他愿意的那样。我决不催他。因此我就出了铺子，在一个有阴凉的旮旯那儿坐下。我坐在那儿，等了又等，原先那个旮旯有阴凉，后来变成有太阳，后来又变成有阴凉，但是我仍旧在那儿等他给我钱。

我希望，做买卖的，可别再有像他那样疯了一般的醉鬼才好。原来附近那一带，无人不知，他把自己卖给魔鬼了，他还特别因为这件事而美名远扬，这是我一会儿就知道了的。因为有些孩子，时来时去，在他的铺子那儿，跟他作散兵战，嘴里喊着那个传说，叫他把金子拿出来。

“你别装穷，查理，你并不穷。你把自己卖给了魔鬼，你把卖来的金子拿出点儿来好啦。快点！你的金子

devil for. Come! It's in the lining of the mattress, Charley. Rip it open and let's have some!'

藏在你的褥子里面哪，查理。你把褥子拆开，拿出点儿来给我们好啦！”

This, and many offers to lend him a knife for the purpose, exasperated him to such a degree, that the whole day was a succession of rushes on his part, and flights on the part of the boys.

他们说了这一类话，同时还屡次要借剪子给他，好拆褥子。这些话和这类情况把他惹得大怒，因此整天价没有别的，就老不断地冲出去追，而那些孩子就老不断地撒开腿逃。

Sometimes in his rage he would take me for one of them, and come at me, mouthing as if he were going to tear me in pieces; then, remembering me, just in time, would dive into the shop, and lie upon his bed, as I thought from the sound of his voice, yelling in a frantic way, to his own windy tune, the 'Death of Nelson'; with an Oh! before every line, and innumerable Go-roos interspersed.

有的时候，他怒不可遏，就把我当做那些孩子里面的一个，朝着我冲来，还满嘴乱动，好像要用牙把我撕成一块一块似的；但是，幸而还没来得及下口，他就又想起来，原来是我，跟着就猛一下有钻回了铺子，在床上躺下（这是我从他的声音上听出来的），像疯子似的，用他那个破嗓子，大唱《纳尔逊之死》[7]；歌儿每一句的起头，都加上一个“哦！”歌儿的中间，还掺杂上许多“咽噜”。

As if this were not bad enough for me, the boys, connecting me with the establishment, on account of the patience and perseverance with which I sat outside,

好像这样还不够我受的，那些孩子，因为我身上

[7]《纳尔逊之死》：为当时流行歌曲之一，也见于狄更斯的另一部小说《我们共同的朋友》地4部第3章。

half-dressed, pelted me, and used me very ill all day.

半遮半露，那样老实、那样有耐性、有恒心，坐在铺子外面，认为我和这个铺子有关系，就整天价老用泥块老远砸我，再不就用别的方法凌辱我。

He made many attempts to induce me to consent to an exchange; at one time coming out with a fishing-rod, at another with a fiddle, at another with a cocked hat, at another with a flute. But I resisted all these overtures, and sat there in desperation; each time asking him, with tears in my eyes, for my money or my jacket. At last he began to pay me in halfpence at a time; and was full two hours getting by easy stages to a shilling.

那个老头子，试了好多次，想法引诱我，要我跟他换东西。有一次，他拿出一根钓鱼竿儿来；另一次，拿出一个提琴来；又一次，拿出一个三角帽来；又一次拿出一个笛子来。不过我对于他所有的诱惑，一概拒绝，咬紧牙关坐在那儿，每次他出来的时候，我都满眼含泪，跟他要钱，再不就要我的夹克。后来，他开始给起钱来，一回给半便士，一点儿一点儿地给，给了整整两个钟头的工夫，从容不迫地给到了一先令。

'Oh, my eyes and limbs!' he then cried, peeping hideously out of the shop, after a long pause, 'will you go for twopence more?'

过了很大的工夫，他把他那副可怕的嘴脸，扒在铺子外面瞧，同时嘴里喊，"哦，我的胳膊腿儿！再给你两便士，你走不走？"

'I can't,' I said; 'I shall be starved.'

"不成，"我说，"那样我就要饿死了。"

'Oh, my lungs and liver, will you go for threepence?'

'I would go for nothing, if I could,' I said, 'but I want the money badly.'

'Oh, go-roo!' (it is really impossible to express how he twisted this ejaculation out of himself, as he peeped round the door-post at me, showing nothing but his crafty old head); 'will you go for fourpence?'

I was so faint and weary that I closed with this offer; and taking the money out of his claw, not without trembling, went away more hungry and thirsty than I had ever been, a little before sunset. But at an expense of threepence I soon refreshed myself completely; and, being in better spirits then, limped seven miles upon my road.

My bed at night was under another haystack, where I rested comfortably, after having washed my blistered feet in a stream, and

"哦，我的心肝肺，再给你三便士，你走不走？"

"我要是不等钱用，那你一个不给都可以，"我说，"但是我可急着等钱用！"

"哦，啯—噜！"他扒着门框，往外瞧我，只露出他那奸猾的脑袋，别的部分都瞧不见，所以他把这个声音憋出来的时候，他的身子都怎样又扭又歪，我没法儿说。"再给你四个便士，你走不走？"

我当时又疲乏，又发晕，所以我听说他再给四个便士，就答应他了。我两手有些哆嗦，从他那像爪子的手里接过了钱，转身走去，又饥又渴，比以前更厉害。那时太阳已经快要西下了。不过我花了三便士以后，就又不饿、又不渴了。我那时精神又恢复了，我就趁着机会，往前一瘸一颠地又挨了七英里路。

我先把磨得起了泡的脚在河沟里洗了一洗，用一些凉爽的叶子尽可能地包扎起来，然后在一个草垛下面躺

dressed them as well as I was able, with some cool leaves.

When I took the road again next morning, I found that it lay through a succession of hop-grounds and orchards. It was sufficiently late in the year for the orchards to be ruddy with ripe apples; and in a few places the hop-pickers were already at work. I thought it all extremely beautiful, and made up my mind to sleep among the hops that night: imagining some cheerful companionship in the long perspectives of poles, with the graceful leaves twining round them.

The trampers were worse than ever that day, and inspired me with a dread that is yet quite fresh in my mind. Some of them were most ferocious-looking ruffians, who stared at me as I went by; and stopped, perhaps, and called after me to come back and speak to them, and when I took to my heels, stoned me.

着，舒舒服服地睡了一夜。

我第二天早晨又上了路，只见路两旁，一块跟着一块，都是啤酒花和果园[8]。那是已经快到秋末，所以果园里红润的熟苹果，累累皆是。有一些地方，摘啤酒花的工人已经工作起来了。我认为，这都是很美的，打算那天晚上，在啤酒花地里睡一夜，因为我想，那一溜一溜的杆子[9]，上面缠绕着啤酒花美丽的梗儿和叶儿，是使我高兴的伴侣。

那天路上的无业游民，比以前更坏，他们在我心里，引起了一种恐惧，直到现在，还是记忆犹新。其中有一些，是形貌最凶、恶霸一般的匪徒，我从路上走过的时候，直拿眼盯我，有时还站住了脚，叫我回来和他们搭话，我撒腿跑走的时候，他们就用石头砸我。

[8] 大卫经过的地方，都属于肯特郡(Kent)；肯特郡是英国专产啤酒花和水果的地方，水果主要为樱桃和苹果。

[9] 啤酒花蔓生，杆子上绑以细绳，供酒花缠缚之用，高丈余，成行林立。

I recollect one young fellow—a tinker, I suppose, from his wallet and brazier—who had a woman with him, and who faced about and stared at me thus; and then roared to me in such a tremendous voice to come back, that I halted and looked round.

我现在还记得，有一个年轻的家伙从他背的袋子和带的火炭炉子看来，我知道他是个补锅匠。跟他在一块儿的还有一个女人。他就像我前面说的那样，转身朝着我，只瞪我。跟着就叫我回来，叫的声音大极了，因此我站住了脚，回头看去。

"Come here, when you're called," said the tinker, "or I'll rip your young body open."

"叫你回来，你就回来，听见了没有？"那个补锅匠说，"不价，我就把你那小嫩肚子给豁了。"

I thought it best to go back. As I drew nearer to them, trying to propitiate the tinker by my looks, I observed that the woman had a black eye.

我一想，还是回去的好。我在脸上带着安抚那个补锅匠的样子，往他们那儿去，那时候，只见那个女人鼻青脸肿的。

"Where are you going?" said the tinker, gripping the bosom of my shirt with his blackened hand.

"你要往哪儿去？"补锅匠说，同时用他那只熏黑了的手，抓住了我的衬衫胸前那一块儿。

"I am going to Dover," I said.

"往多佛去。"我说。

"Where do you come from?" asked the tinker, giving his hand another turn in my shirt, to hold me more securely.

"你是从哪儿来的？"补锅匠说，同时把我的衬衣又扭了一个轸儿，为的是好抓得更牢。

"I come from London," I said.

"从伦敦来，"我说。

"What lay are you upon ?" asked the tinker. "Are you a prig ?"

"N-no," I said.

"Ain't you, by G—? If you make a brag of your honesty to me," said the tinker, "I'll knock your brains out."

With his disengaged hand he made a menace of striking me, and then looked at me from head to foot.

"Have you got the price of a pint of beer about you ?" said the tinker. "If you have, out with it, afore I take it away!"

I should certainly have produced it, but that I met the woman's look, and saw her very slightly shake her head, and form "No!" with her lips.

"I am very poor," I said, attempting to smile, "and have got no money."

"Why, what do you mean?" said the tinker, looking so sternly at me, that I almost feared he saw the money in my pocket.

"你是哪一条路儿上的?"补锅匠说。"你是不是合字儿?[10]"

"不——不是,"我说。

"不是?妈的。你要是在我跟前,不老实,我就把你的脑浆子给你砸出来。"

他说到这儿,就把他空着的那只手举起来,威吓我,做出要打我的样子来,跟着把我上上下下地端量。

"你身上带的钱够买一品脱啤酒的吧?"补锅匠说。"要是够的话,快拿出来。别让你老爷费事!"

我本来很想把钱拿出来,但是我的眼光却和那个女人的眼光碰巧一对。我就看见她轻轻把头一摇,同时用嘴唇作出"别!"字的样式。

"我很穷,"我说,一面想装出一副笑脸却又装不出来,"我没有钱。"

"什么,你这话怎讲?"补锅匠说,同时狠狠地往我身上直瞧,把我吓得以为他

"贼"黑话的叫法,也叫"老合"。原文"prig"也是黑话。[10]

"Sir!" I stammered.

"What do you mean," said the tinker, 'by wearing my brother's silk handkerchief! Give it over here!' And he had mine off my neck in a moment, and tossed it to the woman.

The woman burst into a fit of laughter, as if she thought this a joke, and tossed it back to me, nodded once, as slightly as before, and made the word 'Go!' with her lips.

Before I could obey, however, the tinker seized the handkerchief out of my hand with a roughness that threw me away like a feather, and putting it loosely round his own neck, turned upon the woman with an oath, and knocked her down.

（6）I never shall forget seeing her fall backward on the hard road, and lie there with her bonnet tumbled off, and her hair all

已经看见我口袋里的钱了。

"先生！"我结结巴巴地说。

"我兄弟的绸子手绢怎么围在你的脖子上啦？那是怎么回事？快快还我好啦！"跟着他一下就从我的脖子上把我的绸手绢揪了下来，扔给了那个女人。

那个女人一下笑起来，好像那个补锅匠只是跟我开玩笑似的，把那块手绢又扔给我了，同时和先前摇头的时候一样，轻轻地点了点头，又用嘴唇作出"跑！"字的样式来。

但是，还没等到我照着她的启发办的时候，那个补锅匠又从我手里把手绢拽走了，拽的时候，非常粗鲁，把我一下甩的老远，好像我只是一片羽毛一样。跟着他把手绢松松地围在自己脖子上，转身朝那个女人骂了一句，把她打得趴在地上。

我看到她来了个仰趴，倒在挺硬的路上，把帽子都跌掉了，她的头发沾满了尘

whitened in the dust; nor, when I looked back from a distance, seeing her sitting on the pathway, which was a bank by the road-side, wiping the blood from her face with a corner of her shawl, while he went on ahead.

土，都成了白的了[11]：那种情况，我永远也忘不了。我当时撒腿就跑，跑了一会儿，回头看去，只见她坐在步行路上（那是大路旁边的一个坡儿）用她那披巾的角儿擦她脸上的血，补锅匠就自己往前走去；那种情况，也是我永远忘不了的。

This adventure frightened me so, that, afterwards, when I saw any of these people coming, I turned back until I could find a hiding-place, where I remained until they had gone out of sight; which happened so often, that I was very seriously delayed.

这一场险局，把我吓得很厉害，因此，从那时候开始，我老远看见这种人来了，我就回身转到一旁，先找个地方躲藏起来，等到他们走得看不见了，我才再上路。这种情况，发生的次数太多了，因此我在路上，耽误了许多工夫。

But under this difficulty, as under all the other difficulties of my journey, I seemed to be sustained and led on by my fanciful picture of my mother in her youth, before I came into the world. It always kept me company. It was there, among the hops, when I lay down to sleep; it was with me on my waking in the morning; it went before me all day.

但是我遇到这种困难的时候，也和我在路上遇到别的困难一样，我想象中我母亲在我还没出生的时候那种少女之美的形象，好像老使我坚持下去，好像老领我往前进行。这幅形象，永远和我作伴。我在啤酒花藤蔓之

[11] 因当地的土为白垩质。

中躺下睡觉的时候，这幅形象也就在藤蔓之中。我早晨醒来的时候，它也和我一块醒来。我白天走路的时候，它也整天在我面前走。

I have associated it, ever since, with the sunny street of Canterbury, dozing as it were in the hot light; and with the sight of its old houses and gateways, and the stately, grey Cathedral, with the rooks sailing round the towers.

我从那时以后，永远把这幅形象和坎特伯雷阳光辉煌的街道联系在一起：和它那好像在暖洋洋的太阳地里打盹儿的街道，它那古老的屋舍和城门，它那古老、庄严的大教堂，和它那围着高阁飞绕的乌鸦，联系在一起[12]。

When I came, at last, upon the bare, wide downs near Dover, it relieved the solitary aspect of the scene with hope; and not until I reached that first great aim of my journey, and actually set foot in the town itself, on the sixth day of my flight, did it desert me. But then, strange to say, when I stood with my ragged shoes, and my dusty, sunburnt, half-clothed figure, in the place so long desired, it seemed to vanish like a dream, and to leave me helpless and dispirited.

后来我走到了多佛附近那些空旷宽敞的丘陵上面了，那时候，那幅图画里使我感到的希望，丘陵的荒凉面目，也变得不荒凉了。一直到我走到了这番旅程的第一个大目标，当真踏上了那个市镇的时候（那是我逃出伦敦的第六天），那幅景象才离我而去。说也奇怪，那时候，我脚上穿着破鞋，身上半遮半露，满是尘土，晒得黢黑，站在我那样渴望已

[12] 坎特伯雷（Canterbury）为英国古城，以大教堂著称。城门是中古遗迹。它是从伦敦往多佛必经之路。

久的地方，那幅形象忽然像一个梦一样，一去无踪，把我撂在那儿，使我觉得毫无办法，精神萎靡。

I inquired about my aunt among the boatmen first, and received various answers. One said she lived in the South Foreland Light, and had singed her whiskers by doing so; another, that she was made fast to the great buoy outside the harbour, and could only be visited at half-tide; a third, that she was locked up in Maidstone jail for child-stealing; a fourth, that she was seen to mount a broom in the last high wind, and make direct for Calais.

我现在渔夫中间，打听我姨婆的消息。他们回答我的话，真是形形色色。有一个说，她住在南崖头[13]灯塔上，因而把胡子燎了。另一个就说，她牢牢地绑在港外的大浮标上，只有潮水半落的时候才能去看她。第三个就说，她因为拐小孩儿，关在梅得斯屯[14]的监狱里了。第四个就说，上一次刮大风的时候，有人看见她驾着扫帚一直往加莱[15]去了。

The fly-drivers, among whom I inquired next, were equally jocose and equally disrespectful; and the shopkeepers, not liking my appearance, generally replied, without hearing what I had to say, that they had got nothing for me. I felt more miserable and destitute than I had done at any period of my running away. My money was all gone, I had nothing left to dispose of; I was hungry, thirsty, and worn out; and seemed as distant from my end as if I had remained in London.

我跟着又在马车夫中间打听她，那些马车夫也同样地诙谐，同样地对她毫无敬意。我又想往开铺子的人中间去打听她，但是那般人，一看我那种样子，就厌恶起

[13]在多佛东北四英里。那里的灯塔上的灯光，三十英里外可见。

[14] 梅得斯屯（Maidstone）为肯特郡郡城。

[15] 加莱（Calais）：法国海口，和多佛隔水相对。英国迷信的说法，女巫驾扫帚飞行。

来，还没等我开口，就说，他们没有什么可以卖给我的东西。我这次逃亡，一路之上，不论哪一会儿，都没有这阵儿那样苦恼，那样孤独。我的钱都花光了，我又没有别的东西可以卖的、可以当的；我又饥、又渴、又疲乏；我离我的目的地，好像和我还在伦敦那时候一样地遥远。

The morning had worn away in these inquiries, and I was sitting on the step of an empty shop at a street corner, near the market-place, deliberating upon wandering towards those other places which had been mentioned, when a fly-driver, coming by with his carriage, dropped a horsecloth.

我这样不断打听，可就把一个上午的时光都消磨了。于是我看到，在靠近市场那条街的犄角上，有一家空无一人的铺子，我就在那个铺子的台阶上坐下，琢磨是否瞎走到前面说过的那些地方再去打听，正在犹豫的时候，碰巧来个一个赶马车的，他赶着车走过去的时候，把马衣掉了。

Something good-natured in the man's face, as I handed it up, encouraged me to ask him if he could tell me where Miss Trotwood lived; though I had asked the question so often, that it almost died upon my lips.

我把马衣递给他的时候，我看他脸上的样子，觉得他这个人大概心眼儿不坏，就大胆地问他，是否知道特洛乌小姐住在哪儿；虽然我这句话问得次数太多了，它几乎没说出口来就又噎回去了。

'Trotwood,' said he. 'Let me see. I know the name, too. Old lady?'

“特洛乌?”他说。“我想想看。我脑子里有这么个人。她是不是个老太太?”

'Yes,' I said, 'rather.'

“不错,是,”我说,“有点儿老。”

'Pretty stiff in the back?' said he, making himself upright.

“腰板挺直的,是不是?”他说,同时把自己的腰伸直了。

'Yes,' I said. 'I should think it very likely.'

“不错,”我说,“我想是那样。”

'Carries a bag?' said he-'bag with a good deal of room in it-is gruffish, and comes down upon you, sharp?'

“老拿着个手提包,是不是?”他说,“一个大提包,里面能装好些东西,是不是?脾气挺倔的,对你说话的时候,老斩钉截铁似的,是不是?“

My heart sank within me as I acknowledged the undoubted accuracy of this description.

我嘴里承认这番形容非常正确,心里却不由得凉了半截儿。

'Why then, I tell you what,' said he. 'If you go up there,' pointing with his whip towards the heights, 'and keep right on till you come to some houses facing the sea, I think you'll hear of her. My opinion is she won't stand anything, so here's a penny for you.'

“这样的话,你听我说好啦,”他说。“你要是从这儿上那个坡儿,”一面用鞭子指着高地,“一直往前走,走到冲着海的几所房子那儿,你再打听,准打听得着。我觉得,她这个人,你求她,她也不会给你什么的，所以我这儿给你一个便士好啦。”

I accepted the gift thankfully, and bought a loaf with it. Dispatching this refreshment by the way, I went in the direction my friend had indicated, and walked on a good distance without coming to the houses he had mentioned. At length I saw some before me ; and approaching them, went into a little shop (it was what we used to call a general shop, at home), and inquired if they could have the goodness to tell me where Miss Trotwood lived. I addressed myself to a man behind the counter, who was weighing some rice for a young woman ; but the latter, taking the inquiry to herself, turned round quickly.

我很感激地接了他这一便士，用它买了块面包。我一边走，一面把这块面包吃了。我照我那位朋友指给我的方向往前走了老远，还没有看见他说的那所房子。后来又走了一气，才看见前面果然有些房子。我又往前走到那片房子那儿，进了一间小铺子（那就是我的家乡一带叫作杂货铺的），跟铺子里的人道了劳驾，打听他们知道不知道特洛乌小姐住在哪儿。我本来是跟柜台后面的一个人打听的；他正在那儿给一个年轻的女人称米。那个年轻的女人，听见我这样一问，却把话接了过去，一下子转身朝着我。

“My mistress ?” she said. “What do you want with her, boy ?”

“你问的是我们的小姐吗？”她说，“你找她有什么事儿，你这孩子？”

“I want,” I replied, “to speak to her, if you please.”

“劳你的驾，我找她，有几句话跟她说，”我回答说。

“To beg of her, you mean,” retorted the damsel.

“你是说，跟她告帮吧？”那个大姐驳正我的话说。

“No,” I said, “indeed.” But suddenly remembering that in

truth I came for no other purpose, I held my peace in confusion, and felt my face burn.

“不是，”我说。“完全不是。”但是我忽然想起来，我到这儿来，实在不为别的，实在就是为了告帮，这样一来，我就无话可答了，一时觉得不知怎么样才好，同时觉得脸上都烧起来了。

My aunt's handmaid, as I supposed she was from what she had said, put her rice in a little basket and walked out of the shop; telling me that I could follow her, if I wanted to know where Miss Trotwood lived. I needed no second permission; though I was by this time in such a state of consternation and agitation, that my legs shook under me. I followed the young woman, and we soon came to a very neat little cottage with cheerful bow-windows: in front of it, a small square gravelled court or garden full of flowers, carefully tended, and smelling deliciously.

我姨婆的大姐（因为我从她说的话里，知道她是我姨婆的大姐），把米放在一个小篮子里，出了铺子，告诉我，想知道特洛乌小姐住在哪儿，让我跟着她走就好啦。我当然很乐意。不过我那时候，心里又害怕，又慌乱，所以我的腿不觉得都哆嗦起来了。我跟着那位大姐，一会儿就走近一所整齐干净的小房儿，带着使人心清神爽的凸形窗户；房子前面，有一个夹杂着石头子儿的沙子铺的小方院子或者园子，里面满种着花儿，修剪得很整齐，到处都是清香之气。

“This is Miss Trotwood's,” said the young woman. “Now you know; and that's all I have got to say.” With which words she hurried into the house, as if to shake off the responsibility of my

“特洛乌小姐就住在这儿。”那个大姐说。“你知道了吧，我没有别的可说的了。”说完了，就急忙进了屋里，好像怕人说是她把

appearance; and left me standing at the garden-gate, looking disconsolately over the top of it towards the parlour window, where a muslin curtain partly undrawn in the middle, a large round green screen or fan fastened on to the windowsill, a small table, and a great chair, suggested to me that my aunt might be at that moment seated in awful state.

My shoes were by this time in a woeful condition. The soles had shed themselves bit by bit, and the upper leathers had broken and burst until the very shape and form of shoes had departed from them. My hat (which had served me for a night-cap, too) was so crushed and bent, that no old battered handleless saucepan on a dunghill need have been ashamed to vie with it. My shirt and trousers, stained with heat, dew, grass, and the Kentish soil on which I had slept-and torn besides-might have frightened the birds from my aunt's garden, as I stood at the gate. My hair had known no comb or brush since I left London.

我带到这儿似的。她把我撂在庭院的栅栏门那儿站着，孤独凄凉地隔着栅栏门，看着房间的窗户。只见那儿纱布窗帘子半遮半掩，窗台上钉着一个绿色的小圆屏风或者扇子，窗里有一张小桌子和一把大椅子；我心里想，我姨婆也许正在那儿凛然端坐呢。

我的鞋这时候惨极了，底子早已一块一块地脱落去了，帮儿上的皮子也都裂开了，弄得早就不成个鞋样了。我白天戴的帽子（同时也就是我夜里戴的睡帽）都压扁了，弄歪了，早就不成其为帽子，就是垃圾堆上没把的破汤锅[16]都可以和它比一比而毫无逊色。我的衬衣和裤子，让汗渍、露湿、草染、土沾（沾的是肯特郡的土，我就在这样的土地上睡），同时还撕破了。所以我这样站在栅栏门外的时候，我姨婆园里的鸟儿都要

[16] 深而有长柄之锅。

被我吓飞了[17]。我的头发，自从我离开伦敦那一天起，再就没见过梳子，也没见过刷子。

My face, neck, and hands, from unaccustomed exposure to the air and sun, were burnt to a berry-brown. From head to foot I was powdered almost as white with chalk and dust, as if I had come out of a lime-kiln. In this plight, and with a strong consciousness of it, I waited to introduce myself to, and make my first impression on, my formidable aunt.

我的脸、我的脖子和我的手，因为风吹日晒，多日不洗，都成了浆果一样的紫色了。我从头到脚，全叫尘土和粉末弄得一身白，好像刚从石灰窑里出来似的。我就落到了——并且还强烈地意识到自己落到了——这种地步。站在门外，我等着把自己介绍给我那位凛然不可犯的姨婆，等着给我那位凛然不可犯的姨婆初次见面的印象。

The unbroken stillness of the parlour window leading me to infer, after a while, that she was not there, I lifted up my eyes to the window above it, where I saw a florid, pleasant-looking gentleman, with a grey head, who shut up one eye in a grotesque manner, nodded his head at me several times, shook it at me as often, laughed, and went away.

我待了一会儿，只见房间的窗户那儿，仍旧静悄悄的，我就断定，我姨婆并没有在那儿。我于是就抬起头来，往房间上面的窗户那儿看去，只见那儿有一个和蔼可亲的绅士，满面红光，满头苍白的头发，先很古怪地对着我把一只眼睛一闭，跟

[17] 指自己像一个扎在地里用来吓鸟的草人而言。

I had been discomposed enough before; but I was so much the more discomposed by this unexpected behaviour, that I was on the point of slinking off, to think how I had best proceed, when there came out of the house a lady with her handkerchief tied over her cap, and a pair of gardening gloves on her hands, wearing a gardening pocket like a toll-man's apron, and carrying a great knife.

I knew her immediately to be Miss Betsey, for she came stalking out of the house exactly as my poor mother had so often described her stalking up our garden at Blunderstone Rookery.

'Go away!' said Miss Betsey, shaking her head, and making a distant chop in the air with her knife. 'Go along! No boys here!'

(7) I watched her, with my

着对着我把头点了好几下，又摇了好几下，最后笑一笑，走开了。

在这以前，我心里本来就够乱了，但是我看了这位绅士这种意外的举动以后，我的心更乱了；所以当时我很想偷偷地溜到外面，好仔细琢磨琢磨，我应怎样办，才是上策；正在要溜还没溜的时候，只见屋里走出一位女士来，帽子上系着一条条手绢，手上戴着一副园丁用的手套，身上挂着一个园丁用的布口袋，和收路税的人戴的围襟一样，手里拿着一把大刀子。

我一见她，就知道她一定是贝萃小姐，因为她从屋子里大踏步地走了出来，和我母亲常常说的那种大踏步地走上布伦得屯栖鸦庐的庭院那一次，完全一模一样。

“去！”贝萃小姐说，一面摇头，一面把刀子在空中一比划，在远处作出要砍我的样子来。“去！这儿不许小孩子来！”

我提心吊胆，老远瞧着

heart at my lips, as she marched to a corner of her garden, and stooped to dig up some little root there. Then, without a scrap of courage, but with a great deal of desperation, I went softly in and stood beside her, touching her with my finger.

'If you please, ma'am,' I began.

She started and looked up.

'If you please, aunt.'

'EH?' exclaimed Miss Betsey, in a tone of amazement I have never heard approached.

'If you please, aunt, I am your nephew.'

'Oh, Lord!' said my aunt. And sat flat down in the garden-path.

'I am David Copperfield, of Blunderstone, in Suffolk- where you came, on the night when I was born, and saw my dear mama. I have been very unhappy since she died. I have been slighted, and taught nothing, and thrown upon myself, and put to work not fit for me. It made me run away to you.

她，只见她往院子的一个角落走去，在那儿弯下腰，要刨什么小东西的根子。于是，我虽然半点勇气都没有了，却完全豁出去了的样子，轻轻悄悄地进了院子，站在她身边，用手指头去碰她。

“对不起，小姐，”我开口说。

她惊了一下，把头抬起来。

“对不起，姨婆！”

“嗯？”贝萃小姐喊道，那种惊讶的口气，我还从来没有听见过有和它相近的。

“对不起，姨婆，我就是你的侄孙儿。”

“哎呀，我的天！”我姨婆说，同时啪地一下坐在园子的路径上。

“我就是大卫·科波菲尔，住在色弗克的布伦得屯——你不是在我出生的那一天到那儿去过，见过我的亲爱的妈妈吗？我妈故去了以后，我的生活非常苦恼。没有人理我，没有人教给我任何东西。他们叫我自己维

I was robbed at first setting out, and have walked all the way, and have never slept in a bed since I began the journey.' Here my self-support gave way all at once; and with a movement of my hands, intended to show her my ragged state, and call it to witness that I had suffered something, I broke into a passion of crying, which I suppose had been pent up within me all the week.

My aunt, with every sort of expression but wonder discharged from her countenance, sat on the gravel, staring at me, until I began to cry; when she got up in a great hurry, collared me, and took me into the parlour.

Her first proceeding there was to unlock a tall press, bring out several bottles, and pour some of the contents of each into my mouth. I think they must have been taken out at random, for I am sure I tasted aniseed water, anchovy sauce, and salad dressing.

持生活，叫我干不该我干的活儿。所以我就逃了，逃到你这儿来了。

我到这儿来的时候，刚一上路，就叫人抢了，一路都是走着的，从我上路那一天起，再就没在床上睡过一夜觉。”我说到这儿，完全忍不住了，用手指了一指我身上褴褛的样子，叫我姨婆看一看，我的确受了些苦，跟着就一下痛哭起来。我想，这是我这一个星期以来，一直憋到现在的。

我说这番话的时候，我姨婆脸上，一切表情全都离她而去，只剩下了惊讶，一直坐在石子甬路上，拿眼盯着我。但是等到我一哭，她却急忙站起来，揪着我的领子，把我拽到屋里。

她到了那儿以后，先是把一个锁着的大橱子开开，拿出好几个瓶子来，把每一个瓶子里的东西，都往我嘴里倒了一点儿。我现在回想起来，那些瓶子，一定是随便乱拿的，因为毫无疑问，我当时喝

When she had administered these restoratives, as I was still quite hysterical, and unable to control my sobs, she put me on the sofa, with a shawl under my head, and the handkerchief from her own head under my feet, lest I should sully the cover; and then, sitting herself down behind the green fan or screen I have already mentioned, so that I could not see her face, ejaculated at intervals, 'Mercy on us!' letting those exclamations off like minute guns.

After a time she rang the bell. 'Janet,' said my aunt, when her servant came in. 'Go upstairs, give my compliments to Mr. Dick, and say I wish to speak to him.'

Janet looked a little surprised to see me lying stiffly on the sofa (I was afraid to move lest it should be displeasing to my aunt), but went on her errand. My aunt, with her hands behind her, walked up and down the room, until the gentleman who had squinted at me from the upper window came in laughing.

的东西里面，有茴香水，有凤尾鱼酱，有色拉油。

她把这些补精益神的东西都给我服下去以后，我还是犯歇斯底里，不住抽打抽打地哭，她就叫我躺在沙发上，用披肩给我垫着头，用她头上的手绢给我垫着脚，免得我把沙发套儿弄脏了；这样安置好了，她就在我刚说过的绿扇子或者小屏风后面坐下（因此我看不见她的脸），过一会儿，就喊一声“我的天！”好像放“分炮”[18]似的。

待了一会儿，她拉玲儿。“捷妮，”她的大姐进来了的时候，她说，“你到楼上，就说我问狄克先安好，再告诉他，说我有话给他说。”

捷妮看见我直挺挺地躺在沙发上（我一点也不敢动，怕的是会招惹我姨婆不高兴），觉得很惊讶，不过她还是上楼传话去了。我姨婆就背着手，在屋里来回地

[18]“分炮”每过一分钟，连续放一次，多半作求救的信号，或丧礼的仪式。

走，一直到在楼上冲着我挤眼的那位绅士笑着进了房间的时候。

'Mr. Dick,' said my aunt, 'don't be a fool, because nobody can be more discreet than you can, when you choose. We all know that. So don't be a fool, whatever you are.'

"狄克先生，"我姨婆说，"你不要犯傻，因为只要你想不犯傻，就没有比你再明白的了。这是咱们都知道的。所以，你怎么都成，可就是别犯傻。"

The gentleman was serious immediately, and looked at me, I thought, as if he would entreat me to say nothing about the window.

那位绅士一听这话，马上作出正颜厉色的样子来，往我这儿瞧，瞧的神气，我只觉得，好像是求我千万不要把他刚才在楼上对我做的那种样子说出来似的。

'Mr. Dick,' said my aunt, 'you have heard me mention David Copperfield? Now don't pretend not to have a memory, because you and I know better.'

"狄克先生，"我姨婆说，"你记得我对你提起过大卫科波菲尔吧？你可不要假装着记性不好，因为你和我都知道，你不是那样。"

'David Copperfield?' said Mr. Dick, who did not appear to me to remember much about it. 'David Copperfield? Oh yes, to be sure. David, certainly.'

"大卫·科波菲尔？"狄克先生说，他的样子，据我看来，好像并不大记得似的。"大卫·科波菲尔？哦，是啦，不错。有个大卫。一点不错，有个大卫。"

'Well,' said my aunt, 'this is his boy—his son. He would be as like his father as it's possible

"好啦，"我姨婆说，"这就是他的小子，这就是他的

to be, if he was not so like his mother, too.'

儿子。这孩子要不是因为也像他妈一点儿，那他就完完全全，丝毫不差和他爸爸一样了。”

'His son?' said Mr. Dick. 'David's son? Indeed!'

“他的儿子”狄克先生说。“大卫的儿子？真个的！”

'Yes,' pursued my aunt, 'and he has done a pretty piece of business. He has run away. Ah! His sister, Betsey Trotwood, never would have run away.' My aunt shook her head firmly, confident in the character and behaviour of the girl who never was born.

“不错，是真个的，”姨婆接着说，“不但是大卫的儿子，他还干了一件真有出息的事儿哪。他是逃到这儿来的。啊！他的姐姐，贝萃特洛乌，可决干不出这样事来。”姨婆坚决地摇头，对于那位并没出生的女孩子满怀信心，认为她的品质和行动，绝不会有错儿。

'Oh! you think she wouldn't have run away?' said Mr. Dick.

“哦！你认为，她不会逃跑？”狄克先生说。

'Bless and save the man,' exclaimed my aunt, sharply, "how he talks! Don't I know she wouldn't? She would have lived with her god-mother, and we should have been devoted to one another. Where, in the name of wonder, should his sister, Betsey Trotwood, have run from, or to?"

“哎呀，你这个人真可以的，”我姨婆峻厉地说，“你都瞎说了些什么！难道我还不知道她不会逃跑吗？她一定要跟着她教母一块儿过的；我们一定要你亲我爱的。我真想知道知道，他姐姐贝萃特洛乌要是逃跑的话，她从这哪逃，逃到哪儿去？”

"Nowhere," said Mr. Dick.

“没有地方啊，”狄克先生说。

"Well then," returned my aunt, softened by the reply, 'how can you pretend to be wool-gathering, Dick, when you are as sharp as a surgeon's lancet? Now, here you see young David Copperfield, and the question I put to you is, what shall I do with him?'

"What shall you do with him?" said Mr. Dick, feebly, scratching his head. 'Oh! do with him?'

"Yes," said my aunt, with a grave look, and her forefinger held up. "Come! I want some very sound advice." '

"Why, if I was you," said Mr. Dick, considering, and looking vacantly at me, "I should—" The contemplation of me seemed to inspire him with a sudden idea, and he added, briskly, "I should wash him!"

"Janet," said my aunt, turning round with a quiet triumph, which I did not then understand, "Mr. Dick sets us all right. Heat

"既是这样，那么，"姨婆回答说，这时他听了狄克先生的回答，柔和一点了，"你本来又尖又快，像外科大夫的刀子似的，怎么可又假装着定不住神儿，发起傻来了哪？现在，你瞧，这就是小大卫·科波菲尔。我现在要问你的是：我对他该怎么办才好？"

"你对他该怎么办才好？"狄克先生有气无力地说，同时直挠脑袋。"哦！你对他怎么办才好？"

"不错，"姨婆说，同时样子很严厉地把食指举着。"说！我要你给我出了妥当的主意。"

"啊，我要是你的话，"狄克先生一面琢磨，一面说，同时，茫然弟看着我，"我就——"他这一琢磨我，好像灵机一动，忽然想起一个主意来，所以跟着就急忙地说，"我就给他洗个澡！"

"捷妮，"我姨婆满心得意，而却不动声色（这种情况是我当时还不了解的），转过身去说，"狄克先生说

the bath!"

Although I was deeply interested in this dialogue, I could not help observing my aunt, Mr. Dick, and Janet, while it was in progress, and completing a survey I had already been engaged in making of the room.

My aunt was a tall, hard-featured lady, but by no means ill-looking. There was an inflexibility in her face, in her voice, in her gait and carriage, amply sufficient to account for the effect she had made upon a gentle creature like my mother; but her features were rather handsome than otherwise, though unbending and austere.

I particularly noticed that she had a very quick, bright eye. Her hair, which was grey, was arranged in two plain divisions, under what I believe would be called a mob-cap; I mean a cap, much more common then than now, with side-pieces fastening under the chin. Her dress was of a lavender colour, and perfectly neat; but scantily made, as if she desired to be as little encumbered

得对。烧洗澡水去。"

这番对话，虽然对我关系重大，使我用心细听，但是在对话进行的时候，我还是忍不住要对我姨婆、对狄克先生、对捷妮，观察一番，同时把我在屋里还没看到的情况，补看一下。

姨婆是个身材高大，面目峻厉的老小姐，但是却不难看。她的面容，她的声音，她的举止和体态，都带一种绝不通融、毫不苟且的意味；因此我母亲那样一个柔顺的人，那样怕她，完全可以从这种意味里看出道理来。但是她脸上虽然表示不折不挠，显得凛然森然，她的眉目却生得齐整。

我特别注意到，她的眼睛奕奕有神，犀利明快。她的头发已经苍白了，朴朴实实地分成两半，上面戴着我认为是叫"懒妆头巾"[19]的帽子。我的意思是说，这种帽子，那时很普通，现在却

[19] 懒妆头巾（）通用于十八世纪及十九世纪初年，为妇女家常日间所戴。

as possible. I remember that I thought it, in form, more like a riding-habit with the superfluous skirt cut off, than anything else.

少见了，它的两边，一直搭拉到下巴那儿，有带儿在那儿系着。她的长袍是浅紫色的，非常整洁，但是做得却非常洁净，好像她愿意能多轻便就多轻便才好[20]。我记得，我当时觉得，她的袍子，样子不像别的，只好像是一身骑马的服装，而且把多余的下摆绞掉了。

She wore at her side a gentleman's gold watch, if I might judge from its size and make, with an appropriate chain and seals; she had some linen at her throat not unlike a shirt-collar, and things at her wrists like little shirt-wristbands.

她在腰上戴了一个男人用的金表（我这是根据它的大小和样式作的判断），还带着和它相称的链子和坠子。她脖子上系着一件纱东西，说它像一个衬衫领子，倒还差不离；她在手腕子上戴着像衬衫小袖头的东西。

Mr. Dick, as I have already said, was grey-headed, and florid: I should have said all about him, in saying so, had not his head been curiously bowed—not by age; it reminded me of one of Mr. Creakle's boys' heads after a beating—and his grey eyes prominent and large, with a strange kind of watery brightness in them that made me, in combination with his vacant manner, his submission to my aunt, and his

狄克先生呢，像我已经说过的那样，头发苍白，满面红光。我这样说，本来是可以概括他的全貌的，不过他的头老是很稀奇地有些搭拉着的样子，那并不是由于年纪大的关系。那种情况让我想到撒伦学舍的学童挨了

[20] 这是因维多利亚时代，英国妇女服装，多繁重不便而言。

childish delight when she praised him, suspect him of being a little mad; though, if he were mad, how he came to be there puzzled me extremely.

打以后的样子。同时，他那一双灰色的眼睛，大而凸出，里面奇怪地含有一种水汪汪的亮光；这种情况，再加上他那样恍恍惚惚、愣愣傻傻，他对于我姨婆那样驯服，她夸他的时候他那样和小孩子一样地快乐，这都使我疑心，他这个人，精神可能有些不太正常。不过，如果他真是神经不太正常的话，那他怎么会到我姨婆这儿来了呢，这真叫我非常的纳闷儿。

He was dressed like any other ordinary gentleman, in a loose grey morning coat and waistcoat, and white trousers; and had his watch in his fob, and his money in his pockets: which he rattled as if he were very proud of it.

他的穿戴打扮，和一般的绅士一样，上身是平常白天穿的那种又肥又大的灰褂子和背心，下身是白色的长裤子，表放在裤子上的表袋里，钱放在褂子上的口袋里；他老把钱弄得哗啦哗啦直响，好像他对于钱很得意似的。

Janet was a pretty blooming girl, of about nineteen or twenty, and a perfect picture of neatness. Though I made no further observation of her at the moment, I may mention here what I did not discover until afterwards, namely,

捷妮是一个好看的女孩子，正是容光焕发之际，年纪大约有十九岁或者二十岁，十分干净俏利。我当时虽然没再对她作更进一步的观察，但是有一种情况，我

that she was one of a series of protegees whom my aunt had taken into her service expressly to educate in a renouncement of mankind, and who had generally completed their abjuration by marrying the baker.

可以在这儿说一下，那是我后来才发现的。原来我姨婆曾把一些女孩子，一个接着一个，放在她的保护之下，雇她们做仆人，她的用意分明是要把她们教育得和男人永断纠葛，结果她们总是嫁给了面包师，以了却她们和男人永断纠葛的心愿。捷妮就是这种女孩子中间的一个。

The room was as neat as Janet or my aunt.（8）As I laid down my pen, a moment since, to think of it, the air from the sea came blowing in again, mixed with the perfume of the flowers; and I saw the old-fashioned furniture brightly rubbed and polished, my aunt's inviolable chair and table by the round green fan in the bow-window, the drugget-covered carpet, the cat, the kettle-holder, the two canaries, the old china, the punchbowl full of dried rose-leaves, the tall press guarding all sorts of bottles and pots, and, wonderfully out of keeping with the rest, my dusty self upon the sofa, taking note of everything.

屋子里也和捷妮或者我姨婆同样地干净整齐。我刚才不大的工夫曾把笔放下，想回忆一下当时的情况：那时候，从海上来的微风，还带着花香，又吹进了屋子。我又看见了擦得晶光耀眼的旧式家具，有看见了凸形窗里绿团扇旁我姨婆那把神圣不可侵犯的椅子和那张神圣不可侵犯的桌子，又看见了那个上盖覆毯[21]的地毯，又看见那个猫，那个水壶手垫[22]，那两个金丝鸟儿，那

Janet had gone away to get

[21] 覆毯（drugget）：一种粗毛毯，平日用覆地毯，以防地毯磨损。

[22] 水壶手垫（kettle holder）：用泥、石棉等不传热的材料所作，六英寸见方，至少三层厚。一角有眼儿，可以挂在炉旁，拿水壶时，用它垫手，以免壶把儿烫伤。

the bath ready, when my aunt, to my great alarm, became in one moment rigid with indignation, and had hardly voice to cry out, 'Janet! Donkeys!'

Upon which, Janet came running up the stairs as if the house were in flames, darted out on a little piece of green in front, and warned off two saddle-donkeys, lady-ridden, that had presumed to set hoof upon it; while my aunt, rushing out of the house, seized the bridle of a third animal laden with a bestriding child, turned him, led him forth from those sacred precincts, and boxed the ears of the unlucky urchin in attendance who had dared to profane that hallowed ground.

些老瓷器，那个满装着干玫瑰花瓣的盆吃酒钵[23]，那个满装着各式各样的瓶子和罐子的大橱；同时，我又看见了我自己，满身尘土，和所有这些东西，都特别不协调，躺在沙发上，仔细地观看着一切一切。捷妮给我做洗澡的准备去了，她还没回来的时候，我姨婆忽然使我大吃一惊：她有一会儿的工夫，气得全身发直，几乎都喊不出声来的样子叫道："捷妮！驴！"

捷妮听到这一喊，就好像房子着了火似的，急忙从台阶[24]那儿跑上来，往外冲到房前一块青草地上，那儿有两头驴驮着两个妇人，竟大胆要从那上面过，现在

[23] 盆吃酒（）：普通为烈酒加水、柠檬、糖和香料制成，临时以盆吃酒钵酿之。一度为日常饮料，现只于新年等时，偶一饮之。盆吃酒钵，亦一度为英国家庭必备之物，木制银器，或银制，十七世纪所作，样式精工，故亦为装饰品。贝萃小姐用它盛玫瑰花瓣，表示她不常喝这种酒。

[24]这里的台阶，是地下室通到地面上的台阶。前面第9章里提到"门后面，有几磴台阶"，也是通到地下室的。地下室为厨房所在。

她把这两头驴从那儿赶走了。同时，我姨婆也冲出屋外，把另外驮着一个小孩子那头驴的缰绳抓住了，叫驴转过去，拽着它离开了那块神圣的地方；同时把那个倒霉的赶驴顽童打了一顿耳光，因为他竟敢亵渎了这片神圣的地方。

To this hour I don't know whether my aunt had any lawful right of way over that patch of green; but she had settled it in her own mind that she had, and it was all the same to her. The one great outrage of her life, demanding to be constantly avenged, was the passage of a donkey over that immaculate spot.

一直到现在，我都不知道，我姨婆对于那一片青绿的草地，在法律上是否有任何权利把它算作自己的。不过她自己心里却认定了她有那种权利。这样一来，真有假有，对她说来，完全没有关系。她认为她一生里对她最大的凌辱，经常需要报复的，就是驴在那块纯洁神圣的草地上践踏这件事。

In whatever occupation she was engaged, however interesting to her the conversation in which she was taking part, a donkey turned the current of her ideas in a moment, and she was upon him straight. Jugs of water, and watering-pots, were kept in secret places ready to be discharged on the offending boys; sticks were laid in ambush behind the door;

不管她正做着什么事，也不管她和别人谈得多么兴高采烈，只要一有驴出现，她的思路就马上转变了，她就马上跑了出去，亲自去对付那种畜生。她把盛满了水的罐子和喷壶，放在人看不见的地方，预备好了，往触犯了她的孩子们身上浇，把

sallies were made at all hours; and incessant war prevailed.

Perhaps this was an agreeable excitement to the donkey-boys; or perhaps the more sagacious of the donkeys, understanding how the case stood, delighted with constitutional obstinacy in coming that way.

I only know that there were three alarms before the bath was ready; and that on the occasion of the last and most desperate of all, I saw my aunt engage, single-handed, with a sandy-headed lad of fifteen, and bump his sandy head against her own gate, before he seemed to comprehend what was the matter.

These interruptions were of the more ridiculous to me, because she was giving me broth out of a table-spoon at the time (having firmly persuaded herself that I was actually starving, and must receive nourishment at first in very small quantities), and, while my mouth was yet open to receive the spoon, she would put

棍子放在门后面埋伏着，预备往那种孩子身上打；突然的出击，无时无刻停止；不断的冲突，成为家常便饭。

在那些赶驴的孩子看来，也许这种情况又兴奋，又好玩儿；对那些更懂事的畜生说来，大概它们了解当时的情势，所以就随着它们生来就倔强的天性，偏偏爱往这块青草地上走。

我只知道，洗澡的准备作好以前，就发生了三场冲突。在最后一场，也就是最激烈的一场，我看见我姨婆，和一个十五岁的黄发少年，单人独马交起手来，她把那孩子的头往她的栅栏门上直磕的时候，那孩子好像还没明白是为的什么。

我姨婆那时正在那儿用大匙子喂我喝汤（她坚决地相信，我实实在在地挨了好几天的饿，肠胃很弱，所以不能一开始就吃得太多），我刚张开嘴要接她喂我的东西，还没到口，她就把匙子放回汤碗里，大喊，“捷妮！驴！”同时自己冲出去，和

it back into the basin, cry 'Janet! Donkeys!' and go out to the assault.

人打闹。所以这种搅扰、停顿，在我看来，更觉可笑。

The bath was a great comfort. For I began to be sensible of acute pains in my limbs from lying out in the fields, and was now so tired and low that I could hardly keep myself awake for five minutes together. When I had bathed, they (I mean my aunt and Janet) enrobed me in a shirt and a pair of trousers belonging to Mr. Dick, and tied me up in two or three great shawls. What sort of bundle I looked like, I don't know, but I felt a very hot one. Feeling also very faint and drowsy, I soon lay down on the sofa again and fell asleep.

我洗了个澡，觉得很舒服。因为我曾在田野里睡过觉，身上已经开始觉得，剧烈地痛起来；我那阵儿非常疲乏，非常没有精神，所以叫我的眼睛一连睁五分钟的工夫，都办不到。我洗完了澡以后，她们（我是说我姨婆和捷妮）把狄克先生的一件衬衣和一条裤子给我穿在身上，又用两三个大披肩把我捆扎起来。我当时让她们这样一捆扎，看着像个什么，我现在说不上来；我只觉得，我这样一捆扎，身上非常地热，同时觉得又晕、又困，所以我又在沙发上躺下，一下睡着了。

It might have been a dream, originating in the fancy which had occupied my mind so long, but I awoke with the impression that my aunt had come and bent over me, and had put my hair away from my face, and laid my head more comfortably, and had then stood looking at me. The words, 'Pretty fellow,' or 'Poor fellow,' seemed to be in my ears,

我醒来以后，我有一种印象，觉得仿佛我姨婆，曾来到我跟前，弯着身子，俯在我上面，把我的头发给我从脸上撩开了，把我的头放得更舒服一些，然后站在那儿瞧我。我这种印象，也许只是一场梦，由于我长期的想象而来。我还好像耳边上

too; but certainly there was nothing else, when I awoke, to lead me to believe that they had been uttered by my aunt, who sat in the bow-window gazing at the sea from behind the green fan, which was mounted on a kind of swivel, and turned any way.

听见她说"漂亮的孩子"、"可怜的孩子"这一类话来着。但是我醒来以后，却绝没有任何情况，使我相信，我姨婆说过那些话，因为我只看见她坐在凸形窗前，从绿团扇后面，看着外面的海。那把绿扇是安在一种转轴上的，能朝着任何方向转动。

We dined soon after I awoke, off a roast fowl and a pudding; I sitting at table, not unlike a trussed bird myself, and moving my arms with considerable difficulty. But as my aunt had swathed me up, I made no complaint of being inconvenienced. All this time I was deeply anxious to know what she was going to do with me; but she took her dinner in profound silence, except when she occasionally fixed her eyes on me sitting opposite, and said, 'Mercy upon us!' which did not by any means relieve my anxiety.

我醒了以后不久，我们就吃正餐，吃的是一只烤鸡和一个布丁。其实我那时坐在桌子前面，和一个串扎紧了的鸡[25]并无两样，那即便我觉得有什么不方便，我也决不敢说出来。我坐在桌旁，心里一直都焦灼地想要知道，她要把我怎么办。但是她吃放的时候，却不作一声，只有偶尔的时候，一面把眼睛盯着我（我坐在她对面），一面说一声"我的天！"但是这句话丝毫也不能减少我的焦虑。

The cloth being drawn, and

桌布撤走了，雪里酒放

[25]英国烹调，煮的、烤的或其它做法的鸡等禽类，去毛，去内脏以后，把翅膀和腿，紧扎在身上，从前用铁杵或木扦（skewer）串，现在用粗线缝。

some sherry put upon the table (of which I had a glass), my aunt sent up for Mr. Dick again, who joined us, and looked as wise as he could when she requested him to attend to my story, which she elicited from me, gradually, by a course of questions. During my recital, she kept her eyes on Mr. Dick, who I thought would have gone to sleep but for that, and who, whensoever he lapsed into a smile, was checked by a frown from my aunt.

在桌子上了（我也有一杯），那时候，我姨婆又打发人到楼上去请狄克先生。狄克先生来到楼下，我姨婆告诉他，说她问我话的时候，他可得仔细听；跟着她就问了我一连串的问题，慢慢地把我的情况都套问出来了。狄克先生听的时候，尽力作出明白晓事的样子来。我说我那番遭遇的时候，我姨婆就拿眼盯着狄克先生，要不是那样，我想他早就睡着了；同时，不论多会儿，只要他稍微露出一丁点儿要笑的样子来，我姨婆就把眉头一皱，这样它他就急忙收敛了笑容。

“Whatever possessed that poor unfortunate Baby, that she must go and be married again,” said my aunt, when I had finished, “I can’t conceive.”

“我真不明白，那个可怜的倒霉的娃娃，到底受了什么神差鬼使，偏偏想起来去再嫁一次人！”我说完我的身世以后，我姨婆说。

“Perhaps she fell in love with her second husband,” Mr. Dick suggested.

“那也许是因为她爱上了她第二个丈夫了吧，”狄克先生接着说。

“Fell in love!” repeated my aunt. “What do you mean? What business had she to do it?”

“爱上了！”我姨婆重复说。“你这个话是什么意思？爱上了！那是她应当应

"Perhaps," Mr. Dick simpered, after thinking a little, "she did it for pleasure."

"Pleasure, indeed!" replied my aunt. 'A mighty pleasure for the poor Baby to fix her simple faith upon any dog of a fellow, certain to ill-use her in some way or other. What did she propose to herself, I should like to know! She had had one husband. She had seen David Copperfield out of the world, who was always running after wax dolls from his cradle. She had got a baby—oh, there were a pair of babies when she gave birth to this child sitting here, that Friday night!—and what more did she want?'

Mr. Dick secretly shook his head at me, as if he thought there was no getting over this.

分的吗？"

"也许，"狄克先生想了一想，强作笑容说，"她那时要寻开心吧？"

"寻开心！不错，可就开心啦！"我姨婆回答说。"那个可怜的娃娃，对那样一个狗一般的家伙，对那样一个谁都能看出来非这么那么虐待她不可的家伙，发起痴情来，可就太开心啦。她对自己到底打的什么主意，我真不明白！她已经嫁过一个丈夫了。她已经眼看着大卫·科波菲尔伸了腿了（他从在摇篮里的时候起，就老追蜡油冻的娃娃[26]了）。她也有了孩子了……哦，那个星期五晚上，她生下了坐这儿这个孩子，真可以说是一对娃娃！她还有什么不满足的呢？"

狄克先生偷偷地对我摇了摇头，好像他认为，要叫我姨婆别这样没完没了，是

[26]. 蜡油冻的娃娃：在英语中为美丽而无头脑的女孩子之意。

"She couldn't even have a baby like anybody else," said my aunt. "Where was this child's sister, Betsey Trotwood? Not forthcoming. Don't tell me!"

Mr. Dick seemed quite frightened.

"That little man of a doctor, with his head on one side," said my aunt, "Jellips, or whatever his name was, what was he about? All he could do, was to say to me, like a robin redbreast—as he is—" "It's a boy." A boy! Yah, the imbecility of the whole set of "em!"

The heartiness of the ejaculation startled Mr. Dick exceedingly; and me, too, if I am to tell the truth.

"And then, as if this was not enough, and she had not stood sufficiently in the light of this child's sister, Betsey Trotwood," said my aunt, "she marries a second time—goes and marries a Murderer—or a man with a name like it—and stands in THIS child's light! And the natural

办不到的。

"她连养孩子都和别人不一样，"我姨婆说。"这个孩子的姐姐贝萃特洛乌，在哪儿呀？永远没出世。真是哪儿的事！"

狄克先生好像十分惊吓的样子。

"那个又瘦又小的家伙，那个把脑袋歪在一边的大夫，那个齐利浦，反正不管他叫什么吧，他会什么？什么也不会，就会跟我说，像个红胸鸟[27]一样（一点儿不错，像个红胸鸟），跟我说"是个小子"。小子！呀！那一群东西，没有一个不是白痴！"

这一声突然的猛叫，把狄克先生吓了一大跳，把我也吓了一大跳，如果我得把实话说出来的话。

"这还不算，仿佛这样还不够糟的，仿佛她要把这孩子的姐姐，贝萃特洛乌，还害得不够厉害的，"我姨婆说，"她还要嫁第二次，

[27]红胸鸟性最驯服，不畏人，喜与人亲近。

consequence is, as anybody but a baby might have foreseen, that he prowls and wanders. He's as like Cain before he was grown up, as he can be."

她还要嫁一个"没德性"，真是又没德行，又损——把这个孩子也害了！这样一来，自然而然的结果是，这孩子只好到处自己觅食，到处自己流浪了。其实这种情况，除了一个娃娃，谁都能看出来。现在这个孩子还没长大，就和该隐[28]一模一样了。"

（9）Mr. Dick looked hard at me, as if to identify me in this character.

狄克先生使劲瞧我，好像要仔细认一认，原来我就是这样一个角色。

"And then there's that woman with the Pagan name," said my aunt, "that Peggotty, she goes and gets married next. Because she has not seen enough of the evil attending such things, she goes and gets married next, as the child relates. I only hope," said my aunt, shaking her head, "that her husband is one of those Poker husbands who abound in the newspapers, and will beat her well with one."

"还有那个名字像异教徒的妇人，"我姨婆说，"那个坡勾提，她也跟着嫁人去了。据这孩子说，因为她没有看得够嫁人带来的苦头，她也跟着嫁人去了。我只希望，"我姨婆说，一面摇晃脑袋，"她丈夫是报上老登的那种通条丈夫，老拿通条狠狠地揍她才好。"

I could not bear to hear my old nurse so decried, and made the subject of such a wish. I told my aunt that indeed she was mistaken.

我听了我那个老看妈叫我姨婆这样咒骂，这样糟蹋，就忍不住了。我对姨婆说，她实在错怪了坡勾提了。

[28] 该隐杀死他兄弟亚伯，因而受耶和华的诅咒，永远流离飘荡。见《旧约 创世纪》第 4 章第 1-15 节。

That Peggotty was the best, the truest, the most faithful, most devoted, and most self-denying friend and servant in the world; who had ever loved me dearly, who had ever loved my mother dearly; who had held my mother's dying head upon her arm, on whose face my mother had imprinted her last grateful kiss. And my remembrance of them both, choking me, I broke down as I was trying to say that her home was my home, and that all she had was mine, and that I would have gone to her for shelter, but for her humble station, which made me fear that I might bring some trouble on her—I broke down, I say, as I was trying to say so, and laid my face in my hands upon the table.

我说，坡勾提是世界上最好、最可靠、最实心、最忠心、最能自我牺牲的朋友和仆人。她一直最疼我，她一直疼我母亲；我母亲临死的时候，是她抱着我母亲的头的，我母亲最后感激的吻，是留在她脸上的。我说到这儿，想起我母亲和坡勾提来，就忍不住哽咽，哭起来了；我哽咽难言、勉勉强强地哭着说，她的家就是我的家，她所有的也就是我所有的，我本来想到她那儿去安身，只是因为她家道寒微，我去了，恐怕要给她添麻烦，所以才没去。刚才我说过，我说那些话的时候，忍不住哭起来；我把头趴在桌子上，用手捂着脸哭。

"Well, well!" said my aunt, "the child is right to stand by those who have stood by him—Janet! Donkeys!"

"好啦，好啦，"我姨婆说。"这孩子知道对他忠心的人忠心，很不错。……捷妮！驴！"

I thoroughly believe that but for those unfortunate donkeys, we should have come to a good understanding; for my aunt had laid her hand on my shoulder, and

我绝对相信，如果不是因为不幸有那条驴闯来把我们搅了，那我和我姨婆，一定会非常融洽，言和语顺的；因为我姨婆曾把手放在我的

the impulse was upon me, thus emboldened, to embrace her and beseech her protection.

肩头上来着，而我受到这样鼓励，胆子大起来，也很想把她抱住，求她保护来着。

But the interruption, and the disorder she was thrown into by the struggle outside, put an end to all softer ideas for the present, and kept my aunt indignantly declaiming to Mr. Dick about her determination to appeal for redress to the laws of her country, and to bring actions for trespass against the whole donkey proprietorship of Dover, until tea-time.

但是驴来这一打扰，同时她又去外面和赶驴的争吵起来，可就一时把我姨婆所有的那副软心肠一齐压下去了；那只把她招得老愤怒地对狄克先生嚷嚷，说她决定要诉之法律，把多佛所有养驴的人都告下来，告他们侵犯别人的主权。她就这样一直嚷嚷到吃茶点的时候。

After tea, we sat at the window—on the look-out, as I imagined, from my aunt's sharp expression of face, for more invaders—until dusk, when Janet set candles, and a backgammon-board, on the table, and pulled down the blinds.

吃完了茶点，我们坐在窗前。我看我姨婆脸上那种严厉样子，我就猜想，她守在那儿，为的是好瞧着是不是再有驴来冒犯。直坐到暮色苍茫，那时候，捷妮把蜡点起来放好，拿出一副双陆来，放在桌子上，把窗帘子都放下来。

'Now, Mr. Dick,' said my aunt, with her grave look, and her forefinger up as before, 'I am going to ask you another question. Look at this child.'

"现在，狄克先生，"我姨婆说，同时像上一次一样，脸上带着郑重的样子，食指往上伸着。"我要问你另一个问题。你瞧着这孩子。"

'David's son?' said Mr. Dick, with an attentive, puzzled face.

"大卫的孩子？"狄克先生说，同时脸上显出又注意，

'Exactly so,' returned my aunt. 'What would you do with him, now?'

'Do with David's son?' said Mr. Dick.

'Ay,' replied my aunt, 'with David's son.'

'Oh!' said Mr. Dick. 'Yes. Do with—I should put him to bed.'

'Janet!' cried my aunt, with the same complacent triumph that I had remarked before. 'Mr. Dick sets us all right. If the bed is ready, we'll take him up to it.'

Janet reporting it to be quite ready, I was taken up to it; kindly, but in some sort like a prisoner; my aunt going in front and Janet bringing up the rear. The only circumstance which gave me any new hope, was my aunt's stopping on the stairs to inquire about a smell of fire that was prevalent there; and janet's replying that she had been making tinder down in the kitchen, of my old shirt.

又莫名其妙的样子来。

"一点不错，"我姨婆说。"你现在要把他怎么办？"

"把大卫的孩子怎么办？"狄克先生说。

"不错，"我姨婆回答说，"把大卫的孩子怎么办？"

"哦！"狄克先生说。"是啦。把他怎么……我要叫他去睡觉。"

"捷妮！"我姨婆喊道，喊的时候，带着我前面说的那种同样志得意满而却不动声色的样子。"狄克先生给我们大家指出明路来了。床铺好了没有？铺好了，我们就带他睡觉去。"

捷妮回主人的话，说床早已铺好了；跟着她们就带我上楼。她们带我的时候，态度很温柔，但是方式却有些像押解犯人一样：我姨婆在前面带路，捷妮就在后面押着。只有一种情况，使我生出一种新的希望来：原来我姨婆走到楼梯上面，停了一下，问捷妮为什么到处都是烟味儿；捷妮就说，她把我的衬衣，在下面厨房里，燎成引火的东西了[29]。

But there were no other clothes in my room than the odd heap of things I wore; and when I was left there, with a little taper which my aunt forewarned me would burn exactly five minutes, I heard them lock my door on the outside. Turning these things over in my mind I deemed it possible that my aunt, who could know nothing of me, might suspect I had a habit of running away, and took precautions, on that account, to have me in safe keeping.

但是我的寝室里，却除了我穿的那一堆怪东西而外，再没有别的衣服。她们给我留了一只小蜡，我姨婆还预先警告我，说那支小蜡，只能点五分钟的工夫；说完了她们就走了，把我一个人撂在一那儿。我听见他们在外面把门锁上了。她们为什么锁门呢？我把这种情况在心里面琢磨了一阵，我认为，可能是由于我姨婆，对于我还什么都不知道，疑心我有喜欢逃跑的习惯，所以为了预防，把我锁在屋里，免得我出漏子。

（10）The room was a pleasant one, at the top of the house, overlooking the sea, on which the moon was shining brilliantly. After I had said my prayers, and the candle had burnt out, I remember how I still sat looking at the moonlight on the water, as if I could hope to read my fortune in it, as in a bright book; or to see my mother with her child, coming from Heaven, along that shining path, to look upon me as she had looked when I last saw her

我那个屋子很叫人可心，它坐落在这所房子最高的一层，俯临大海，那时月光正清澈明亮地照在海面上。我记得，当时祷告做完了，蜡也着完了，我仍旧坐在那儿，瞧着海上的月光，有的时候觉得，好像那就

[29] 英国从前的家庭里，把旧布破布，用火燎得要焦而没焦，作为引火物。

sweet face.

I remember how the solemn feeling with which at length I turned my eyes away, yielded to the sensation of gratitude and rest which the sight of the white-curtained bed—and how much more the lying softly down upon it, nestling in the snow-white sheets!—inspired. I remember how I thought of all the solitary places under the night sky where I had slept, and how I prayed that I never might be houseless any more, and never might forget the houseless.I remember how I seemed to float, then, down the melancholy glory of that track upon the sea, away into the world of dreams.

是一本发亮的书，我能从那上面看到我的命运似的，又有的时候就觉得，好像我看到我母亲，怀里抱着婴儿，沿着那条晶明澄澈的路从天上来到，像我最后一次看见她那慈爱的面容那样，往下瞧我。

我记得，我带着肃穆的心情，把眼光从海上转到挂着白帐子的床那儿的时候，我那种庄严之心，怎样一变而为感激之情，安乐之感。至于躺在轻软暖和的床上，盖着雪白的单子，那我的感激之心，安乐之感，就更大了。我记得，我怎样想到所有我夜里睡过的那些寂寞偏僻、一无屏蔽的地方，跟着就祷告，永远可别再受无家可归之苦，同时祷告，永远也别忘了那些无家可归的人。我记得，我祷告完了以后，好像飘飘然沿着海上那道使我黯然的辉光入了睡乡。

# 第七章

# *Wuthering Heights*
# 呼啸山庄

*"Nelly, make me decent, I'm going to be good."*

## 背景介绍

英年早逝总是令人心痛，艾米丽·勃朗特 30 岁去世的时候，说不定也预测到了，很多很多年以后，她唯一的小说《呼啸山庄》会成为一座别人无法逾越的高山，令人仰而望之。她笔下的希克厉（Heathcliff）是一个看似简单却复杂得令人难易琢磨的角色。他集宠爱与憎恨于一身，自己又去宠爱和憎恨他人。他的爱和恨都是高强度 的，具有摧毁性的力量。这种超出常人的力量和他生活的凄厉的荒野融为一体，好像在冰天雪地里却看到滚烫的鲜血一样令人止住呼吸，希腊悲剧 catharsis（净化）的效果在艾米丽 • 勃朗特的小说里实现了。

方平 (1921—2008 年 ) 于 1984 年 12 月 1 日的夜里完成了《呼啸山庄》的翻译工作，他读原著肯定是细读，这种阅读方式把他拉入到了故事里，体会作者不同于一般人的情节设计技巧和人物刻画的力度，他不吐不快，写了一篇长长的译本序。我们则从这篇有名的序里看到了译者的热切和认真，想必他的译本肯定也不错。那么，读读看。

## 细读节选

本书节选了第七章，一个危机四伏的章节。希克厉和卡瑟琳亲密无间的关系就要被迫中断，另一个家族将被卷入冲突，仇恨的种子开始入土并萌芽。叫它命运也罢，叫它机缘也罢，这个捡来的希克厉将在这一章里失去他唯一的知己卡瑟琳。他的倔强和自尊与他的地位很不相符，可是他愿意为了卡瑟琳作出改变，他为她哭泣，为她挨打。卡瑟琳则受了现实的诱惑，无意中要抛却她对希克厉的信仰，真是一个无情的女子呀。果真如此吗？两小无猜的日子结束了。我们一起来经历这永远不会消失的心痛吧。

## 拓展思考

1. 凭借记忆，写出 3 句划线的原文与译文。

| 原文 | 译文 |
|---|---|
| | |
| | |
| | |

2. 你能说出希克厉的心里话吗？

3. 卡茜对希克厉的感情是怎么表达出来的？

4. 如果你是希克厉，你会打算复仇吗？

# Chapter vii

# 第七章

Cathy stayed at Thrushcross Grange five weeks: till Christmas. By that time her ankle was thoroughly cured, and her manners much improved. The mistress visited her often in the interval, and commenced her plan of reform by trying to raise her self-respect with fine clothes and flattery, which she took readily; so that, instead of a wild, hatless little savage jumping into the house, and rushing to squeeze us all breathless, there 'lighted from a handsome black pony a very dignified person, with brown ringlets falling from the cover of a feathered beaver, and a long cloth habit, which she was obliged to hold up with both hands that she might sail in.

卡茜在画眉山庄一住五个礼拜，直到圣诞节。这时候她的脚脖子完全好了，举止也文雅多了。在这段时间里，女主人经常去探望她，而且着手实现改造她的计划，那就是用漂亮的衣裳和殷勤的奉承来抬高她的自尊心；她果然乖乖地接受了。所以她回家那天，并不是一个粗野的披头散发的小蛮子一下子跳进宅子，冲过来把我们紧紧地拥抱得透不过气来；却只见从一头漂亮的小黑马上跳下来一位好大气派的贵人儿，头戴一顶插羽毛的海狸皮帽，棕色的鬈发从帽檐下挂下来，穿的是一身长长的布骑服，她的双手提起了裙子，才一步三摇地走进来。

Hindley lifted her from her horse, exclaiming delightedly, "Why, Cathy, you are quite a

亨德莱把她从马背上扶下来的时候，高兴地喊了起来："嗨，卡茜，你可真是

beauty! I should scarcely have known you: you look like a lady now. Isabella Linton is not to be compared with her, is she, Frances?"

"Isabella has not her natural advantages," replied his wife: "but she must mind and not grow wild again here. Ellen, help Miss Catherine off with her things—Stay, dear, you will disarrange your curls—let me untie your hat."

I removed the habit, and there shone forth beneath a grand plaid silk frock, white trousers, and burnished shoes; and, while her eyes sparkled joyfully when the dogs came bounding up to welcome her, she dared hardly touch them lest they should fawn upon her splendid garments.

She kissed me gently: I was all flour making the Christmas cake, and it would not have done to give me a hug; and then she looked round for Heathcliff. Mr. and Mrs. Earnshaw watched anxiously their meeting; thinking it would enable them to judge,

个美人儿！我差点儿认不得你了。瞧你，这才是位千金小姐呀。伊莎蓓拉 林敦哪儿能跟她比呢，可不是吗，法兰茜丝？"

"伊莎蓓拉可比不上她长得那么俊俏，"做妻子的回答道，"可是她得记住，不能回到家里又变野了。爱伦，帮卡瑟琳小姐把衣帽脱下来，别走动，心肝儿，你会把鬈发儿碰坏了，让我来给你解开帽子的带儿吧。"

我替她把骑服脱去之后，眼前顿时一亮，在一身出色的方格丝袍底下，闪现出白裤子和发亮的皮鞋。她一双眸子闪烁着快乐的光芒。这时候家里的狗扑过来欢迎她，她简直不敢去碰它们，怕它们会跳到身上来弄脏她簇新的好衣裳。

她轻轻地吻我一下；我正在做圣诞节的蛋糕，一身都是面粉，假如跟我来个拥抱，会成什么样儿呢？接着她把头转来转去，要找希克厉。欧肖先生和他的太太很焦急地在一边注视着，因为

in some measure, what grounds they had for hoping to succeed in separating the two friends.

从这两个人见面的情形，他们认为大致可以看出他们想拆开这一对朋友究竟有多大把握了。

Heathcliff was hard to discover, at first. (1) If he were careless, and uncared for, before Catherine's absence, he had been ten times more so since.

一下子还真难找到希克厉。如果说，卡瑟琳还没有住到林顿家去之前，他不成个体统，也没人照顾；那么从这以后，更是十倍地糟糕。

Nobody but I even did him the kindness to call him a dirty boy, and bid him wash himself, once a week; and children of his age seldom have a natural pleasure in soap and water. Therefore, not to mention his clothes, which had seen three months' service in mire and dust, and his thick uncombed hair, the surface of his face and hands was dismally beclouded.

除了我，再没有人理睬他，甚至在一个礼拜中，没人肯行个好，骂他一声脏孩子，叫他去洗洗干净。像他这样大的孩子，对于肥皂和清水原本不会有多大好感的；所以也不提他的衣服——那是穿了三个月，泥里滚过，灰里爬过，也不提那常年不梳，一头浓密的乱发，就是他那蒙上一层乌光的脸儿和手儿，也够瞧了。

He might well skulk behind the settle, on beholding such a bright, graceful damsel enter the house, instead of a rough-headed counterpart of himself, as he expected.

算他做得有道理，他一看见宅子里进来这么一位娇艳优雅的闺秀，而不是他期望中的蓬头垢面，可以跟他配对的同伴，就躲到长靠背椅子后面去了。

"Is Heathcliff not here?" she demanded, pulling off her gloves,

"希克厉不在这儿吗？"她问道，把手套脱了下来，

and displaying fingers wonderfully whitened with doing nothing and staying indoors.

露出来好白好白的手指儿，那是因为成天呆在室内，又不干活的缘故。

“Heathcliff, you may come forward,” cried Mr. Hindley, enjoying his discomfiture, and gratified to see what a forbidding young blackguard he would be compelled to present himself. “You may come and wish Miss Catherine welcome, like the other servants.”

“希克厉，你走过来好了，”亨德莱嚷道，瞧着他那种狼狈的样子，心里好不得意，他就是要叫他硬着头皮走出来现眼——原来他是这么一个叫人作呕的小下流胚。“你可以过来向卡瑟琳小姐表示欢迎，跟别的仆人一样。”

Cathy, catching a glimpse of her friend in his concealment, flew to embrace him; she bestowed seven or eight kisses on his cheek within the second, and then stopped, and drawing back, burst into a laugh, exclaiming,

卡茜一眼瞅见她的朋友躲在什么地方，便飞快地奔去跟他拥抱，一口气在他脸上连亲了七八个吻，这才停下来，倒退了一步，迸出来笑声，嚷道：

“Why, how very black and cross you look! and how—how funny and grim! But that’s because I’m used to Edgar and Isabella Linton. Well, Heathcliff, have you forgotten me?”

“哎呀，瞧你，多黑，多别扭呀，还多么——多么好笑，脸子绷得多紧呀！不过那是因为我看惯了埃德加，伊莎蓓拉 林顿。得啦，希克厉，你可把我忘了吧？”

She had some reason to put the question, for shame and pride threw double gloom over his countenance, and kept him immovable.

她这话不是问得没理由的，原来羞愧和自尊心在他脸上笼罩了双重阴云，叫他纹丝不动。

“Shake hands, Heathcliff,’ said

“握握手吧，希克厉，”

Mr. Earnshaw, condescendingly; "once in a way that is permitted."

"I shall not," replied the boy, finding his tongue at last; (2) "I shall not stand to be laughed at. I shall not bear it!" And he would have broken from the circle, but Miss Cathy seized him again.

"I did not mean to laugh at you," she said; "I could not hinder myself: Heathcliff, shake hands at least! What are you sulky for? It was only that you looked odd. If you wash your face and brush your hair, it will be all right: but you are so dirty!"

She gazed concernedly at the dusky fingers she held in her own, and also at her dress; which she feared had gained no embellishment from its contact with his.

"You needn"t have touched me!' he answered, following her eye and snatching away his hand. (3) "I shall be as dirty as I please: and I like to be dirty, and I will be dirty."

With that he dashed headforemost out of the room, amid the merriment of the master and

欧肖装得宽大为怀地说道，“偶尔一次是允许的。”

“我才不能，”那孩子总算开了口，说了话，“我不能让人当做笑话，我受不了这个。”他当真要从一圈人中间直冲出去，但是卡茜又把他捉住了。

“我并没有意思想笑你呀，”她说道，“我是不由自主地笑了起来呀。希克厉，至少也得握一握手！你恼的是什么呢？那只是你看起来有点怪罢了。只要你洗个脸，梳梳头，那就完全可以了；可是你真脏！”

她很关心地瞧着握在她手里的那几只黑手指儿，还看了看自己那身衣服，担心他的手指儿会给它添上什么并不美观的花纹。

“你不用来碰我！”他跟着她的眼光看，回答道，又一下子把手抽了回来。“我爱多脏就多脏，我高兴脏，我就要脏！”

这么表白之后，他就把头一低，直向室外冲去，真让东家和东家娘心花怒放，

mistress, and to the serious disturbance of Catherine; who could not comprehend how her remarks should have produced such an exhibition of bad temper.

可叫卡瑟琳心慌意乱，不知该怎样才好。她想不通为什么她这句话会惹得他发那么大的脾气。

After playing lady's-maid to the new-comer, and putting my cakes in the oven, and making the house and kitchen cheerful with great fires, befitting Christmas-eve, I prepared to sit down and amuse myself by singing carols, all alone; regardless of Joseph's affirmations that he considered the merry tunes I chose as next door to songs.

我伺候过了这位新到的贵人儿，又把蛋糕放进了烘炉，生起了熊熊的炉火，给正屋和厨房增添生气，显出一派圣诞节前夕的光景；这之后，我就准备坐下，独个儿唱几只圣歌，让自己高兴高兴，不管约瑟夫认定，我选的那几只欢乐的圣歌简直就是小曲儿了。

He had retired to private prayer in his chamber, and Mr. and Mrs. Earnshaw were engaging Missy's attention by sundry gay trifles bought for her to present to the little Lintons, as an acknowledgment of their kindness.

他已回到自己房中独个儿做祷告去了；而欧肖夫妇正逗着卡茜看各种各样的小玩意儿，那是替她买来，准备送给林顿家的两个孩子，算是表示一点谢意。

They had invited them to spend the morrow at Wuthering Heights, and the invitation had been accepted, on one condition: Mrs. Linton begged that her darlings might be kept carefully apart from that "naughty swearing boy."

他们还约了小兄妹两个明天到呼啸山庄来玩，这个邀请他们接受了，不过有一个条件；林顿太太拜托欧肖家费心，别让她的一对宝贝接触到那个“赌神罚咒的坏孩子”。

Under these circumstances I remained solitary. I smelt the

大家都忙自己的事儿，于是就只剩我一个人在那

rich scent of the heating spices; and admired the shining kitchen utensils, the polished clock, decked in holly, the silver mugs ranged on a tray ready to be filled with mulled ale for supper; and above all, the speckless purity of my particular care—the scoured and well-swept floor.

I gave due inward applause to every object, and then I remembered how old Earnshaw used to come in when all was tidied, and call me a cant lass, and slip a shilling into my hand as a Christmas-box; and from that I went on to think of his fondness for Heathcliff, and his dread lest he should suffer neglect after death had removed him: and that naturally led me to consider the poor lad's situation now, and from singing I changed my mind to crying. It struck me soon, however, there would be more sense in endeavouring to repair some of his wrongs than shedding tears over them: I got up and walked into the court to seek him.

He was not far; I found him

儿。我闻到烧热了的香料发出一股浓郁的香味，一边儿欣赏那些擦得亮光光的厨房里的器皿，那用冬青装饰、上了蜡的钟，那些摆好在盘子里的银杯子、只等吃晚饭时拿来盛加香料的麦酒；尤其让我得意的是那一片儿无可挑剔的干干净净——我特别出力洗刷、打扫过的地板。

我为每样东西在暗地里喝一声好，于是我记起在从前，一切都收拾整齐之后，老欧肖总会走进来夸我是个好姑娘，拿一个先令塞进我手里，算是圣诞节的礼。从来我又想到了他对希克厉的宠爱来，想到他老是担心，只怕他死了之后再没人照顾那孩子了；这样我自然又不免想到那可怜的孩子眼前的处境了。我本来在唱歌，唱着唱着，我忽然要哭起来了。不过我随即想到，为他洒泪，还不如想办法帮他减轻些他所受的委屈来得有意义呢。我站起身来，到院子里去找他。

果然，他就在不多远的

smoothing the glossy coat of the new pony in the stable, and feeding the other beasts, according to custom.

“Make haste, Heathcliff!” I said, “the kitchen is so comfortable; and Joseph is up-stairs: make haste, and let me dress you smart before Miss Cathy comes out, and then you can sit together, with the whole hearth to yourselves, and have a long chatter till bedtime.”

He proceeded with his task, and never turned his head towards me.

“Come—are you coming?” I continued. “There’s a little cake for each of you, nearly enough; and you’ll need half-an-hours donning.”

I waited five minutes, but getting no answer left him. Catherine supped with her brother and sister-in-law: Joseph and I joined at an unsociable meal, seasoned with reproofs on one side and sauciness on the other. His cake and cheese remained on the table all night for the fairies. He managed to continue work till nine o’clock, and then marched dumb

地方。我看见他正在马房里给一匹新来的小马刷平它那身光洁的毛头，又在喂别的牲口，这原是他的日常工作。

“快些儿，希克厉！”我说道；“厨房里可舒服呢，约瑟夫又正在楼上。快些儿，趁卡茜小姐出来之前，让我替你打扮得整整齐齐，你们两个可以坐在一块儿，整个炉火归你们俩受用，你们畅畅快快地谈心，直到上床睡觉的时候。”

他只管干他的活儿，连头都不朝我转一下。

“来吧！……你来不来呀？”我把话说下去道，“我给你们每人留着一小块蛋糕，差不多够吃了；你总得要半小时的打扮呢。”

我等了他五分钟也没得到他的回话，就舍下他走了。卡瑟琳跟她的哥哥嫂嫂一起吃晚饭。约瑟夫跟我一起吃了一顿不愉快的饭，点缀着他那方面的训斥和我这方面的毫不相让。他的一份蛋糕和干酪都留在桌子上，让半夜里仙人来享受。他这摸摸

and dour to his chamber.

Cathy sat up late, having a world of things to order for the reception of her new friends: she came into the kitchen once to speak to her old one; but he was gone, and she only stayed to ask what was the matter with him, and then went back.

In the morning he rose early; and, as it was a holiday, carried his ill-humour on to the moors; not re-appearing till the family were departed for church. (4) Fasting and reflection seemed to have brought him to a better spirit. He hung about me for a while, and having screwed up his courage, exclaimed abruptly—

"Nelly, make me decent, I'm going to be good."

"High time, Heathcliff," I said; "you have grieved Catherine: she's sorry she ever came home, I daresay! It looks as if you envied her, because she is more thought of than you."

The notion of envying Catherine was incomprehensible to

那摸摸地干到了九点钟，于是一言不发、板着脸儿、迈着大步回房去了。

卡茜睡得很迟，为了招待她的新朋友，她有数不清的事儿要吩咐呢。她到厨房来了一次，找她的老朋友谈天；可是他已经走了，她只问了一声他到底怎么啦，便又回到客室里去了。

第二天早晨，他一早就起身；这一天是节日，他却带着一肚子坏脾气独个儿到原野去；直到一家人都上教堂里去了，他才回来。空空的肚子，沉甸甸的心事，似乎叫他的火气也退了些。他在我面前转了一阵之后，突然鼓足勇气，这样宣布道：

"纳莉，把我收拾得像样些，我要学好了。"

"正是时候了，希克厉，"我说道；"你呀，已经伤了卡瑟琳的心啦。她真后悔她回家来，我敢这么说！看样子你像是在妒忌她，只因为人家理会她，就不理会你。"

"妒忌"卡瑟琳，这观念他可没法理解，但是什么

him, but the notion of grieving her he understood clearly enough.

"Did she say she was grieved?" he inquired, looking very serious.

"She cried when I told her you were off again this morning."

"Well, I cried last night," he returned, "and I had more reason to cry than she"

"Yes: you had the reason of going to bed with a proud heart and an empty stomach," said I. 'Proud people breed sad sorrows for themselves. But, if you be ashamed of your touchiness, you must ask pardon, mind, when she comes in. You must go up and offer to kiss her, and say—you know best what to say; only do it heartily, and not as if you thought her converted into a stranger by her grand dress.

And now, though I have dinner to get ready, I'll steal time to arrange you so that Edgar Linton shall look quite a doll beside you: and that he does. You are young-

叫伤了她的心，这回事他是很明白的。

"她说过她伤了心吗？"他盘问道，很认真的样子。

"她哭了，当我告诉她，今天早晨你又不知道到哪儿去了。"

"好吧，我是昨晚上哭的，"他回答道，"而我比她哭得更有理由。"

"不错，你有理由带着你那颗骄傲的心和一个空肚子上床睡觉去，"我说道，"骄傲的人替自己带来烦恼和痛苦。你昨天无缘无故地闹别扭，假使你自己也觉得不好意思的话，那听着，等她回来的时候，你得向她赔个不是。你得上前去跟她亲个吻，就这么说一该怎么说……你一定最清楚不过，只是要说得亲亲热热的；不要看到她穿上了漂亮的衣裳，就当作她已经变成了陌生人。

这会儿我要做饭去了，不过我还是可以抽工夫来替你收拾，保管叫埃德加 林顿跟你一比，成了个洋娃娃——其

er, and yet, I'll be bound, you are taller and twice as broad across the shoulders; you could knock him down in a twinkling; don't you feel that you could?'

实他也真像。你年纪比他小，可是我敢担保，你长得比他高，有他两个肩膀阔。你一眨眼就能把他打倒了。你觉得你有这本领吗？”

Heathcliff's face brightened a moment; then it was overcast afresh, and he sighed.

希克厉的脸儿亮了一下，可是随即又笼罩上一层乌云，他叹了口气。

"But, Nelly, if I knocked him down twenty times, that wouldn't make him less handsome or me more so. I wish I had light hair and a fair skin, and was dressed and behaved as well, and had a chance of being as rich as he will be!"

“可是，纳莉，就算我打倒他二十次也没用呀，他不会变得难看，我也不会变得好看起来呀。我恨不得也有淡淡的头发，白白的皮肤，穿着好衣裳，又懂那一套礼节，而且就像他那样，将来会有很多的钱。”

"And cried for mamma at every turn," I added, "and trembled if a country lad heaved his fist against you, and sat at home all day for a shower of rain.

“还要碰一碰就直叫妈妈，”我接过来说道，“只要村里的孩子像你扬一扬拳头，就吓得直发抖；老天下一阵骤雨就在家里待一整天。

Oh, Heathcliff, you are showing a poor spirit! Come to the glass, and I'll let you see what you should wish. Do you mark those two lines between your eyes; and those thick brows, that, instead of rising arched, sink in the middle; and that couple of black fiends, so deeply buried, who never open their windows

噢，希克厉，你这话真泄气！来找找镜子，我要叫你看到你应该希望的是什么。你看到了吗，那横在鼻梁上的两道皱纹？还有，那两条浓浓的眉毛？人家是往上拱起的，你可是在中间往下陷；还有，那一对深深嵌

boldly, but lurk glinting under them, like devil's spies?

在里面的黑小鬼，从不曾看到它们痛痛快快地把“窗子”打开过，却总是悄悄地在里面一闪一闪地溜来溜去，像是魔鬼的探子。

Wish and learn to smooth away the surly wrinkles, to raise your lids frankly, and change the fiends to confident, innocent angels, suspecting and doubting nothing, and always seeing friends where they are not sure of foes.

你希望把这些阴沉沉的皱纹除掉吧，学会坦率地抬起你的眼皮吧；让一对小魔鬼变成信任的、纯洁的小天使吧，一点也不懂得疑神疑鬼；如果不能断定对方是仇敌，就把他当成朋友看吧。

（5）Don't get the expression of a vicious cur that appears to know the kicks it gets are its desert, and yet hates all the world, as well as the kicker, for what it suffers.'

别学恶狗的那种神气，明知道它挨这几下踢一点都不冤枉，可是因为自己吃了亏，不但恨那踢它的人，而且对整个世界都怀恨在心了。”

"In other words, I must wish for Edgar Linton's great blue eyes and even forehead," he replied. "I do—and that won't help me to them."

“换句话说，我得希望长着埃德加·林顿的那双蓝蓝的大眼睛和他的光滑的额头，”他回答道，“我是希望的，可是有什么用呢？”

"A good heart will help you to a bonny face, my lad," I continued, "if you were a regular black; and a bad one will turn the bonniest into something worse than ugly. And now that we've done washing, and combing, and sulk-

“只要心地好，相貌自然会变得好，我的孩子，”我接着说，“哪怕你是个地地道道的黑鬼。心地不好，就算你长着最漂亮的面孔，也会变得比丑还要遭！得啦，现

ing—tell me whether you don't think yourself rather handsome?

I'll tell you, I do. You're fit for a prince in disguise. Who knows but your father was Emperor of China, and your mother an Indian queen, each of them able to buy up, with one week's income, Wuthering Heights and Thrushcross Grange together? And you were kidnapped by wicked sailors and brought to England. (6) Were I in your place, I would frame high notions of my birth; and the thoughts of what I was should give me courage and dignity to support the oppressions of a little farmer!"

So I chattered on; and Heathcliff gradually lost his frown and began to look quite pleasant, when all at once our conversation was interrupted by a rumbling sound moving up the road and entering the court.

He ran to the window and I to the door, just in time to behold the two Lintons descend from the family carriage, smothered in cloaks and furs, and the Earnshaws dis-

在脸也洗了，头也梳了，脾气也发过了，告诉我，你觉得自个儿很漂亮吗？

对你说吧，我就这么想呢。说你是一个王子也并不过分，谁知道你的爸爸不是中国的皇帝，你的妈妈不是印度的女王呢？他们每个人一星期的收入，就可以把呼啸山庄连同画眉山庄一起买下来啊。你是给坏心眼儿的水手拐到英国来的呀。要是换了我，我可要把自己的出身往高处想；我想到了我本是谁的时候，我还怕没有勇气和尊严来对付那个小小的庄稼汉的压迫吗？”

我就这么唠叨个没完，希克厉的眉心慢慢儿解开了，神情变得很高兴了。正在这个时候，只听得辚辚的车声从路那边传过来，进入了院子。那一阵车声把我们的谈话打断了。

他奔到窗边，我赶到门口，正好看到林顿兄妹俩从家庭马车里跨下来，都是大衣皮袄裹得紧紧的；欧肖一家人从马背上跳下来。冬天

mount from their horses: they often rode to church in winter. Catherine took a hand of each of the children, and brought them into the house and set them before the fire, which quickly put colour into their white faces.

里，他们多半骑着马儿上礼拜堂。卡瑟琳一手拉着一个孩子，把他们带进宅子，安排他们坐在壁炉前。一会儿，那两张白白的脸泛起了红意。

I urged my companion to hasten now and show his amiable humour, and he willingly obeyed; but ill luck would have it that, as he opened the door leading from the kitchen on one side, Hindley opened it on the other.

我怂恿我的伙伴赶快出去，让大家瞧瞧他开眼开眉的样子，他高高兴兴地听从了我的话。谁知道偏有这样倒霉的事，他刚好打开厨房这一边的门，那一边亨德莱也开门进来了。

They met, and the master, irritated at seeing him clean and cheerful, or, perhaps, eager to keep his promise to Mrs. Linton, shoved him back with a sudden thrust, and angrily bade Joseph "keep the fellow out of the room—send him into the garret till dinner is over. He'll be cramming his fingers in the tarts and stealing the fruit, if left alone with them a minute."

两人撞见了。东家看见他收拾的干干净净，又高高兴兴，反而生气起来。也许呢，他是一心要做到答应了林顿夫人的话。他伸手一推，把他猛地推了回去，还怒气冲冲地吩咐约瑟夫道："不许这家伙闯进房间来，把他送到阁楼去，等吃过了晚饭，再放他下来。他会伸手去乱抓糕饼，还偷水果吃，只要有一会儿旁边没有人看住他。"

"Nay, sir," I could not avoid answering, "he'll touch nothing,

"不会的，先生，"我忍不住替他说话，"他什么都不会碰的，他不会的呀；我

not he: and I suppose he must have his share of the dainties as well as we."

"He shall have his share of my hand, if I catch him downstairs till dark," cried Hindley. "Begone, you vagabond! What! you are attempting the coxcomb, are you? Wait till I get hold of those elegant locks—see if I won't pull them a bit longer!"

"They are long enough already," observed Master Linton, peeping from the doorway; "I wonder they don't make his head ache. It's like a colt's mane over his eyes!"

He ventured this remark without any intention to insult; but Heathcliff's violent nature was not prepared to endure the appearance of impertinence from one whom he seemed to hate, even then, as a rival. He seized a tureen of hot apple sauce (the first thing that came under his gripe) and dashed it full against the speaker's face and neck; who instantly commenced a lament that brought Isabella and Catherine hurrying to the place.

Mr. Earnshaw snatched up the

想他也跟我们一样，该有他自己的一份糕点吧。"

"请他吃我一个巴掌吧，要是天还没黑，让我在楼下又撞见了他，"亨德莱嚷道。"滚开，你这个流氓！怎么！你想打扮成公子哥儿啦，不是吗？等着吧，等我一把抓住你那好文雅的鬈发儿，看我不把它拉得长长的！"

"不拉也够长啦，"小少爷林顿从门口往里张望说，"我倒不懂，这一头头发没叫他害头疼。就像小马的马鬃那样披在他的眼睛上！"

他巴巴儿地插进这句话来，本没有侮辱的意思；可是希克厉的火爆的性子却容不得旁人有半点取笑他，何况即使在当时，他已经差不多把对方当作情敌一样仇恨了。他拿起一盆热热的苹果酱汁（他顺手抓到的第一件东西），对准对方的脸上、脖子上泼去。那孩子顿时哇的一声哭了起来，闹得伊莎蓓拉和卡瑟琳急忙赶了来。

欧肖先生当场抓住他，

culprit directly and conveyed him to his chamber; where, doubtless, he administered a rough remedy to cool the fit of passion, for he appeared red and breathless. I got the dishcloth, and rather spitefully scrubbed Edgar's nose and mouth, affirming it served him right for meddling. His sister began weeping to go home, and Cathy stood by confounded, blushing for all.

把他押到自己的房中去；不用问，到了那里，施出强硬的手段来镇压他那股蛮横劲儿，因为他回来的时候，脸色通红，气都喘不过来。我拿起一块擦碟子的布，没好气地给埃德加擦鼻子、擦嘴巴，明白跟他说，活该这样，谁叫他多嘴。他的妹妹哭着要回去了。卡茜站在一旁，不知该怎样才好，这一切叫她脸红。

"You should not have spoken to him!" she expostulated with Master Linton. "He was in a bad temper, and now you've spoilt your visit; and he'll be flogged: I hate him to be flogged! I can't eat my dinner. Why did you speak to him, Edgar?"

"你就不该跟他说话！"她埋怨小少爷林顿道。"正好碰在他脾气不好的当儿；这一下，你这次做客可扫兴了。他又得挨鞭子啦，我最恨他给拖去挨鞭子！我吃不下饭了。你干吗要跟他说话呀，埃德加？"

"I didn't," sobbed the youth, escaping from my hands, and finishing the remainder of the purification with his cambric pocket-handkerchief. "I promised mamma that I wouldn't say one word to him, and I didn't."

"我不曾呀，"那小伙子抽抽噎噎地说，从我的手里逃了出来，掏出白麻手绢，把还没擦到的地方自己擦干净了。"我答应妈妈不跟他说一句话，我就不曾跟他说话。"

"Well, don't cry," replied Catherine, contemptuously; "you're not killed. Don't make more mischief; my brother is

"得啦，别哭啦，"卡瑟琳轻蔑地回答道，"你又没给人杀死。别再招惹麻烦

coming: be quiet! Hush, Isabella! Has anybody hurt you?"

了。我哥哥来了，安静些吧！别开口，伊莎蓓拉！有什么人碰了你没有？"

"There, there, children—to your seats!" cried Hindley, bustling in. "That brute of a lad has warmed me nicely. Next time, Master Edgar, take the law into your own fists—it will give you an appetite!"

"好啦，好啦，孩子们；到你们的座位上去吧！"亨德莱急匆匆地走进来嚷道。"那个小畜生叫我的手脚暖和了许多。下一次，埃德加少爷，你用自己的拳头来执行王法好了，这会让你开胃的！"

（7）The little party recovered its equanimity at sight of the fragrant feast. They were hungry after their ride, and easily consoled, since no real harm had befallen them.

香味扑鼻的筵席一摆出来，这小小宴会中的几个人把气恼全忘了。他们从礼拜堂骑马乘车赶来，肚子都饿了，因此吃起来格外香，何况他们又并没有真发生什么了不起的事儿。

Mr. Earnshaw carved bountiful platefuls, and the mistress made them merry with lively talk. I waited behind her chair, and was pained to behold Catherine, with dry eyes and an indifferent air, commence cutting up the wing of a goose before her.

欧肖先生在席上割鸡分肉，替每个人装了满满一盘；女主人谈笑风生，逗得大家非常高兴。我在她的椅子后面伺候着，看见卡瑟琳眼膛干干的，满不在乎地开始切她面前的鹅翅膀，我感到痛心，

"An unfeeling child," I thought to myself; "how lightly she dismisses her old playmate's troubles. I could not have imagined her to be so selfish."

"好没有情义的孩子呀，"我私下想到；"她的老朋友正在吃苦头，她却已经一下子想不起来啦。我真想

She lifted a mouthful to her lips: then she set it down again: her cheeks flushed, and the tears gushed over them. She slipped her fork to the floor, and hastily dived under the cloth to conceal her emotion. I did not call her unfeeling long; for I perceived she was in purgatory throughout the day, and wearying to find an opportunity of getting by herself, or paying a visit to Heathcliff, who had been locked up by the master: as I discovered, on endeavouring to introduce to him a private mess of victuals.

In the evening we had a dance. Cathy begged that he might be liberated then, as Isabella Linton had no partner: her entreaties were vain, and I was appointed to supply the deficiency.

We got rid of all gloom in the excitement of the exercise, and our pleasure was increased by the arrival of the Gimmerton band, mustering fifteen strong: a trumpet, a trombone, clarionets, bassoons, French horns, and a bass viol, besides singers. They go the rounds of all the respectable

不到那会那么自私。”

她把满满一叉举到了嘴边，可是又放了下来；她的脸蛋儿红了，有两颗泪珠从眼眶里滚了下来。她失手把叉掉到了地板上，便急忙钻到台布底下掩藏她内心的感情。我也并没有一直把她称作没有情义的，因为不久我就看出来，她一整天都在活受罪，苦苦地想找一个脱身的机会，独个儿待着，或是去探望一下希克厉，他被主人锁在房里，这是后来我在想法送些东西给他吃的时候发觉的。

到晚上，我们举行了一个舞会。卡茜为他求情：把他放出来吧，因为伊莎蓓拉没有舞伴；可是没有得到允许。东家指派我顶这个缺。

在兴奋地跳啊蹦啊的当儿，大家把一切烦恼都抛了。等到吉牟屯的乐队来到时，我们的劲头儿更高了。那个乐队拥有十五人之多——一个小喇叭，一个长号，高音和低音单簧管、大管、圆号，一个低音大提

houses, and receive contributions every Christmas, and we esteemed it a first-rate treat to hear them.

琴，还加上一组歌手。凡是体面的人家，他们都去巡回演奏过，每逢圣诞节便受收受一些捐款；我们认为能够听他们的演奏真是了不起的享受呢。

After the usual carols had been sung, we set them to songs and glees. Mrs. Earnshaw loved the music, and so they gave us plenty.

在照例演奏了几曲圣诞欢颂之后，我们便要他们演唱民歌和无伴奏重唱曲。欧肖太太很喜欢音乐，所以他们为我们演唱了一个又一个节目。

Catherine loved it too: but she said it sounded sweetest at the top of the steps, and she went up in the dark: I followed. They shut the house door below, never noting our absence, it was so full of people. She made no stay at the stairs'head, but mounted farther, to the garret where Heathcliff was confined, and called him. He stubbornly declined answering for a while: she persevered, and finally persuaded him to hold communion with her through the boards.

卡瑟琳也是喜欢音乐的，可是她说，如果在楼梯顶端听来，那才美到极点呢；所以她就在黑暗中上了楼。我跟在后面。他们在底下把大厅的门儿关了，根本不曾理会到溜走了两个人，那里挤满了那么多人。她到了楼梯头并不停步，却只顾往上爬，只爬到希克厉被禁闭着的阁楼上。她在门外叫他，起先他硬是不搭理；她只管一声声叫，最后终于叫他回心转意，隔着板壁跟她说话。

I let the poor things converse unmolested, till I supposed the

我由着这两个可怜的小东西谈心，不去打扰他们。

songs were going to cease, and the singers to get some refreshment: then I clambered up the ladder to warn her.

Instead of finding her outside, I heard her voice within. The little monkey had crept by the skylight of one garret, along the roof, into the skylight of the other, and it was with the utmost difficulty I could coax her out again.

When she did come, Heathcliff came with her, and she insisted that I should take him into the kitchen, as my fellow-servant had gone to a neighbour's, to be removed from the sound of our 'devil's psalmody,' as it pleased him to call it. I told them I intended by no means to encourage their tricks: but as the prisoner had never broken his fast since yesterday's dinner, I would wink at his cheating Mr. Hindley that once.

He went down: I set him a stool by the fire, and offered him a quantity of good things: but he was sick and could eat little, and my attempts to entertain him were thrown away. He leant his two elbows on his knees, and his chin

直到我认为歌唱快要停止，歌手要吃茶点了，这才爬上楼去催促她。

可是不见了她这人，只听得她的声音从房里传出来。这小猴子先从一个阁楼的天窗爬到了屋顶上，再从另一个天窗爬进那个阁楼去了。我好容易才算把她哄了出来。

她走出来，希克厉也跟着出来了。她逼着我一定要把他领到厨房里去。好在我那位“同事”已到邻居家去了，说是可以让耳根清静些，免得听我们那种“魔鬼的赞美诗”（他就是这么说的）；我就跟他们说，我怎么也不能帮着他们耍花招；只是那小囚犯自从昨天中饭以后，还不曾吃过一点儿东西，这一回他背着亨德莱先生的行动，我就只当做没有看见吧。

他走下楼来，我给他在炉火边安放了个凳子，拿了许多好东西给他吃；可是他病了，吃得很少，我想款待他的一番热心算是白费。他把双肘支撑在膝盖上，两手

on his hands and remained rapt in dumb meditation. On my inquiring the subject of his thoughts, he answered gravely—

"I'm trying to settle how I shall pay Hindley back. (8) I don't care how long I wait, if I can only do it at last. I hope he will not die before I do!"

"For shame, Heathcliff!" said I. "It is for God to punish wicked people; we should learn to forgive."

"No, God won't have the satisfaction that I shall," he returned. "I only wish I knew the best way! Let me alone, and I'll plan it out: while I'm thinking of that I don't feel pain."

"But, Mr. Lockwood, I forget these tales cannot divert you. I'm annoyed how I should dream of chattering on at such a rate; and your gruel cold, and you nodding for bed! I could have told Heathcliff's history, all that you need hear, in half a dozen words."

Thus interrupting herself, the

托着下巴，半天不吭一声，想他的心事。我不禁问他，呆呆的在想些什么？谁知道他一本正经地回答道：

"我在打算，怎样才能找亨德莱算账。要等到哪一天我都不在乎，只要最终给我报了仇就行。但愿他不要在我报仇还没报成之前先死去！"

"亏你说得出口，希克厉！"我说道。"坏人是由上帝来惩罚的，我们应当学着宽恕人。"

"不，上帝也不能剥夺我的满足，"他回答道。"我只想知道有什么最好的办法。别来打扰我吧，我会琢磨出一个主意来，在我琢磨的时候，我就不觉得痛苦了。"

"可是，洛克乌先生，我忘了这些故事不能给你解闷儿。真可恼，想不到我会这么一股劲儿地只顾唠唠叨叨；你的粥也凉了，你在打瞌睡啦！你要听的就是希克厉的身世，我本来三言两语就可以交代完的。"

那位女管家就这样打断

housekeeper rose, and proceeded to lay aside her sewing; but I felt incapable of moving from the hearth, and I was very far from nodding.

了自己的话头，站了起来，打算把她手里的针线活儿放下了。可是我觉得自己离不开壁炉，再说，我一点儿也没有瞌睡的意思。

"Sit still, Mrs. Dean," I cried; "do sit still another half-hour. You've done just right to tell the story leisurely. That is the method I like; and you must finish it in the same style. I am interested in every character you have mentioned, more or less."

"坐着别动，丁恩太太，"我嚷道，"请再坐半个钟头吧！你这样慢悠悠地把故事讲下去，再好不过。这正对我的劲儿。你一定要照这个样儿讲到底。你所讲到的每一个人物或多或少都让我感到兴趣。"

"The clock is on the stroke of eleven, sir."

"钟打十一下了，先生。"

"No matter—I'm not accustomed to go to bed in the long hours. One or two is early enough for a person who lies till ten."

"没关系，我是想赖不过半夜十二点不睡觉的。一个人睡到十点钟才起身，那么到一两点钟睡觉已经够早啦。"

"You shouldn't lie till ten. There's the very prime of the morning gone long before that time. A person who has not done one-half his day's work by ten o'clock, runs a chance of leaving the other half undone."

"你可不要睡到十点钟才起床啊，到了十点钟，一清早的大好光阴早已错过了。一个人要是十点钟还没干好一天的一半活儿，说不定连剩下的一半儿也干不成啦。"

"Nevertheless, Mrs. Dean, resume your chair; because to-morrow I intend lengthening the night till afternoon. I prognosticate for myself an obstinate cold,

"不过，丁恩太太，还是再坐下来吧。因为我打算这一觉睡到明天下午呢。我有个预感，明天我少说要得

at least."

"I hope not, sir. Well, you must allow me to leap over some three years; during that space Mrs. Earnshaw—"

"No, no, I'll allow nothing of the sort! Are you acquainted with the mood of mind in which, if you were seated alone, and the cat licking its kitten on the rug before you, you would watch the operation so intently that puss's neglect of one ear would put you seriously out of temper?"

"A terribly lazy mood, I should say."

"On the contrary, a tiresomely active one. It is mine, at present; and, therefore, continue minutely. I perceive that people in these regions acquire over people in towns the value that a spider in a dungeon does over a spider in a cottage, to their various occupants; and yet the deepened attraction is not entirely owing to the situation of the looker-on. They do live more in earnest, more in themselves, and less in surface, change, and frivolous external things. I could fancy a love for life here almost possible; and

一场重感冒。"

"我希望不致如此吧，先生。好吧，你得容许我把时间跳过约莫三年光景。在那几年里，欧肖太太……"

"不，不，我不容许有这一类事情！你可曾体会到那样一种心情——假使你独个儿坐在那里，有一只母猫在你面前的地毯上舔它的小猫，你只顾盯着它看，出了神，到后来老猫漏舔了小猫的一只耳朵，也会叫你老大的不舒服。"

"我得说那可是懒散得要命的心情哪。"

"恰好相反，是一种活跃得叫人厌倦的心情；我眼前就是这样。所以你原原本本地讲下去吧。我觉得这一代的人比起城里人来，自有一种好处——就像是地窖里的蜘蛛比起茅屋里的蜘蛛那样。可是那深深吸引人的地方，并不是因为你处在旁观者的地位上。他们确实是生活得更认真、更执著于自己，而不在乎浮面的东西，不在乎翻花样和那身外的琐屑事

I was a fixed unbeliever in any love of a year's standing. One state resembles setting a hungry man down to a single dish, on which he may concentrate his entire appetite and do it justice; the other, introducing him to a table laid out by French cooks: he can perhaps extract as much enjoyment from the whole; but each part is a mere atom in his regard and remembrance."

物。我可以想象，在这儿，终生信守不渝的爱情几乎是可能得了。而我向来怎么也信不过有哪一种爱情能够维持一年的。这种情况就有些像你在一个饿肚子的人面前放一盘子菜，那他的食欲就全都集中在这一盘子菜上，吃得津津有味；另一种情况就像你给那饿肚子的人安排了一席法国厨师烹调的菜肴，也许他能从整桌酒席上得到同样多的享受，可是每一套菜只占有他当时的注意和日后的回忆的一小部分罢了。"

"Oh! here we are the same as anywhere else, when you get to know us," observed Mrs. Dean, somewhat puzzled at my speech.

"噢，在这点上我们跟别地方的人并没两样，以后你跟我们熟识了，就知道了，"丁恩太太说道，我这番话有点儿把她弄迷糊了。

"Excuse me," I responded; "you, my good friend, are a striking evidence against that assertion. Excepting a few provincialisms of slight consequence, you have no marks of the manners which I am habituated to consider as peculiar to your class. I am sure you have thought a great deal more than the generality of servants think. You have

"请原谅，"我回答道。"你，我的好朋友呀，就是你那段话的一个很明显的反证。你除了稍微带一点儿无关紧要的乡土习气外，我一向认为那些属于你那一阶级的特征，并没有在你的举止上留下痕迹。我敢说，你香的要比一般仆人多得多。你不得

been compelled to cultivate your reflective faculties for want of occasions for frittering your life away in silly trifles."

Mrs. Dean laughed.

"I certainly esteem myself a steady, reasonable kind of body," she said; "not exactly from living among the hills and seeing one set of faces, and one series of actions, from year's end to year's end; but I have undergone sharp discipline, which has taught me wisdom; and then, I have read more than you would fancy, Mr. Lockwood. You could not open a book in this library that I have not looked into, and got something out of also: unless it be that range of Greek and Latin, and that of French; and those I know one from another: it is as much as you can expect of a poor man's daughter.

"However, if I am to follow my story in true gossip's fashion, I had better go on; and instead of leaping three years, I will be content to pass to the next summer—the summer of 1778, that is nearly twenty-three years ago."

不培养自己的思考能力，因为你没有机会把生命浪费在那些无聊琐碎的事儿上呀。"

丁恩太太笑了起来。

"的确，我把自己看作一个稳重懂事的人，"她说，"这可不一定因为住在山乡，一年到头只看到那几张面孔，那老一套的行动；我是受过严格教育的，这教给了我智慧。再说，洛克乌先生，你也许想不到我读过不少书吧。在这儿书房里，随你打开哪一本书来，我没有不翻读过，并且从其中学到些东西的——除非那是希腊文、拉丁文，还有是法文的书籍—我只认得它们是什么文。对于一个穷人家的女儿，你所能要求的最多也不过这样罢了。

"不过，假如真要用谈家常的方式把我的故事讲下去，那我还是继续往下讲吧；也不要一跳就是三年，我把故事放到第二年夏天就行了——那也就是一七七八年的夏天，离开现在差不多有二十三年了。"

# 第八章

# *Middlemarch*
# 米德尔马契

*But the door-sill of marriage once crossed, expectation is concentrated on the present.*

## 背景介绍

乔治·艾略特，女，英国维多利亚时期的传奇人物。一生写了 7 部小说，开创了心理小说这种题材。她原名玛丽安（Mary Anne），之所以取一个男性笔名，据说是为了让她的作品能够“被严肃地对待”。她的愿望倒是在西方世界实现了，*Middlemarch* (1871—1972 年) 曾被誉为英语语言所能写就的“最伟大的小说”。这部涵盖大量心理洞见的现实主义作品，以相当的深度探讨了爱情和婚姻，讲述了谋求一生有所建树的女性多萝西娅自掘坟墓式的婚姻。但是遗憾的是她的作品中文译本很少。中国读者除了学英美文学的对她知之甚少。鉴于此，本书特意选取了她比较成熟的作品，被译为《米德尔马契》的长篇小说以飨读者。

项星耀 (1924-1997 年) 是苏州人，以翻译俄国作家赫尔岑的《往事与随想》而闻名。 江南才子的细腻在翻译艾略特的作品中正好可以派上用场。一个女人写的关于女人的心理活动被译者扎扎实实地给翻译成了中文字，使得不认识英语的读者也得以窥探维多利亚时期英国女性的内心世界。

## 细读节选

《米德尔马契》全书共有 8 卷，每卷分若干章节，本书节选了第二卷第二十章。在这一章里女主人公多萝西娅正在罗马度蜜月，然而，就是在本应甜蜜蜜的时候，她有了婚后至关重要的顿悟，她突然意识到她的丈夫卡苏朋先生根本不是她所想象的那样学识渊博，崇高伟大，她所崇拜的太阳花不过是包装精良的狗尾巴草。这种对人的认识的改变不是一句话可以表述出来的，艾略特运用了大量的长句子来扑捉多萝西娅心里微妙而复杂的活动。

艾略特笔下的女性往往对知识和精神而不是物质有极高的向往与追求，因此她们的失望常常是彻底的，一旦发现对方不能够担当自己赋予的角色，就会在认识上来个 180 度大转弯。节选的这一章就是如此。对这部分心理活动的翻译不仅要求译者的英语功夫过硬，对女性心理的把握也很重要。项星耀前辈是怎样处理的呢？我们一起来细读原文和译文。

## 拓展思考

1. 凭借记忆，写出 3 句划线的原文与译文。

| 原文 | 译文 |
| --- | --- |
| | |
| | |
| | |

2. 乔治艾略特的语言有什么风格？译文能传递这种风格吗？

3. 多萝西娅美在哪里？

4. 你在文学作品中遇到过卡苏朋先生这样的角色吗？

# Chapter xx

*"A child forsaken, waking suddenly,*
*Whose gaze afeard on all things round doth rove,*
*And seeth only that it cannot see*
*The meeting eyes of love."*

Two hours later, Dorothea was seated in an inner room or boudoir of a handsome apartment in the Via Sistina.

I am sorry to add that she was sobbing bitterly, with such abandonment to this relief of an oppressed heart as a woman habitually controlled by pride on her own account and thoughtfulness for others will sometimes allow herself when she feels securely alone. And Mr. Casaubon was certain to remain away for some time at the Vatican.

(1) Yet Dorothea had no distinctly shapen grievance that she could state even to herself; and in the midst of her confused thought and passion, the mental act that was struggling forth into clear-

# 第二十章

一个弃儿突然醒来，
用惶恐的目光打量一切，
但是发现再也找不到
那对充满深情的眼睛。

两个小时后，多萝西娅回到了西斯蒂纳街的旅馆，坐在一套漂亮房间的内室或起居室中。

我很遗憾，我只得说她正在哭，哭得那么伤心，好像要尽情发泄心中郁积的烦恼似的。一个女人由于自己的骄傲，也由于对别人的体贴，一直克制着自己，要到她相信周围没有人的时候，才会这样出声痛哭。这时卡苏朋先生无疑还在梵蒂冈，他得在那儿多待一会儿。

然而多萝西娅自己也说不清楚，她的烦恼究竟是什么。在她混乱的思想和情绪中，有一种心理活动正在竭力挣扎，要使自己变成明确

ness was a self-accusing cry that her feeling of desolation was the fault of her own spiritual poverty.

的概念，即一种自我谴责的声音，向她大声疾呼，说她的孤独感是她自己的过错，是她精神贫乏的表现。

She had married the man of her choice, and with the advantage over most girls that she had contemplated her marriage chiefly as the beginning of new duties: from the very first she had thought of Mr. Casaubon as having a mind so much above her own, that he must often be claimed by studies which she could not entirely share; moreover, after the brief narrow experience of her girlhood she was beholding Rome, （2） the city of visible history, where the past of a whole hemisphere seems moving in funeral procession with strange ancestral images and trophies gathered from afar.

她嫁给了一个人，这个人是她自己选中的，她比许多女孩子幸运，因为她把她的婚姻主要看作新的义务的开始。从第一天起她就相信，卡苏朋先生有一颗比她丰富的多的心，他必须经常研究学问，这种研究不是她完全能参与的。此外，在她短暂的少女时代，她接触的只是一个狭隘的世界，现在的她却面对着罗马，这个城市本身就是一部有形的历史，半个地球的过去仿佛仍在这里举行丧葬仪式，把她那些祖先的奇异形象，那来自四面八方的战利品，展示给人们。

But this stupendous fragmentariness heightened the dreamlike strangeness of her bridal life. Dorothea had now been five weeks in Rome, and in the kindly mornings when autumn and winter seemed to go hand in hand like a happy aged couple one of

但是这架庞大的残骸，使她的新婚生活更变得像梦一般光怪陆离。多萝西娅来到罗马已经五周，起先，秋天和冬天像一对幸福的老人，手携着手在一起漫步，但不久便只有一个留了下

whom would presently survive in chiller loneliness, she had driven about at first with Mr. Casaubon, but of late chiefly with Tantripp and their experienced courier.

来，在更寒冷的孤独中打发日子。多萝西娅也是这样，起先，她与卡苏朋先生一起坐了车，在亲切的早晨出外游览，但后来却主要只能跟坦特莉普和那位见多识广的导游人在一起了。

She had been led through the best galleries, had been taken to the chief points of view, had been shown the grandest ruins and the most glorious churches, and she had ended by oftenest choosing to drive out to the Campagna（3）where she could feel alone with the earth and sky, away-from the oppressive masquerade of ages, in which her own life too seemed to become a masque with enigmatical costumes.

她们陪着她穿过琳琅满目的画廊，浏览主要的景物，参观最伟大的古迹和最豪华的教堂，但最后，她总是选择康派奈平原作她驱车出游的地点；她要独自与天地为伍，离开那令人窒息的世纪的假面舞会，因为在那里，她自己的生活似乎也戴上了面具，穿上了不可思议的服装。

To those who have looked at Rome with the quickening power of a knowledge which breathes a growing soul into all historic shapes, and traces out the suppressed transitions which unite all contrasts, Rome may still be the spiritual centre and interpreter of the world.

对于那些学识渊博、智慧敏锐的人，他们看到罗马的时候，他们的知识会给一切历史形态注入活的灵魂，找出一切对立现象之间隐蔽的变化轨迹，那么，罗马在他们眼里可能仍是世界的精神核心和说明者。

But let them conceive one more historical contrast: the gigantic broken revelations of that Imperial and Papal city thrust

但是不妨想想，历史在另一些人心头引起的反应，比如，罗马帝国和教皇城残

abruptly on the notions of a girl who had been brought up in English and Swiss Puritanism, fed on meagre Protestant histories and on art chiefly of the hand-screen sort; a girl whose ardent nature turned all her small allowance of knowledge into principles, fusing her actions into their mould, and whose quick emotions gave the most abstract things the quality of a pleasure or a pain; a girl who had lately become a wife, and from the enthusiastic acceptance of untried duty found herself plunged in tumultuous preoccupation with her personal lot.

留的雄伟遗迹，一下子投射到一个少女的意识中，而这个少女是在英国和瑞士的清教精神中长大的，她吸收过的养料只是贫乏的新教历史，她接触过的艺术珍品只是袖珍遮光屏之类的东西；她天性热烈，但知识浅陋，她又把这些知识统统变成了原则，她的行动也以这些模式为依据；她的情绪又极易激动，以致在她眼里，抽象事物也带上了欢乐或痛苦的色彩；而且这个少女最近又成了妻子，她本来热情洋溢，准备迎接从未经历过的义务，现在却发现自己陷入了混乱的心境，以致为个人的命运忧心忡忡。

The weight of unintelligible Rome might lie easily on bright nymphs to whom it formed a background for the brilliant picnic of Anglo-foreign society; but Dorothea had no such defence against deep impressions. Ruins and basilicas, palaces and colossi, set in the midst of a sordid present, where all that was living and warm-blooded seemed sunk in the deep degeneracy of a supersti-

不可理解的罗马对无忧无虑的闺阁名媛说来，也许不致构成什么压力，它只是为英国或外国上流社会提供了举行丰富多采的野餐的背景，但是多萝西娅缺乏这种自卫能力，罗马给她的印象太深刻了。废墟和会堂遗址，宫殿和巨型石像，出现在污浊鄙陋的现实中，这

tion divorced from reverence; the dimmer but yet eager Titanic life gazing and struggling on walls and ceilings; the long vistas of white forms whose marble eyes seemed to hold the monotonous light of an alien world: all this vast wreck of ambitious ideals, sensuous and spiritual, mixed confusedly with the signs of breathing forgetfulness and degradation, at first jarred her as with an electric shock, and then urged themselves on her with that ache belonging to a glut of confused ideas which check the flow of emotion.

Forms both pale and glowing took possession of her young sense, and fixed themselves in her memory even when she was not thinking of them, preparing strange associations which remained through her after-years.

Our moods are apt to bring with them images which suc-

里，一切有生命、有血肉的事物却在堕落，退化，仿佛宗教失去崇敬，变成了迷信；巨人的火热生命仍在墙上和天花板上窥视着，挣扎着，但已显得黯淡朦胧；洁白塑像构成的长廊上，那些大理石眼睛似乎在抵制着一个陌生世界的单调光线；总之，一切热烈的理想留下的这一大堆残余，不论是感性的，还是精神的，都跟现实中退化和懈怠的迹象混合在一起，起先，它们骤然呈现在她的眼前，使她像触电一样，大为震惊，后来，它们又纷至沓来，压到她的身上，使她透不过气，混乱的思想仿佛越积越多，把她的感觉之流也堵塞了。

各种形态的事物，不论是苍白的还是灼热的，都渗入了她年轻的意识，哪怕她不想它们，它们仍照样刻印在她的记忆中，形成种种奇异地结合，在她今后的一生中始终不会消失。

我们的情绪往往有各种幻象伴随着，它们会一个接

ceed each other like the magic-lantern pictures of a doze; and in certain states of dull forlornness Dorothea all her life continued to see the vastness of St. Peter's, the huge bronze canopy, the excited intention in the attitudes and garments of the prophets and evangelists in the mosaics above, and the red drapery which was being hung for Christmas spreading itself everywhere like a disease of the retina.

一个出现，跟一幅幅恍惚迷离的幻灯画一样。每当孤独凄凉、难以排遣的时刻，多萝西娅总是会看到那巍峨壮丽的圣彼得教堂，那巨大的青铜圆顶，想起屋顶镶嵌画中的那些先知和福音传播者，他们的姿态和衣衫中流露的强烈意愿；为圣诞节张挂的大红帷幕，仿佛印在她的视网膜上，到处可见。

Not that this inward amazement of Dorothea's was anything very exceptional: many souls in their young nudity are tumbled out among incongruities and left to "ind their feet" among them, while their elders go about their business.

我并不认为，多萝西娅内心的这种诧异感是绝无仅有的现象，许多年轻人怀着童稚无知的心灵跨入不协调的现实，这时如果大人忙于自己的事，他们便只得在中间自己“学习走路”。

Nor can I suppose that when Mrs. Casaubon is discovered in a fit of weeping six weeks after her wedding, the situation will be regarded as tragic. Some discouragement, some faintness of heart at the new real future which replaces the imaginary, is not unusual, and we do not expect people to be deeply moved by what is not unusual.

我也并不认为，我们发现卡素朋夫人在结婚六个星期之后，竟在独自啼泣，这便是一幕悲剧。在新的真实的未来代替想象的未来时，心头产生一些失望，一些困惑，这并不是罕见的，既然并不罕见，人们也不必为此惶恐不安。

That element of tragedy which lies in the very fact of frequency,

接触频繁本身蕴藏着悲剧因素，好在它还无法渗入

has not yet wrought itself into the coarse emotion of mankind; and perhaps our frames could hardly bear much of it. If we had a keen vision and feeling of all ordinary human life, it would be like hearing the grass grow and the squirrel's heart beat, and we should die of that roar which lies on the other side of silence. (4) As it is, the quickest of us walk about well wadded with stupidity.

人类粗糙的感情，我们的心灵恐怕也不能完全容纳它。要是我们的视觉和知觉，对人生的一切寻常现象都那么敏感，那就好比我们能听到青草生长的声息和松鼠心脏的跳动，在我们本来认为沉寂无声的地方，突然出现了震耳欲聋的音响，这岂不会把我们吓死。事实正是这样，我们最敏感的人在生活中往往是麻木不仁的。

However, Dorothea was crying, and if she had been required to state the cause, she could only have done so in some such general words as I have already used: to have been driven to be more particular would have been like trying to give a history of the lights and shadows, for that new real future which was replacing the imaginary drew its material from the endless minutiae by which her view of Mr. Casaubon and her wifely relation, now that she was married to him, was gradually changing with the secret motion of a watch-hand from what it had been in her maiden dream.

但是，多萝西娅正在啼哭，如果有人问她什么原因，她能够说的，也只是我刚才讲的那些笼统的话。如果再要具体一些，那就无异要把她知道的、不知道的一切统统形诸语言。事实上，新的真实的未来取代幻想的未来，是通过无限众多的细节在潜移默化中进行的，她对苏卡朋先生的看法，也是像时针一样在不知不觉的改变，以致离开她少女时代的梦境的。

It was too early yet for her

目前，哪怕要她充分认

fully to recognize or at least admit the change, still more for her to have readjusted that devotedness which was so necessary a part of her mental life that she was almost sure sooner or later to recover it.（5）Permanent rebellion, the disorder of a life without some loving reverent resolve, was not possible to her; but she was now in an interval when the very force of her nature heightened its confusion. In this way, the early months of marriage often are times of critical tumult—whether that of a shrimp-pool or of deeper waters—which afterwards subsides into cheerful peace.

识，或至少承认这种变化，都还为时过早，更不用说改变他对丈夫的忠诚了，这种忠诚是她精神生活中不可或缺的部分，因此她几乎相信，它迟早会恢复正常。永久的背弃，缺乏坚定的爱和尊重的不正常生活，对她来说是不可能的。只是眼前她正处在一种中间阶段，她的强烈天性也助长了它的混乱状态。婚后的最初几个月总是这样，它往往是充满风波的危机时期，但不论这是小池塘中的风波还是大海中的风波，它迟早会平静下去，变得相安无事。

But was not Mr. Casaubon just as learned as before? Had his forms of expression changed, or his sentiments become less laudable?

再说，卡苏鹏先生不是仍像以前那么渊博吗？他的谈吐难道已有所改变，或者他的情操已不那么值得赞美？

（6）Oh waywardness of womanhood! Did his chronology fail him, or his ability to state not only a theory but the names of those who held it; or his provision for giving the heads of any subject on demand? And was not Rome the place in all the world to give free play to such accom-

啊，女子总是这么任性！难道他的历史研究已经失败？难道他已不能如数家珍似的说明各种理论、以及提出这些理论的人？难道他在必要时，已不能头头是道地回答任何问题？难道罗马不正是全世界最适宜发挥这

plishments? Besides, had not Dorothea's enthusiasm especially dwelt on the prospect of relieving the weight and perhaps the sadness with which great tasks lie on him who has to achieve them?—And that such weight pressed on Mr. Casaubon was only plainer than before.

种才能的地方？再说，多萝西娅翘首以待的，不正是要在未来减轻他为了完成伟大的事业而负起的重担，或者为此而承担的痛苦吗？何况现在，卡素朋先生的这幅担子之重，比以往任何时候都更为明显。

All these are crushing questions; but whatever else remained the same, the light had changed, and you cannot find the pearly dawn at noonday. The fact is unalterable, that a fellow-mortal with whose nature you are acquainted solely through the brief entrances and exits of a few imaginative weeks called courtship, may, when seen in the continuity of married companionship, be disclosed as something better or worse than what you have preconceived, but will certainly not appear altogether the same.

这些都是决定性的问题；但尽管一切依然照旧，光线已经变了，到了中午你便再也看不到彩虹般的曙光。事实是颠扑不破的，有一个人，他的性格你只是在充满幻想的几个星期，在那个所谓求婚阶段，通过断断续续的短暂接触认识到一些，现在到了婚后，在接连不断的朝夕相处中，你所看到的比你预先想象的也许好一些，也许坏一些，但绝不可能完全一样。

And it would be astonishing to find how soon the change is felt if we had no kindred changes to compare with it. To share lodgings with a brilliant dinner-companion, or to see your favorite politician in the Ministry, may bring about changes quite as

要是我们找不到类似的变化作比较，我们不免会对这种变化来得如此之快大吃一惊。跟一位才华横溢的好朋友住在一起，或者看到你钦佩的政治家入阁办事，都会引起同样迅速的变化，开

rapid: in these cases too (7) we begin by knowing little and believing much, and we sometimes end by inverting the quantities.

始时是了解不多，信仰极高，最后却往往适得其反。

Still, such comparisons might mislead, for no man was more incapable of flashy make-believe than Mr. Casaubon: he was as genuine a character as any ruminant animal, and he had not actively assisted in creating any illusions about himself.

不过这种比较仍不免引起误会，因为卡苏鹏先生与别人不同，从不弄虚作假，他是像任何反刍动物一样光明磊落的，他不想费尽心计，为自己制造假象。

How was it that in the weeks since her marriage, Dorothea had not distinctly observed but felt with a stifling depression, that the large vistas and wide fresh air which she had dreamed of finding in her husband's mind were replaced by anterooms and winding passages which seemed to lead nowhither?

那么，多萝西娅在结婚后的几个星期中，虽然没有发现具体的根据，却隐隐意识到，她的美梦已经破灭，她本来指望在她丈夫心头找到远大的前景和清新的气流，现在却发现，她只是走进了阴暗的前室，在曲折的死胡同中打转，找不到出路，她感到寒心，感到窒息，这是为什么呢？

I suppose it was that in courtship everything is regarded as provisional and preliminary, and the smallest sample of virtue or accomplishment is taken to guarantee delightful stores which the broad leisure of marriage will reveal. But the door-sill of marriage once crossed, expectation is concentrated on the present. (8) Having once embarked on your

我想，那是因为在婚前，一切带有临时性质，仿佛只是一场序幕，以致品德和才能的个别实例，也被当作了丰富的宝藏，似乎到了婚后，它们便可在广阔的天地中得到充分表现。但是一但跨过结婚的门槛，希望便集中到了现实上。在你登上

marital voyage, it is impossible not to be aware that you make no way and that the sea is not within sight—that, in fact, you are exploring an enclosed basin.

结婚的汽船开始航行时，你不能不发现，你的面前并没有路，你找不到海洋，事实上，你只是在一个封闭的水坞里打转。

In their conversation before marriage, Mr. Casaubon had often dwelt on some explanation or questionable detail of which Dorothea did not see the bearing; but such imperfect coherence seemed due to the brokenness of their intercourse, and, supported by her faith in their future, she had listened with fervid patience to a recitation of possible arguments to be brought against Mr. Casaubon's entirely new view of the Philistine god Dagon and other fish-deities, thinking that hereafter she should see this subject which touched him so nearly from the same high ground whence doubtless it had become so important to him.

在他们婚前的接触中，卡苏朋先生常常谈到自己的一些看法和点点滴滴的问题，多萝西娅听了，总觉得摸不着头脑，但她想，这种零乱琐碎的现象可能是由于他们不能常在一起的缘故，她对他们的未来仍充满信心，因此总是毫不怠懈，仔细听他讲，他对非利士人的神大衮，以及其他鱼神，怎样有了全新的观念，别人又可能提出什么论点来反驳他等等。她一边听一点想，这问题对他一定很重要，她今后也得跟他站在同一高度来看待它才是。

Again, the matter-of-course statement and tone of dismissal with which he treated what to her were the most stirring thoughts, was easily accounted for as belonging to the sense of haste and preoccupation in which she herself shared during their engagement.

还有，他在回答最激动她的一些想法时，那种理所当然的谈话方式，那种不愿意多讲的口气，看来是由于时间仓促，事情太多，因此是不足为怪的，她自己在订婚之后也处在这种状态呢。

But now, since they had been in Rome, with all the depths of her emotion roused to tumultuous activity, and with life made a new problem by new elements, she had been becoming more and more aware, with a certain terror, that her mind was continually sliding into inward fits of anger and repulsion, or else into forlorn weariness.

How far the judicious Hooker or any other hero of erudition would have been the same at Mr. Casaubon's time of life, she had no means of knowing, so that he could not have the advantage of comparison; but her husband's way of commenting on the strangely impressive objects around them had begun to affect her with a sort of mental shiver: he had perhaps the best intention of acquitting himself worthily, but only of acquitting himself. (9) What was fresh to her mind was worn out to his; and such capacity of thought and feeling as had ever been stimulated in him by the general life of mankind had long shrunk to a sort of dried preparation, a lifeless embalmment of knowledge.

When he said, "Does this interest you, Dorothea? Shall we

但现在，他们已经到了罗马，随着她的感情深处出现的翻腾起伏的浪潮，随着生活中新的因素造成的新问题，她逐渐怀着惴惴不安的心情发觉，她的心正在不断滑进愤怒和厌恶的漩涡，或者滑进凄凉失望的深渊。

贤明的胡克，或者其他博学之士，处在卡苏明先生的这个生活时期，是否也像他一样，这一点她无从知道，因此他也无法从这种比较中沾光。但是她丈夫对周围那些引起她深思和惊异的事物的态度，却使她的思想受到了震动，看来她怀着良好的意图，要使自己有所成就，但也仅仅是使自己有所成就而已。她认为新鲜的，在他已经成为老生常谈；从思想和感觉上对一般人类生活反应的能力，对他来说早已成了明日黄花，她的知识只是没有生命的僵尸。

他常常这么说："多萝西娅，你对这有兴趣吗？我

stay a little longer? I am ready to stay if you wish it,"—it seemed to her as if going or staying were alike dreary. Or, "Should you like to go to the Farnesina, Dorothea? It contains celebrated frescos designed or painted by Raphael, which most persons think it worth while to visit."

们要不要再呆一会儿？只要你乐意，我都可以。”这种话使她听后，只觉得离开或待下去同样索然无味。有一次他还问她：“多萝西娅，你想参观法奈斯宫吗？那里有许多著名的壁画，是拉斐尔设计或绘制的，许多人认为这是值得游览的地方。”

“But do you care about them?” was always Dorothea's question.

“但是你对它们有兴趣吗？”她总是这么反问。

"They are, I believe, highly esteemed. Some of them represent the fable of Cupid and Psyche, which is probably the romantic invention of a literary period, and cannot, I think, be reckoned as a genuine mythical product. But if you like these wall-paintings we can easily drive thither; and you will then, I think, have seen the chief works of Raphael, any of which it were a pity to omit in a visit to Rome. He is the painter who has been held to combine the most complete grace of form with sublimity of expression. Such at least I have gathered to be the opinion of cognoscenti."

“我相信，它们得到了很高的评价。其中有些表现了丘比特和赛姬的故事，这大概是文明时期的浪漫主义创造，我认为，不能把它们真正看作神话的产物。但是如果你喜欢这些墙头画，我们不妨去玩玩。我想，这样你就可以见识到拉斐尔的主要作品了，访问罗马而没有看到它们，这是很可惜的。大家公认，拉斐尔是把最完美的形式和崇高庄严的内容结合起来的大师。至少据我所知，这是鉴定家们的共同意见。”

This kind of answer given in a measured official tone, as of a

这类回答四平八稳，像

clergyman reading according to the rubric, did not help to justify the glories of the Eternal City, or to give her the hope that if she knew more about them the world would be joyously illuminated for her. There is hardly any contact more depressing to a young ardent creature than that of a mind in which years full of knowledge seem to have issued in a blank absence of interest or sympathy.

官样文章，仿佛一位教士对着祈祷书照本宣科，既不想独出心裁，对永恒之城的荣耀作过多的揄扬，也不想引起她的幻想，使她觉得，要是她对这一切了解得多一些，世界在她眼里就会变得更加光辉灿烂，充满各种乐趣。也许，一个满腔热情的年轻人，最苦闷的就是接触到一颗冷若冰霜的心，在这颗心里，多年积累的知识，已把它的兴趣和同情统统埋葬掉了。

On other subjects indeed Mr. Casaubon showed a tenacity of occupation and an eagerness which are usually regarded as the effect of enthusiasm, and Dorothea was anxious to follow this spontaneous direction of his thoughts, instead of being made to feel that she dragged him away from it.

确实，在另一些事情上，卡苏朋先生显得十分执着和关心，这通常被认为是热情的表现，多萝西娅要求自己随着他的思想的这种自然趋向行走，丝毫没有意思要把他从这条路上拉开。

But she was gradually ceasing to expect with her former delightful confidence that she should see any wide opening where she followed him. Poor Mr. Casaubon himself was lost among small closets and winding stairs, and in an agitated dimness about the

但是她不再像从前那么乐观，那么充满自信了，她逐渐失去了希望，不再相信跟着他走，会找到任何宽广的道路。可怜的卡苏朋先生，他自己也在狭小的斗室和曲折的楼梯之间徘徊，找

Cabeiri, or in an exposure of other mythologists' ill-considered parallels, easily lost sight of any purpose which had prompted him to these labors.

不到出路呢。关于卡比里神的模糊认识，使他不安，他还发现，另一些神话学家有些类比考虑不够周密，在这中间他自然很容易迷失方向，忘记了当初促使他从事这种研究的任何目的。

With his taper stuck before him he forgot the absence of windows, and in bitter manuscript remarks on other men's notions about the solar deities, he had become indifferent to the sunlight.

他点着蜡烛，却没有想到要打开窗户，他在稿纸上指责别人对太阳神的错误观念，但自己却对太阳本身失去了兴趣。

These characteristics, fixed and unchangeable as bone in Mr. Casaubon, might have remained longer unfelt by Dorothea if she had been encouraged to pour forth her girlish and womanly feeling—if he would have held her hands between his and listened with the delight of tenderness and understanding to all the little histories which made up her experience, and would have given her the same sort of intimacy in return, so that the past life of each could be included in their mutual knowledge and affection—or if she could have fed her affection with those childlike caresses which are the bent of every sweet woman, who has begun by show-

这些特点在卡苏朋先生身上，已经像骨骼一样定型，不可改变，但要是多萝西娅可以自由吐露她那些女孩子的和妇人的感情，要是他能够握着她的手，津津有味、温柔体贴地听她谈她生活中那些琐屑小事，表示他的同感，而且也照此办理，跟她娓娓谈心，使彼此了解过去的生活，互相同情，或者要是她能够靠那些孩子气的爱抚，那种任何温柔女子都有的癖好——它们最初表现在对着秃顶洋娃娃的硬脑瓜如醉如痴地亲吻上，因为她们用自己无穷的爱给那段

ering kisses on the hard pate of her bald doll, creating a happy soul within that woodenness from the wealth of her own love.

木头注入了快活的灵魂——满足自己的感情，那么，他那些特点，她一时也许还觉察不到。

That was Dorothea's bent. With all her yearning to know what was afar from her and to be widely benignant, she had ardor enough for what was near, to have kissed Mr. Casaubon's coat-sleeve, or to have caressed his shoe-latchet, if he would have made any other sign of acceptance than pronouncing her, with his unfailing propriety, to be of a most affectionate and truly feminine nature, indicating at the same time by politely reaching a chair for her that he regarded these manifestations as rather crude and startling.

要知道，多萝西娅是有亲吻的癖好的。尽管她渴望了解与她相隔遥远的事，渴望爱天下所有的人，可是她对身边的一切也不能漠不关心，她有足够的热情来亲吻卡苏朋先生的衣袖，抚摸他的鞋带，只要他露出一点接受她的爱抚的意愿，而不是摆出一副道貌岸然的神态，声称她是最温柔多情、真正具有女性气质的人，同时彬彬有礼的邀请她坐下，表示在他眼里，她那些表现是粗俗，不足为训的。

Having made his clerical toilet with due care in the morning, he was prepared only for those amenities of life which were suited to the well-adjusted stiff cravat of the period, and to a mind weighted with unpublished matter.

早上，他恰如其分地完成了教士的梳洗打扮后，也预备接受生活中的爱抚，但只限于当时那种端端正正的硬领饰，以及那颗时刻挂在尚未出版的著作上的心所允许的范围。

And by a sad contradiction Dorothea's ideas and resolves seemed like melting ice float-

在这种不如人意的情况下，多萝西娅的想法和决心像冰遇到了暖流，融

ing and lost in the warm flood of which they had been but another form.

(10) She was humiliated to find herself a mere victim of feeling, as if she could know nothing except through that medium: all her strength was scattered in fits of agitation, of struggle, of despondency, and then again in visions of more complete renunciation, transforming all hard conditions into duty. Poor Dorothea! she was certainly troublesome—to herself chiefly; but this morning for the first time she had been troublesome to Mr. Casaubon.

She had begun, while they were taking coffee, with a determination to shake off what she inwardly called her selfishness, and turned a face all cheerful attention to her husband when he said, "My dear Dorothea, we must now think of all that is yet left undone, as a preliminary to our departure.

I would fain have returned home earlier that we might have been at Lowick for the Christmas; but my inquiries here have been protracted beyond their anticipated period. I trust, however, that the time here has not been passed

化了，消失了，变成了另一种形态。

她感到委屈，发现自己只是做了感情的牺牲品，她也只能这样理解一切，她的全部力量变成了一阵阵的烦恼、挣扎和失望，她觉得没有出路，只能更进一步放弃一切，把难以忍受的生活条件当做一种义务接受下来。可怜的多萝西娅！她无疑烦恼重重，但主要是自怨自艾，直到今天早上，她才第一次使卡苏朋先生感到烦恼。

在他们喝咖啡的时候，她本来是要决心要排除她所说的自私的观念，因此她露出愉快的脸色，注意听她丈夫的话："亲爱的多萝西娅，我们现在必须考虑还有什么没有做，做离开前的准备了。

我本想早一些回国，在洛伊克过圣诞节的，但我在这里收集材料的工作超过了预计的时间。不过我相信，这段时间对你说来不是毫无收获的。

unpleasantly to you.

Among the sights of Europe, that of Rome has ever been held one of the most striking and in some respects edifying. I well remember that I considered it an epoch in my life when I visited it for the first time; after the fall of Napoleon, an event which opened the Continent to travellers.

在欧洲各个游览中心，罗马一向也是令人流连忘发的地方，在某些方面，它还能给人以启发。我记得很清楚，我对它的第一次访问，在我看来一直是我一生中一件划时期的事件。那是在拿破仑失败之后，那时欧洲大陆才重又向旅游者开放。

Indeed I think it is one among several cities to which an extreme hyperbole has been applied—'See Rome and die:' but in your case I would propose an emendation and say, See Rome as a bride, and live henceforth as a happy wife."

确实，我认为它是为数不多的城市中的一个，有一句极端夸张的话这么说：'到过罗马，死而无怨。'但是就你而言，我得把它略加修改，变成'作为新娘到过罗马，就会作为幸福的妻子度过一生'。"

Mr. Casaubon pronounced this little speech with the most conscientious intention, blinking a little and swaying his head up and down, and concluding with a smile. He had not found marriage a rapturous state, but he had no idea of being anything else than an irreproachable husband, who would make a charming young woman as happy as she deserved to be.

卡苏朋先生是怀着最真诚的的意愿，发表这一席小小的演说的，他偶然眨一下眼睛，点点头，最后还笑了笑。他并不觉得结婚是一件值得庆幸的事，但他要求自己做一个无可皆议的丈夫使年轻可爱的妻子得到应该得到的幸福。

"I hope you are thoroughly

"我希望，你对我们这

satisfied with our stay—I mean, with the result so far as your studies are concerned," said Dorothea, trying to keep her mind fixed on what most affected her husband.

"Yes," said Mr. Casaubon, with that peculiar pitch of voice which makes the word half a negative. "I have been led farther than I had foreseen, and various subjects for annotation have presented themselves which, though I have no direct need of them, I could not pretermit.

The task, notwithstanding the assistance of my amanuensis, has been a somewhat laborious one, but your society has happily prevented me from that too continuous prosecution of thought beyond the hours of study which has been the snare of my solitary life."

"I am very glad that my presence has made any difference to you," said Dorothea, who had a vivid memory of evenings in which she had supposed that Mr. Casaubon's mind had gone too deep during the day to be able to get to the surface again. I fear there was a little temper in her reply. "I hope when we get to

次旅行感到完全满意，我这是就你的研究工作所取得的成果说的。"多萝西娅说，竭力使自己的心情适应丈夫最关切的事。

"是的，我很满意，"卡苏朋先生说，他那种异样的音调使他的话有些像反话。"我的研究比我预料的更为复杂，各种需要注释阐明的问题愈来愈多，虽然它们跟我并无直接关系，但也不能避而不谈。

尽管有抄写员的协助，这工作还是相当繁重，幸好有了你，使我可以在业余时间不致陷入孤独生活的罗网，老是为此苦闷惆怅。"

"我很高兴，我的存在能使你的生活得到一些调剂，"多萝西娅说，但是有几个晚上的情景，她还历历在目，那是她曾想，卡苏朋先生的心在白天已陷的太深，再也不会浮到上面来了，因此她的回答可能包含着一些情绪。"我希望我们

Lowick, I shall be more useful to you, and be able to enter a little more into what interests you."

"Doubtless, my dear," said Mr. Casaubon, with a slight bow. "The notes I have here made will want sifting, and you can, if you please, extract them under my direction."

"And all your notes," said Dorothea, whose heart had already burned within her on this subject, so that now she could not help speaking with her tongue. "All those rows of volumes—will you not now do what you used to speak of?—will you not make up your mind what part of them you will use, and begin to write the book which will make your vast knowledge useful to the world? I will write to your dictation, or I will copy and extract what you tell me: I can be of no other use." Dorothea, in a most unaccountable, darkly feminine manner, ended with a slight sob and eyes full of tears.

The excessive feeling mani-

回到洛伊克以后，我能对你更加有用，也可以分享你的乐趣。"

"这是毫无意义的，亲爱的，"卡苏朋先生说，略微点了点头。"我在这里记下的笔记需要整理，你如果愿意，可以在我的指导下作些摘录。"

"你的全部笔记，我都愿意帮你整理，"多萝西娅说，一提起这些事，她的心就开始燃烧了，这使她现在讲的话不能带一点锋芒。"你那一摞摞笔记本，你老说要整理，为什么现在还不动手？难道还不能决定，哪些材料是有用的？你怎么还不开始写那本书，让你的渊博知识得到公认，发挥作用？我可以替你作记录，也可以根据你的要求抄抄写写，作些摘要，因为我也只有这些能耐。"多萝西娅说到最后，不知为什么，在那种无法理喻的女性气质的影响下，发出了轻轻的啜泣，眼眸中噙满了泪水。

感情的过多流露，本来

fested would alone have been highly disturbing to Mr. Casaubon, but there were other reasons why Dorothea's words were among the most cutting and irritating to him that she could have been impelled to use.

只会使卡苏朋先生手足无措，不知如何应付，但是现在，由于其他原因，多萝西娅那些情不自禁的话却伤了他的自尊心，使他非常生气。

She was as blind to his inward troubles as he to hers: she had not yet learned those hidden conflicts in her husband which claim our pity. She had not yet listened patiently to his heartbeats, but only felt that her own was beating violently.

原来，她对他心头的烦恼一无所知，他对她也是这样。隐藏那个在她丈夫胸中的那些值得我们怜悯的矛盾，她是想象不到的。她也从未耐心地静听他心脏的跳跃，只是觉得自己的心跳得非常厉害。

In Mr. Casaubon's ear, Dorothea's voice gave loud emphatic iteration to those muffled suggestions of consciousness which it was possible to explain as mere fancy, the illusion of exaggerated sensitiveness: always when such suggestions are unmistakably repeated from without, they are resisted as cruel and unjust.

在卡苏朋先生耳中，多萝西娅那些话无异把他隐藏在内心的模糊意识，变成了明确无误的语言，要是她不讲，他本来可以说，这只是他的想象，是他自己神经过敏引起的幻觉，事实上，每逢他发现别人确实在暗示这点时，他也总是听不入耳，认为这只是残酷而不公正的指责。

We are angered even by the full acceptance of our humiliating confessions—how much more by hearing in hard distinct syllables from the lips of a near observer,

哪怕不光彩的自我忏悔，要是别人完全信以为真，我们也难免愤愤不平，那么，如果我们心中那些含

those confused murmurs which we try to call morbid, and strive against as if they were the on-coming of numbness!

混的低语，那些连我们自己也不愿承认，要把它们说成是病态的表现，竭力加以抵制，仿佛全属子虚乌有的东西，忽然由我们身边的一位旁观者，用清晰响亮的声音讲了出来，这结果会如何，就可想而知了！

And this cruel outward accuser was there in the shape of a wife—nay, of a young bride, who, instead of observing his abundant pen-scratches and amplitude of paper with the uncritical awe of an elegant-minded canary-bird, seemed to present herself as a spy watching everything with a malign power of inference.

何况现在这位站在一旁的残酷的谴责者是以妻子的面目出现的——不，还是一位年轻的新娘，她非但对他的手不停挥，以及堆积如山的稿子视若无睹，没有像体贴入微的金丝雀那样对他肃然起敬，表示心悦诚服，反而像一个暗探那样，怀着恶意在窥测他的动静。

Here, towards this particular point of the compass, Mr. Casaubon had a sensitiveness to match Dorothea's, and an equal quickness to imagine more than the fact.

正是在罗盘的这一点上，卡苏朋先生是和多萝西娅同样敏感，也同样会超过事实想入非非。

He had formerly observed with approbation her capacity for worshipping the right object; he now foresaw with sudden terror that this capacity might be replaced by presumption, this worship by the most exasperating of all criti-

以前他赞扬过她，说她有判断力，懂得尊敬应该的一切；现在他却突然怀着惶恐的心情预见到，这种能力可以变成自以为是，这种尊敬也可以变成令人愤慨的指

cism,—that which sees vaguely a great many fine ends, and has not the least notion what it costs to reach them.

For the first time since Dorothea had known him, Mr. Casaubon's face had a quick angry flush upon it.

"My love," he said, with irritation reined in by propriety, "you may rely upon me for knowing the times and the seasons, adapted to the different stages of a work which is not to be measured by the facile conjectures of ignorant onlookers.

It had been easy for me to gain a temporary effect by a mirage of baseless opinion; but it is ever the trial of the scrupulous explorer to be saluted with the impatient scorn of chatterers who attempt only the smallest achievements, being indeed equipped for no other. And it were well if all such could be admonished to discriminate judgments of which the true subject-matter lies entirely beyond their reach, from those of which the elements may be compassed by a narrow and superficial survey."

责——这种指责只知向往许多美好的成果，对取得这些成果的辛勤劳动却视而不见，一无所知。

自从他们认识以来，多萝西娅第一次看到，卡苏朋先生的脸色突然掠过了一丝悻悻不平的愠色。

"亲爱的，"他说，由于礼貌，没有让愤怒发泄出来，"你可以相信，我知道在我的工作的不同阶段，应该做什么，这不是一位无知的旁观者可以凭肤浅的猜测得知的。

在我看来，用虚无缥缈、毫无根据的议论哗众取宠，赢得一时的效果，这话很容易；但是谨慎严格的探索着应该经得起急功好利的饶舌者的嘲笑，那些人企求的只是一些渺小的可怜的成就，事实上他们也别无所能。我希望所有这样的人都懂得，在评论时怎样区别两类不同的事物；一类是他们完全不理解的，也是不能理解的，另一类则只要靠他们浮光掠影、一知半解的印

This speech was delivered with an energy and readiness quite unusual with Mr. Casaubon. (11) It was not indeed entirely an improvisation, but had taken shape in inward colloquy, and rushed out like the round grains from a fruit when sudden heat cracks it. Dorothea was not only his wife: she was a personification of that shallow world which surrounds the appreciated or desponding author.

Dorothea was indignant in her turn. Had she not been repressing everything in herself except the desire to enter into some fellowship with her husband's chief interests?

"My judgment was a very superficial one—such as I am capable of forming," she answered, with a prompt resentment, that needed no rehearsal. "You showed me the rows of notebooks—you have often spoken of them—you have often said that they wanted digesting. But I never heard you speak of the writing that is to be published. Those were very simple facts, and my judgment went no farther. I only begged you to let me be of

象，就可以信口雌黄。"

一篇话讲得振振有辞，激昂慷慨，跟卡苏朋先生平时的谈吐大不一样。确实，这不是一时的急就章，而是经过内心的酝酿才形成的，现在只是像果实遇到炎热的天气突然裂开，一颗颗种子便滚滚而下了。多萝西娅不仅是她的妻子，也成了这位怀才不遇、或者牢骚满腹的作者周围那个浅薄的世界的化身。

现在轮到多萝西娅发怒了。她放弃了一切，仅仅要求参与丈夫的主要活动，分享他的一点乐趣，难道这不应该吗？

"我的议论是很浅薄的，我能做到的也仅此而已说，"她回答，一下子变得怒气冲冲，这是用不到排练的。"你给我看那一摞摞笔记本，你也常常讲到它们，你还常常说，它们需要整理。但我从没听你谈到，你什么时候动手写那本预备发表的著作。这些是非常简单的事实，我的议论没有越出这个范围。

some good to you."

我只是要求帮助你，为你多出些力而已。"

Dorothea rose to leave the table and Mr. Casaubon made no reply, taking up a letter which lay beside him as if to reperuse it. Both were shocked at their mutual situation—that each should have betrayed anger towards the other.

多萝西娅站起来，离开了餐桌，卡苏朋先生没有回答什么，只是拿起手边的一封信，好像预备重读一遍似的。他们对彼此的态度都有些吃惊，想不到竟会剑拔弩张，怒目相向。

If they had been at home, settled at Lowick in ordinary life among their neighbors, the clash would have been less embarrassing: but on a wedding journey, the express object of which is to isolate two people on the ground that they are all the world to each other, the sense of disagreement is, to say the least, confounding and stultifying.

如果他们是在家中，是在洛伊克的左邻右舍中过千篇一律的日常生活，这样的冲突也许还情有可原，但现在是在蜜月旅行中，这种旅行的目的显然是要使两个人与世隔绝，因为他们彼此就是整个世界，这样，不论怎么说，任何意见不合都是十分荒谬、愚不可及的。

To have changed your longitude extensively and placed yourselves in a moral solitude in order to have small explosions, to find conversation difficult and to hand a glass of water without looking, can hardly be regarded as satisfactory fulfilment even to the toughest minds.

大幅度改变了自己的地理位置，从精神上使自己处在与外界隔绝的状态，可是却为一些小事争争吵吵，找不到共同语言，给对方端一杯水也低头不语，这哪怕对嘴冷漠的心来说，恐怕也不能认为是满意的效果吧。

To Dorothea's inexperienced sensitiveness, it seemed like a ca-

就涉世未深、天性敏感的多萝西娅而言，这无异是

tastrophe, changing all prospects; and to Mr. Casaubon it was a new pain, he never having been on a wedding journey before, or found himself in that close union which was more of a subjection than he had been able to imagine, since this charming young bride not only obliged him to much consideration on her behalf (which he had sedulously given), but turned out to be capable of agitating him cruelly just where he most needed soothing. Instead of getting a soft fence against the cold, shadowy, unapplausive audience of his life, had he only given it a more substantial presence?

一场天翻地覆的灾难，改变了她周围的一切；就卡苏朋先生而言，这是一种新的痛苦，他以前既没经历过蜜月旅行，也从未与一个女子有过如此密切的关系，而这种关系他必须无条件服从，这也是他未从想到的，因为他发现，这位年轻美貌的新娘不仅使他有负义务，必须处处为她着想（这是他已经在尽量做的），而且在他最需要的安慰的时候，她却可能与他发生龃龉，弄得他不得安生。难道他非但没有找到温柔乡，使他可以躲避生活中一切冷酷，阴险，讨厌的骚扰，反而让它们更具体地呈现到了他的面前？

Neither of them felt it possible to speak again at present. To have reversed a previous arrangement and declined to go out would have been a show of persistent anger which Dorothea's conscience shrank from, seeing that she already began to feel herself guilty.

这时他们谁都没法开口。改变原来的安排，拒绝出门，那无异表示还在继续发怒，这是多萝西娅的良心所不允许的，它发现她已在开始后悔，觉得自己错了。

However just her indignation might be, her ideal was not to claim justice, but to give tender-

不论她的愤怒多么有道理，她的根本目的不是分清是非，是给予温情。因此在

ness. So when the carriage came to the door, she drove with Mr. Casaubon to the Vatican, walked with him through the stony avenue of inscriptions, and when she parted with him at the entrance to the Library, went on through the Museum out of mere listlessness as to what was around her.

马车来到门口的时候，她仍随同卡苏朋先生前往梵蒂冈，跟他一起穿过排列成行的石碑；到了图书馆门口，两人才分手。然后她独自在博物馆茫无目标的地闲走，对周围的一切毫无兴趣。

She had not spirit to turn round and say that she would drive anywhere. It was when Mr. Casaubon was quitting her that Naumann had first seen her, and he had entered the long gallery of sculpture at the same time with her; but here Naumann had to await Ladislaw with whom he was to settle a bet of champagne about an enigmatical mediaeval-looking figure there.

她没有心思回过头去告诉他，她要坐车前往别处。瑙曼第一次看到她，就是在卡苏朋先生离开的时候。然后他与她同时走进了狭长的雕塑陈列室。但是他必须在这里等候拉迪斯拉夫，因为他们赌了一瓶香槟，要解决那儿一个带有中世纪色彩的人像的谜。

After they had examined the figure, and had walked on finishing their dispute, they had parted, Ladislaw lingering behind while Naumann had gone into the Hall of Statues where he again saw Dorothea, and saw her in that brooding abstraction which made her pose remarkable.

在仔细研究那个人像之后，他们一边走一边争论，争论结束后，两人分手了，拉迪斯拉夫仍在那儿闲逛，瑙曼来到了塑像厅，又在那儿见到了多萝西娅，她站在一边沉思默想，那副出神的姿态引起了他的注意。

She did not really see the streak of sunlight on the floor more than she saw the statues: she was inwardly seeing the light of years to come in her own home

她实际并不在看地板上那一条阳光，也没有看那些塑像，她在心中看到的只是她未来的岁月——她自己的

and over the English fields and elms and hedge-bordered high-roads; and feeling that the way in which they might be filled with joyful devotedness was not so clear to her as it had been.

But in Dorothea's mind there was a current into which all thought and feeling were apt sooner or later to flow—the reaching forward of the whole consciousness towards the fullest truth, the least partial good. There was clearly something better than anger and despondency.

家，英国的原野和榆树，两边密布树篱的大陆。她觉得，那本来可以充满快乐和忠诚的道路已经不如以前那么明朗了。

但是在多萝西娅心中，有一条永不停息的潜流，她的一切思想和感情迟早都会汇集到那儿，而它在不断向前，把她的全部意识引向最完美的真理，最公正无私的善。很清楚，愤怒和失望不是她所有的一切。

# 参考书目

## 英文书目

1. Bronte，Emily, Wuthering Heights, Beijing, Foreign Language Teaching & Research Press, 1996.

2. Eliot, George，Middlemarch, London, Penguin Books, 1994.

3. Dickens，Charles, David Copperfield, London, Wordsworth Editions Ltd,2000.

4. Thackeray, William Makepeace, Vanity Fair: A Novel without a Hero , Cambridge, Cambridge University Press, 2013.

5. Cao Xueqin, Gao E, A Dream of Red Mansions, translated by Yang Xianyi and Gladys Yang, Beijing, Foreign Language Teaching & Research Press, 2010.

6. Luo Guanzhong, Three Kingdoms, translated by Moss Roberts, Beijing, Foreign Language Teaching & Research Press,1995.

7. Shi Naian and Luo Guanzhong, Outlaws of the Marsh, translated by Sidney Shapiro, Beijing, Foreign Language Teaching & Research Press,1995.

8. Wu Chengen, Journey to the West, translated by W.J.F.Jenner, Beijing, Foreign Language Teaching & Research Press, 2010.

## 中文书目

1. [ 英 ] 艾米丽•勃朗特 :《呼啸山庄》，方平译，上海 : 上海译文出版社，2012 年 7 月。

2. [ 英 ] 狄更斯 :《大卫•科波菲尔》: 张谷若译，上海 : 上海译文出版社，2011 年 5 月。

3. [ 英 ] 萨克雷 :《名利场》，杨必译，北京 : 人民文学出版社，2012 年 1 月。

4. [ 英 ] 乔治•艾略特 :《米德尔马契》，项星耀译，北京 : 人民文学出版社，2007 年 5 月。

四大名著采用的是人民文学出版社的权威定本，2013 年 6 月出版

**特别声明：**

因为没有联系到相关译本的译者或其家人，在此本人特向翻译界前辈表示最诚挚的敬意和感谢，看到本书后，若有任何需要，请联系本书编者。